# FIVE SURVIVE

# Also by Holly Jackson

A Good Girl's Guide to Murder series

*A Good Girl's Guide to Murder*
*Good Girl, Bad Blood*
*As Good as Dead*

FIVE
SURVIVE

HOLLY JACKSON

**Delacorte Press**

Text copyright © 2022 by Holly Jackson
Jacket art copyright © 2022 by Christine Blackburne
Map copyright © 2022 by Mike Hall
Jacket design by Casey Moses

Visit us on the Web! GetUnderlined.com

Educators and librarians, for a variety of teaching tools, visit us at RHTeachersLibrarians.com

Library of Congress Cataloging-in-Publication Data is available upon request.
ISBN 978-0-593-37416-0 (trade) — ISBN 978-0-593-37418-4 (ebook)
ISBN 978-0-593-70489-9 (international edition)

The text of this book is set in 10-point Utopia.
Interior design by Ken Crossland

Printed in the United States of America
10 9 8 7 6 5 4 3 2 1
First American Edition

*To Harry Collis, who, at a hundred years old,*
*is probably the oldest Young Adult reader*
*in the world . . .*

# THE GETAWAY VISTA 2017 31B FLOOR PLAN

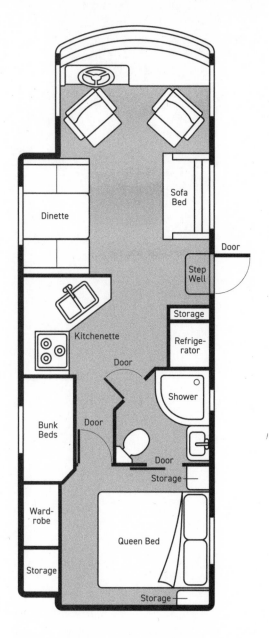

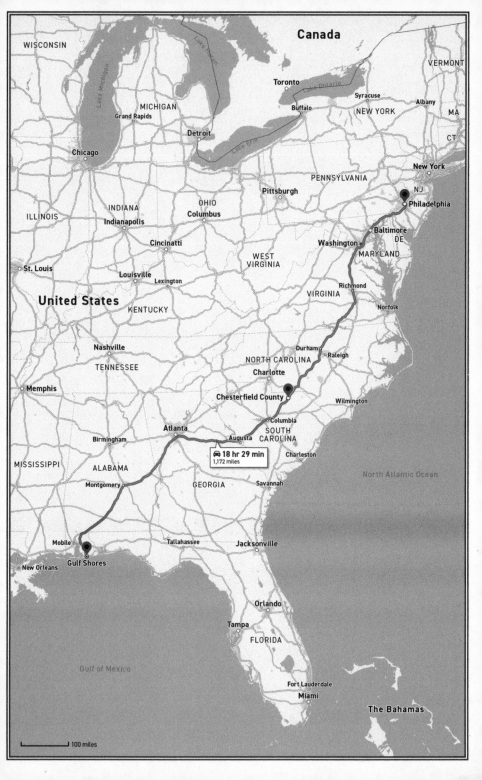

# 10:00 P.M.

# ONE

Here and not. Red and black. One moment there, another gone. Her face in the glass. Disappearing in the light of oncoming headlights, reappearing in the dark of outside. Gone again. The window kept her face for its own. Good, it could keep it. Back, the window didn't want it either.

Red's reflection stared through her, but the glass and the darkness didn't get her quite right, blurring the details. The main features were there: the too-pale glow of her skin and the wide-set dark blue eyes that weren't hers alone. *You look so much alike,* she used to hear, more than she cared to. Now she didn't care to hear it at all, even think it. So, she looked away from her face, their face, ignoring them both. But it was harder to ignore something when you were trying.

Red shifted her gaze, looking instead at the cars in the lane beside and below. Something wasn't right; the cars seemed too small from up here at her window, but Red didn't feel any bigger. She watched a blue sedan edging forward to pass, and she helped it along with her eyes, pushing them ahead. There you go, bud. Ahead of this thirty-one-foot-long metal can, speeding down the highway. Which was strange when you thought about it; that you traveled *down* a highway when *high* was right there in the name.

"Red?" The voice opposite interrupted her thoughts of lowways and highways. Maddy was looking at her through the dimmed inside lights, skin screwed up around her sandy-brown eyes. She gave a small kick under the table, jabbing Red in the shin. "Did you just forget we were in the middle of playing a game?"

"No," Red said, but yes, yes she had. What had they been playing again?

"Twenty Questions," Maddy said, reading Red's mind. Well, they had known each other all their lives; Red had only gotten a seven-month head start and she hadn't done a lot with it. Maybe Maddy had learned to read her mind in all that time, more than seventeen years. Red really hoped not. There were things in there no one else could ever see. No one. Not even Maddy. Especially not Maddy.

"Yeah, I know," Red said, her eyes wandering to the other side of the RV, to the outside door and the sofa bed—currently sofa—where she and Maddy would sleep tonight. Red couldn't remember; which side of the bed did Maddy like again? Because she couldn't sleep if she wasn't on the left side, and just as she was trying to read Maddy's mind back about that, her eyes caught on a green sign outside in the night, flying over the windshield.

"That sign says Rockingham, aren't we getting off this road soon?" Red said, not loud enough for anyone at the very front of the RV to hear, where it would have been more use. She was probably wrong, anyway, best to say nothing. They'd been driving on this same road for the past hour, I-73 becoming I-74 and then US 220 without much fanfare.

"Red Kenny, focus." Maddy snapped her fingers, a hint of a smile on her face. It never creased, though, Maddy's face, not even with the widest of smiles. Skin like cream, soft and clearer than it had any business being. It made the freckles on Red's face stand out even more, side by side in photos. Literally side by side; they were almost the exact same height, down to the highest-standing hair, though Red's was dark blond where Maddy's was more light brown, a shade or two separating them. Red always had hers tied back, loose bangs at the front that she'd cut herself with the kitchen scissors. Maddy's was untied and neat, the ends soft in a way Red's never were. "I'm the one asking questions, you're the one with the person, place or thing," Maddy prompted.

Red nodded slowly. Well, even if Maddy also liked to sleep on the left, at least they weren't on the bunks.

"I've asked seven questions already," Maddy said.

"Great." Red couldn't remember her person, place or thing. But really, they'd been driving all day, setting off from home around twelve hours ago, hadn't they played enough road trip games? Red couldn't wait for this to be over so she could finally sleep, whether left side or right. Just get through it. They were supposed to arrive at Gulf Shores around this time tomorrow, meet up with the rest of their friends, that was the plan.

Maddy cleared her throat.

"And what answers did I give, remind me?" Red said.

Maddy breathed out, an almost sigh or an almost laugh, hard to tell. "It was a person, a woman, not a fictional character," she said, counting them off on her fingers. "Someone I would know, but not Kim Kardashian or you."

Red looked up, searching the empty corners of her mind for the memory. "No, sorry," she said, "it's gone."

"Okay, we'll start again," Maddy said, but just then, Simon stumbled out of the small bathroom, saving Red from more Organized Fun™. The door bounced back into him as the RV sped up.

"Simon Yoo, have you been in there this whole time?" Maddy asked, disgusted. "We've played two whole rounds."

Simon pushed his black, loosely waved hair away from his face and held an unsteady finger to his lips, saying, "Shh, a lady never tells."

"Shut the door, then, jeez."

He did, but with his foot, to make some point or other, almost overbalancing as they hurtled along the highway, changing lanes to pass. Wasn't their exit soon? Maybe Red should say something, but now she was watching as Simon waded forward, leaning on the tiny kitchen counter behind her. In one awkward motion, he slid onto the booth beside her, knocking his knees on the table.

Red studied him: his pupils were sitting too large in his dark, round eyes, and there was an incriminating wet patch on the front of his teal-colored Eagles shirt.

"You're drunk already," she said, almost impressed. "I thought you'd only had like three beers."

Simon moved close to whisper in her ear, and Red could smell the sharp metallic tang on his breath. She couldn't miss it; that was how she knew when her dad was lying to her, *No I didn't drink today, Red, I promise.* "Shh," Simon said, "Oliver brought tequila."

"And you just helped yourself?" Maddy asked, overhearing.

In answer, Simon balled both his fists and held them in the air, yelling: "Spring break, baby!"

Red laughed. And anyway, if she just asked, maybe Maddy wouldn't mind sleeping on the right tonight, or for the rest of the week. She could just ask.

"Oliver doesn't like people touching his things," Maddy said quietly, glancing over her shoulder at her brother, sitting just a few feet behind her in the front passenger seat, fiddling with the radio as he chatted to Reyna in the driver's seat. Arthur was standing just behind

Oliver and Reyna, now shooting a closed-mouth smile as he caught Red's eye. Or maybe it was actually Simon he was smiling at.

"Hey, it's my RV, I have a claim to anything in it," Simon hiccupped.

"Your uncle's RV." Maddy felt the need to correct him.

"Weren't you supposed to have a driving shift today too?" Red asked him. The plan was to share the drive equally among the six of them. She had taken the first two-hour shift, to get it out of the way, driving them out of Philly and down I-95 until they stopped for lunch. Arthur had sat with her the whole time, calmly directing her, as though he could tell when she was zoning in and out, or when she was panicking about the size of the RV and how small everything looked from up here. Mind readers everywhere, clearly. But she'd only known Arthur six or seven months; that wasn't fair.

"Reyna and I swapped," Simon said, "on account of the beers I'd already drunk." A wicked smile. Simon had always been able to get away with anything, he was too funny, too quick with it. You couldn't stay mad at him. Well, Maddy could, if she was really trying.

"Hey, Reyna's really cool, by the way," Simon whispered to Maddy, as though she had some claim over the coolness of her brother's girlfriend. But she smiled and took it anyway, a glance over at the couple, picture-perfect, even with their backs turned.

A break in the conversation; now was the time to ask before Red forgot.

"Hey, Maddy, about the sofa bed—"

"—Shit!" Oliver hissed up front, an ugly sound. "This is our exit right here. Move over, Reyna. Now! NOW."

"I can't," Reyna said, suddenly flustered, checking her mirrors and flipping the turn signal.

"They'll move for you, we're bigger, just go," Oliver said, reaching forward like he might grab the wheel himself.

A screeching sound, not from the RV but from Reyna, as she pulled the hulking vehicle across one lane. An angry Chevrolet screamed on its horn, and the guy at the wheel threw up a middle finger, holding it out the window. Red pretended to catch it, slipping it into the chest pocket of her blue-and-yellow-check shirt, treasuring it forever.

"Move, move, move," Oliver barked, and Reyna swerved right again, making the exit just in time. Another horn, this time from a furious Tesla they left behind on the highway.

"We could have just come off at the next one and worked it out. That's what Google Maps is for," Reyna said, slowing down, her voice strange and squished like it was working its way through gritted teeth. Red had never seen Reyna flustered before, or angry, only ever smiling, wider each time she checked in with Oliver's eyes. What was that like, to be in love? She couldn't imagine it; that was why she watched them sometimes, learning by example. But Red should have said something about the exit earlier, shouldn't she? They'd made it almost all day without any raised voices. That was her fault.

"I'm sorry," Oliver said now, tucking Reyna's thick black hair behind her ear so he could squeeze her shoulder, imprinting his fingers. "I just want to get to the campsite ASAP. We're all tired."

Red looked away, leaving them alone in their moment, well, as alone as they could get in an RV with six people, thirty-one feet long. Apparently that extra foot was so important they couldn't round it down.

The world on her side of the RV was dark again. Trees lined the road, but Red could hardly see them, not past her own reflection and the other face hiding beneath it. She had to look away from that too, before she thought about it too much. Not here, not now.

The truck in front slowed as it passed a SPEED LIMIT 35 sign, its brake lights staining the road red ahead of them. The color that followed her wherever she went, and it never meant anything good. But the road moved on, and so did they.

Oh wait, what was it she needed to ask Maddy about again?

# TWO

A strange yawning in Red's gut, the sound hidden by the wheels on the road. She couldn't be hungry, could she? They'd only stopped for dinner at a rest stop a few hours ago. But the feeling doubled down, twisting again, so she reached out for the bag of chips in front of Maddy. She removed a handful, placing them carefully in her mouth one by one, cheese dust coating her fingertips.

"Oh yeah," Simon said, standing up and sidling out of the booth, heading toward his bunk beyond the mini-kitchen. "And youse all owe me seven bucks for the snacks I got at the gas station."

Red stared down at the chips left in her hand.

"Hey." Maddy leaned over the table. "I'll cover you for the snacks, don't worry about it."

Red swallowed. Looked down even farther to hide her eyes from Maddy. Not worrying wasn't a choice, not one Red had anyway. In her darkest moments, those winter nights when she had to wear her coat to bed, over two pairs of pajamas and five pairs of socks, and still shivered anyway, Red sometimes wished she were Maddy Lavoy. To live in that warm house as though it belonged to her, to have everything they had and everything she didn't anymore.

Stop that. She felt a flush in her cheeks. Shame was a red feeling, a hot one, just like guilt and anger. Why couldn't the Kennys heat their home on guilt and shame alone? But things would get better soon, right? Real soon, that was the plan, what it was all for. And then everything would be different. How freeing it would be to just do or think, and not have to double-think or triple-think, or say *No thank you, maybe next time.* To not beg for extra shifts at work and lose sleep either way. To take another handful of chips just because she wanted to.

Red realized she hadn't said anything yet. "Thanks," she mumbled, keeping her eyes to herself, but she didn't take any more chips, it didn't feel right. She'd just have to live with that feeling in her gut. And maybe it wasn't hunger after all that.

"No worries," Maddy said. There, see, she didn't have any. Maddy had no need for worries. She was one of those people who was good at everything, first try. Well, apart from that time she insisted on taking up the harp. Unless Red was one of Maddy's worries. It did seem that way sometimes.

"Are we in South Carolina yet?" Red said, changing the subject, one thing *she* was good at.

"Not yet," Oliver called behind, though he wasn't the Lavoy she'd asked. "Soon. I think we should be at the campsite in around forty minutes."

"Woohoo, spring break!" Simon yelled again in a high-pitched voice, and somehow he had another bottle of beer in his hand, the refrigerator door swinging open behind him.

"I got it," Arthur said, passing an unsteady Simon in the narrow space between the sofa bed and the dining table, clapping him on the back. Arthur darted forward to catch the refrigerator door and pushed it shut, the dim overhead lights flashing against his gold-framed glasses as he turned. Red liked his glasses, standing out against his tan skin and curly dark brown hair. She wondered whether she needed glasses; faraway things seem to have gotten farther and fuzzier lately. Another thing to add to the to-worry list, because she couldn't do anything about it. Yet. Arthur caught her looking, smiling as he ran a finger over the light stubble on his chin.

"Given up on Twenty Questions, have you?" he asked them both.

"Red forgot her person, place or thing," Maddy said, and that made Red think: Wasn't there something else she'd forgotten, something she wanted to ask Maddy?

"Chip?" Maddy offered the bag to Arthur.

"Ah, I'm good, thanks." He backed away from the bag, almost tripping over the corner of the sofa bed. A look clouded his eyes, and now that she was looking, was there a slight sheen of sweat on his forehead? Red didn't normally catch these things, but this one she did. Did that mean she looked at him too often?

"What's up?" she said. "Deathly allergic to cheese puffs?"

"No, thankfully," Arthur said, feeling his way as he sat down on the sofa bed.

Oh yes, Red needed to ask Maddy about which side she slept on. Shit, Arthur had just said something and she hadn't listened. Best to go with a well-placed "Huh?"

"I said at least I don't feel as dizzy as Simon probably does."

"Carsick?" Red said. "Well, RV-sick?"

"No, it's not that." Arthur shook his head. "Probably far too late to be telling you all this, but I'm not that great with tight spaces." He looked around at the crammed-in furniture and the compact kitchen. "I thought it would be wider—"

"That's what she said!" Simon interrupted.

"For god's sake, Simon, enough with *The Office* references," Maddy

12

said. "He's been doing that since middle school, before he even knew what it meant."

"I'm standing right here, Mads, don't third-person me."

"Can you all shut up for a second?" Oliver spoke over Maddy's retort. "We're trying to navigate over here."

Red turned back to Arthur. "Well, good thing you're not spending a whole week in this cramped RV. Oh . . . wait." Red smiled at him.

"I know, right."

Arthur was Simon's friend, really, but he was all of theirs by now. He didn't go to their high school, he went to one in South Philly, but he and Simon were on the same basketball team, both joined last year sometime. Red guessed Arthur didn't much like his friends at his own school, because he'd been coming to all their parties and hangouts since senior year began. And that was okay, because she liked having him around. He always asked how she was and how was her day, even though Red usually answered with lies or exaggerated stories with only faint traces of the truth. He showed interest when Red wasn't interesting at all. And there was that time he dropped her home after that New Year's Eve party and let her sit in his car, warming up in the dry air of the heater before she had to go inside the cold house and find whatever mess her dad had left for her. Arthur didn't know that was happening, he thought they were just talking, talking the night away at two in the morning outside her house. A small kindness he never knew he'd given her. She should give him one back.

"We'll be at the campsite soon, I think," she said. "You can get out and stretch your legs in the great big outdoors. I'll come with you."

"Yeah." Arthur smiled. "I'll be fine." His gaze dropped from her face to the table, where she was resting one hand. "I was meaning to ask earlier, but I didn't want to distract you from driving. What does your hand say?"

"Oh." Red blushed, raising the hand and rubbing at it self-consciously, realizing as she did that there was something written on the back of that one too. To-do lists everywhere, even on her own body. To-do lists and never-get-done lists. "I've got a two-for-one special for you," she said. "On our left hand, we have: *Call AT&T.*"

"Ah, I see. Fascinating. What about?" he asked.

"You know," Red said. "Just to check in with them, see how they're doing, whether they had a good day."

Arthur nodded, a wry smile to match hers. "And did you do it?"

Red pursed her lips, looking at the empty box she'd drawn near her knuckle. "No," she said. "I ran out of time."

"And hand number two?"

"On hand number two," Red said, drawing out the suspense, "we have the very elaborate and detailed instruction: *Pack.*"

"You must have done that one," Arthur said.

"Just about," she replied like it was a joke, but she was telling the truth this time. Packed literally right before she left the house this morning, no time to even double-check her bag against her list. She'd been too busy making sure there was enough food in the house for her dad while she was away.

"Well, if you did it, why haven't you checked it off?" Arthur said, pointing to the small empty box on the see-through flesh of her hand. "Here." He stood up, grabbing one of Maddy's pens from the table that she'd used in an earlier game of Hangman. He uncapped it and leaned toward Red, pressing the felt-tip end against her skin. Gently, he drew two lines: a check mark in the little box. "There you go," he said, standing back to admire his handiwork.

Red looked at her hand. And it felt stupid to admit it to herself, but the sight of that little check mark did change something in her. Small, minuscule, a tiny firework bursting in her head, but it felt good. It always felt good, checking off those boxes. She held out her hand proudly for Maddy to examine and got the nod of approval she was looking for.

Arthur was still watching her, a look in his eyes, a different one that Red couldn't decipher.

"Brazil nuts," Red said.

Arthur's face screwed up. "What?"

"I used to be allergic to them as a kid, but I'm not anymore. Isn't that weird, that a person can just change like that?" she said, fidgeting with the front pocket of her light blue jeans. She'd been sitting here in this spot a long time now. Too long. "My mo—p-parents had to write it on my hand, so I wouldn't forget. Also, does the pattern in the curtains remind anyone of something?" She touched the white-and-blue curtain hanging down next to her, running her hand between the pleats. "It's been bugging me all day, can't work out what it is. A cartoon or something."

"It's just a random pattern," Maddy answered.

"No, it's something. It's something." Red traced her finger over it. Like the silhouette of a character she couldn't quite place. From a book she was read at night, or a TV show? Either way, best not to think back to that time, to when she was little, because of who else might be there.

"Tomatoes," Arthur said, saving her from the memory. "Give me a rash around my mouth. Only when raw, though." He straightened up, as did the wrinkles in his white baseball jersey, navy on the arms. "Anyway, I think I better help with the directions. I'm sensing that Simon is being a hindrance."

"I'm doing a stellar job, thank you very much," Simon said, looking over Oliver's shoulder at an iPhone with a marble orange case; must be Reyna's. There was a map on the screen, a blue dot moving along a highlighted road. The blue dot was them, the six of them and all thirty-one feet of RV. Thank god it wasn't a red dot. Blue was safer.

Arthur sidled to the front, blocking Red's view of the screen, her eyes falling instead to Maddy, who gave her a not-so-subtle wink.

"Huh?"

Maddy shushed her silently, nodding her head ever so slightly in Arthur's direction. "Checks all the boxes," she whispered.

"Stop it," Red warned her.

"You stop it."

They both stopped, because just then Maddy's phone rang, an angry-wasp buzz against the table. The screen lit up with the view from the front camera: the off-white ceiling and a sliver of the under-side of Maddy's chin. Across the top was the word *Mom* and *FaceTime video,* with a *slide to answer* button waiting patiently at the bottom.

Maddy's reaction was instant. Too quick. She tensed, bones sharpening beneath her skin. Her hand darted out to grab the phone, holding it up and away to hide it from Red.

Red knew that was what she was doing, she always knew, though Maddy didn't know she knew.

"I'll call her when we get to the campsite," Maddy said, almost too quiet to hear over the wheels, pressing the side button to reject the call. Looking anywhere but at Red.

*Mom.*

Like Maddy thought Red would split open and bleed just to see the word.

It had been the same for years. In freshman year, Maddy used to take kids to the side and tell them off for saying *yo Momma* jokes in front of Red. She didn't think Red would ever find out. It was a forbidden word, a dirty word. She even got weird talking about the Mummers Parade in front of Red.

How ridiculous.

Except, the thing was, Maddy wasn't wrong.

Red did bleed just to see the word, to hear it, to think it, to remember, the guilt leaving a crater in her chest. Blood, red as her name and red as her shame. So, she didn't think it, or remember, and she wouldn't look to the left to see her mom's face in her reflection in the window. No, she wouldn't. These eyes were just hers.

# THREE

Red concentrated on staring ahead. She wanted to think about the pattern in the curtains again, but she couldn't risk looking that way. Instead, she looked down at the check mark drawn on her hand, eyes tracing the lines, trying to summon back that tiny firework.

Maddy placed her phone facedown.

"Shall we play another game?" she said.

If Red had to sit here any longer, she might go mad. Even just walking a few laps of the RV might help. Thirty-one feet, you know, not just thirty. The 2017 GetAway Vista 31B. 2017 was also the year that—no, stop.

She was about to stand up when the sound of a duck quacking stopped her, mechanical and insistent. It was coming from behind her head.

"Oh, that's me," Oliver said, jumping up from the passenger seat and squeezing his wide shoulders past Arthur and Simon. "Mom's calling," he said.

Red breathed in.

"How do you know it's your mom without looking?" Simon asked, a look of genuine confusion on his face.

"Personalized ringtone," Oliver said, walking past the dining table to the tiny kitchen, running his hands through his golden-brown hair, the exact same shade as his eyes. His backpack was sitting on the counter. He unzipped it. "My mom started it; has personalized ringtones for the whole family," he explained, digging his hand inside. "She has duck à l'orange for her birthday meal every year. Hence the duck." He found the ringing phone, pulled it out. "Arthur, can you take over directions?"

"No problem." Arthur took the empty seat.

"Hey, Mom," Oliver said, holding the phone out to get a good view of his face. He stepped forward and slid onto the booth beside Red. Catherine Lavoy's face filled the screen, her hair the same color as Oliver's, neat and curled. Faint lines around her eyes as she smiled out of the phone. She looked tired, her face full of shadows.

"Hello, sweetie," she said, an uncharacteristic croakiness catching her voice. She cleared her throat. "I just tried Madeline but she wasn't picking up."

"I'm here, Mom," Maddy said, with an awkward glance at Red, but Red pretended not to notice. It was stupid anyway because Red liked Catherine. More than liked her. Catherine had been there Red's entire life. She was kind and caring, and she always knew just how to help her. And, most importantly, she always cut sandwiches into triangles. Oliver pressed the button to activate the rear camera so Maddy could wave at her mom. "Sorry, I didn't hear it ringing."

"That's okay," Catherine said. "Just calling to check how you guys are doing. Are you at your stopover point yet?"

Oliver pressed the front camera on again, and Red could see from the direction of his gaze that he was looking into his own face, shifting his angles so the light found his cheekbones. "No, not yet, we're close to the campsite I think, though. Hey, where are we?" he called to those at the front.

Arthur checked over his shoulder. "Driving through a *Morven Township*. Should be around twenty-five minutes."

"Who was that?" Catherine asked, searching the corners of her screen as though they could give her the answer.

"Maddy's friend, Arthur," Oliver said.

"Who's driving?" Catherine asked.

"Reyna is currently."

"Hi, Mrs. Lavoy," Reyna called from the front, not taking her eyes off the dark road.

"Hello, Reyna," Catherine shouted back, too loudly, her voice crackling against the speakers. "Okay, so you're almost there?"

"Correct."

"Great. Oh, is that Red there?" Catherine asked, peering into her screen, raising it closer to her eye.

Oliver tilted the phone, trapping Red inside the camera. She smiled.

"Oh, it is! Hello, sweetie, how's it going?"

"Yeah, good. No official complaints to file."

Catherine laughed. "And are my children behaving? You know I trust you the—"

Catherine froze on the screen, dead pixels distorting her face.

"The—"

Her hand jolted across the screen, blending into the mess of her face. No longer a person, just blocks of muted color.

"Mom?" Oliver said.

"Th . . . th . . ."

Her words scattered into layers, robotic and strange.

Red's image was frozen too, eyes wide, afraid she'd be stuck in Oliver's phone forever.

"Mom, can you hear me?" Oliver said. "Mom?"

"Ca . . . n you g . . . uys hear me? Hello?" Catherine's voice broke through, but her face couldn't keep up, mouthing words that already existed, talking before she could speak.

"Got you," Oliver said. "Well, sort of. Guess the service must be spotty around here."

"Okay, well." Catherine's face fast-forwarded, twitching as it dragged itself to the present. "I'll let you get on with . . . is that a beer bottle?" Catherine's eye moved to the camera again, staring at a shape on the counter behind Oliver's shoulder.

"Yeah, it's mine," Oliver said smoothly, without a beat. He might just be a better liar than Red.

"You aren't drinking on this trip, are you, Maddy?" Catherine raised her voice to find her daughter off-screen.

"No, Mom," Maddy began. "I know—"

"—You are seventeen, I don't want to hear from anyone that you've been drinking. You can have fun without it."

Which reminded Red; Maddy turned eighteen in just a couple of weeks. She was already worrying about how to get her a birthday present.

"Yes, I know. I am. I won't," Maddy said, leaning forward so her mom could hear her more clearly.

"Oliver?"

"Yes, Mom. I'll watch her. Take chaperone duties very seriously, won't we, Reyna?"

"Yes ma'am," Reyna called.

"All right." Catherine eased back from the camera. "I'll let you go, then. I've got some prep to get on with. Text me in the morning before you head off again."

"Will do, Mom," Oliver said.

"Okay, bye everyone, bye Red."

They called "Bye" in clashing tones, Simon going high and shrill for some reason.

"Love you, Oliver, Maddy."

"Love you, Mom," they said in perfect Lavoy synchronization, and Oliver thumbed the red button, disappearing Catherine back to that warm house in Philadelphia.

"Whew." Maddy breathed out. "What more does she want? My big brother and his girlfriend are already accompanying me on spring break at her insistence. It's so annoying."

She was talking to Red, she must have been, because just then her eyes flashed and she snatched them away, realizing she'd been complaining to the one with the dead mom. But that was okay because Red was thinking about the cartoon *Phineas and Ferb;* they weren't a match for the pattern in the curtains, but now the full theme song was running through her head.

"It's fine," Oliver said to his sister. "Reyna and I are renting our own condo. You won't even see us; we'll leave you and all your friends to it. Wouldn't catch me staying in an RV for a whole week with a bunch of teenagers."

"Yeah," Maddy said, directing her voice at her brother now, "but Mom doesn't know about that part."

"And what Mom doesn't know can't hurt her. She's just stressed with work stuff at the moment," Oliver said, coming to his mom's defense. He did that a lot.

Red really wanted to stand up now, to escape this conversation, to go stand with Arthur at the front, but Oliver and his wide shoulders were trapping her here. Simon came and sat down too, just to make the situation worse, dropping in beside Maddy and digging his hand through the bag of chips. He shoveled an entire fistful into his mouth.

"Yeah, I know," Maddy said, cheeks still flushed. "But she doesn't have to take it out on me."

"She's just protective of you," Oliver countered.

"What are youse all talking about?" Simon said, spewing orange crumbs from his mouth as he did.

"My mom," Oliver explained. "She's stressed because she's in the middle of this huge case at the moment."

"Oh yeah, she's a lawyer, right?" Simon asked, going in for more chips.

Oliver did not look amused. "She's assistant district attorney," he said, and it was hard to miss the pride in his voice, the way he over-pronounced those three words. Which Red translated to mean: *No, Simon, you idiot, she's not* just *a lawyer.*

"What's the case?" Simon said, oblivious to the disdain on Oliver's face.

"You've probably heard about it on the news," he said, pointedly. "It's a pretty big deal."

*A huge deal,* Red thought.

"It's a homicide case; a murder involving two members of the biggest organized crime gang in the city," Oliver said, a shadow of disappointment in his eyes as he didn't get the reaction he was looking for from Simon. He elaborated: "The *literal* Philadelphia Mafia."

"Oh, cool," Simon said, between bites. "Didn't know the Mafia was still a thing, I love *The Godfather.* 'Revenge is a dish best served cold,'" he said in a dreadful Italian American accent.

"Very much still a thing," Oliver said, settling in to his story now that he had Simon's attention.

Could Red climb under the table to get out? Urgh, no: too many legs.

"There was some leadership dispute going on in the crime family, I won't bore you with the details. And at the end of August last year, one of the leaders, Joseph Mannino, was killed by another, Francesco Gotti. Allegedly, I should say. Shot him twice in the back of the head."

Red tried not to picture it, studying the curtains again. She had heard it all so many times; she probably knew the details even better than Oliver. Not that she was going to say so.

"We are officially in South Carolina!" Arthur called, pointing to a green sign out the front, illuminated by the RV's headlights.

Oliver kept talking: "Mom is the lead prosecutor taking Frank Gotti to trial for the murder. The pretrial conference is in a couple of weeks—"

April 25 to be exact, Red thought, surprised she had remembered that particular detail. That wasn't like her.

"—and then it's jury selection and the actual trial."

"Cool," Simon said again. "Mrs. Lavoy, taking on the mob."

Oliver seemed to swell a little, sitting up taller, blocking Red in even more. "But it's not just all that. She had to fight to even get this case. Normally a crime like this would be considered a federal case and would be tried by the US attorney's office. They've tried to prosecute Frank Gotti multiple times, on various charges like drug trafficking and racketeering, and have never once got a conviction. But Mom managed to argue that this murder was under the DA's jurisdiction because it wasn't specifically related to drug trafficking and because Frank Gotti killed Mannino himself; he didn't pay a hit man like they normally do."

Simon yawned; Oliver was losing his crowd. But he didn't take the hint.

"And we know that," Oliver continued, "because there was an eyewitness. Someone actually saw Frank Gotti walking away after shooting Mannino dead. And that's why Mom's so stressed—because the entire case rests on this witness's testimony. And, as you can imagine, in cases against the Mafia, lead witnesses are often intimidated out of testifying or straight-up killed. So Mom has had to make sure the witness has been kept entirely anonymous in all the court documents. *Witness A* is what the press are calling him."

"I see," Simon said. Did he regret asking? Red certainly regretted having to hear it all again.

"But if she wins this case," Oliver said, eyes flashing as though this were the most important part of the story, so Simon better stay with him, "it will be career-defining. The current DA is retiring after this term, and if Mom gets this conviction, she's basically guaranteed to win the Democratic primary this year and be elected DA."

"Let's not jinx it," Maddy chimed in, and it was nice to hear someone else's voice for a change, other than Oliver's and the one in Red's head.

"No"—Oliver nodded down at his sister—"but I'm saying, if Frank Gotti is found guilty, Mom has a great chance of becoming DA." He turned back to Simon. Poor Simon. "Her biggest competition at the moment is Mo Frazer, another assistant DA. He's very popular, especially with the African American communities, but if Mom gets this conviction, I think it will give her the edge over him."

Oliver finally drew back, bowing his head like he was waiting for someone to personally congratulate him.

"Congratulations," Red said, resisting the urge to add one small clap. Simon took the opportunity to escape.

"Shut up, Red," Oliver replied, trying to make it a joke. There were times when Red thought of Oliver as a borrowed big brother; she'd known him her entire life, longer than Maddy if you thought about it like that. But then there were other times she wasn't even sure he remembered her name. Not like it was a difficult one: think primary colors.

"She's done incredibly well for herself. DA before the age of fifty. Of course, by that time I'm going to be US attorney general," he said, again like it was a joke, but it really really wasn't. Oliver managed to turn everything into a dick-measuring contest. Red snorted at that, giving the voice in her head a pat on the back.

"What?" Oliver turned to her, his wide shoulders even wider now, a blockade either side of his neck. "Okay, so what are you doing with your life? I actually can't remember which college you're going to this year, remind me?"

A lump in Red's throat.

"Harvard," she said without blinking. "Full-ride scholarship."

Oliver's eyes snapped wider, bottom lip hanging open. She had just one-upped his prelaw at Dartmouth with a premed girlfriend, how dare she? Red enjoyed the look while she could.

"Wh . . . R-really?" he said.

"Yeah," she said. "Early admission."

"Red," Maddy said in a mock-warning voice, her eyes silently scolding. She used to enjoy annoying Oliver too.

"What?" Oliver looked between them.

"I'm not going to college this year," Red said, relenting. It was fun while it lasted, living that other life.

Oliver laughed, a sigh of relief buried in there somewhere. "I was going to say. Full scholarship at Harvard, ha! Didn't think so."

Oh he didn't, did he?

"You're not going anywhere?" he asked now, fully recovered from the shock.

"Red missed the application deadline," Maddy explained for her. Which wasn't the truth, but it was a good lie, a convenient one, because how very *Red* it was.

"You know me," Red said, just to hammer it home.

"How could you miss the deadline?" Oliver turned to her, a look of cold concern on his face, and Red didn't like where this was going, but she was trapped right here in this fucking booth forever.

She shrugged, hoping that would shut him down.

It did not, Oliver opening his mouth to speak again.

"I don't understand it," he said. "You were such a smart kid."

Don't say it, please don't say it.

"Seems a shame," Oliver went on. "You had so much potential."

And there it was. The line that ripped her open. She'd lost count of the number of times it had been said to her, but there was only one that truly mattered. Red was thirteen and Mom was alive, screaming at each other across the kitchen, back when it used to be warm.

"Red?" Maddy was saying.

It was too hot in here.

Red stood up, knocking her knees against the table, swaying as the RV turned.

"I gotta go—"

But she was saved by Arthur, calling: "Shit, I think we went the wrong way."

# FOUR

"What do you mean?"

Oliver got up from the booth—thank God, Red was free—and walked the four strides to the front, nudging Simon out of his way.

"Let me see," he said to Arthur, holding his hand out for the phone with the directions.

Red was free and she wasn't about to sit at this table any longer. She sidled along and out, moving toward the congregation at the front, perching on the corner of the sofa bed. Oh yes, now she remembered.

"Maddy, which side—"

"—No, it's fine." Oliver spoke across her, swiping his finger on the screen. "It's redirected us. Just keep going down this road, it takes us past a small town called Ruby. Then it should be a left turn and we go south for a bit, toward the *Carolina Sandhills National Wildlife Refuge*," he read from the screen. "Campsite is right around there. We should be just over ten minutes, everyone."

"Perfect," Reyna said, taking one hand off the wheel to rub at her eyes.

"You getting tired?" Oliver asked her. "I can take over?" His voice was different when he spoke to Reyna. Softer at the edges.

"No, I'm good," she said, shooting him a quick smile over her shoulder, stretching wide across her light brown skin. It seemed almost a waste, that a smile that nice was meant for Oliver. That was a mean thought. He meant well. Everyone always meant well.

"You okay?" Arthur asked Red, vacating the passenger seat so Oliver could take it and coming to stand beside her.

She nodded. "RV feels smaller when you've been in it for ten-plus hours."

"I hear that," he agreed. "We'll be there soon. Or we could both get shit-faced like Simon and we won't care anymore."

"I'm not shit-faced," Simon said from behind Arthur. "I'm a very comfortable-amount drunk."

"I'm not so sure Tomorrow Morning Simon will agree," Red said.

"I'm not sure Now Maddy agrees either," Maddy said, turning around and perching on her booth so she could see them all. "You don't want to peak too soon. We have a whole week ahead of us."

Simon finished off his beer in one large gulp, eyeballing Maddy as he did so.

"Is it this left turn here?" Reyna asked, slowing down. "Oliver?"

"Sorry, um . . ." He stared down at the phone in his hands. "The GPS has gone weird. I think I've lost service. I'm not sure where we are."

"I need an answer," Reyna said, idling to a stop just ahead of the intersection, hand hesitating over the turn signal.

A car horn sounded behind them. And again.

"Oliver?" Reyna said, her voice rising, the knuckles bursting out of her skin like bony hilltops as she held the wheel too hard.

"Um, yes, I think so. Left here," he said, uncertainly.

But it was all Reyna needed; she pushed off and took the turn, the car behind screaming its displeasure as it zipped off across the intersection.

"Asshole," she said under her breath.

"Sorry," Oliver said. "Your phone isn't working."

"Not you, the car," Reyna clarified.

"I can't get the map to work," Oliver said, swiping furiously at the screen, closing the map app and reopening it. It was blank; a yellow background and empty grid lines and nothing else. "It doesn't know where we are. Zero bars. Hey, does anyone have any service?"

Red had left her phone over there on the table. But if she had zero bars, it could mean she had no signal, or it could mean that AT&T finally cut off her service after the last unpaid bill.

"I've got a bar," Arthur said, his phone cupped in his hand.

"Who's your provider?" Oliver looked up at him.

"Verizon," he said. "Hold on, I'll get the route up." He tapped at his screen. "Already had it loaded from when I was directing Red. Okay, so yeah we took the correct turn. You keep on this road for two miles, then it's a right down Bo Melton Loop."

"My phone is struggling too," Maddy said, holding it up and shaking it, like that might spark some life back into it.

"We're deep in the country now, folks," Simon said, leaning on his words in an atrocious Southern accent, spliced with a touch of *crazy old man.* Sober Simon was normally quite good at accents. He prided himself on them, in fact, always guaranteed a part in the school play. You should hear his upper-class English gentleman.

Red watched out the wide windshield, a panoramic view of darkness, the two headlights carving up the night, bringing it into existence. There was no world anymore, only this RV and the six of them, and whatever the dark brought them.

Arthur made a small noise: a groan in the back of his throat as he stared down at his screen. Red stood up, looking over his shoulder to see what it was. He glanced back at her and cleared his throat. Maybe she was standing too close.

"Looks like I just lost service too," he said, right as Red's eyes registered the zero bars at the top of the screen.

"Shit," Oliver hissed, tapping Reyna's phone again, like he could make it work through sheer force of will. If anyone could, a Lavoy could.

"It's okay," Arthur said to him, "I still have the route up, just can't see where we are on it. We'll have to look for road signs."

"Old-school navigation," Reyna commented.

"Let me help," Simon said, shuffling over to Arthur and Red, crowding them. "I'm good at maps."

"You say you're good at everything," Red said.

"I *am* good at everything," Simon answered. "Except being humble."

There was no one else on the road. No passing headlights, no red glow of brake lights up ahead. Red stared out the windshield, concentrated.

"When's the turn?" Reyna asked.

"Not yet," Red answered, her eyes now following the highlighted road on Arthur's screen, no blue dot to guide them, trying to match it with the darkness outside.

"Wouldn't trust Red with directions," Maddy said.

"Hey."

"Well, I mean, it's not like you're ever on time, is it?"

Red leaned back to look at Maddy perching on the booth, head resting on the bed of her knuckles. "I'll have you know," she said, "that everyone else was later than me this morning. I was first by like ten whole minutes."

Maddy looked sheepish, biting one lip.

"What?"

"Nothing."

Red knew it wasn't nothing.

"Maddy, what?"

"I, um, I told you we were meeting at our house at nine. But I told everyone else we were meeting at ten."

"You told me a whole hour earlier?" Red said, and why did it sting that she had? It was a lie, yes, but it was a considerate lie. Maddy knew Red would be late: she didn't know all the reasons why, but she knew the end result and that was the same, wasn't it?

"So technically, you were fifty minutes late and everyone else was on time."

"I missed the bus," Red said, which wasn't true: she spent the last of her change on her dad's favorite cereal and then walked the whole way, bag wheeling behind her.

"Ha, look, that road's called Wagon Wheel Road," Simon snorted, pointing at the screen.

"Is that the right I make?" Reyna asked, hand darting to the turn signal, though there was no one to signal for.

No, it wasn't here.

"No, no, no," Arthur said quickly. "It's the next one. I think."

Reyna sped up again, following the road as it curved around.

"Wagon Wheel." Simon was still chuckling to himself.

"Here, this right," Oliver said, taking charge. "Turn, Reyna."

"I'm turning," she said, the faintest trace of irritation in her voice. Too many cooks. Which made Reyna, what? A spoon? The Lavoys had fancy spoons at their house: pearly handles and no stains.

There was a new sound, joining with the wind as it rushed against the sides of the RV: a rasping noise beneath them. The road was growing rougher, gravelly, the RV lurching as it rolled down. There were no more yellow markings, no more *my lane* and *your lane,* and from the light of the high beams Red could see rows and rows of trees standing either side, silent sentinels on the dead-of-night road.

She felt watched, which was stupid; trees didn't have eyes. But neither did doors, yet her mom used to stick googly ones on Red's so she felt safe in her bed in the dar— No, stop, she needed to concentrate on where they were going.

"Looks like we're in the middle of nowhere," Maddy commented from her perch, cupping her hands around her eyes so she could look out the side window.

"As is the campsite, so we're good," Oliver replied.

The RV staggered as it hit a pothole.

Arthur was chewing his lip, eyes narrowed behind his glasses. "I think it's left here," he said, not sure, not loud enough to reach Reyna.

"Left, left here!" Simon didn't have the same problem. But Reyna didn't listen, didn't trust the drunk one.

"It's left," Red said.

"You sure?" Oliver asked her, but Reyna had already pulled the RV into it, and the road wasn't even paved anymore, just dirt and rocks, dust kicking up into the headlights. "This can't be right, let me look at the map." He snapped his fingers for Arthur to pass his phone over. "Reyna, turn around."

"I can't turn around!" she said, more than a hint of irritation in her voice now: a full underlayer. "This road is way too narrow and this RV is way too big."

"Where are we?" Red asked Arthur, leaning across to see, like it made any difference.

"I think we're here somewhere." He pointed at the screen. "McNair Cemetery Road. Maybe."

"That's definitely wrong," Oliver said. "We have to turn ba—"

"—I can't!" Reyna shot him a look.

"Is there a turn?" Red nudged Arthur.

"Wait, I think there's a left soon," he said, zooming in to the mouth of the small road on his phone. "Might circle us back to that other road." He glanced at Red and she nodded.

"For fuck's sake," Oliver said, one of his knees rattling against the dashboard. "We wouldn't have gone the wrong way if I was directing."

"This is stressful," Maddy said, her hands buried in her loose hair. "We should have just flown and rented a condo like everyone else from school is."

A flush in Maddy's cheeks as she realized what she'd said, their eyes meeting for half a second. Red was the reason they didn't fly and rent a condo like everyone else. That was why Maddy came up with the RV idea. *Way cheaper—just gas and spending money. Come on, it will be fun.* It was all Red's fault.

"Just keep going," Red said to Reyna, blocking everyone else out.

"I don't see a left turn." Reyna leaned closer to the wheel, straining to see.

As they followed the corner around, the headlights got lost in the woods, recoiling as they bounded off some body of water: a creek hiding somewhere behind the trees.

"Where's the left turn?" Reyna pushed forward.

"There!" Simon pointed out the windshield. "It's here. Go left."

"Sure?"

Red glanced down at the map in Arthur's hands. This was it. "Yes," she said. "Down there."

"Doesn't even look like a real road," Oliver said as they peeled down it, dirt and gravel loud against the wheels.

It was narrower, tighter, the trees pressing in on them, barring the way with low-hanging branches that scraped the top of the RV.

"Keep going," Red said. Her fault that the others were here and not on a nice plane tomorrow instead, with all their other friends.

"I've lost the map," Arthur said, blank grid lines taking over his screen.

"Keep going," she said.

"Not like we have a choice," Oliver retorted.

The trees broke away from the road, cutting their losses, giving way to low-lying scrubland and long grass on either side.

"Is it a dead end?" Oliver asked, staring out the front.

"Keep going," Red said.

"Pretty sure it's a dead end," Oliver decided, though none of them could see. "Reyna, it's wide enough here, you can turn around and head back."

"Okay." Reyna gave in, pushing her foot against the brake.

The RV slowed, rattling against the barely-there road.

A sharper sound, like a crack, splitting the night in half.

"What was that?" Simon asked.

The RV hitched, drooping down at the front left side, Red stumbling into Arthur as it did.

"Fuck," Oliver said, staring at Reyna over there on the sunken side, slamming his fist into the dashboard. "I think we just punctured a tire."

# 11:00 P.M.

# FIVE

Reyna turned the engine off and the night grew too quiet, only the sounds their own bodies made, Red's breath catching in her throat.

"I'll go first." Oliver stood up, pushing past the others as he walked over to the door of the RV, just beyond the sofa bed. His steps were heavy, shaking the ground. He opened the door and let the outside in.

A wash of cool night air hit Red in the face as she watched Oliver take the four steps down to the outside world.

Maddy went next, sliding out of the booth to follow her brother.

"You okay?" Arthur asked Reyna, who was standing up from behind the wheel, stretching out her neck.

"Yeah," she said, the slightest tremor in her voice. "I don't understand what we could have hit. There's nothing on the road."

"Let's go see." Arthur gave her a kind smile and then turned, heading out the door, Simon trailing closely behind him, slightly less steady on the steep steps.

"After you," Red said, gesturing Reyna ahead of her. "I'm sure it'll be okay."

"It will be all my fault somehow," Reyna said to her, a secret flash from her deep brown eyes. "Just you watch."

Was she talking about Oliver? Red knew that feeling, but she didn't know Reyna had felt it too. The two of them, Lavoy-adjacent but not Lavoys and didn't they know it. Except lots of things were actually Red's fault. This, even.

"No, it'll be fine," Red said as she scooped up her phone from the table. Oliver couldn't blame Reyna; they were happy, they were perfect, small touches and soft voices.

Reyna's shoes tapped down the stairs and then it was Red's turn, her legs aching from sitting down too long as she took each step. One, two, three, four, and by the end, as her sneakers scraped against the dirt road, she was wondering whether Reyna had seen a dead body yet, as part of her studies. Maybe she could ask if they still looked like the people they once were. Or whether it was true that blood was sometimes blue, not always red.

Red followed Reyna, who followed Simon, walking around the front side of the RV, into the too-bright light of the high beams, dust from the road floating upward through them.

"Oh fuck!" came Oliver's voice. He was already there, crouched down beside the wheel, lighting it up with the flashlight on Reyna's phone. "Definitely punctured."

"You sure?" Arthur asked as he stepped out of the blinding high beam.

"Yes I'm sure. I was actually downplaying it: there's a huge fucking hole and a giant tear in the tire."

"What from?" Maddy said, crouching down beside Oliver as Red came around the corner of the RV and saw the tire for herself. There was a large split in the rubber, about the size of her hand, the two sides peeling away from each other. No air at all, the bottom pooling out under the weight of the RV. Thirty-one feet long, but how heavy?

"I don't know," Oliver said, searching around with the flashlight, running his hand carefully over the road. "Maybe there's glass here, or a sharp rock. Maybe a nail. Reyna?" He pivoted to look up at her, shining the light in her eyes. "You didn't see anything?"

"No, I didn't see anything," she replied, exchanging a quick look with Red.

"Well, you must have driven over something. Why weren't you looking?" Oliver returned to his search, a harder edge to his voice.

Reyna had been right. Well, she did know Oliver better than Red did.

"None of us saw anything. It's pitch-black outside." That was Red's best attempt at helping, but the small sideways smile on Reyna's face showed that it was appreciated all the same.

"I can't find anything. Maybe it got thrown by the wheel. Or maybe it was just a piece-of-shit tire that broke over nothing." Oliver stood up, shining the light on Simon now. "Does your uncle ever get this RV serviced?"

"How the fuck should I know?" Simon hiccupped. But, really, how the fuck should he know, especially in his current state.

"Well, how long has your uncle owned the RV?" Oliver pressed.

"I don't know."

"How do you not know that?" Oliver's voice sharpened.

"Because he's drunk," Maddy said, an apologetic glance at Simon, swaying on his feet.

"Listen," Arthur said, "we've driven over five hundred miles on the tire today, and it's been fine." Defending the tire or defending Simon, Red wasn't sure.

"It doesn't really matter how it got punctured," Reyna said, stepping forward. "What matters is what we can do about it."

"Someone call Triple-A," said Maddy.

"There's no signal, remember?" Oliver looked down at her, Reyna's phone raised in his hand.

"The police?" Maddy tried again.

"Still need service to call them, unfortunately," Arthur answered this time, much softer than Oliver had.

"Does anybody have any service at all?" Oliver turned to the group. "Check your phones."

Red pulled hers out of her jeans pocket, the screen lighting up the underside of her face. No bars. No 3G or 4G or GPRS. Nothing. Except 67% battery, which, hey, was pretty good for her.

"Nothing," she said for good measure.

"Who are you with?" Oliver asked, in a way that sounded as though Red could only give him wrong answers.

"AT&T." She glanced down at the unchecked box scrawled on her hand.

"Shit," Oliver said. Yep, see, wrong answers only. "That's what me, Reyna and Maddy are on. Arthur, you still got nothing with Verizon?"

"Nothing," Arthur confirmed, showing Oliver his home screen.

"Everyone has zero bars? Simon?"

"Yeah, I'm the same. T-Mobile. Nothing."

"We must be in a dead zone," Red said.

"Okay, so calling for help is out." Reyna looked at them all. "We—"

"—Maybe not," Oliver cut across her. "We could walk back to that small town we passed. Ruby. Find a landline there to call for help if there's still no service. It was only a few miles back."

"More like five miles," Reyna said. "That's too far."

"Well, maybe we'll find a house or a farm or something with a landline on the way," Oliver said.

"It's really dark," Maddy said in a small voice. "And we're in the middle of nowhere."

"Not all of us have to go," Oliver replied. Neither of the Lavoys were volunteering for walking-in-the-dark duty, then. Red had another idea.

"Why can't we just sleep here tonight?" she suggested. "I bet no one else will be driving this way until morning, and then we can get help once it's light."

"No," Maddy said, and Red was surprised. She'd assumed Oliver would be the one to shoot it down. "If we wait till tomorrow to fix the tire, then we won't set off in time, and we'll be late getting to Gulf Shores. Everyone else from school will be there and we'll miss the first night out with everyone."

"Not to just swoop in and save the day here, but I'm gonna," Simon said, leaning his elbow on Red's shoulder. "Can't believe I'm the observant one here, but: there's a spare tire on the back of the RV."

Maddy's face rearranged, her relief obvious even through the darkness that separated them. She gave Simon an amused smile, and Arthur gave him a pat on the back, the vibration passing through Red too.

"Yes," Oliver said. "I was just going to ask you whether there was a spare."

Of course he was.

"I assume there's a jack somewhere?" he asked.

"I'm a Simon, not a Jack," Simon replied, with a wry smile that Oliver clearly hadn't noticed.

"I mean the device to lift the—"

"Oh right, *that* jack," Simon said in an exaggerated tone, miming smacking himself on the head. He really did belong on a stage somewhere. "Yeah, I think there's probably one in those lower storage units."

"Right, okay." Oliver clapped and it was too loud, echoing through the quiet scrubland, patches of grass bristling at the intrusion. "Let's get this done as quick as we can, then get back on the road to that fucking campsite."

The darkness held its breath, listening as they made their plans. Then the wind let go, dancing through Red's hair, and the grass chattered and the trees whispered, and Red wondered what it was they were saying to each other.

# SIX

Was now a bad time for Red to say she had to pee?

"Reyna." Oliver turned to her. "You and Maddy go with Simon to find the jack, and we'll need a wrench too. Something to remove the nuts."

"That's what she said," Simon whispered so only Red could hear.

"Arthur." Oliver pointed to him. "You and me will get the spare tire."

"Okay."

"What about me?" Red said as the others picked up their feet and started to move.

"Think we are all heading in the same direction," Arthur said, beckoning for her to follow.

They were, moving as a group to the rear side of the RV, Maddy swiping the flashlight up on her phone to help light the way. She pointed it at the side of the RV, the light glaring against the glossy off-white sides and the red-and-blue-stripe motif along the center. The RV seemed bigger from out here, a faint yellow glow leaking out of the windows. Maddy moved the beam lower, the flashlight revealing three large storage units around the rear wheel, under the overhanging side.

Maddy opened the one at the very end, and Reyna knelt to have a look.

"No, that's the generator in there," she said. "Next one."

Red moved past them, following Arthur and Oliver as they walked around the back of the vehicle. A black ladder was attached here, running to the roof of the RV. And mounted beside it, in a canvas cover, was the spare tire.

Oliver gave it a slap.

"Let me just see something," Arthur said, planting one foot on the bottom rung of the ladder. He pushed up, climbing fast, his phone a lump in the back pocket of his jeans. Not that Red was looking.

"What are you doing?" Oliver called up to him as Arthur stepped out onto the roof of the RV. He might have lost himself to the dark sky if it weren't for his white sweatshirt, glowing like the moon. Red looked up even farther and, hey, she could see the actual moon.

"Just wondering if I can see any lights nearby," Arthur replied, disappearing from sight as he walked farther along. The sounds of his shoes pattering. Red and Oliver waited for the answer.

"Anything?" Oliver said. "Arthur?"

"Er, let me look over here and . . ." Arthur grunted. "No, I can't see any." He came back, looming large over them as he turned and carefully guided his foot back to the ladder. "No sign of civilization anywhere."

"Doesn't matter," Oliver said as Arthur climbed down. "We'll get this tire changed in no time and be on our way."

Arthur jumped to the ground, brushing off his knees as Oliver unzipped the canvas cover from the spare tire. He pulled at it and it rattled against its mount.

"Hey, have you found a wrench or something?" Oliver called to the others. "We need it to get the spare down."

"Yeah, gimme a sec," Reyna replied. She needed two seconds, actually, and then a four-pronged wrench appeared around the corner, before she even did. She held it out for Oliver. "Here. And we found a jack in the same compartment, with some wooden blocks, I think to get it high enough under the RV."

"Great," Oliver said, handing Reyna back her phone. He braced the wrench in his hand, securing it over the first lug nut. "Can you carry it all over to the front wheel?"

"Already on it," she said, disappearing again behind the RV.

"Need a hand?" Arthur asked as Oliver leaned his weight onto the wrench. The nut started to give and Oliver turned with it.

"All good, I got it," he said, loosening it the whole way and removing the nut. Three more to go. "Actually, could you shine a light?"

"Sure," Arthur said, removing his phone from his front pocket and flicking on the flashlight.

Red wasn't any help, was she? Standing here looking at the moon.

"It's big tonight," Arthur said, following her eyes to the sky.

*"That's what she said!"* came Simon's faint call from the side of the RV.

Red snorted, looking away when she noticed a flush in Arthur's cheeks.

"Hey, at least we're out of the RV for a bit." She gestured to the wide-open nothing all around them, wrapped in darkness. Dirt, low bushes, patches of high grass, and space. Lots of space. Up and down, this way and that. "Must say, exploding the tire with your mind was a slightly drastic measure."

Arthur clicked his tongue. "Desperate times," he said.

"What do you think it could have been, really?"

He shrugged. "Probably a sharp rock or glass, like Oliver said."

And was Red imagining it, or did his voice sometimes soften for her? No, he was just nice to everybody.

"We should never have come this way," Oliver said, summoned by his name. He removed the third nut. "I knew it couldn't be right."

"It's no one's fault." Arthur sniffed. "Not easy navigating without a working map."

Oliver's silence said all it needed to; it was everyone's fault except his.

"At least it's only raw tomatoes," Red said, "so you can still eat pizza."

"What is she talking about?" Oliver said, almost there with the final nut.

"Oh, my allergy." Arthur smiled, somehow staying with her. That was rare. Red lost most people at least a few times a day, sometimes a few times per conversation. "I know, not sure life would be worth it without pizza. I'd just have to have a perma-rash."

"Hey, grow a beard and no one would know," she said. It would probably look good on him too.

"Don't know what the fuck you two are talking about, but I'm done," Oliver said, straightening up. "Here, Red, run this up to the front." He placed the wrench in her hand, the metal warm where he'd been holding it. "They can start loosening the nuts on the flat before we jack it up."

"Yes sir, right away sir." But she did it, she even ran, just like he said, rounding the RV and along the side, stones scattering under her feet.

She slowed, holding the wrench out to Reyna, who was crouched in front of the wheel, the metallic cover already removed and a bright red metal jack beside her, its lever up and ready. A pile of wide wooden blocks there too. "Oliver said to—" Red began.

"—Yeah, I heard him," Reyna said, taking the wrench and positioning it over the first nut. "He's got one of those voices that carries."

Reyna leaned into her arms, pushing down on the nut until it gave, loosening it a few turns before moving on to the next.

"How often does your uncle use the RV?" Maddy was asking Simon, picking at the side of her lip.

He shrugged, and it almost tipped him. "Don't know. He's a bit weird." And then in explanation: "My white uncle."

"Ah," Maddy said, spinning on her heels at the sound of footsteps. Oliver and Arthur were walking over, the spare tire cradled in Arthur's arms. Guess Oliver decided to let him help after all.

He dropped the tire down, the rubber jumping up to meet his hand again before he laid it on its side.

"How you getting on?" Oliver asked Reyna, leaning over her.

"Last one," she said with a grunt as it gave way, and she spun the wrench a couple of times. "All loosened."

"Great." Oliver rested his hand on her shoulder. A small touch. "Let's get the jack in place."

A *12-ton hydraulic bottle jack,* it said on the side in large black letters against the red. Oliver bent down, unscrewing the black top of the jack, the device growing taller with each turn.

"That's as high as it gets. Someone pass me those blocks."

Simon pushed them over with one foot.

Oliver piled the blocks up, four high, beneath the outer metal frame of the RV, just behind the wheel. Then he placed the steel-plated bottom of the jack on top of the highest block, jiggling it to check it was secure enough. It would do, apparently, because Oliver turned his attention to the lever. He pulled it up and down, and again, and slowly the top of the device began to emerge from the base, reaching up for the bottom of the RV. Oliver's arm pumped and pumped again. He settled down on his knees; this would take a minute.

Which was good, because Red just remembered—

"Hey, Maddy, which side of the bed do you normally sleep on again?" she said. "Because I—"

"—The left normally," Maddy said, watching as the jack disgorged itself, metallic and rigid. "But I'm easy."

"Oh, that's fine, I'm normally the right," Red lied. And why did she need to? Maddy had just said she didn't mind.

The top of the jack made contact with the frame of the RV, metal on metal, shining ghostly white as Maddy captured the moment in the flashlight. A creaking sound as Oliver pulled the lever up and down and up. Slowly, the RV began to lift, the flat tire unpuddling from the ground.

"Ladies and gentlemen, we have liftoff!" Simon whooped, and the scrubland stole his voice, echoing it back, stripping it of anything human. An otherworldly cry in the night.

Red watched the RV, inching higher and higher, relieving the pressure on the torn-open tire.

"I have to pee." She suddenly remembered, voicing it as she did.

"Ever the lady," Simon commented.

"Well, you can't go in the RV now we've jacked it up," Oliver said, slightly breathless, slightly irritated, still pumping away at the lever. "You'll have to find a bush."

"I might upgrade to a tree, thanks," Red said, turning toward the back end of the RV and the thick trees they'd come through that way. She couldn't go somewhere in front of the RV; she didn't know how far the headlights would reach. Imagine: Arthur seeing her white ass, floating in the night. Red avoided his eyes.

"You can't go on your own," Maddy said, grabbing her arm. "It's pitch-black."

"I have my phone."

"No, but, I mean it might not be safe." She breathed out. "What if there's an axe-murderer or something?"

"No axe-murderers in South Carolina," Simon said. "Only in North Carolina. It's chainsaws you've gotta watch out for. And vampires."

"Chainsaws. Vampires. Got it," Red said. "I'll keep my eyes peeled."

"Vampires *love* peeling eyes."

"Red?" Maddy said.

"I could—" Arthur began.

"—I'll be fine, I'm just going over there. Be right back."

Red kept going toward the back, doubling her pace when Oliver called: "Quickly, we won't be long here!"

She'd pee in her own time, thanks. Except now she was moving at a slow jog, and now more of a run, shoes scuffing against the rough road. The voices of the others faded behind her as she moved, just her and the moon now, and the whispering in the grass. She slowed to pull out her phone—11:21 p.m. and 65% battery, still very good for her—and swiped up to flick on the flashlight. Shadows stretched and shrank as she pooled the light around her, searching for a spot. There were plenty of shrubs and bushes around, but they were short, not much to hide behind. And she still wasn't that far from the group.

Red went farther, farther, holding up the light to carve a path through the darkness. Her eyes alighted on a tree right ahead, alone, broken away from the others. Just like her. Branches spring-full of leaves, quivering as she approached. Had the tree been pushed out by the others or left of its own accord? Anyway, Red circled around the back of it, checking to be sure the trunk covered her. All good.

She put her phone down on the grass over there, a white glowing halo around it as the rest of the world fell to darkness. She fumbled for the button on her jeans, unzipped, and pulled them down with her underwear, strapped around her ankles.

She squatted.

Sometimes it was difficult to pee when she thought about it too hard. So she thought about something else, thought about how good it would feel when this night was finally over. Thought about whether her dad had managed to find one of the ready-meals she'd left him tonight, or if he'd passed out before he could. It wasn't enough. Nothing she could do for him was enough. There was a ghost in Red's house, and it wasn't her mom. Dad needed help, proper help, and you needed money for that. But Red would take care of that for him soon; that was the plan. She just had to see everything through. Not that she could see anything right now, apart from the outline of her phone.

A snap in the trees. Red's eyes flicked up. It was dark, too dark, just black shapes among more black shapes. But there, right over there, something moved in the trees.

# SEVEN

"Hello?" Red called, her voice hollow, her eyes alive, sorting through shadows.

Perfect.

This was the absolute worst way to die. Mid–squat-pissing behind a tree while Maddy's axe-murderer charged at her from the front. Dignified till the end. No, the worst way to die must be suffocating, no, no, actually, the worst was on your knees, two shots to the back of the—all right, all right, let's finish up here.

There wasn't anyone in the trees. Red knew that. She did. The only people were the ones she knew of, behind her on the scrubland. It was just a rat, or a bat, or a raccoon, or maybe a vampire. But it didn't matter because she was finished.

Her legs shook as she straightened, pulling her underwear and jeans back up, fastening the button and zipper in a hurry. She lurched for her phone and held it up, the flashlight her weapon against the night.

"Aha!"

See, no one in the trees. Told you.

But even so, Red decided to run back to the others. Oliver would probably say she'd been too long already. Her ponytail flicked against the back of her neck and she could hear her heart in her ears; was that from the running or because of the axe-murderer? The light swung forward and back in her hand, flashing along the road. Red stumbled over a rock she hadn't seen, swearing as her ankle buckled beneath her, trying to bring her down.

"Red?"

Red held the phone up. Arthur was just ten feet in front of her on the road, walking toward her, his glasses reflecting the light.

"You okay?" he called. "We thought we heard you yelling."

"Oh, yeah I was," she said, panicking and quickly double-checking that she'd done up her fly before Arthur could see. "Just shouting at the axe-murderer."

"Well, I hope he's having a good evening," Arthur said as they finally met on the road, turning on his heels to walk back together.

"He's having a great time, skulking through the trees, watching girls pee."

Arthur snorted. He pushed his glasses up his nose, a sudden awkwardness in the movement of his arms. "I was going to cover my eyes and call out before I got close, by the way," he said, like it was important she knew that. "So I didn't—"

"—see me peeing?" she asked.

"Exactly. I don't think we're quite there yet."

And what did he mean by that? Where *were* they? As far as Red knew, they were just awkwardly flirting, neither of them very good at it, and in a few months he'd move on with his life, like everyone else. Probably get a nice college girlfriend he could take home for Thanksgiving.

"Red?"

Crap, she hadn't been listening. Had he said anything else?

"Yeah?"

"You know, in all this time, I've never asked you," he said. "Why did your parents call you Red?"

"Oh, well, that's easy," she said. "Because of my natural bright red hair color." She reached back to tug at a strand of her dull blond hair.

Arthur smiled, shook his head.

"And the real reason?" he asked.

"It's not Red, it's Redford," she said, eyes on the RV as their steps brought it closer. Did Red imagine it, or was the RV steadily lowering on one side? They must have changed the tire. "I was named after my grandpa. Redford Foster."

"That's quite a name," he laughed.

"Isn't it?"

"Very serious."

"Well, he was," Red said. "He was a police captain."

A pause.

"Like your mom?"

The word punched through Red's chest, a hole left behind, air bleeding around it. She slowed to catch her breath. Yes, like her mom. Grace Kenny, captain of the Philadelphia Police Department, Third District. She didn't know Arthur knew about all that.

Arthur drew to a stop, catching her arm, the RV twenty feet ahead of them.

"You know, early on, Maddy pulled me aside and told me to never ask you about your mom," he said. "Or to even mention moms in general in front of you. And if that's what you want, then that's fine, but if you can't talk to your best friend about her, I was wondering, maybe, whether you wanted someone else to talk to about her. And I could do that sometime. If you want."

No. She didn't want. She could not speak of her, would not think of her. Arthur hadn't known Red in the before time, he was new, he wasn't supposed to know about her mom. Maybe that was what Red liked most about him, that he was untainted by knowing. Except he did know, Maddy had told him. Did that change everything? Was that why he was always nice to her, why he softened his voice? She looked down. That was enough. Red refused to think about Arthur knowing, pitying her, or about Mom. Push it away, out of her head, skip to the next thought. Gone.

"What are you doing when we finish senior year?" she asked, a question she never asked because she hated when people asked her, and Arthur bristled at the brush-off, dropping his eyes. "You going to college?"

"Um, no, actually," he said, recovering. "No, for me it's straight to joining the family business." He grimaced. What was the family business—kicking puppies?

"Which is?" she asked.

"Flipping houses, essentially. But I'll be in the office."

"That's not so bad."

"No," he agreed. "Except it means I'll spend all day every day inside."

"Ah, the ol' claustrophobia," she said.

He raised a finger. "Exactly."

Red sniffed. "What, did you get locked inside a closet as a kid, or something?"

It was a joke, but Arthur didn't smile. His eyes hardened on the road, shoulders hitched up to his ears.

"Yeah," he said, flatly. "Just a prank but . . . my brother sometimes takes things too far."

Well, shit. Now it was clearly Red's turn to put her foot in it. Arthur's eyes were still clouded, an awkward twist in his mouth. Maybe he didn't want to talk about his brother, just as much as Red didn't want to talk about her mom. She made a silent deal with him; he agreed, even if he didn't know about it. There were more important things to think about tonight, anyway. Now she just had to change the subject, quick, distract them both.

"Need to get yourself an outside job, then," she said. "Dog-walker?"

Arthur shook the expression out of his face, recovering as he turned to her.

"Farmer?" he countered.

"Nature conservationist?" she said.

"Ooh, nice."

Red had another one: "Axe-murderer?" she said.

"I hear that's taken."

Red had almost forgotten what it was they were listing, and why, but before she could say her next one, a sound erupted across the wide clearing. Clapping. Cheering. Another loud whoop from Simon.

"They must be done. Come on," Arthur said, leading Red up to the RV and along the side. And she might have been wrong, but there was a moment where it looked like he had reached for her hand.

They approached the others at the front, the torn-open wheel lying discarded on the road, the RV lowered back down on its new tire. Simon was cradling the jack like it was an old friend. Smiles on everyone's faces as the flashlight landed on them.

"There you are," Maddy said to Red. "I was getting worried."

"Thanks for all your help there, Red," Oliver added, his arm tucked through Reyna's. Red was pretty sure Reyna had done most of the work anyway.

"You're very welcome," she replied.

"Oh and, by the way, I checked," Oliver continued, speaking to both Red and Arthur now. "This *is* a dead-end road. Well, it goes through some trees over there, but it's so tight we'd never get the RV through."

"Okay, sorry," Arthur said, and what was he apologizing for? They had all gotten lost. And Red was the one who told them to keep going, who brought them down here.

"That's fine," Red said. "We can turn around."

"Right, let's get this show on the road." Oliver clapped again. "Red, can you take the old tire, shove it in the storage compartments? Maddy, grab the blocks and the wrench."

Red picked it up, the tire limp and awkward in her arms. She looked down at the tear, eyes tracing along its frayed edges. Completely destroyed.

"This way," Simon said to her, gesturing with the jack.

Arthur, Reyna and Oliver headed off into the high beams, glowing as they made their way back around to the door.

"So," Maddy said, the blocks and wrench gathered precariously in her arms. "Arthur came looking for you. Worried you were lost in the dark."

"And he found me," Red said. "End of story."

"Oh, what's this?" Simon asked, opening the closest storage compartment and pushing the jack inside. "Girl gossip?"

"Nothing," Red said, brushing past him to chuck the tire in too. It made a loud *thwack* as it landed.

"Oh, come on, include me." He stuck out his bottom lip, tugging on Red's sleeve.

"There's nothing to be included in."

"Arthur went looking for Red," Maddy said, the blocks and wrench falling from her arms into the compartment with a loud clatter. She pushed the door shut and locked it in place with the handle.

"Ooh, saucy," Simon said with a click of his tongue and an exaggerated wink.

"We were gone for like three minutes," Red said, walking toward the back side of the RV, the others on her heels.

"That's enough," Simon said, and Maddy laughed.

"Will you two—"

"—fuck off?" was Simon's suggestion.

"—shut up?" was Maddy's.

"—make out?"

"Ew, Simon." Maddy's face crumpled in disgust.

"Oh as if you wouldn't," Simon said, overtaking Red and turning around. "I'm very good-looking. Check out these cheekbones. Camera loves these cheekbones."

"That's not what Camera says behind your back," Red said, pushing him on.

"Huh, betrayal!"

They rounded the other side of the RV.

"Well, anyway," Simon whispered to Red. "I approve of the pairing."

"You approve of all pairings," Maddy added.

"Not true." Simon paused again by the door, his foot on the lowest step. "I think it's weird that Jess T's new boyfriend is twenty-two, and that they've only been together two months and she's bringing him on spring break. *And* that he's called Marco. Red flags everywhere."

With another push, Red finally got him into the RV, stepping up behind him and shuffling in. Everyone was at the front, Reyna settling back into the driver's seat.

"Really, I can take over," Oliver was saying. "I only had one beer earlier."

"It's fine, I got it," Reyna said.

"Can you make the turn?"

"Yes I can make the turn."

"Right, okay," Maddy said, pulling the door closed behind her. "All in. Let's get out of here."

"Finally." Oliver looked back at them all, a wide smile cracking his face. "Well done, everyone. Overcoming adversity."

Probably the most adversity Oliver Lavoy had ever encountered.

"It makes for a good story, at least," Maddy said. "Much more exciting than everyone else's journey tomorrow."

"Yeah." Simon nodded. "Unless *Marco* murders them all on the plane."

Reyna turned the keys in the ignition, and the RV roared into life, ready to go.

Simon whooped again, Arthur clapped and Maddy cheered.

"Oh wait," she said, fumbling for her phone. "Let's get a victory selfie. Come on, everyone in."

Maddy outstretched her arm, trying to fit them all in the screen.

"Red, in closer. Reyna, turn around."

Red shuffled in closer to Arthur and Simon. She'd already been smiling too long, her cheeks aching. Maddy held up two fingers on her spare hand.

"Okay, everyone say: *Team RV!*"

"Team RV!" they called, voices out of time and out of tune.

Maddy pressed the button on the *V,* and Red could see everyone's teeth in the photo.

"Perfect," Maddy said, lowering her arm to study the picture.

"Team RV," Simon called again, turning it into a chant. "Team RV! Team RV!" He stopped when no one else joined in. There was such a thing as too much celebration.

Reyna released the parking brake and the RV rolled steadily forward. She pulled to the left, slowly coming off the road and into the surrounding dirt and grass, headlights scaring away the shadows. But there were always more behind. Expectant, waiting. Reyna turned the steering wheel as far as it would go, bringing the RV almost parallel to the road.

"Okay, back up now. Back up," Oliver said.

"I know." Reyna put the RV in reverse, and the screen in the center console lit up. A grainy black-and-white image from the rearview parking camera mounted at the back. Red watched the screen as the RV reversed over the road, Reyna pulling the wheel all the way to the right. The rough gravel and dirt gave way to a high patch of grass, beckoning to them in the wind. Or waving them goodbye. But there was something else in the image now, hidden behind the grass. Something crouching, dark and still.

"There's a rock," Oliver said, leaning closer to the screen. "Careful, there's a huge rock right behind us."

"I can see it," Reyna said coolly, backing up a couple more feet before stopping and shifting into drive. She inched forward, straightening up the wheel as the RV staggered back onto the road, facing the way they'd come in.

"Let's go." She pressed down on the gas.

Red thought they'd never leave. She cradled her hands, fingernails biting into the skin of her wrist.

"Team RV!" Simon shrieked again, more frantic this time, and Maddy gave a light round of applause for Reyna and her three-point-turning skills.

Maybe that was why they didn't hear the first one, but Red did. A crack that split the night again, and the RV sank behind her, scraping on the gravel.

Another crack and hiss, and the front right of the RV buckled, tipping them off balance.

"What the f—" Simon began, falling into Red.

Another.

The back left burst, the RV collapsing with it.

Another. The last one.

The RV grated against the road, screeching as it rolled to a stop.

All four tires. Gone.

# EIGHT

Nobody said anything for a second. Then for a moment. Then two, as Red stared at them all, breath picking up in her chest.

Oliver was the first to break the silence.

"What the fuck, Reyna?" He turned to her. "What have you driven over?"

"I didn't do anything!" she broke, shouting back at him. "It wasn't me. Must be something wrong with the tires."

"I can't believe this." Oliver ran his hands through his hair, making it stick up at the front. "We should have checked for glass or sharp rocks before we moved. I can't believe this," he said again, storming toward the door, his shoulder knocking hard into Red's as he passed.

He wrenched open the door, feet crashing against the steps.

Reyna switched off the engine and pulled out the keys, scrambling out of her chair to follow Oliver outside.

"What's going on?" Maddy asked, the first note of fear in her voice.

"Let's go see," Simon said, already halfway out the door, jumping down. Maddy went after him, cradling her phone in her hands, the Team RV selfie still up on her screen.

"You okay?" Arthur asked Red, catching her eye.

She rubbed her shoulder. "Fine." She turned to the steps and skipped down them.

She looked left. The wheel at the front had a gaping hole across it, like a downturned mouth in a silent scream.

She looked right. She couldn't see the hole in the back tire, but she could see it was flat, rubber splaying out on the road, even chunks that had come loose.

Arthur came down the steps, standing behind her, one thumb hooked in the pocket of his jeans.

"Are we ever going to get out of here?" Red asked him.

"I don't know," he said, walking away around the front of the RV, following Oliver's voice.

"And this one!" Oliver shouted, from the other side. "And, let me see, yes the one at the back too. All punctured. All four tires. How the fuck does that happen!?" Red could hear him clearly, even with the width of the RV standing between them, his voice filling the empty scrubland. "How do you puncture all four tires?"

"Oliver, it was not my fault. We were hardly even moving!"

Guess Reyna had been right. But whose fault would it have been if Oliver had been driving, Red wondered.

Maddy was standing in the headlights, chewing her thumb, glowing around the edges like she was lit from within. She did that when she was nervous. The thumb-chewing, not the glowing.

Red didn't know where Simon was, he must be on the other side somewhere too, quiet for once.

Red followed her eyes over to the back tire on this side, searching for the hole, the tear, the point of origin. If a thing was destroyed, she needed to know how. She knew her own point of origin. That day.

That last phone call. But maybe the tire didn't have one, or maybe it was underneath, hiding it like she hid hers.

"It's no one's fault, youse guys." Simon's voice sailed over.

"What the fuck are we going to do now?!" Oliver's next.

"Stop shouting and we'll work it out!" Reyna.

And then something new, a flicker in the corner of Red's eye, pulling at her attention. She turned to look at it. There was a red dot, right over there on the off-white side of the RV, near the open door. That wasn't there before. It was too low down to be part of the red-stripe blue-stripe pattern along the side. And it wasn't just a dot, was it? Too bright for that. It was a little red light, clinging to the side of the RV. No bigger than a fingernail.

"Guys," she called.

Someone else had to see this.

But wait. The red dot was moving now, shuddering as it lowered down the side of the RV. Red watched it go, blinking as it came to a stop, a few inches above the edge of the frame.

"Guys!"

Someone else needed to see this.

The red dot moved again, toward the wheel. Toward Red.

She backed away and the dot disappeared, reemerging on the other side of her, moving, moving, beyond the back wheel.

"Guys!"

A crack in the darkness, louder now that she was outside with it. Red flinched, hands up to her ears, and the red dot wasn't there anymore. But there was something else.

A splintered hole in the RV.

Not the size of a fingernail.

The size of a bullet.

That was when she knew.

"It's a gun!" Red screamed to the others.

"What was that?" Oliver's voice, fast and unnerved.

"It's a gun," Red said, turning to face the darkness. There was someone out there, in that wide-open nothing full of shifting shadows. Someone in all that nothing, someone with a gun. A rifle.

"Someone's shooting at us!" Oliver yelled, finally understanding. "Go, Reyna, go around the front. Back in the RV."

"Oliver!" Maddy screamed.

"Maddy, go get inside! RUN!"

Red couldn't move. Why couldn't she move? The voices of the others blurred into a high-pitched hum in her head. Arthur sprinted past her in the ringing silence, scrabbling for her arm, but she couldn't move.

"Red!" he screamed from the steps.

She smelled something, bitter and strong and—

"Move, Arthur, get inside!" Oliver barked, pushing Reyna in front of him and up. "Come on, Simon, hurry! Take my hand! Okay, is everyone inside? Red? Where's Red?"

Red faced down the darkness, breath trapped in her throat. Why wasn't she moving? Just move. And then the voice wasn't hers anymore, it was her mom's. There'd been a shooting in the city, downtown. And Mom wanted her to know something. *You have to run, Red. If there's ever an active shooter. Run, don't hide. It's harder to hit you when you're moving, so run! Run now, sweetie. Run!*

Run, Red. She should run. She needed to run, out into the wide-open nothing.

"RED! Get inside the RV now!"

But Oliver's voice was louder than her mom's, and Red listened to him.

She chose.

Her shoes pushed off against the dirt and she flew. To the steps and up, taking Oliver's outstretched hand as he dragged her inside.

The door slammed shut behind her.

# NINE

"Everyone get down!"

Red dropped to her knees, her chest tightening around her hummingbird heart. She couldn't breathe, she felt like she couldn't breathe.

"Maddy, get away from that window," Oliver said, the panic cutting up his voice. "Come here."

Simon was huddled in front of the refrigerator, Reyna by the kitchen counter. Maddy crawling up beside Oliver under the dining table. And Arthur was crouched here, next to her.

"I tried to get you," he said quietly. "I'm sorry."

"What did you see, Red?" Reyna asked her, her dark brown eyes too wide, shoulders hitching as she spoke. "You saw them?"

Red shook her head, gulping to force the air through. "No. No, I didn't see anybody. I saw a dot," she said. "A red dot, on the side of the RV. Before we heard the shot. Someone shot at the RV."

"A red dot?" Simon stared at her. "Like a laser sight?"

"I think so."

Simon screwed up his face. "This can't be real," he said, tilting his head. "No, this really can't be real. Are you sure it was really a gun?

Couldn't someone just have a laser pointer, and made the sound to scare us?"

"What are you talking about?" Arthur asked him.

"I'm saying, let's not panic." Simon's words slurred as he forced them out. "Maybe it's not what it seems. This could just be a prank. The guys from school knew we were stopping over near here. Maybe they followed us. Trying to scare us."

"Why would they do that?" Maddy's voice shook.

"I don't know. Rob and Taylor are always pulling shit like this. Fucking sadists. And they don't like me. You know they—"

"It's real, Simon," Red said, cutting him off. "I saw the bullet hole in the side of the RV. I was right next to it."

His face rearranged, cold fear taking over his eyes. It made it all worse somehow, watching the sudden change in Simon.

"Oh my god," Maddy said, trying not to cry. Red knew that face well. "He shot at you, Red?"

Not really, but it had been close enough. A couple of feet. The red dot must have touched her on its way. She didn't like that.

"Calm down." Oliver squeezed Maddy's hand. "Someone shot at us, but I'm sure this is all some kind of misunderstanding, okay?"

Simon scoffed. "Sure, just a misunderstanding. There's a sniper out there with a high-powered rifle and a laser sight who's decided to use us as target practice. But yeah, just a misunderstanding."

He'd changed his tune.

"Maybe it was a warning shot," Oliver said.

"Six," Arthur corrected him. "Six shots. He shot out all the tires."

"Right. But maybe we're trespassing on his land or something."

"Oliver," Reyna said.

"What? This is the South." He shuffled forward, out from under the table, leaving Maddy behind. She looked so small under there. "I've got an idea," he said, crouching low as he moved forward, toward the sofa bed, eyes on the window above it.

"Oliver, what are you doing?" Reyna hissed.

"I'm just going to explain what we're doing here. I'm sure this is all a misunderstanding."

Not sure enough to stand up, though. Clearly Oliver had never been in a situation he couldn't talk his way out of. Red didn't think this would be one of those.

Keeping his head low, behind the sofa, Oliver slowly reached up and unlatched the window, sliding it a few inches open, letting the darkness in.

"Hello!" he called, up and out the gap in the window. "I'm sorry if we're on your land, we got lost!"

Red should tell him it was pointless. The shooter was using a laser sight to help him aim, which meant he was probably more than shouting distance away, out there in the wide-open nothing. Oliver wouldn't listen, though, even if she did.

"We were just trying to leave!" Oliver shouted, louder now. "We won't say anything if you let us leave! I'm sure you have a license!"

Red looked back at Arthur. He was fidgeting, nervously tapping the top of his leg. And so was she, it turned out, picking at the seams of her front pocket. She checked in with Maddy on the other side, half under the table, strange downward shadows on her face.

Then Simon gasped. He pointed, and Red whipped her head around, following the line of his finger. To the front of the RV, and the back of the driver's seat. Right there, against the very top of the headrest, was the red dot.

"It's inside," Simon whispered, terror reshaping his face again.

"What?" Reyna couldn't see.

Red looked away from the dot, tracing it back to its point of origin.

"It's coming through that window. Oliver, watch ou—"

She didn't finish and the window exploded above him. Shattering into a million million pieces that rained down as he covered his head with his arms. Shards that shimmered as they fell, scattering around Red and Arthur too.

Maddy screamed.

"Oliver!" Reyna shouted. "Are you okay?"

He raised his head carefully, surveying his arms, touching his face as though afraid it might not still be there.

"I'm fine," he said, his voice emptied out with the shock. "Fine." He shook his shoulders, glass glittering as it clung to his shirt. He swiped at his arms, and the last few shards dusting his hair. Lucky he didn't seem to be cut anywhere. Lucky like a Lavoy.

"Yeah, just a warning shot," Simon said, a tremble in his hand as he flicked a piece of glass away. Had Red ever seen him scared before? Ever? Simon Yoo was supposed to be fearless.

"Well, you're the one who thought it was a fucking prank," Oliver growled suddenly, coming through the shock. "Fuck this. There's obviously some maniac out there. We need to get out of here, right now. First we need to cover the windows. Turn down the lights so he can't see us inside. Simon, can you?"

Simon was closest to the light switches. He glared at Oliver.

"Just reach up and dim them. You aren't by a window. You'll be okay."

Simon's legs shook as he raised himself up from the floor, using the handle on the refrigerator for balance. He reached out to the panel of switches beside the fridge, quickly turning the knobs as far as they would go without clicking off. The lights in the living area of the RV lowered to their darkest setting, a weak, murky yellow.

"Good. Okay." Oliver nodded to the rest of them, digging a small shard of glass out of his collar. "Right, now we need to close all the blinds and curtains."

Red nodded. They had to keep out that deadly red dot.

Oliver saw her. "Okay, Red, you do the blind on the broken window."

Why? He was right next to it.

"Arthur, you take the curtain on the front right window."

"I see," Arthur said to Red. "We get the side with the sniper."

Oliver ignored him. "Maddy and I will do the windows by the dining table."

Yep, on the safe side, Arthur had called it.

"Reyna, you take the curtain front left, by the driver's seat, once Arthur has closed his. We'll leave the windshield so we can drive out of here. And Simon, you get the one by the bunks."

So Simon had made it to the non-sniper side too, then.

"Oh and close the bedroom door while you're there; there's a big window at the back there too."

"What about the window on the door?" Simon said, gesturing to it with his head.

"Oh yeah. Red, can you grab that one too?"

Sounds fair.

"Okay, everyone." Oliver clapped his hands and they all flinched at the sound, too close to the crack of the rifle. "Let's do it. Go, go, go!"

Red pushed up into a low crouch, her shoes crunching against the sparkling glass as she lunged forward, passing Oliver. She took a breath and stood up, slowly, her leg catching on the small fire extinguisher mounted to the wall here. She turned and tucked herself sideways in the thin gap between the blown-apart window and the one in the door. Trying not to think about the red dot, but of course now she had. With her left hand, she reached out for the chain hanging by the window, quivering in the outside breeze that wasn't outside anymore. She pulled, and the cream-colored shades started to descend. Too slowly.

"Come on," she willed it, glancing aside to see Arthur ripping the black curtain closed ahead of her in the cockpit, Reyna now venturing out to hers.

Red pulled, too hard, the shade jamming. "Fuck you," she said, reversing the chain a few turns to set it right and then drawing it down the rest of the way. The wind laughed at her, playing with the bottom of the shade, pushing it out a few inches and sucking it back in.

Red turned her head the other way, catching Simon as he closed the door to the bedroom at the back. She reached up with her right hand, over and out to the catch at the top of the window in the door. She held her breath and dragged it down in one quick movement, the dark shade locking in place at the bottom.

Only now did Oliver rise up, beckoning Maddy to do the same. They leaned over the booths at the dining table, unhooking the tiebacks and pulling both sides of the curtains across. Red still couldn't work out what the patterns in those curtains reminded her of. It was on the tip of her brain, really. So annoying. It wasn't that guy from *SpongeBob,* was it? The grumpy one with the clarinet. Oh, damn it, what was his name again? And what was that smell that was following her, bittersweet and cloying? Was it coming from her? Red looked down and raised her shoe. The bottom of her sole was dirty and wet with something. She sniffed. Was that gas?

"Okay, good work everyone," Oliver said, out of breath, like he'd had the difficult job there. A *thanks* would be nice. "Right, let's get out of here. Reyna, where are the keys?" He held out his palm toward her.

"How?" Maddy asked him. "All the tires are blown out."

"The RV will still move," Oliver said. "Slowly, and it will likely cause irreparable damage to the wheels, but I think we have bigger problems right now."

Why would there be gas on Red's shoes?

"Reyna, keys!" He snapped his fingers impatiently.

She patted the pockets on her hoodie, at the back of her jeans, a look of horror dawning in her eyes.

"I don't have them. I don't know where they are."

Red had seen her take them, after the four tires were shot out.

"What do you mean?" Oliver rounded on her. "You had them. You were driving!"

"I know, I know." She ran her hands nervously through her black hair. "Maybe I dropped them when I was running, I don't know."

"Outside?!" Oliver was shouting again.

"Maybe, I don't know, I'm sorry!"

"Well, who's going to go outside and get them, Reyna?!"

"Nobody's going outside," Simon interjected.

"I've got them," Arthur said. Nobody listened except Red. "I've got them!" he shouted over the others, pointing to the kitchen, behind the counter where Reyna had hidden. Arthur stepped forward and picked the keys up, rattling them to make the point. "Here," he said, chucking them over to Oliver, who barely caught them, fumbling them against his chest.

"Okay, fine," he said, shooting a quick "Sorry" over in Reyna's direction. And Red couldn't help but wonder: Who would Oliver have made go outside to get them?

"I'll drive," he said, passing his sister and his girlfriend on the way up to the driver's seat. And Red hadn't noticed before, but there was now a bullet-sized hole in the headrest, white stuffing escaping through the ripped plastic. Imagine if that hole was inside one of them. No, don't, because then she'll think of two bullets to the back of the head . . . right, see? And anyway, she needed to concentrate on thinking about why her shoes smelled like gas, and everything else.

Oliver settled down into the seat, cricking the bones in his neck. He cleared his throat. "I'll get us out of here," he said, like a promise or a threat. He pushed the key into the ignition and turned it.

The engine coughed, empty sputters one after the other. That sound you never wanted to hear.

"What?" Oliver said, staring down at the key in disbelief.

He tried again.

The engine gasped and spluttered, taking its dying breath.

"What?!" Oliver roared. He flicked his head to check the fuel gauge. "We're out of gas. That doesn't make sense. We filled up again at nine o'clock. It should be three-quarters full, at least. How is it empty?"

He punched the steering wheel. Again. And again. An inhuman sound in his throat.

"That's what he was aiming for," Red said, glancing down at her shoes, understanding now. "Not me. He was aiming for the gas tank."

"What?" Oliver turned back, his face patchy and red.

"He shot out the gas tank," she said.

"Why?" Maddy asked.

Red had an answer. The others probably did too, but Simon was the one who gave voice to it.

"So we can't leave."

The RV was going nowhere. And here they were, the six of them, trapped inside it, the wide-open nothing and the red dot waiting for them out there.

12:00 A.M.

# TEN

Trapped.

Shut in.

Only thirty-one feet to share between them, that extra foot important enough not to round down.

"Why would he want to trap us here?" Maddy asked, her pupils too wide, dark pools eating away the color of her eyes. "What does he want with us?"

"I don't know," Oliver answered, pushing up from the driver's seat, one more punch to the wheel for luck. "He probably lives around here, and we are in the wrong place at the wrong time. I told you we should never have come down this road."

"Like you predicted this was going to happen?" Simon said, a surprising note of anger in his voice, an unsteadiness to his tread. Red should get him some water. He needed to sober up, fast. His instincts were dulled, his reactions, and he would need those tonight.

"I said it was the wrong way and none of you listened!"

In the kitchen, Red opened the cupboard mounted high beside the microwave. She removed a glass and guided it to the shiny-clean sink, flicking on the faucet and filling it near full.

"We had no service. We were lost," Arthur said, a forced calm in his voice that no one else had right now.

"Here." Red handed the glass of water to Simon, telling him with her eyes to drink it. At least she didn't have to hold the glass for him, like with her dad sometimes.

"It was Red," Oliver said, not looking at her. "She insisted we come down this road. And you two." He pointed at Arthur and Simon. "You three were navigating. This is your fault."

Simon stepped forward, splashing some of the water on his shirt. The other patch had finally just dried. "By the same logic, I could say it was Reyna's fault we got stuck here. Because she was driving and refused to turn around."

"I couldn't turn around!" Reyna said.

"Everyone, please!" Maddy slapped her hand on the dining table three times. "This is not helping. It's no one's fault we're here. But we are, okay? And we have to work together to figure out what to do."

"There's nothing we can do," Simon said, near hysterical now. "Unless someone also happened to pack a rifle for spring break and we can snipe him back."

Red mimed for him to drink up.

"Is there still no service?" Maddy said, answering her own question as she looked down at the lock screen on her phone. "Shit. Nothing."

"Can't you call emergency services without a signal?" Simon said, still not drinking. "I swear I've seen it in a movie before."

It didn't work like that, Red knew. She'd asked that question before herself, years ago on a family vacation in Yellowstone.

"Yeah, 'cause sometimes it comes up saying *No service— emergency calls only*," Reyna added.

"That's only if your phone can piggyback onto another network,"

Red said, her mom's answer now becoming hers. "There's clearly no service from any network here."

"Try it," Oliver said, ignoring her. "Try, Maddy."

Maddy unlocked her phone, her tongue tucked between her teeth as she concentrated. She brought up the keypad and carefully typed in *9-1-1*.

She waited for a nod from Oliver, then she pressed the green button and raised the phone to her ear.

They waited. The seconds stretching into eternity as Maddy closed her eyes to concentrate harder. It was one of those things she did that made her Maddy. Like when they were ten and she thought you had to ring the doorbell every time you left or came home, even if no one else was in and you had the key. That shrill, insistent bell in one held note, standing outside the Lavoys' house. Funny how Red could remember some things like that, yet she couldn't remember to call AT&T. She wondered what were the things that Maddy thought made Red Red?

Maddy exhaled, her chest sinking. "Nothing," she said quietly, letting the phone fall to her side.

Oliver swiped at her arm, grabbing the phone. "*No network connection,*" he read from the alert on the screen. "Fuck." He dropped the phone back into Maddy's hands, worthless to him.

Well, Red did say.

"Someone might have called the cops, though," Maddy said, not ready to give up yet. "I know it's late." She glanced at her phone. "It's four minutes past midnight, and most people are probably in bed. But someone must have heard the gunshots and called the police, right? There were farms and houses not too far back."

"The shots weren't loud," Red said. "Even we couldn't tell what it was at first. Just the sound of the tires bursting."

"It's a rifle?" Maddy doubled down.

But Red had heard these guns before, a memory she tried to push away. The three-volley rifle salute at the funeral. A line of officers in uniform, aiming over the flag-draped casket. The road beyond the cemetery blocked with what felt like every squad car in the city, top lights spinning, painting the world red and blue. *Ready to aim. Fire.* Three times. A crack like thunder, riding through the sky, shaking the bones inside you. And those had even been blanks. So loud. Unmistakable. Piercing through the bagpipes as they played "Amazing Grace," which was funny in a way because her name had been Grace. The Lavoys should know; they were all there too. Catherine standing with one hand on Red's shoulder, squeezing when the rifles went off. Red's dad didn't even cry, standing on her other side. No, he saved all his falling apart for after.

"Red?" Arthur said.

Oh no, they'd been talking without her.

"I think Red's right," Simon said, the glass in his hands only half full now. "It wasn't even loud enough for us to know it was a gunshot. I think he must be using a suppressor."

"A what?" asked Reyna.

"A silencer," Simon explained. "And yes, all of my worldly knowledge does come from movies, but that doesn't mean it isn't valid."

"So you think nobody heard?" Maddy deflated even more, if that was possible. "Nobody called the cops?"

Simon shrugged. "I think we can't count on it."

"No, we can't count on it," Oliver repeated, picking up the sentiment, chewing on some silent thought. "We make our own luck," he said to Maddy alone, a Lavoy expression that often got wheeled out. Which must mean that Red was terrible at making hers.

Maddy looked back at her brother, a new glint in her eye. "Make our own luck," she said. "Well, if no one heard the gunshots, then maybe they'll hear this."

Before anyone could say anything, Maddy charged to the front of the RV, leaned across the driver's seat and pressed her thumb into the wheel.

The horn screamed, rupturing the quiet of just-past-midnight. One long note, then four short bursts.

"Maddy?" Red said. She didn't like her standing so close to that bullet hole in the driver's seat. On the other side, the shade over the smashed window swayed in the wind, like a silent threat from the outside world. No, not Maddy.

Maddy leaned the heel of her hand into the horn, as though she could make it louder that way.

"Maddy," Arthur said, a tension in his jaw as he eyed the broken window. "Maybe we shouldn't—"

Three loud beeps cut him off.

"Someone will hear!" Maddy shouted, determined. "Someone will—"

Red felt it more than she heard it. A rush of air to her right. The shade shuddering, dancing against its fixings, a new hole ripped through it.

Maddy screamed.

"No, Maddy!" Red screamed harder.

# ELEVEN

The small window on the driver's side must have blown out, a clinking of broken glass as it cascaded out onto the road, out of sight.

There was a hole in the black curtain hanging across it, at the top, only a foot above Maddy's head. But she still had a head, eyes blinking at them all. It had missed her.

"Are you hit?" Oliver bounded forward, dragging his sister back from the cockpit.

"No, I . . . no," Maddy said, shaking her still-there head.

Red took her hand, held on to it. If Maddy had been standing up straight, or a few inches back . . . well, it didn't bear thinking about. And Red was good at not thinking about things like that.

"He really didn't like you doing that," Simon said, another wet patch on his shirt, the glass empty as he placed it back on the counter.

"No, he did not," Red agreed.

"Right, okay, everyone," Oliver said, pushing Maddy down to sit on the booth. "New rule. No one does anything without checking with me first. Not one thing unless it has been discussed with the whole group, okay?" He looked around at each of them for confirmation.

Red nodded.

"I won't even take a piss without preapproval," Simon said,

holding up his hands. Red should refill that glass for him. She wasn't sure there was a worse time to be drunk than right now.

"Right." Oliver pushed himself up, half sitting on the table as the others gathered around him. A determined set to his jaw, like he knew he was the only possible leader here. Twenty-one years old, prelaw, a sister and a girlfriend to protect, a mom who would soon be DA. "We've already lost two windows, which is not good news. So, the first thing I want us to do is to board up those broken windows, for extra protection."

"With what?" Reyna asked, shrugging her empty arms.

"We must have something. Everyone, check around the RV and in your bags and suitcases. Look for any resources we can use and bring them back to this table."

"Resources?" Arthur asked.

"Things to help us survive. Something to cover the windows. Anything that could be used as first aid. Or as a weapon."

"A weapon?" Simon snorted. "Yeah, that sniper won't know what's hit him when I slowly charge at him with my Gillette razor."

Oliver ignored him. "Now. Five minutes, guys."

No one protested, shuffling away from the table in various directions, knees bent, keeping their heads low. Simon and Arthur headed toward their bunk beds—Simon on the bottom, Arthur on top—and the bags they'd dumped there this morning. Oliver and Reyna pushed past them, drawing to a stop outside the closed bedroom door. The queen-sized bed beyond it, where they were supposed to be sleeping tonight. Red wasn't sure anyone would be sleeping tonight.

"The window at the back is still exposed," Oliver said to Reyna. "You crawl into the room, take cover against the back wall and lower the shade. I'll hit the lights and close the door so the sniper can't see anything."

He wasn't speaking to her in that soft voice anymore. But that was the first rule of leadership, wasn't it: delegation. Still, Red couldn't believe he hadn't asked her or Arthur or Simon to cover the window for them instead, or gone ahead and been the hero himself. Reyna stared back at Oliver, like she couldn't believe it either.

"Fine." She swallowed.

"Okay, three, two, one."

Oliver pulled open the door, and Reyna slipped inside on her hands and knees. She disappeared as Oliver reached in to switch off the light, closing the door after her.

He caught Red's eye, watching, and gave her a grim nod.

A few seconds later, Reyna's voice called through, "Okay, done!" and Oliver followed it back into the bedroom, flicking on the light, heading toward the closet and out of Red's view.

"Red, come on," Maddy said, pulling at her shirt and jolting her back.

Maddy stopped short of the sofa bed, her eyes up on the large overhead cupboards, where Red and Maddy had stored their bags. Getting them would mean standing right in front of the broken window. The shade was still breathing in and out, wind whistling through the ripped bullet hole, a faint trace of gasoline finding its way inside. Maddy's hand shook as she studied the hole, looking back to where she had been standing to re-create the path of the bullet. Or that was what Red imagined she was doing; she knew Maddy and Maddy knew her.

"I'll get the bags," Red said, pushing Maddy aside, back into the safety by the table. She walked forward, crunching through the fallen glass, then raised one foot and stood up on the sofa bed. The fake leather squeaked against her shoes as she pushed up, her other leg hovering behind her. She opened the first cupboard, grabbing the dark purple side handle of Maddy's new bag and swinging it out, muscles in her arms straining.

"How much did you pack?" she said, dropping the heavy bag onto the sofa, scattering more glass. Maddy darted forward to retrieve her suitcase, holding it in both arms, almost like a shield.

Red opened the other cupboard and reached for her bag, only noticing now that the seams were breaking at the side, loose black threads tickling her skin as she grabbed it. Dad wouldn't like that; this was her mom's old suitcase, *Grace Kenny—Philadelphia* still scribbled in the luggage tag at the top. One of the last pieces of her handwriting they had left. Not the time to think of that, though. Not ever the time.

Red stepped down with the bag in her hands, turning back to Maddy, who was sitting cross-legged on the floor between the door and the kitchen counter, unzipping her stiff, new bag. The zipper snarled as she pulled it around the corner.

Red brushed some glass aside with her foot and settled down beside Maddy, her back arching as she leaned against the door, buttressing the side of her suitcase against Maddy's.

She unzipped it, pushing the top flap open so it slapped the floor of the RV.

"No sudden noises," Simon called over his shoulder, annoyed.

"Sorry," Red called back over hers. She stopped; Maddy was staring at her.

"This is crazy," Maddy said quietly, shaking her head, pausing to bite down on her lower lip. "I can't believe this is happening."

Red still couldn't believe it either. For different reasons, probably, because she always half expected the worst to happen. Maddy was half full and Red was half empty, which reminded her: she needed to get Simon some more water.

"Are we gonna be okay?" Maddy asked, and suddenly her eyes were filled with tears, one escaping, making a break down her cheek.

Red swiped it away as it reached Maddy's chin. "Yeah, we'll be okay, I promise," Red said, a promise she hoped she could keep. She tried to tell Maddy that with her eyes and nothing else, a slow blink.

"What if one of us gets shot?" Maddy said, her bottom lip threatening to go, ready to take her whole face down with it.

"No one's getting shot." Red held her eyes. "We are getting out of this alive," she said, "you and me." Always *you and me* with them, since before they could walk and talk and think. And even before that, when their moms were best friends, their own *you and me* from the first day they met at college. Lavoys and Kennys, except their moms had had different names back then. Maddy wasn't just her best friend, Maddy was family. "Come on, let's look for *resources*," she said in her Oliver voice that usually made Maddy laugh. It didn't work tonight, so Red tried something else: "Maybe those six bullet-proof vests I packed will come in handy."

Maddy snorted, wiping her nose. "Maybe so will the functioning cell tower I brought in mine."

There we go, a near smile at least. Maddy pushed open the top of her case and it was so packed that maybe she really did have a whole cell tower in there. Tall piles of clothes, neatly folded and separated into sections: underwear there, shorts that side, multiple pairs of jeans, three separate wash bags, shoes in pairs down the middle like grid lines. They were only supposed to be gone seven days, yet Maddy must have packed enough clothes for weeks.

Red glanced at her own case. No piles, no folding, no order. It was all chucked in together. Balled-up underwear buried in each corner, a watered-down mascara and a foundation that didn't match her skin tone somewhere loose in there, never to be seen again. A puddle of marbly-pink goop—which must mean her shampoo bottle had leaked—spreading over a lone sock. Her toothbrush stood up dead center, her nice shirt caught in its bristles. She'd been hoping she could borrow Maddy's toothpaste, not that it mattered now.

"Red," Maddy said, disapprovingly, looking down at the mess of Red's suitcase. She burrowed her hand through, overturning clothes to see underneath. "Did you forget to even pack a bikini?" she asked, searching through the rest of it. Red had one bikini, blue and white, and Maddy was right: it wasn't here.

"Guess I must have missed it," Red said, trying to remember forgetting it.

Maddy turned to her. "And what the hell were you going to do on a beach vacation without a swimsuit?"

Red shrugged.

"Borrow one of mine, I'm guessing?"

She was annoyed, but at least if she was annoyed then she wasn't scared right now. That was better.

"Don't think it really matters anymore," Red said. "We're not making it to the beach."

Maddy didn't say anything.

"I don't have anything useful," Red said, zipping the suitcase shut and kicking it away.

"Let me see," Maddy murmured, turning back to her own bag. She picked up one of the wash bags, shiny plastic zebra print, and opened it. "Yes, I thought so," she said, dipping her hand inside and coming back with a pair of hair scissors.

"You never cut your own hair—?" Red said.

"No, but I always take these when I go away. Never know when you might need a pair of scissors. I had to turn leggings into shorts once when I misjudged the weather."

"Are those for first aid or a weapon?" Red eyed the scissors.

"Both, I guess," Maddy said, pulling out a small roll of Scotch tape from the same wash bag. She placed both items beside her, giving them a quick pat. "Oh yeah." She reached out for the front of the suitcase and the zippered compartment there. "I brought a real flashlight, just in case we were out late on the beach and our phones ran out of battery or something." She pulled out a flashlight about the size of her hand, black with a fluorescent yellow stripe. "I put a beach ball in there too. Guess that was pointless. What the hell is going on, Red?"

"I know!" Arthur said suddenly, loud enough for the others to hear. "We can use the mattress from my bunk to block up the big window behind the sofa."

"That's a good idea," Red said, at the exact same time that Oliver said it, as he reemerged from the bedroom with Reyna on his heels. He had something in both hands, cradling the items as he struggled past Simon in the narrow corridor. He arrived beside the table and stopped to look around at them all, eyes alive and searching.

"Okay, time's up," he said. "What did everybody find to help us survive the night?"

# TWELVE

Oliver went first, of course, placing down a small first aid kit—Red guessed Reyna had packed that—and a headlamp, with a couple of spare batteries. Maddy stepped up and added her scissors and Scotch tape to the collection.

Simon returned to the kitchen empty-handed, like Red. But he stopped there, pulling open one of the drawers.

"I knew there'd be one here somewhere," he said, cutlery rattling and a scraping sound of metal on metal as he pulled his hand out, clutched around the black handle of a kitchen knife. It was sharp, with a serrated edge that caught the dim overhead lights.

"Chekhov's knife," Simon said with a dark smile as he added it to the items on the dining table.

"Huh?" said Oliver.

"Never mind, it's a theater thing."

A clatter and a grunt behind, as Arthur wrestled with the mattress from his bunk, pulling it down and tucking it under one arm, his glasses knocked askew on his face.

Red gave him a thumbs-up, and he returned it with his spare hand.

"Did someone open my tequila?" Oliver said, digging through his backpack on the counter.

"Another mystery to solve," Simon said, by the refrigerator. "Right after we work out why there's a sniper out there shooting at us. That reminds me." He opened the fridge and pulled out a glass bottle of vodka, unopened, adding it to the pile on the dining table. Red questioned him with her eyes. "For disinfecting wounds," he explained. "Or liquid courage."

"Aha," Oliver said, his hand reemerging from the bottom of his backpack clutched around a shiny silver Zippo lighter. Engraved too, bet that was expensive. Onto the pile it went.

"There's a small toolbox in here," Reyna said, voice muffled, her head buried in the closet right by the front door. "I guess we don't need a tape measure, though."

"Not unless we want to measure the length of the RV for fun while we're trapped in here," Simon said.

"It's thirty-one feet," said Red, "not just thirty." Simon should know, he was the one who told her that, and now she couldn't get the damn number out of her head.

Reyna backed up out of the closet, and in her hands were a small hammer, a screwdriver, and a roll of gray duct tape. "There's a mop and a dustpan and brush in there too," she said, adding those new items to the collection.

"Great." Oliver's eyes spooled around, skipping over Arthur, whose hands were full, and flicking between Simon and Red. "Simon," he said. Unlucky. Probably because he was closest. And because everybody knew he drank the tequila. "Can you grab the dustpan and brush and sweep up the glass?"

"Really?" Simon hardened his gaze.

"We don't want anyone cutting themselves," Oliver said, leading him in the direction of the open closet, the movement disguised as a pat on the back. "It will take you two minutes, go on."

Simon muttered something under his breath, but Red only caught the hardest of syllables. She didn't imagine it was anything worth repeating. He picked up the dustpan and brush, struggling for a moment to separate the two, then bent low, sweeping piles of window glass into the pan, glittering as it moved.

"Excuse your feet," he said, maneuvering around Maddy's shoes and her still-open suitcase.

"Okay, this is good," Oliver said, surveying the *resources* they had managed to gather. Red looked too: a pair of scissors, a lighter, a headlamp, a flashlight, spare batteries, a hammer, a screwdriver, duct tape, Scotch tape, vodka and a kitchen knife. Each item disappearing from her head as soon as she moved onto the next, like one of those memory games she always lost.

"Should I get this in place?" Arthur asked, hoisting the mattress up higher in his grip.

"Yeah, go ahead," Oliver said. "Out of the way, everyone."

Arthur walked through slowly, guiding the mattress past corners and people. The handle on the bathroom door tried to grab his shirt and pull him back. Reyna unhooked it for him and he nodded his thanks. He turned awkwardly to avoid Simon on the floor, but the back of the mattress bumped him on the head, and Simon muttered something else unheard.

"It should just slot in here, behind the back cushions," Oliver said, taking the back end of the mattress and helping Arthur to guide it up and forward, in front of the broken window. They pushed it through, sliding it into the gap between the back of the sofa and the wall, wedged in under the overhead cupboards. "Hold on, it's blocking the door," Oliver said, shoving the mattress in farther, tucking the far end in beside the front passenger seat. "There we go," he said, grabbing it and giving it a shake to check. "That's wedged in there good."

It might be wedged in there good, but would a mattress stop a bullet from a precision rifle? Red wasn't sure it would, but at least they could now pretend they were safe in here, without the outside breathing in through that window. Pretending was half the game, and she should know. Her life depended on it.

"Right, that's one window done." Oliver stood back. "We still need to cover the one by the driver's seat. Red?" He turned to her. "Did you find anything we can use?"

No, she was the only one who had failed on that front, staring down at her useless suitcase, its edges fraying as the threads unpicked themselves, like they wanted to break. And, hey, that gave her an idea, if they wanted it so bad.

"Yes," she said, surprising herself most of all. "My suitcase. We can flatten it out and use it to board up that window. It's breaking anyway."

"Good idea," Reyna said, ahead of Oliver. "And we can use the duct tape to keep it there."

Oliver hadn't said it was a good idea, Red was waiting, but he grabbed the knife from the table and held it out to her, handle first.

"You do the honors," he said as she took it. "But also, let's put your stuff somewhere. We don't want all your crap in the way."

"We can put it in my case," Maddy sighed. "I'm sure it will fit, she doesn't have much."

Maddy grabbed Red's suitcase and flipped it over, the upturned contents falling on top of her neatly packed possessions. She sighed again to see it, removing the leaking shampoo bottle and then pressing it all down so the lid would zip shut.

Red hoped Arthur hadn't looked at her balled-up underwear. She knew one pair she'd packed had unicorns on it; Santa had gotten them for her that final Christmas. Red hadn't believed in him since she was eight, of course, but it was tradition that Santa got the Kennys ugly socks and underwear for Christmas. Only, Santa must have died when her mom did.

"Oli, can you help me get my bag back up there and out of the way?" Maddy asked.

Only his little sister was allowed to call him Oli. Believe her, Red had learned the hard way.

"Yep, sure." He grunted as he lifted the double-packed case, Arthur opening the overhead cupboard for him as he drew close, helping him squeeze the stuffed bag inside.

Simon was just finishing up, brushing the last few shards and crumbs of broken glass from the sofa, backing away as he finished. The floor was all clear now. He carried the full pan into the kitchen—Red sucked in a breath as he stumbled, tripping over nothing—but his hand was somehow steady. He opened the cupboard with the trash can and dumped the glass out, tapping the pan against the edge to get the last of the glittering dust.

"Go on, Red." Oliver had returned, standing over her as she crouched by the empty shell of her suitcase. "Let's get this done."

Red tightened her grip on the knife, holding it out to the corner nearest her. She tried not to look at the luggage tag hanging from the top, but her eyes betrayed her. Come on, it didn't matter. Mom wasn't in that luggage tag, Mom was dead. And they needed something to block the window; Red had to be useful, like everyone else was. She pressed the knife against the corner, sawing down with the serrated edge, cutting through the zipper, and the fabric, and the cardboard underneath. The knife chewed up the material with its teeth, splitting the corner apart. Red shifted to get the next one, the handle of the knife growing warm in her hands. Why did she find the word *resources* funny anyway? What she really should be thinking about instead was that red dot out there, and the person in charge of it. Watching. Waiting?

"Good job on the glass, Simon," Oliver said, a delayed *well done,* but a *well done* all the same. A good leader motivates his team. Delegation. Motivation. Would Oliver say *good job* to her when she finished butchering her mom's old suitcase?

"There," she said, sitting back, the final corner cut through, the sides of the suitcase lying prone against the floor.

"All right, get it in place, then."

That was all the *well done* she got. Oliver Lavoy wasn't as liberal with his approval as Maddy or Catherine. They gave Red *well done*s all the time, if she'd earned them.

"I'll help," Arthur said, stepping forward to grab the duct tape and scissors from the table. Three *resources* used already, oh come on, would she stop it with the *resources.* Just think of another word, then. *Stuff. Thingamabobs. Jawn.*

Red stood, picking up the remains of her suitcase, carrying it to the front of the RV, a few steps behind Arthur. He drew the edge of the curtain out a couple of inches and leaned closer to take a quick look.

"Just one of the panes shattered," he said. "This side." He gestured to the one at the front. "Do you want to hold it up and I'll tape it?"

"That's what she said!"

"Simon, come on, really," Maddy snapped. "Now is not the time or place. If that's the last thing I hear before I die, then I swear to God . . ."

She left the threat empty and dangling.

There was a flush in Arthur's face again, a warm pink. He swiped at his cheeks like he could wipe the blush away, hide it from her.

Well, that was fine if he was embarrassed; he'd probably seen her old unicorn underwear anyway.

Arthur busied himself pulling a length of duct tape free and cutting it loose with Maddy's scissors, and Red positioned the un-folded suitcase in front of the curtain, over the gaping hole into the wide-open nothing out there. In the dark, where the red dot lived.

Arthur rested one knee on the driver's seat and pressed the tape along the top edge of the suitcase, cutting off more to secure it.

"Are you okay?" he asked her, moving on to the next side, his hand accidentally brushing past hers.

A tiny firework in her head. What a stupid little fucking firework. Maddy should tell it that now was not the time or place.

"Everything will be okay," Red said, staring forward, losing her eyes to the minute details of the suitcase fabric, crossing over and under, so she didn't think about how close Arthur's face was to hers right now, both leaning across the driver's seat.

"That's not what I asked."

"I don't know," she answered, honestly for once. "Are you sup-posed to be okay when someone's trying to kill you?"

"I don't think you are." And, somehow, Arthur's voice did away with the hard syllables, smoothing them over, gliding one to the next. Someone else might call it mumbling, but Red wasn't someone else. Arthur pressed a long piece of tape down across the width of the suit-case and onto the part of the window that had survived, withdrawing his hand quickly from the curtain and back into the safety of the RV.

A sound interrupted them. The flushing of a toilet. Red checked over her shoulder to see Oliver closing the bathroom door behind him.

"Right, everyone, over here," he called, another loud clap. Red flinched. Someone should tell him to stop doing that.

"Go on," Arthur said to her. Had he noticed the flinch? As long as he hadn't noticed the firework. "I can finish up here." He splayed his hand against the suitcase, taking its remaining weight from her, ready with the last few pieces of tape.

"Thanks." She stepped back, grabbing the scissors and the roll of duct tape, taking them with her back to the dining table. Someone else had already replaced the knife.

Maddy was leaning against the refrigerator, and Red went to lean against her.

"Looks like Arthur is just finishing up with that window," Oliver said, right as Arthur was done, wiping his hands off down the front of his jeans and walking over. The six of them, gathered in and around that tiny kitchen.

"Okay, now that we've secured the RV," Oliver continued, though who could say how secure it really was, against that rifle. They couldn't see outside anymore, the RV was their own little world, but a bullet could come in anywhere, through the wall and anyone in the way, out the other side before they even had a chance to scream. That didn't feel very safe, not as Red understood the word.

"Next, we need to work out what our plan is."

"Plan?" Maddy asked.

"Yeah, so that we all get out of here. Alive," he added, and with that one word, the air grew thick, a strange buzzing in Red's ears as she did that thing where she tried to imagine what it would be like to be un-alive.

Reyna cleared her throat, and Red was grateful for the distraction. "Well, listen." She glanced down at the time on her phone. "It's been like twenty-five minutes now since he last shot at the RV. Maybe he's . . . I don't know, maybe he's gone?" Her voice went up at the end, turning it into a question.

"What, you think he got bored and went home to jack off?" Simon said.

"Maybe."

"Unless he's waiting," Maddy said.

"Waiting for what?" Reyna asked her.

"For us to think he's gone, and to walk out the door right into his crosshairs," she said, darkly.

"It is a fair point," Oliver said, and Red wasn't sure who he was siding with, until he drew closer to Reyna. "How do we know if he's even still out there?"

He wasn't going to make one of them go outside and check, was he? And what were the chances it would be either Red, Arthur or Simon he gave those instructions to? The expendables.

"I'm not volunteering to go see," Simon said. He must have had a similar thought, still annoyed about the glass-sweeping.

There was that fizzing in Red's ears again. Could anyone else hear it?

"Well, put it this way," Oliver said. "The RV is not going anywhere. We can't call for help. So, the only way we're getting out of here is by leaving the RV. And Reyna has a point; it's been a while since his last shot. Maybe he's gone."

"Why would he shoot out all the tires and the gas tank to trap us here if he was just gonna leave right after?" Maddy said.

It seemed no one knew how to answer that. No one said anything for a moment, eyes shifting around the group, Red fiddling in her pocket, Simon staring up at the ceiling. Until a voice dared to break the silence.

"Hello."

Red looked up, at Simon, then at Arthur. Had one of them

spoken? The voice had sounded strange: metallic and muted. But, no, it couldn't have been them because they too were looking around, searching for the speaker. Arthur caught her eye and Red shook her head. It wasn't her.

"Did someone just—" Reyna began.

Oliver shushed her, holding up his finger.

"But I—" Simon now.

"Shut up!" Oliver shouted him down, holding up both hands to control the silence.

But it wasn't silent; there was that empty, fizzing sound again.

It clicked off and—

"—Hello," the voice spoke again, deep and disembodied.

Maddy gasped, and Oliver tapped her on the arm to keep her quiet, brandishing his finger at the rest of them.

"Hello?"

A voice, but no one to claim it. Red scanned over her shoulder. The voice was coming from the front of the RV, and so was that fizzing sound she hadn't imagined.

"Hello," it said. "Come here."

# THIRTEEN

"Nobody move!"

Oliver's eyes were frantic, spinning in his head as he studied the front of the RV, and the darkness of the uncovered windshield. He backed up, feeling for the knife on the table.

"He said, 'Come here,'" Maddy whispered, fear spiking in her voice, hands moving instinctively to protect her head. "Is he right outside? Oh my god he's going to kill us all."

"Hello."

The voice clicked off, replaced by that fizzing hiss, but this time Red knew exactly what it was, the sound passing through her, gathering snapshots of memory. Ones she normally pushed away, the good and the bad. Running around her house, back when it had been warm, a walkie-talkie in her hand as she played Cops and Cops with her mom. They'd invented it, you see, because neither wanted to be a robber. Tiny Red yelling made-up police codes into the radio, sometimes too excited to remember to press the push-to-talk button, but always remembering to finish with "Over!" Running into separate rooms, demanding status reports on the *Bad Guys*. The *Bad Guys* were invisible, but somehow she and her mom always managed to save the day and save the city. Together. They were heroes, if only in the game.

It was static, that sound, the fuzz between her voice and her mom's as they ran to each other, laughing, taking cover. But that was all ruined now, because it was the exact same sound as the one at the funeral, the static between the final call on the police radio. *Central to Officer 819.* Static. *Officer 819, no response.* Static. *Officer 819, Captain Grace Kenny, is End of Watch. Gone but never forgotten.* Static.

Gone, that was right. And Red tried to forget most of the time.

"Hello?" The voice came from Oliver that time, crouching low on the floor, eyes trained on the front of the RV, knife up.

"He's not there," Red said. "It's a two-way radio." Oliver narrowed his eyes at her. "A walkie-talkie."

Oliver straightened up, his grip loosening on the knife. "Where is it?"

"Somewhere over there." Simon pointed toward the driver's seat, the one-eyed bullet hole glaring back at them.

"Inside or outside?" Reyna asked, taking one tentative step forward.

"How would he have gotten it inside?" Oliver snapped. "We are right here and the RV is secure."

Maybe if he said it enough times, it would become true.

"Come here," the voice said, crackling at the edges.

"He wants us to go and get it, I think," Maddy said.

"I don't care what he wants," Oliver barked. "Let me think for a second."

"He wants to talk to us?" Simon asked, exchanging a glance with Maddy.

"Hello."

"He's waiting," Reyna said. "We don't want to piss him off, Oliver."

"What are we waiting for?" Simon said. He stepped forward, not checking back for permission from Oliver. "Come on." He beckoned, not quite brave enough to go alone.

Red stepped up, Arthur too, walking carefully toward the front of the RV behind Simon, keeping their heads low. Red was ready to drop to her knees at the slightest sound or whistle of air, her breath tight in her chest.

The static grew louder, thicker, trying to draw up old and older memories, but Red thought them away. She needed her head here and now. And, anyway, Simon was right, the static was coming from somewhere near the driver's seat. Beyond.

"Excuse me," Oliver said, maneuvering Red out of his way with his elbow. Clearly he'd had his second to think, then. "Where is it?"

"I can't see," Simon said, crouching low to search the footwells in front of the driver and passenger seats. "Not here."

"It's outside," Red said, following her ears. "Outside that window." She gestured to the one she and Arthur had just boarded up with the flattened suitcase. It sounded like the radio was just beyond, hovering in the darkness of outside where the rules were different, waiting for them to let it in.

"Did you hear anything when you were covering the window?" Oliver asked.

"No, nothing." Arthur swallowed.

"He must have put it there after we were done," Red followed up. She would have recognized that sound right away, if it had been only inches from her head.

"We have to get it," Simon said. "He wants to talk to us." He peeled back a few strips of the duct tape that held the lid of the suitcase in place. "Anyone want to take a look? Oliver, you're in charge, aren't you?"

"I'm not putting my face out that hole."

"Hello." The voice was right there, tinny but clear. A shiver passed up Red's spine, climbing it to the back of her exposed neck.

"Well, I'm not putting my face out there either," Simon hissed. "Can't be on Broadway without a fucking face."

"Hey, hey, one of you use your phone," Reyna said, standing with Maddy just behind the gathering. "Take a video on your phone, out the window."

"Good idea," Arthur told her, already retrieving his from his front pocket. He swiped across to find his camera app, sliding to the video option and tapping the lightning bolt to activate the flash. Aggressively bright against the dull yellow of the overhead lights.

"Be careful," Red told him as Arthur pressed the red record button, and the beep it made cut right through her, joining the shiver up her back.

Arthur nodded at Simon, who tucked himself up onto the chair to make room for him, pulling back the corner flap of the suitcase. The gap was small, but enough for Arthur to snake his hand and phone through. He reached forward, losing half his arm to the outside world and the unknown beyond.

"Hello."

Simon sucked in a nervous breath and Arthur flinched, gritting his teeth. The sleeve of his arm shifted and wrinkled around the hinge of his elbow as he moved the wrist beyond, recording a full arc of outside. Red watched his face as he did, the tension in his upper lip, the focus in his eyes, and she reasoned that if she didn't think about the red dot then it couldn't possibly take his arm, or any other part of him. But didn't that count as thinking of it?

"Okay," Arthur said, his face unfurrowing as he drew his arm back inside the RV, quickly, clumsily. He tapped his thumb to the screen to stop the recording. Simon pressed the duct tape back in place and Red leaned across the back of the chair to see the video on Arthur's screen. Oliver did the same, watching over Arthur's shoulder.

The video began with a shaky view of the dashboard, clipping the end of Red's voice as she told him to be careful. It moved over, catching Simon as he pulled his legs up out of the way, glancing back, eyes on a point above the camera. A close-up of Simon's fingers as they bent into ridges, pulling the suitcase aside. The screen zoomed in on the black hole, breaking that barrier between out there and in here as it moved through into the total darkness of outside, the air lit by the ghostly glow of the phone. There was nothing out there, nothing they could see, until the view shifted down and the flash reached the road, picking out stones and pieces of glass.

"Hello," the voice repeated from ninety seconds ago, through the recording.

The shot juddered and then continued, swinging around to the right, the white light reflecting in the driver's-side mirror.

"There!" Simon pointed at the screen.

Arthur paused the video. Hanging from the bottom of the driver's-side mirror was a shape, a small black shape with an antenna out the top. The walkie-talkie glared at them through the darkness with one bright green eye: a small backlit rectangular display.

"Where is it?" Maddy asked from back there.

"Attached to the driver's-side mirror," Oliver answered, straightening up. "Okay, Arthur, reach out and grab it."

"Why does Arthur have to do it?" Simon said.

"Because he's already done it once."

"It's fine," Arthur said, rolling up the sleeve on his right arm, opening and closing his fist like he was practicing, tendons sticking out under his tan skin. There was a small, puckered scar near the base of his index finger that Red had never noticed before. Now definitely wasn't the time to ask about it.

"He wants us to pick up the walkie-talkie, he won't shoot, not yet," Arthur said in a whisper, more to himself than to anyone else. He cricked the bones in his neck and then he was ready, nodding to Simon.

Simon pulled the suitcase back, a bigger gap this time, and Arthur leaned toward it. He balled his fist and pushed through, his arm disappearing outside again. His breaths came too quickly, fogging his glasses, his nose pressed up against the suitcase as he reached, blindly.

"I can feel it," he said, the muscles in his neck straining.

"Grab it," Oliver said, leaning forward.

"I can't, it's attached." Arthur blew out a mouthful of air and closed his eyes behind his glasses. Like Maddy did sometimes, to focus. Had Red ever tried that trick? "Okay, I think I can unclip it . . . hold on . . ."

"Don't drop it," Oliver said, like Arthur wasn't already telling himself the same thing. Probably; Red couldn't read his mind.

"Got it," Arthur exhaled, opening his eyes and blinking slowly as he carefully guided his arm back through the gap, elbow, then wrist, the antenna of the walkie-talkie snagging on the suitcase as he finally pulled it inside. The static hissed, crossing the threshold, and Arthur hissed too, looking across at Red, his green-brown eyes swimming as they readjusted to the light.

"Here," he said, reaching over Simon to pass the walkie-talkie to Red, dropping it into her hand. It was cool against her fingers.

"Hello," it crackled from within her grip. She was holding his voice, he, him, the sniper, the red dot, but she didn't want to and her heart was too loud, reaching up into her ears and the back of her throat. Red stared down at the walkie-talkie, at the numbers on the display, at the buttons below the screen, at the crop-circle holes of the speaker and microphone at the bottom of the device, so like the one she used to play with. All black, apart from the green display and one red button on the side.

"What should we . . . ," she began, but Oliver stepped over and picked the walkie-talkie up out of her open hand.

He studied it, narrowing his eyes.

"What are we going to say?" Reyna asked. "Maybe we should plan beforehand, how to best play it, so he leaves us alone."

"How do I . . ." Oliver shook the walkie-talkie, glancing up at Red. Had he really never played with one of these before, even as a kid? Red only ever remembered him doing homework or telling her and Maddy to keep it down. Oliver Lavoy, born prelaw just like his soon-to-be-district-attorney mom, no time for playing.

"You hold down that red button at the side there to talk." Red showed him, like her mom once showed her. Not now, get out of her head, you don't belong here.

"Right," he said, like it was obvious now. He took a deep breath.

"Oliver," Reyna said, "should we—"

Oliver pressed the button and the static cut out immediately. He raised the walkie-talkie to his face.

"Who is this?" he asked, pushing his voice out so hard that it growled around the edges.

The static returned as Oliver released the button, looking back at the rest of them, eyes wide.

They waited.

The static clicked out.

"Ah, you found me." The walkie-talkie spoke, cold and metallic.

"Who is this?" Oliver said again.

"The button," Red reminded him.

"Who is this?" Oliver repeated, holding down the button this time.

Static.

"You know who this is."

Static.

"No?" Oliver said.

"I'm the one outside with the rifle."

Red swallowed, forcing it down her too-tight throat.

"What do you want from us?" Oliver said, pacing away from the cockpit and down the length of the RV. The rest of them followed. "If it's money, I don't think we have much cash on us right now. But you can have it all. And my credit card. I'll give you the PIN. Take as much as you want. It's yours. Just let us go."

Click.

Static.

"I don't want your money," the voice said.

A shadow crossed his face, confusion in the draw of his eyebrows. If only it had been that easy, Oliver. Throw money at the problem.

"What do you want, then?" Oliver paced. "I'm sorry if we're on your land. We didn't mean any offense. We got lost. We were never supposed to be here. Just the wrong place at the wrong time."

Static.

The walkie-talkie crackled, a strange, hitching sound. Was he laughing at them?

"What if I said you were the right people, in the right place at exactly the right time."

Oliver lowered the walkie-talkie, glancing up at the rest of them, eyes drawn. His mouth flickered silently, words dying before he could breathe life into them.

Maddy's arm tensed, pushing against Red. Simon on her other side, holding on to her sleeve. She didn't move, staring at the walkie-talkie in Oliver's hand, molding the static into empty whispered words in her head. *Right people, right place, right time.*

"What does he mean?" Arthur said, voice rasping and low, catching on the sides of his throat. His eyes darted to Red's, but she couldn't give him any answers there.

Oliver sucked in a shaky breath and raised the walkie-talkie to his lips. He pressed the button, and the only sound in the RV, in the world, was Red's breath, too heavy in her chest.

"What do you mean?" Oliver asked of the man out there in the wide-open nothing.

Static.

"I'll tell you what I mean."

Static.

"Oliver Charles Lavoy.

"Madeline Joy Lavoy.

"Reyna Flores-Serrano.

"Arthur Grant Moore.

"Simon Jinsun Yoo.

"Redford Kenny."

# FOURTEEN

Chaos.

When had Maddy started screaming? Red couldn't remember now. Like the sound had always been there in her head, along with the static.

Simon's shoulders bucked, thrashing as he choked on air.

The walkie-talkie dropped to Oliver's side, chaos in the golden swirl of his eyes, moving too fast to be in real time.

Arthur stuttered.

Reyna swore.

Red listened, the chaos creeping into her own brain as she realized that something new was beginning now, a shift in the air and a hitch in her chest.

"How does he know our names?" Simon choked. "How the fuck does he know our names?!"

"No, no, no," Maddy shaped her scream. "He's here to kill us. He's going to kill us all!"

"I—I don't u-understand . . ." Arthur shook his head. "H-how—"

"Fuck!" Reyna held the sides of her face, strands of black hair clinging to her skin. "This was planned. This was all planned. He was waiting for us here."

Not random, no. Not wrong place, wrong time. Planned. It was all planned. And why was Maddy's scream still in her head?

Oliver's eyes kept spinning, like they were broken, spooling loose right out of his skull.

"Oliver, do something!" Reyna shouted. "Say something. He knows who we are!"

He snapped back into life. "What can I say, Reyna? What can I do? I'm trying to think what this means!"

"What this means is that he trapped us here on purpose. He knew we were coming."

"How could he know?" Simon said, eyes watering as he coughed on the words. "We got lost."

"Why? Why?" Maddy wailed.

"Everyone, let me think!" Oliver roared into the chaos, patches of red climbing up his neck, threatening to take his face.

Maddy cried.

Simon coughed.

Arthur stared and Reyna shook her head.

Red listened, filling herself with the static to push out the scream.

But the static cut out, and in its place that deep, tinny voice.

"I can tell you your dates of birth and home addresses too, if you like."

Oliver recoiled from the walkie-talkie in his hands, placing it down on the table. He stood back and studied it, arms hugged around his chest.

"Is it possible he searched the RV license plate after he shot out the tires?" he asked the others. "That it might have led him to Simon's uncle, then Simon, then to finding the rest of us?"

Red could tell from Oliver's face that he didn't believe it even as he gave voice to it, that an answer wasn't needed because it had already been given in the asking.

"He knew who we were before we got here," Reyna said, joining Oliver to stare down at the walkie-talkie. "He brought us here, trapped us here."

"Why?" Maddy wiped her face.

"He's going to kill us," Simon said, and his voice didn't match the words, hollow and flat.

"I don't want to die," Maddy cried, a new tear cascading to the cliff edge of her nose. It jumped free, splattering on the floor.

Red took Maddy's hand again, gave it a squeeze. Not quite an *it'll be okay* anymore, but an *I'm here too*.

Oliver nodded to himself, once, twice, then he lurched forward to pick up the walkie-talkie again.

"We've already called the cops," he said. "A while ago. They say they'll be here any minute."

Static.

A crackling sound, cold and inhuman. He was laughing again.

Oliver waited for the static to return, then he held down the button.

"Yeah. Hilarious, isn't it? They'll be here in less than five minutes, so you should probably pack up and start running if you want to get a head start."

"The cops aren't coming. No one's coming to help you."

A muscle twitched in Oliver's cheek.

"Yes they are. We called them," he said, a new hint of desperation in his voice.

Static.

"You didn't call anyone. There's no service. I made sure of that."

Oliver lowered the walkie-talkie, his thumb straying away from the button.

"FUCK!" he screamed, holding on to the word as it ripped at his throat. Flecks of spit in the air.

"He knocked out the cell service?" Reyna said, her hand moving to the back of Oliver's neck as he bent forward, elbows to his knees, head to his hands. Defeated already.

"How could he do that?" Simon said, turning to aim the question at each of them. Nothing.

"The more important question is why," Reyna replied. "What does he want? We give it to him and maybe he lets us go."

"He wants to kill us," Maddy said, squeezing Red's hand back, so hard that she felt their bones crunching together.

Oliver sniffed, straightening up. He wiped his mouth with the back of his hand and pushed the button.

"Please don't kill us," he said.

Oliver Lavoy was not ready to die. Were any of them?

A crackle from the walkie-talkie.

"That depends on you," the voice said. "I want something from you. And I will get it before the night is over."

"I said you can take my credit card. All of our cards. Take whatever we have."

Red had nothing.

Static.

"I told you, it's not money I want."

"Ask him what he wants," Simon said, flapping one hand to get Oliver's attention. "Ask him."

Oliver held down the button.

"What do you want?"

Static.

"One of you knows something. A secret. You know who you are and you know what it is."

Red's eyes crossed in front of her, and she imagined she could see the sound of the static, staining the air a speckled gray, closing in around her. Maddy's shoulders dropped, her hand growing sticky and uncomfortable in Red's. Arthur was blinking, too fast, turning to watch Simon as he coughed and spluttered. Reyna's eyes dropped, and Oliver chewed the inside of his cheek. No one was looking at Red, but she looked at them all.

Oliver raised the walkie-talkie to his mouth again. He waited one moment, then two.

"What secret?" he asked, releasing the button.

Static.

"That's for the six of you to figure out. And remember one thing: you can't see me but I can see you. If you try to run, I will shoot."

# FIFTEEN

The air was too thick in here, syrupy with the smell of gasoline, with the quickening of their breaths. It plugged Red's nose and her ears until she could close her eyes and pretend she wasn't here at all, forcing herself to think of that pattern in the curtains. *You can't see me but I can see you,* and Red could see nothing here at all with her eyes shut.

"He'll shoot us if we leave the RV," Oliver said, like they hadn't all been listening, like they hadn't all just heard that together.

Red opened her eyes, twisting her hand out of Maddy's grip. She watched as Oliver dropped the walkie-talkie down on the table, a heavier thud than it should have made. It stood end up, the green LCD display watching them.

"We are never getting out of this RV." Simon sniffed, running his hand down his face, pulling the skin out of shape, revealing the red underneath his eyes. "If we're going to die here, fuck it, I'm having more tequila."

"No, Simon," Red croaked, her voice raw and unused.

"Fuck it!" he barked, strolling over to the kitchen counter. "Come on, everyone, let's do shots in the dark."

Reyna sidestepped, blocking his way to the counter and Oliver's open backpack.

"No," she said sternly. "We need to stay rational."

"What are you, the tequila guardian?" He pointed at her.

"Right, because I'm Mexican?"

"No, because you're standing in the way." He hiccupped. "If I want to die drunk, then I'll die drunk, thank you and good night."

"We're not going to die," Arthur said, stepping forward to pull Simon back, hand on his shoulder. "We just need to give him what he wants. What's the secret he's talking about?"

"And who?" Maddy added quickly, picking at her fingernails.

Red looked straight ahead, blinked slowly, clearing her eyes like someone who had no secrets. Someone who wasn't thinking of them right now. Everyone had secrets, though, didn't they? Somebody else here had to. Were hers any worse, any bigger? Most likely, at least the one she was keeping now. The plan. But no one could ever know about that, that was the point. Oh, and there was the fact that her mom was dead and it was probably her fault, all her f—could it be Bart Simpson, the pattern in the curtain?

"It's not me," Simon said, giving up on the tequila. He pushed past Red and Maddy to drop back on the sofa, head resting against the mattress wedged there. "My only secret is that I haven't told my parents I want to be an actor, not work in finance. Don't think someone's threatening to kill me over being a secret theater kid. Apart from my dad, that is," he said, adding in an exaggerated stage whisper: "He's Korean."

"I can't think of anything," Arthur said, pausing to scratch his eye. "Nothing big enough for this."

"Me either," Maddy said, almost too fast. Red noticed. And the way she wouldn't look up or hold anyone's gaze.

Oliver stepped forward, cleared his throat. "I know who it is. I know what this is about."

Red looked at him. Maddy looked at him. Arthur and Simon looked at him. Reyna didn't.

"It's me and Maddy," he said.

Maddy stiffened. "I don't—" she began.

"—It's obvious, isn't it?" Oliver cut across her. "This is about our mom."

Now Reyna *was* looking at him. "What do you mean?" she asked.

"This must be about her case. The Frank Gotti case."

"What's that?" Arthur said.

"Our mom is assistant DA, and she's the lead prosecutor on an upcoming homicide case."

"In the Mafia," Simon said, gesturing with his beer bottle. Wait, where did he get a beer from?

"Yeah, exactly." Oliver snapped his fingers at him. "This whole thing seems exactly like something they'd pull."

"Why? What's the case?" Arthur made the mistake of asking him.

Could Red really stand to listen to this one more time? Oliver glanced at her and she kept her face straight.

"So, about a year ago," he began, leaning back on the table, "the boss of the organized crime group—"

"The Mafia," Simon offered.

"Yes, the Mafia." Oliver's jaw tightened, clearly irritated at the interruption. "The boss of the family, a man called John D'Amico, died of throat cancer in the hospital last year. He left behind a bit of a power vacuum, with three members of the family vying for the top job to replace him."

Yep, Red thought, first up was—

"Tommy D'Amico," Oliver said, holding up one finger. "John's oldest son."

Number two:

"Joseph Mannino, who had been John's underboss, which is a second-in-command-type thing."

And finally:

"Francesco Gotti, who had been John's consigliere, which is like the top adviser role."

Oliver tucked away his three upheld fingers, and Frank Gotti was the one who flashed into Red's mind, that photo of his face she'd seen and seen again, one dark curl of hair falling down to cover his left eye.

"The three of them split the family into factions, as it were," Oliver continued, glancing around to make sure they were all listening. "There was fighting but no one got seriously hurt. Not until last August, when Frank Gotti killed Joseph Mannino himself. Shot twice in the back of the head. And my mom—our mom—is the one who's prosecuting Frank. The trial is in a few weeks and she's going to get a guilty conviction. We know it. They clearly know it."

Arthur looked down, eyes flickering back and forth like he was sifting through everything Oliver just said.

"So you think this"—he gestured around at the RV, at the wide-open nothing outside the blocked-up windows—"us being here, that sniper out there, is about that murder case?"

"Yes, that's clearly what's going on," Oliver replied, his eyes unfaltering. "This is all about my mom. They're trying to get to her. And they are using me and Maddy to do it."

"You mean, like, holding us for ransom?" Maddy said, uncertain.

"In a way." Oliver nodded. "They've probably already contacted her, told her they are holding us hostage somewhere."

"But why?" Reyna chimed in now. "What would they want from her?"

"If they go to trial, Mom is going to put Frank in prison for the rest of his life. They can't let that happen; he's their leader. Well, to some of them. They are probably demanding she find a way to drop the charges to stop the case going to trial. Or . . ." He trailed off.

"Or they'll k-kill us," Maddy finished it, stumbling over the word.

Oliver didn't say anything, but his silence was answer enough, the static from the walkie-talkie filling in for him. "And, now that I'm thinking it through, maybe this secret he's talking about, the secret he wants . . . maybe it's the identity of the eyewitness. The one the whole case rests on. And they want Mom to give it to them."

"So they can kill the witness and stop the trial?" Reyna asked, eyes narrowing, a knot of lines forming across her forehead. Red looked to Oliver, waiting for the answer.

"Yeah," he replied. "Wouldn't be the first time a witness for the prosecution was killed right before trial with these kinds of people. That's why Mom tried so hard this time to protect the witness's anonymity. This whole thing has organized crime written all over it."

"And will she give it up?" Red asked then, trying to catch up with the others, to see the whole picture and their place within it. "Will she give them the witness?"

Oliver looked across at her. He blinked.

"If it's a choice between me and Maddy and the witness, Mom will give them the name," he said. "Life or death. She'll have to."

Red nodded. Something tightened in her chest, uncomfortable and warm, as Oliver's words became real. Fuck. Either way it went, someone was going to die here. If Oliver was right, that was. And, it seemed, he usually was.

"That's why we can't let that happen," Oliver continued, hardening his gaze, sharing it with the others. "We have to stop them. We have to escape. We can't let my mom give up that name. This trial is too important. It would be the end of her career."

"And someone would die," Maddy reminded him. "She would be killing the witness, giving them up."

"Right. I already said that," Oliver snapped, missing the point. Red caught it, though, glad that Maddy was here to offset her brother. Between saving a life and his mom's career, it was clear which was most important to Oliver. And probably, by extension, his own career. Red bit her lip so she didn't say anything, not that it would probably change his mind at all.

"Are you sure that's what this is about?" Reyna asked Oliver, looking up at him, something in her eyes, a glint that Red couldn't read. A silent conversation in half a second.

Oliver brushed her off. "Yes, it has to be about that. I mean, if you just think logically, Maddy and I are the most high-value targets here. It has to be about us."

Red couldn't disagree.

"Any reason anyone else here would be held hostage by a sniper?" he asked the room.

The others shook their heads, Red too.

"Nobody loves me," she said with a sniff, not like Catherine loved Maddy and Oliver. That hurt, thinking about it, a twist in her gut and a hole in her heart.

"Right, okay. We're all agreed?" he said, not looking for an answer. "So now we have to work out how to escape."

# SIXTEEN

*Escape* was a strange word, wasn't it? One of those ones that tripped Red up. Funny like *resource* but not in the same way. A word that, if you thought it too much, grew spiky and nonsensical in your head. Please someone say something else. Escape. *Eeescape. ESCAPÉ.*

"Just to float an alternative," Simon said from the sofa, his head bouncing back against the mattress. Thank you, Simon. "Why don't we just wait this whole thing out, here in the RV? Look, sunrise must be at about six a.m., right? And when it's light, the sniper loses his advantage, because we'll be able to see where he is. Then we can escape"—there it was again—"and because it's morning we're more likely to be able to flag down help." He sat back, hands raised as though his plan were there, sitting on top of them, held out like an offering.

"My mom will give up the name before sunrise." Oliver shook his head, dismissing the plan.

"And the witness will be killed," Maddy said, a grim set to her jaw. "Mom would be responsible for someone dying."

*Someone dying.* Red's chest tightened again.

"Right." Simon nodded, raising his hands and the plan even higher. "And that's very sad for the witness, of course. Poor guy. But it's not really our fault. And I'd prefer the six of us to survive. We're safest in the RV. I mean, come on." Simon glanced around. "Arthur? Red?" he said, looking for agreement in their eyes.

But Red didn't agree, she couldn't. She looked down. "I think we should do what Oliver says," she answered, keeping her voice flat. What other choice was there? Oliver was in charge: the natural leader, the highest value. This was about surviving, and this RV wasn't safe, no matter how hard they pretended.

Simon dropped his hands, a flicker of betrayal in his eyes as he shot them at Red. He shrugged it off and returned to his beer.

"Majority rules." Oliver clapped his hands, returning to business. "Let's start thinking about how we can escape, then."

*ÉSCÄPÈ.*

"Or get help," Maddy added.

Arthur sighed, removing his glasses to wipe them against his sweatshirt. "Both seem pretty impossible right now. No cell service. No one around. A rifle. And we don't know where he is, out there in the darkness." A pause. "He has all the cards."

Oliver exhaled, conceding the point, and Red bet he didn't like being someone without any cards. Cards. Pokémon cards? Was that the pattern in the curtains? If she thought about that, then she couldn't think about anything worse, like what was happening here.

The static filled the room again, in the absence of voices, and Oliver glanced down at the walkie-talkie.

"Maybe he doesn't have *all* the cards," he said, scooping the walkie-talkie up, cradling it between his hands like it was spun from glass. "We have this. He's overlooked something here. He's given us a communication device!" His voice picked up speed, mouth trying to keep up, as was Red. "Can't we use this to contact someone? Walkie-talkies don't need cell service, I mean, clearly. And don't emergency services use walkie-talkies, anyway? Can't we somehow connect this to the police radio and ask for help?"

"Can't believe we didn't think of that sooner." Simon sat forward. "That's a plan I can get on board with."

It didn't work like that. None of it worked like that.

"How would we . . ." Oliver trailed off, studying the LCD display.

"What's wrong, Red?" Arthur had been watching her, he must have read it in her eyes. She thought she was better at keeping a straight face; she'd had enough practice.

"I'm sorry," she began, looking at Maddy instead of Oliver, the softer of the Lavoys. "Two-way radios don't work like that. Radio frequencies are regulated. Emergency services, like the police, have their own frequencies specifically so they don't get interference from other signals, like you're suggesting."

"Right, I know," Oliver said. Had he, though? "But, in an emergency, can't we make it do that?"

There was a simple answer to that, the one Oliver didn't want to hear. But he was asking, so: "No," she said, looking away from him as she did, so his eyes didn't bully a different response out of her. "No, it's not physically possible to make this radio transmit on the emergency frequencies that police use."

"Fuck" was Oliver's simple answer in return.

"How do you know?" Reyna turned to Red, but Oliver answered for her:

"Her mom was a cop."

And that *was* still hurt. It always did. But that wasn't why she knew so much about walkie-talkies. Well, not directly. Her mom was a cop, but so was Red when they played that game together. And that was how she knew. Four days after the funeral, Red found a box in the attic, a box of her mom's old stuff. And there, nestled between old jackets and shoes, were the walkie-talkies. A piece of masking tape across the back of each, one with *MOM,* one with *RED.* She hadn't been looking for them, not really, just looking to look, to preserve her mom for another day, and then another. Red left her own walkie-talkie there, took the one labeled *MOM* down to her room. She stole a screwdriver from her dad—he was already mostly lost by then, but he could still pretend to function, still went to work—and, in the quiet of her room past midnight, she took apart the walkie-talkie. Piece by piece, wire by wire, but she never did find her mom's voice hiding inside.

"It's probably an FRS radio," she said, approaching Oliver, holding her hand out, waiting for him to let it go. He placed it in her hand, and she felt the familiar weight of the device. She knew it, inside and out.

"FRS?" Oliver said, not stepping back, like he couldn't be too far from the walkie-talkie, couldn't trust her to even hold it.

"Family Radio Service," she said. "It's the radio frequencies most amateur devices like this use. If I remember right"—and she did remember right, how could she ever forget this—"it has twenty-two channels." She knew more than that, that those twenty-two channels were found somewhere between 462 and 467 megahertz, and that the speaker also functioned as the microphone, built from the same bones: a magnet, a coil of wire, a cone made of plastic. She'd learned all that, putting Mom's walkie-talkie back together again, until it turned on and hissed at her. For days that was all she did, took it apart, rebuilt it, did it again on her mom's birthday the year after, and the one after that. You couldn't do that with dead moms, though, rebuild them. They stayed gone.

"So, we can't use it to contact anyone else?" Oliver asked, still standing too close.

Red stepped back if he wasn't going to. "Yes, we could," she said, and the light returned to Oliver's eyes. "In theory, if someone else is using another two-way radio on the same frequency channel within range, we would be able to talk to them. The sniper is using channel three."

Red and her mom always used number six, for some reason. It was lucky, at least until it wasn't anymore.

"What's the range?" Reyna asked, studying Red as though she couldn't wait for the answer.

Red sighed, unable to give them what they wanted. "It's not great with something like this," she said. "It depends on the terrain, the weather, how many trees and buildings are in the way, but . . ." She thought about it. "A couple of miles, maybe. A few at most."

Red and her mom once picked up interference from a wedding planner barking orders down her end. Must have been someplace close. The groom had been late, apparently, but Red pretended it was a surveillance mission and they took notes. Laughing. The kind of laugh that hurt during and after.

"Oh," Reyna said in response. No, it wasn't good news, not for them. They were in the middle of nowhere, a range of three miles still left them pretty much in nowhere. But there were houses and farms within all that nowhere.

Reyna pulled out her phone to check the time. "It's almost one a.m.," she said, deflating. "I guess it's unlikely anyone will be out using a walkie-talkie."

Silent agreement from the rest of them, the walkie-talkie laughing at them from Red's hands.

"Unlikely, but they might?" Red said. "Or someone might have a baby monitor on in range. We could keep cycling through the channels, see if we pick up any interference?"

Red hadn't found her mom's voice on channel six, or any of the others she'd tried. But it was harder when the person you were looking for wasn't alive.

"Yes." Oliver snapped his fingers at her, a smile cracking his face. "This is what I'm talking about! Some initiative. Okay, Red, you're in charge of the walkie-talkie. You cycle through the channels, but make sure you always return to three, every couple of minutes or so. In case we miss the sniper trying to talk to us. We don't want him to know what we're up to."

Red glowed, despite herself, nodding as she accepted the order from Oliver. Was she *useful*? What a plot twist that was. A smile from Maddy too, full house. Red bet Arthur was secretly impressed as well; look at her, knowing stuff.

Right, focus. There was a man with a rifle outside, and Red was trying to be useful. She wouldn't want to die, not like that. Although she supposed it wouldn't take two shots to the back of the head this time. Just the one, just anywhere. Red pressed the *menu* button and then the + on the right, switching to channel four instead and the empty static there. She could pretend the tone of the static changed each time, a different swirl of sound, like a new song. But it didn't, it sounded the same. An empty hiss. Up to five now, then six. Red waited longer there, just in case.

"Okay," Oliver said, looking around at the group. He stepped over to the sofa and, in one quick motion, removed the beer bottle from Simon's hand, walking it over to the kitchen counter. "So Red is on part one of the plan; trying to get outside help. But we need part two. An escape plan."

*ÊŚĊĄPË.*

Stop that. Up to channel eight now. Should she go back to three and make sure the sniper wasn't trying to talk to them?

"Like our mom always says." Oliver turned to Maddy. "A plan

126

must have two parts, and you have to make sure either way plays out in your favor."

"That's win-win," Maddy said, completing it for him.

Yes, Catherine Lavoy always had a plan, Red knew that. Birthday presents and reserves. Two different flavors of ice cream. Red herself preferred the lose-lose system: no plan at all and no backups. She pressed the down button back to three to check for the sniper's voice. Nothing. Back up to eleven. Click, static, click.

"And what is the plan?" Simon said, his words more slurred now, but Red couldn't tell if he was putting it on to irritate Oliver. "You're the leader, the most high-value person here. What is your brilliant plan to escape the active shooter out there in the pitch-black who can see us but we can't see him?"

Oliver's jaw snapped open, hanging ajar as his eyes spooled in his head again, working loose.

"That's it," he laughed, slapping one hand against his hip. "That's his only advantage, that we don't know where he is."

"I'd say his advantage is the giant fucking rifle with the laser sight," Simon muttered.

Oliver didn't hear him, or didn't listen. "That's the plan, that's all we have to do. Work out exactly where he is out there. Find the sniper."

1:00 A.M.

# SEVENTEEN

"Find him?" Arthur said, at the same time as Reyna, voices clashing, each leaning on a different word.

Finding a sniper in the pitch-black wide-open nothing. Something about needles and haystacks, Red thought, or a shot in the dark. Literally. She scrolled up through the channels on the walkie-talkie, the flickering of the static not quiet enough to be just background noise. Nothing. More nothing.

"Yes," Oliver said, his eyes too wide and his voice too loud. "Don't you see, if we work out exactly where he is, we can use the RV to cover us while we run the other way. He'll never even know."

Oliver turned his wide shoulders, head following a moment later. He looked up at the mattress covering the broken window as though imagining the bullet, bringing it back to life in his head.

"From the positioning of the shots through both windows, and the first tire he shot out, he was definitely on this side." He gestured beyond the front door. "I guess at an angle, though, if he was able to shoot out the tires on the other side, most likely aiming underneath the RV. So he must have been somewhere over there, low to the ground, hiding in the long grass."

Oliver held out his arm at a diagonal, pointing his finger between the right side and back end of the RV.

"Okay." Reyna swallowed, letting her hand skim Oliver's as she came to stand beside him. "That narrows it down."

Oliver moved his hand away, shaking his head. "No, he *was* there. But then he came up to the RV to plant the walkie-talkie on the driver's-side mirror. He could have moved position after that, knowing we'd think about this." He sighed. "Realistically, he could now be anywhere, on either side."

Arthur nodded, eyes darting to the corners of the RV, like it was starting to shrink around him. At least it had that extra foot, thirty-one feet instead of thirty. "So how would we find him now?" he asked.

Oliver scrunched his face, thinking. And if that wasn't enough, he said: "I'm thinking."

How to find a shooter in the dark? Red should make another joke to cheer Maddy up, talk about the night-vision goggles she'd packed in her suitcase.

"Is now a good time to mention I packed my thermal imaging goggles?" Simon said, rising from the sofa. Hey, that was her line. A bit better, actually. Simon could have it.

"Shh," Oliver hissed, pressing his fingers to his temples to think even harder. "Red?" he said suddenly, turning his attention to her.

The static fizzed as she looked up.

"When someone shoots a rifle, is there something other than the noise? Does it give off any light, a flash?"

Red shrugged. Why was he asking *her* that? Oh, right, because her mom was a police captain and she would have known the answer. Oliver seemed like he was waiting for more.

"I don't—" she began.

"—Yeah, there's a muzzle flash," Simon said, his arm knocking into Red's as he rejoined the group. Arthur was right; it was too small in here, and it was getting warm now too.

Everyone turned to look at Simon.

"It's like that little explosion of light when you fire," he said, finally looking up, noticing their eyes. "Why are youse all staring at me? What, you don't watch movies? I mean the muzzle flash is not really there, it's normally added in postproduction. But yeah: gun goes off, there's a flash."

Turned out Simon was *useful* too. Who would have thought, the two of them, Red and Simon? Certainly not Oliver, it seemed, judging by the stunned look in his eyes, pupils sitting too large among all that golden brown.

He stepped forward, clapping Simon hard on the back, twice. That must be the best *well done* you could get, beyond words.

"Right, okay," Oliver said, talking it through with himself. "Gun goes off, there's a flash. That's it, there's our plan."

"How?" Maddy asked, and to which part, Red wasn't sure. Didn't sound like a full plan, not one up to Catherine Lavoy's standards at least.

"We position ourselves at every window in the RV. Someone watching the front, back, both sides. Every angle. We watch, and then we bait a shot from the sniper—"

"—Sounds safe," Simon commented.

"—and one of us will see it, see the flash. Then we'll know exactly where he is. And then"—Oliver's eyes glinted—"we run, in the opposite direction, using the RV as cover. We're going to get out of here."

That sounded more like a full plan, except there was one part missing.

"How do we bait a shot from him?" Arthur asked, spotting it too. "Without one of us getting killed?"

Red cycled through channel one, then two, back to three. Empty static, all of them.

"We—"

"—Hello?" The voice crackled into life in her hands. The sniper. "Hello. Are we all still alive in there?" he asked.

Red sniffed, breath stalling, heart kicking up in her chest. She scanned the faces of the others quickly. What should she do?

Oliver was there before she could ask him. He grabbed the walkie-talkie out of her hand and pressed the button.

"We're here," he said, trying to disguise the tremor in his voice. "We're working on that secret you want."

Static.

"Good," the voice answered. "Keep working. Time's running out."

Static.

"Can we just ask him to take a shot?" Reyna suggested.

Oliver rounded on her. "Why would we ask him to take a shot, Reyna? Come on, think. We can't give away that we're trying to escape."

He dropped the walkie-talkie back into Red's hands.

"Sorry, I'm just trying to help." Reyna shrank back, sliding into the booth at the dining table.

"Why has he taken shots before?" Oliver said, not really speaking to the others. "He shot at the tires and the gas tank to trap us here. Then at the window, maybe to scare us. Then—"

"The horn!" Maddy said, eyes lighting up. She pointed to the steering wheel. "He shot at us when I was beeping."

Oliver snapped his fingers. "Bingo."

# EIGHTEEN

They were really doing this, were they? Asking to be shot at. Inviting the red dot in.

Red pressed the button, clicking up through the channels on the walkie-talkie, swapping one static for another while she waited, eyes on Oliver.

"Okay, let's think about our angles, then," he said.

Yes, let's.

"Windows. We've got a big one at the back of the RV. Then on the left we have the small one by the bunks, two windows at the dining table." He nodded his head at them, Red's eyes catching on the curtains. "The two side windows at the front and the windshield." The windshield was the only window they hadn't covered, their only view out into the total darkness of outside. "Then on the right we have the big one behind the sofa, and the small one in the front door. And that's it, isn't it? There isn't one in the bathroom."

"There's the rearview camera, too," Reyna said quietly from the table, picking at her thumb. "Should come up if we put the RV in reverse. I think."

"Yes, okay, great," Oliver said, turning to shoot her a smile. Reyna didn't return it. "That means we might not need someone to cover the back. The person pressing the horn can use the camera to get that angle. Okay."

He studied them all and they waited to be assigned their windows, Red skipping back to channel three.

"I'll take the rearview camera and I'll press the horn." He swallowed, like his was the hardest job, but he didn't have to put his face up to a window with a sniper watching outside. "Reyna, you'll be with me, you watch out the front, through the windshield. Maddy, you take the front left side, watching out the dining table window. Simon, back left, through the bunk window. Arthur, you're front right, through the window behind the sofa. And Red, you're back right, the window in the door."

Red nodded. At least her window still had glass in it. She glanced at Arthur, a knot forming in her gut. He'd pulled the short straw here; the last two times the sniper shot at them, it had come through that window. He looked okay, though. Nervous, not scared. Not yet, at least. He glanced at her, and she gave him a quick half smile. He caught it from her, stretching onto the other side of his face. Together they made one whole smile, tight and tense.

"I'm taking the riskiest job," Oliver said. Was he? "He'll shoot toward whoever is at the steering wheel, like with Maddy. So I'm going to need some protection."

"You're not going to ask one of us to be your human shield, are you?" Simon said, backing away with his hands raised.

Red snorted, though none of this was really funny, was it? They might die tonight, all of them, some of them, her. A bullet could come anytime, anywhere. Was that what made these smaller moments funnier, because they might not get any more? Last chances to smile, to laugh, to tell Arthur she liked him and it was okay that he didn't like her back because she was unlikable at times, she knew that. To tell Simon that, yes, his cheekbones were amazing and it would be a damn shame if he didn't end up onstage or in front of a camera. To thank Maddy for always being there by her side, to share all those big moments, and small, some so small that Red had probably forgotten them by now. To tell Reyna that maybe she could do better. To tell Oliver, well, Red wasn't sure what she would tell Oliver. And that didn't matter because she wasn't going to say any of that anyway. Red wasn't good at last chances, at final moments, was she? *I hate you.*

She'd never said it since.

A swarm of guilt in her gut as she came back to the room, cooling to shame as she watched Oliver studying the pile of resources on the table. Nothing big enough to protect him there.

"Oh, I know," he said, darting forward to grab the screwdriver. "Excuse me." He pushed past Red and Simon, elbow butting hers, walking over to the small closet beside the front door. He pulled it open.

"There's only a mop and a dustpan and brush in there," Simon told him.

"I know," Oliver replied, bending down to look at the hinges on the inside of the door. "Arthur, will you help me here? Hold the door while I remove the hinges?"

"Sure." Arthur nodded, rolling up the sleeves of his sweatshirt. He walked between Red and Simon, gently resting his hand on her back as he guided himself through. Fingers warm, then gone, leaving something behind. That stupid, pathetic firework again, at the back of her eyes. Didn't it know there was a man outside with a gun?

Arthur curled his hands around the top corners of the closet door while Oliver guided the screwdriver, slotting it into the first screw.

Red's eyes returned to the walkie-talkie. Her job. Her

responsibility. Her plan. Partly, anyway. She clicked up again, shaping the static with her ears, making it say whatever she wanted it to. You could do that with memories too, sometimes. Lie to yourself, think fake thoughts to cover the ones you didn't want. Like that time Catherine Lavoy took Red to the mall, because she'd finally outgrown her last pair of jeans, and it was Red's first good day since everything happened. She'd even smiled. But sometimes Red changed it, and it was *her* mom instead, not dead anymore, not angry anymore. A lie. Impossible. But it was nicer than the truth.

"So before we get into position, everyone," Oliver said, one screw removed, turning his attention to the next. "We will have to turn off all the lights in the RV, so we can see out the windows better. Turn off the headlights too, so Reyna can see out front. So grab one of the flashlights or use your phone's light to get yourselves into position."

Simon waded forward, snatching the headlamp from the dining table with a whispered "Yes." He pulled the elastic over his head, wearing the light over his eye like an eye patch.

Red shook her head at him. She thought the adrenaline would have sobered him up by now. She thought wrong, clearly. She crossed to the kitchen and turned on the faucet, filling Simon another glass of water, pushing it into his chest.

"All right, *Mom*." Simon swayed, taking a sip.

"Simon," Maddy hissed at him, angry lines crisscrossing her forehead. He'd said the forbidden word.

Oliver grunted as he removed one of the hinges, the muscles in Arthur's arms stretching as they took the weight of the door. Oliver bent low to remove the hinge at the bottom.

Turning the screwdriver, he said, "You are all responsible for your angle. So you have to be ready when I say I'm about to beep. No blinking, no sneezing, no nothing. We cannot miss the muzzle flash. Simon?"

"Aye aye, Captain."

No, Red had already worked out it wasn't anyone from *Sponge-Bob* in the curtains. She was going to die before she figured it out, wasn't she? Her eyes tripped up on Reyna's face on their way back from the curtains, sitting there, staring straight ahead. Chewing on her tongue and some silent thought, a strange faraway look in her dark eyes. Was she thinking about the plan, about what they were about to do, or something else?

Simon noticed too. He sidled over and whispered in Red's ear, "You see the way she looked at Oliver when this secret was mentioned? Something going on there."

Red didn't respond, but she blinked, and Simon seemed to think that was the same thing. He nodded, too hard, and now Red couldn't help but think he was trying to deflect somehow.

"Okay." Oliver placed the second hinge inside the closet and straightened up, his knees clicking. He took the freed closet door from Arthur and swung it sideways, tucking it under one arm. "Let's do this. Reyna, look alive."

She got to her feet, wiping her hand across her face, taking the look in her eyes away with it.

"Flashlights on, everyone."

Red placed the walkie-talkie down on the dining table, leaving it on channel three, ready for the sniper. She reached into her pocket for her phone. No service of course but, hey, 51% battery, still pretty good for her. She knew that Maddy panicked whenever her own was below 50%, wouldn't even leave the house.

She swiped down and clicked on the flashlight.

"Arthur, hit the lights. Reyna, headlights."

Reyna leaned across the steering wheel and out went the headlights. Arthur reached up to the control panel by the refrigerator and twisted the lights all the way off. The darkness from outside found its way into the RV, disappearing them all, broken up only by the white swinging beams of their flashlights. A yellow glow from Simon's headlamp as he readjusted it onto his forehead. Red lit up Maddy as she came to stand next to her, ready to take her position at her window. Her face was ghostly pale, almost blue, white dots in the pools of her eyes.

"Into your positions."

*"That's what she said,"* Simon whispered, walking past Red toward the window by the lower bunk.

Red turned, bumping into Arthur.

"Sorry, after you," she said.

Arthur approached his window, resting one knee up on the sofa. Red took her place at the front door, waiting behind the closed shade. She watched over her shoulder as Oliver awkwardly spun the closet door to stand end up and he crouched beside the steering wheel. He shifted the gear into reverse, and the image from the rearview camera flickered into life in the center console. The road eerie white at the bottom of the screen, the sky molded from shades of black and gray.

Oliver shuffled the closet door against himself. A shield. A barricade. But could wood that thin stop a bullet from a high-powered rifle?

Red turned to her own window. She swallowed, fast-forwarding the next few seconds, to her putting her face and eyes up against the bottom of the glass to study the darkness beyond. She imagined the red dot floating right there on her face, joining the freckles on her nose, moving up to her forehead, or against her teeth, and she'd never even know about it. Maybe she'd hear the crack in her last moment, but she wouldn't know, would she, as it hit its target? Dead too fast for the fear to live. Like how she imagined Mom had died, in those early days when her dad and the other officers spoke in jagged circles around it. *Killed in the line of duty* was all some would say to her. *Your mom was a hero,* others.

In Red's head, Mom didn't have time to be scared, no time to think her goodbyes, she didn't know it was her end, she didn't know and with one blink she was gone. But she wasn't afraid, and that was one good thing as the world fell apart. Except that wasn't what happened. At all. Red looked it up, the night before the funeral. Multiple articles about the fatal shooting of Police Captain Grace Kenny of the Philadelphia PD, Third District. She shouldn't have, because then she wouldn't know. But it was too late. And the picture in her head changed. Mom on her knees. Begging for her life—the articles didn't say that part, but Red filled in the gaps. On her knees, terrified, knowing what was about to happen. And then it did: two shots to the back of the head. Killed with her own service weapon. She had time to be afraid, all the time in the world, lifetimes in seconds, there on her knees. *Executed* was another word the articles used, a word almost too big for thirteen-year-old Red to understand. It didn't fit in her head, not in the same sentence as her mom.

She understood now, though, thinking about putting her face up to that window. Thinking about that red dot searching her out in the darkness. Even a fraction of the fear her mom felt, right there at the end of all things.

"Red, are you listening?" Oliver raised his voice. "I said flashlights off!"

"S-sorry," she mumbled, pressing the button, and the pitch-black claimed the RV for itself, the others no longer full people, just shadows, nightmare figures on this nightmare night. No moonlight even, now that Reyna had pulled down the shade on the windshield.

"Now," Oliver said, clearing his throat. "If you pull your curtains or shades just a little bit, from the bottom corner, so you can look out."

"Do we really have to put our fucking faces up against the windows?" Simon's voice called behind her. "Sounds like a death wish to me."

"Yes," Oliver replied. "Because that's the plan."

Have to stick to the plan, Red thought. Always. Like she was doing right now. She just had to see through the rest of tonight, the rest of the plan.

"Oh, I know!" Maddy shouted, directly opposite Red at her window. Always side by side. "We can use our phones, like Arthur did before. Record a video of outside, then we definitely won't miss the flash."

"Okay, if you'd prefer," Oliver conceded.

"Yes, I'd fucking prefer," Simon said, a sound of clumsy rustling from his corner.

"Right, phones out!" Oliver called.

Red watched the dark shape of Arthur struggle with his, fiddling with the front of his jeans. Close enough to reach out and touch. To hold hands, even, if they didn't need both hands for this plan.

"Put them up against the windows now, make sure they are facing your assigned angle."

Red unhooked the shade, her fingers gripped hard around the clasp. Do not let it go. She raised it a couple of inches from the bottom and, with her other hand, pressed the camera of her phone against the glass. She shifted her body so she wasn't directly behind the phone, in the line of sight, and she watched the screen. There was nothing out there. Only black.

She checked over her shoulder at Arthur. His hand had disappeared beyond the lower corner of the mattress, out there in the night, the other still fiddling nervously with his jeans.

"Okay, start recording now!" Oliver shouted, and the dark RV was filled with a chorus of high-pitched bleeps, singing to each other, as they all pressed record.

One second. Two seconds. Three seconds on the recording.

"Ready?" Oliver called, a shadowy arm reaching up behind his shield.

Red's breath stuttered, the sound of her heart too loud in her ears, too loud and too fast. And then her heart was lost to a scream, the scream of the horn piercing the night and piercing her ears. One long note, then four short bursts.

"Come on." Oliver's voice strained as he pressed the horn again.

Three short beeps.

One long note.

The RV wailing into the darkness.

And again.

Nothing. Not the crack Red's ears were waiting for, not the clap of the gun. Her phone screen dark and empty.

"Come on!" Oliver tried again, ten sharp beeps, sharper, shorter.

The RV screamed and screamed again.

"Why is he not taking the fucking shot?!"

Nothing.

The screaming stopped, the ghost of the sound ringing in Red's ears in the after-silence.

# NINETEEN

The dark shape of Oliver's head, emerging from behind the closet door.

"Why the fuck didn't he take the shot?" he barked.

Red's eyes adjusted to the darkness, built a home there in it.

"I don't know," Arthur said, breathless, pulling his hand back inside the RV and stopping the recording on his phone. A deflated double beep. Red did the same, hooking the window shade back down to the bottom.

More double-tone bleeps, from the others' phones as they withdrew from the windows.

The ringing in Red's ears faded, taken over by the ever-present static.

"I don't understand," Maddy said, frustrated, slumping down on the booth. "He did it last time."

The walkie-talkie crackled on the table and Maddy flinched, jumping away from it.

"Was that for me?" The voice came through, a low hiss. "You know you already have my full attention."

A new sound through the speaker, metal grating on metal, the sound of the rifle cocking. It cut out and the static took over again.

Filled the room, filled Red's head. But the cocking gun, it stayed somehow, working its way down into her bones. She could feel it, in the turn of her elbow and the bend of her knee.

"Fuck." The shape of Oliver stood up, resting his closet door against the driver's seat. "That should have worked. It doesn't . . . that should have worked."

A sigh from Reyna, because Red knew Maddy's sighs and that wasn't it. Reyna's silhouette floated away from the windshield.

"He's only going to shoot now if he sees one of us try to leave the RV, isn't he?" she said, but Red couldn't see her eyes and didn't know who she was talking to.

"Again," Simon said, his voice drawing closer in the darkness behind her. "I am not nominating myself for self-sacrificing duty." He didn't sound drunk anymore.

"Maybe you're right," Oliver replied, close enough now that Red could make out his face. Well, just the glint of his eyes and the glint of his teeth. "Maybe those first shots at the RV were just to scare us, but now that we know what this is about, what he wants, he'll only shoot to stop one of us from getting away."

The long-winded way of saying exactly what Reyna just had. Red wondered if he did that to her a lot.

"So, maybe . . . ," Maddy said, uncertainly, and Red could picture the look on her face, the exact pull in her eyes and the fold to her mouth. "Maybe we make it look like one of us *is* leaving the RV. That's how we bait the shot."

Oliver nodded his head. "Just what I was going to say. We make him think one of us is escaping out the door, enough to take the shot."

"How, without actually getting shot?" Simon replied. "Are we going to build a fake human or something?"

"That's exactly what we're going to do, Simon." The trace of a smile in Oliver's voice now. Red bet he somehow thought it was all his idea, even though it was Reyna, Maddy and Simon who'd reasoned it out. "Red," he said then, like he'd read her thoughts. "Can you hit the lights."

She stepped toward the refrigerator and reached up to click the lights back on. Even on their lowest setting, the brightness of the dim overhead lights made her eyes water, rebuilding the RV and the six of them from the darkness.

Maddy squinted at Red, a nod to ask if she was okay. Red nodded back.

"And what are we going to build a fake human out of?" Reyna asked now, not disguising the doubt in her voice.

"Well, we already have that closet door." Oliver gestured back to his shield. "That could be the body, if we put one of my hoodies over it."

"The mop!" Simon said, louder than he needed to. "We snap it in half and those could be arms, inside the sleeves."

Oliver nodded, considering it.

"Oh," Maddy interjected. "I have a beach ball in my suitcase. Not blown up yet, but that could be the head, right?"

"That could work," Oliver said.

No, it couldn't, what were they all talking about? Even on her worst day, Red didn't look like a closet door with stick mop-arms and a giant beach ball head. The shooter would never believe it was one of them; he had a telescopic sight mounted to his rifle. But she didn't say anything. How could she say anything? That was part of *the plan.* Red looked over at Arthur and Reyna. They were silent, like her.

Oliver clapped and, my god, he had to stop doing that.

"Right, Maddy, can you go grab one of my hoodies? The green one. Reyna, grab that mop. Simon, bring the duct tape."

"Red, come with me," Maddy said, pulling on Red's sleeve. She didn't want to walk into the back bedroom on her own. And, sure, because even though this RV was thirty-one feet, Red had been in the same ten feet for far too long.

She followed Maddy, past the kitchen and the bunks, through the open door into the back bedroom. Maddy flicked on the light.

The black-and-white patterned sheets on the bed were crumpled under the weight of a blue suitcase.

"That must be Reyna's," Maddy said, walking past the foot of the bed to the large closet along the back right, as they faced it.

"This isn't going to work," Red said, now that it was just the two of them and Oliver couldn't hear. "This plan. The shooter will never believe it's a person."

"He might," Maddy said, reaching for the handle and pulling the closet open. There was a long mirror on the inside of the door. Red hadn't known it was there. She flinched as it doubled the people in the room, catching eyes with herself over Maddy's shoulder.

"Would you think closet-beach-ball-mop-man was real if you saw him out and about?" she asked, looking at Maddy's reflection.

"I might, at a quick glance."

"Why don't you just ask him out while you're at it? You'd have cute kids."

Red made a face at her in the mirror, eyes wide and nostrils flared, wrinkles disappearing the freckles on her nose. Mom used to pull that same face at her, in the mirror opposite their kitchen table, making Red laugh over sugarcoated cornflakes. Red pushed the memory away. It wasn't Mom in the mirror, it was her and Maddy, and that didn't help anybody. It never did. Put her away. Red needed to focus on tonight, on the people still here, not the ones who were gone and never coming back.

Maddy bent low, back to her, blocking the view. But in the mirror, Red could see Maddy's double, rifling through Oliver's open suitcase on the floor of the closet.

Two Maddys, two Reds.

Wait a second.

"The mirror," Red said quietly, not sure yet, the idea still forming. "Can't we use the mirror to make a double of one of us? A reflection." She tried to imagine it in her head, placing the mirror at the door of the RV, re-creating the angles. She couldn't quite get there on her own, not all the way. "At the door. Can't we . . ." She trailed off, but Maddy's reflection had straightened up now, staring her dead in the eye.

"That's brilliant," she said.

# TWENTY

*Brilliant.* Not a word people often used about Red or her ideas. She felt heat rise to her cheeks, but it wasn't a bad feeling like it normally was.

"Good job, Red." Maddy sounded so much like her mom when she said that. "Guys!" she shouted now, turning away from the mirror so Red could see her real face. "Scratch the fake human plan, the sniper will never believe it. We've got a better idea!"

"What?" Oliver's and Reyna's voices called in unison.

"But we've already started building Larry," Simon followed up.

"There's a full-length mirror in here," Maddy called as Oliver approached down the hall. "We put this by the door, at the right angle, he'll think he's shooting at one of us, but it will just be our reflection."

Maddy put it better than Red could have.

Oliver caught sight of himself in the mirror, above Red's head. She turned to see the real him, a light growing behind his eyes.

He smiled. "Yes. Yes, that could work. It will work. That's the new plan." He stepped forward, past Red, narrowing his eyes as he studied the mirror, flicking to the small black framing on each corner. "What's it attached with? Just those screws? We'll get that down, easy. Simon, can you pass the screwdriver!"

A clattering sound from the front of the RV, Simon's voice calling: "Coming, boss."

Oliver looked down at his sister. "Well done, Maddy. Really good idea."

"Well, actually—" Maddy began.

"—Mom will be proud of you," Oliver continued, patting her on the shoulder. "When we get out of here, she'll be so proud of you. That's a Lavoy plan if ever I heard one."

Maddy dropped her eyes, chewing on her bottom lip. Red watched her, a tightening in her chest, shifting with her ribs.

"Thanks," Maddy said, quietly. Nothing more.

Red didn't mind, though, or maybe she did. What was that too-full feeling at the back of her throat, then? Or that hollow one in her gut? It was fine. Maddy could have that plan, if it would make her mom proud. Red had her own.

"Special delivery," Simon said, jogging up the length of the RV, screwdriver held out in front of him.

"Excuse me," Red said, shuffling past Simon as he reached the bedroom, Reyna walking in behind him. A look passed between them, Reyna and Red, as they converged. Red wasn't sure what it meant but she returned it anyway.

"You okay, Red?" Arthur asked, standing in the kitchen.

Red joined him, leaning back against the counter, arms hugged around her ribs, to protect them.

"Just dandy," she said.

"So," he said, nodding his head back the way she'd just come. "Using a mirror to reflect one of us to bait a shot," he summarized, again, better than Red ever could. "That's smart," he added.

"The Lavoys are very smart," Red said.

"Want to know a secret?" Arthur said, his voice dipping into whispers, eyes flashing from behind his glasses. "I think you're smarter."

Red smiled in spite of herself. Had he been listening to her and Maddy in the bedroom? Or was he just trying to be nice? *Smart.* Another word Red didn't belong in a sentence with. She had *potential,* though, remember. Had it, but didn't use it, that was why people said it.

"I think you're wrong," she said, voice flat, barricade up.

"I think you're lying," Arthur retorted, knocking away at it.

She looked up at him, that same drunk-warm feeling behind her eyes. Why was he so kind to her? And why did that make her want to be un-kinder back? Because she didn't deserve it, that was why. She was just Red. Just Red and Just Arthur, and they should probably just stay that way, because she didn't know how to be somebody's someone.

"That's okay," Arthur said, like he could read the thoughts racing behind her eyes. But he couldn't, he didn't know what lived back there, in her head. "Your secret is safe with me. It always is."

"I don't have secrets." She hid behind a smile again. Oh, stop it, grinning like an idiot.

"International spy?" Arthur asked.

"I wish."

"Your real name is Agatha?"

"Only if yours is Edgar."

"Secret frog-racing champion?"

"You got me," she said.

"Nice." He smiled too, but he didn't grin like an idiot. He wore it better. "I won't tell anyone, promise."

"Won't tell anyone what?" Simon said, walking down the corridor, knocking into the wall on one side and the bunks on the other. How did he seem more drunk again?

"Red's big secret," Arthur replied.

"Right, move, move, move," Oliver raised his voice as he walked backward, carrying one end of the mirror, Reyna on the other side. They scattered, out of the way, Red moving over to the sofa and dropping down. It was nice to sit, her legs bone-tired. But she knew it wouldn't last long. The purple plastic mop was lying in front of her, already snapped in half, the mopping end removed.

Oliver and Reyna gently lowered the mirror down, close to the front door, Oliver wrapping one arm around it to take its weight.

"Let's think this through," he said, motioning with his head for them all to gather around.

See, not long at all. Red stood up, Simon on one side, Maddy on the other, the three of them repeated again in the mirror.

"Right, so if someone is standing there"—Oliver motioned to the gap in front of the closet, now missing its door—"they aren't in the line of fire, they're protected by the wall of the RV. And if the mirror is in front of the door, angled that way, the sniper will see their reflection, right?"

"Science, bitch!" Simon erupted then.

"Simon," Maddy warned.

"Sorry," he sniffed. "But we're in an RV. I was going to have to say it one time. Think I'd rather be cooking meth, though. Less risky."

Oliver shot him a look, hardening his eyes.

"Sorry."

"Yes, that works," Reyna said, walking around to the front side of the mirror. "But only if the sniper is somewhere in this direction." She held out both arms in a wedge, a quarter circle, one arm facing straight out through the door, the other toward the back of the RV. "If he's this way"—she gestured out through the front right of the RV—"he won't see the reflection. And that's if he's even on this side at all."

"Well, of course this only works if he's on this side," Oliver said. "We'll have to repeat it in one of the windows on the other side if it doesn't work."

Reyna didn't listen to him, continuing with her own thought trail. "If there was a way to pivot the mirror quickly, and someone else could be standing here"—she gestured to the small gap between the sofa and the front door—"then their reflection could be seen this way." She held out her arms again, another quarter circle. "And we'd cover this whole side."

Oliver nodded. "Right, okay. How do we pivot the mirror? And, saying that, how do we hold the mirror up? No one can be standing behind or beside it; they'd get hit."

Simon darted forward, scooping up the broken mop from the floor, holding up Larry's arms. "Could we attach these, as handles? Got a whole roll of duct tape."

Oliver snapped his fingers at him. "Yes. You get started on that. I want one on either side, at the top corners. Wrap the tape all the way around multiple times so it's really secure. And use some extra tape to lengthen the handles; we want them as long as possible so no one has to stand in the line of fire. Reyna, maybe you should help," he added, watching Simon struggle to find the end of the duct tape.

Reyna slid the broken mop handles out from under Simon's arm, and Maddy stepped forward to relieve him of the tape. They got to work, the duct tape droning like an angry wasp as Maddy pulled lengths and lengths from the roll.

"Wouldn't we need to slide the mirror over too, Reyna?" Oliver said. "Like a foot or so, to get the correct angle."

Reyna looked down, studying the floor for a moment as she held up one handle for Maddy to tape.

"Yeah," she said. "Because in its first position, the mirror needs to be slightly off-center, to the left to catch the person standing there."

"Thought so." Oliver nodded to himself. "We need to put the mirror on something then, something that slides easily. Oh." He gestured for Arthur to step forward and hold the mirror, moving away to the front of the RV and the abandoned closet door still resting against the dashboard. "This," he hissed, bringing it over.

That won't slide easily, Red thought.

"That won't slide easily," Arthur said.

"Easier than the mirror against the ground," Oliver countered.

"You almost need something round under it." Arthur hugged the mirror. "So that it rolls, like a skateboard."

"Good idea," Reyna said, testing how secure the first handle was.

Everyone had good ideas—not Red, though. She stood back, useless, unused. She hoped the others didn't think she was doing it intentionally. She couldn't even think of anything round, everything that popped into her head was full of sharp edges. Including that fucking pattern in that fucking curtain.

"I got it!" Simon shouted, too loud, darting behind the mirror to the refrigerator. He opened it and came back with his hands full. A can of beer clenched in both fists. He held them out to Oliver.

"That works," Oliver said. "Grab four more."

Simon grinned, disappearing behind the refrigerator door again. "See," he muttered, "this is why it's stupid that they tell teenagers not to drink. Drinking saves lives."

That hadn't worked with Red's dad, though, had it? Taking whatever life he'd had left after Mom.

Simon passed the rest over, and Oliver placed the beer cans down on their sides, a few feet in front of the entrance, spacing them equally. Picking up the closet door again, he placed it on top of the cans, parallel to the front door. Sliding it forward and back for good measure, nodding to himself.

"We're done too," Reyna said, not holding on to the mirror anymore, just the handle that side, Maddy on the other, testing it. Reams and reams of duct tape were wrapped around the top of the mirror and the purple plastic, binding them together. It was ugly, but it worked. "Yeah, it will stay up," Reyna said needlessly.

"All right, let's put it on the door, then. In its first position." Oliver picked the mirror up by its middle. He turned on his heels and shifted his arms, carefully balancing the mirror on the center of the closet door, pointing at a diagonal, at the space between the closet and the front door.

"Simon, stand there, will you?" he asked.

Simon did, commenting, "Handsome as ever," as he stared at his reflection.

"Reyna, will you hold that side?" Oliver said, taking the purple handle on the right while she took the one on the left. They fiddled for a moment, making sure the mirror stood up straight.

"Maddy, stand by the front door for a second."

She did, winding around Red on her way. She pressed against the door, standing as far back as she could.

"What do you see?" Oliver asked her.

"I see Simon," she said, trying not to react as Simon winked at her through the mirror.

"Okay, now Arthur stand there, by the sofa."

Arthur shuffled sideways into the gap.

"Okay, so let's see." Oliver used his foot, pushing the closet door several inches toward Reyna, the mirror moving with it, one beer can rolling free. "Now, Reyna, pull your handle forward while I pull mine back." The bottom of the mirror protested, scraping against the door, but it shifted into its new angle. "And now what do you see, Maddy?"

"Arthur," she said, which, judging by her brother's reaction, was the correct answer.

"Okay," he said. "It's clumsy, but it works. Arthur, can you come hold this?" Arthur stepped forward, taking the handle from Oliver, the mirror tipping forward as it passed hands.

"The only problem is," Oliver continued, both hands free now, one moving to his chin, "I think the two people being the reflections also have to control the mirror. There's no space for anyone else, and the rest of us need to be at the windows, recording to find the muzzle flash when he shoots. So, which two are going to be our reflections?"

The room was silent, only the fizz of static to mark the passing seconds by.

"Well, it can't be Maddy or me," Oliver said, gaze moving across them all. "We're the ones he's holding hostage. He won't take a shot at either of us."

Arthur cleared his throat. "The sniper never actually said that."

"No, but he wouldn't, would he?"

Arthur didn't seem to have an answer for that one. Well, that left all the non-Lavoys, then. What else had Red expected?

"Simon, Arthur, it should be you two," Oliver said, brows drawing low, darkening his eyes with shadows.

"Why me?" Simon glared back. "Who died and left you in charge?"

"You really want to make Reyna and Red do it?" Oliver replied. "Besides, you're the actor here, aren't you?"

Simon shrugged.

"Act like it, then."

Oliver looked over his shoulder at Arthur, checking to see if he had any complaints. Arthur nodded his head, just once, chewing on the inside of his cheek. He would do it.

"Right, okay, Simon, you're there by the closet, Arthur by the sofa. Take the handle, Simon, there we go, let's practice this a couple of times. So Arthur, I think you'll have to open the door, push it hard so it opens the whole way. And then once it's done, Simon you'll have to close it."

Simon coughed. "How am I going to close the door without walking down the steps right into his line of sight?"

Oliver faltered, a good point there.

"Rope," Red said quietly, a stupid suggestion really because they didn't have any.

"We can make one out of clothes," Maddy added, and now it made sense.

"There's some sweatshirts in the top of my bag," Arthur said. "You can use those. On my bunk."

"Okay," Red said, Maddy giving her the *go-ahead* eyes. She walked around the mirror contraption, past the kitchen to the bunks. She stepped one foot up on the bottom bunk to reach Arthur's bag, sitting there on the empty plastic frame of his bed.

"Right," Oliver was saying behind her. "Let's reset the mirror into its first position here and run it a couple of times so you know what you're doing."

Red unzipped the bag, spreading the two canvas sides. Arthur had folded his clothes, not quite as neat as Maddy, and not quite as strict.

"So the door opens," Oliver continued. "We leave it a few seconds on Simon. Arthur, I think you can hold the mirror on your own now, so Simon can step into view. Simon, make it look like you're walking down the steps or something, don't just stand there."

"Walking, walking," Simon replied angrily, the sound of his sneakers stomping on the floor.

There were a few baseball shirts at the top of one of Arthur's piles, more blues, more grays, one dark red. Red pulled out three of them, studied the lengths across the sleeves, and then grabbed one more to be sure.

She stepped down, the shirts bundled in her arms. They smelled clean, and yet somehow they still smelled like him. The same as the hoodie he'd let her borrow after New Year's Eve when he dropped her home. She'd slept in it that night, under her coat, and in the morning it only smelled like her. Arthur had never asked for it back. Maybe he was used to losing things too.

Red walked over to the dining table, Maddy joining her there, picking up the first shirt.

"Now, Arthur, kick the door across. About eight inches, I think. Whoa, stop, that's it."

Red picked up two of Arthur's shirts by their sleeves, knotting them together at the ends and pulling them tight.

"Arthur, you pull the handle back, Simon, grab yours, pull it forward. Yes. Now, Arthur, get back in position, Simon can hold the mirror now."

Maddy took Red's shirts, tying them to the two of hers and stretching the jumble out to its full width. "Rope," she said, a pinch at the corners of her eyes, the face she made when she said sorry. Not about the rope, Red knew, about the mirror plan.

"It's fine," Red told her. "I don't care."

"How did it look, Reyna?" Oliver asked.

Red looked up to see Reyna shooting a thumbs-up from the front door.

"You done with the rope?" Oliver's eyes were on them.

Maddy jumped up with it, hurrying over to tie it to the metal handle on the inside of the front door. Double knot. Then passing the other end to Simon, who was shaking his head for some reason.

"Okay, let's get this over with. We need to leave the lights on this time, so the sniper can see the reflection. Red, you take the window behind the sofa, this corner, point your phone in a diagonal toward the back of the RV."

Red followed the order, phone ready in her hand, resting one knee on the sofa, just a few inches behind Arthur.

"Maddy, take the same window, the other end, but point your phone straight forward."

The sofa sank as Maddy planted both knees on the other end, glancing at Red.

"Reyna, the passenger-side window, aiming your phone diagonally to the front. And I'll take the rearview camera again."

He walked over to the dashboard behind Reyna, dropping to his knees, head lowered to the screen. Red watched him and something stirred in her head, switching Oliver out with someone else. Didn't he know people sometimes died like that, on their knees?

"Press record," he said.

Red thumbed the red button on her screen. The birdsong high-pitched beeps from her phone, answered by Maddy's, then Reyna's.

"Get into position."

Red pulled the bottom corner of the mattress up, sliding the hand with the phone through to the unknown outside, her wrist pressing against a shard of broken glass, but there was nothing she could do about it. She pointed her phone in the right direction and looked away, eyes on the back of Arthur's head.

Red held her breath, counting the seconds.

"Is everyone ready?"

# TWENTY-ONE

"NOW!"

"Wait!" Arthur shouted back, shifting his position, wiping his spare hand down the front of his jeans.

"Arthur, now!" Oliver screamed. "Open the door!"

"Fuck!"

Arthur reached forward, slamming his hand down on the handle and pushing hard.

The door to the RV swung open, the darkness waiting for them there, gaping and black. It must be a rectangle of light, looking from the other side.

Simon raised his knees like he was running, hurrying down the steps, his teeth gritted, eyes wild and afraid and—

*Crack.*

The mirror shattered.

"Fuck!" Arthur screamed as the mirror jumped out of his hands, crashing back against the counter.

"Close the door!" Oliver's frantic voice filled Red's ears. "Simon, pull the rope!"

Simon scrabbled with it, the rope almost sliding through his hands. He fell back against the closet and he pulled.

The door slammed shut with a thump, lock clicking into place, sealing them inside once more.

"Holy fuck!" Simon said, sinking to the floor, laughing or crying Red couldn't quite tell. "We did it."

Arthur was bent double, breathing hard. His hands were pressed against his thighs, head hanging upside down. Was he all right?

"Who's got it?" Oliver was standing now. "He shot! Who got the muzzle flash on their phone?"

Red pulled hers inside, slotting the mattress back into position. There was a bead of blood there on the see-through skin of her wrist, where the glass had pierced through. Her very own red dot.

She stopped the recording, phone twittering at her, the same sound from Maddy and Reyna. She navigated to the video file and pressed play.

"Get into—"

"—Get into posi—"

"—Get into position," Oliver's voice said three times, overlapping. Reyna's video was playing half a second before hers, Maddy's just after.

The sound of Red's breath from the speaker at the bottom of her phone. Rustling as the image on-screen went from light to pitch-black, inside to out.

"Is every—"

"—Is everyone r—"

"—Is everyone ready?"

Red brought the screen closer, studying the pixelated darkness.

"N—"

"—NOW—"

"—NOW!"

Red didn't blink.

"Wai—"

"—Wait—"

"—Wait!"

The three layers of Arthur's voice in a frenetic rush, splicing together.

"Arthur—"

"—Arthur, now—"

"—Arthur, now! Open the door!"

"Fu—"

"—Fuck—"

"—Fuck!"

The Arthur from here and now turned; Red felt his eyes on her, but she didn't look away from the screen because it was coming, it was—

*Cr—*

*—Cra—*

*—Crack.*

A tiny flash of light in all that black as the three shots split the air. But it had only been one, and she had it, right here. Red had it. She paused the video, spooled it back.

"I've got it," she said, looking up at Arthur. His eyes looked drawn, mouth tight. "I've got it." Louder now.

"Let me see." Oliver rushed over, leaning to watch behind her shoulder. "Play it again."

Red pressed the play button.

"Fuck!" Arthur's voice said one more time.

"It's there," Red said. "Wait one second."

*Crack.*

A pinprick flash of white light in the dark background of her screen. Small, tiny. Like the little firework in her head. She dragged

163

back through the frames again to play it one more time. There, a quick burst of light, just right of the center.

The muscles in Oliver's mouth twitched.

"Which way were you pointing the phone, Red? Exactly." His eyes fixed on hers, so hard that she had to look away, and yet she could still feel them when she blinked, like they'd marked her.

"This way." Red pointed at a diagonal, out to the right toward the back of the RV.

Oliver straightened up, his eyes following the direction of her arm.

"So, he's over there still," he said. "Hard to say, but maybe a few hundred yards that way. Likely where he was when he first shot out the tires and the windows. He must have gone back to the same position after planting the walkie-talkie."

The walkie-talkie fizzed, hissing in silent agreement. Red was surprised, almost, that the sniper had nothing to say after what just happened.

The muscles in Oliver's mouth shuddered again, but this time they broke into a wide smile that cracked his face in two.

"We did it, guys," he said, looking around. The others didn't react. "I said we did it!" Oliver laughed, hitting Red on the shoulder, moving to do the same to Arthur. Arthur still didn't look right, eyes unfocused, picking at the pocket of his jeans. He was a fiddler, like Red, but maybe only when he was nervous, scared. Simon still didn't look right either, puddled there on the floor, legs outstretched among large shards of broken mirror, staring up at the ceiling, breath heavy in his chest.

"Come on, guys! We did it, we're getting out of here. Alive!"

Oliver pulled Reyna into a hug, burying a kiss in her thick black hair. He wrapped an arm around Maddy and then offered a hand to Simon, to pull him up off the floor.

Maddy was smiling now, hugging her own arms.

"Woohoo, spring break!" Simon said again, stumbling to his feet.

Oliver stood in the middle, grinning at them all.

*Delegate. Motivate. Celebrate.* All the qualities of a natural leader, which made Red more than an unnatural one.

Oliver clapped his hands, somewhere between an applause and to get their attention. He already had it. "Right, the sniper is back that way." He pointed. "So, if we climb out the driver's-side window and run in that direction"—he pointed with the other arm, the exact opposite way—"the sniper won't see us, because the RV will cover us. He won't even know we're gone. He won't. And even if he does, he's not going to be able to catch us. We have a head start, and he's carrying a rifle."

"You can't shoot a rifle like that while running," Red agreed.

"We did it," Reyna said now, nodding, like she could only believe it if she heard it out of her own mouth.

"Fuck yeah we did!" Simon answered, a fist raised as pieces of mirror crunched under his shoes. "Although that's seven years' bad luck, isn't it? Broken mirror?"

"Well, it's good luck for us now," Maddy replied.

Behind Simon, there was a splintered hole in the wooden base of the dining booth, where the bullet had struck through after the mirror, probably out the other side of the RV back into the dark night. Through glass and wood and wood and plastic and metal. Skin and bone would be nothing in its path.

"Right then." Oliver rubbed his hands together, the sound grating. "Let's get the fuck out of this RV! Don't bring anything with you. Just essentials. Just your phones. Hopefully we will run into some service at some point so we can call the police to catch this fucker before he runs off. And call our mom to let her know we escaped."

Would Catherine have given up the name they were looking for by now, Red wondered, mind already leaving the RV, skipping away to the next part.

Her ears fizzed, but was that just the static?

"Shall we take this?" she asked, stepping across the broken mirror to grab the walkie-talkie from the table.

"No, leave it," Oliver said, looking over his shoulder. "We don't need it. We're not playing his game anymore."

He walked over to the driver's seat, leaning across it to rip off the duct tape securing Red's gutted suitcase across the window. With one hard jerk he pulled it all down, dropping it in the footwell. He ripped the curtains aside, baring the pitch black of outside, waiting for them with open arms.

One windowpane was already open, smashed to pieces, but Oliver flicked the catch and slid the other panel across, uncovering that side instead. Easier to climb out of when standing on the driver's seat.

"Will be a bit tight," Oliver observed, rolling his shoulders. "Everyone got their phones? Yes? Okay." He stood up on the driver's seat, ducking as his head grazed the ceiling. "I'll go first. Then Maddy, then Reyna, Red, Arthur, Simon." He looked at them in order. "Get in line, get ready. No flashlights on yet, we don't want him to be able to see anything. You drop down and just run as fast as you can in this direction." He pointed out beyond the driver's-side mirror. "Through the trees there. Keep going, don't wait for anyone. We'll regroup on that road and then get the fuck out of here. Got it?"

Red nodded, taking her place between Reyna and Arthur, Maddy shuffling to the front. Lavoys first.

"I tell you what," Simon said, from the back of the line. "I never want to see another fucking RV again as long as I live."

"Tell me about it," Reyna sniffed, almost a laugh.

Fiddling, nervous energy, in front and behind Red.

"I'm going," Oliver said, bending down and lowering one leg out the window, coming to sit on the frame, exactly halfway inside and halfway outside. He dipped his head under and out.

The static cut off, silence taking its place. Before:

"Hello." The voice crackled to life behind them.

Oliver paused, looking back inside the RV, listening.

"Cute trick with the mirror," it said, a bark of laughter in his dark, metallic voice. "But there's one thing I should tell you before you make the mistake of climbing out that driver's-side window, Oliver. I probably should have told you sooner, that's my fault."

Static.

Red's chest constricted, ribs folding in one by one like fingers as she turned to look back at the walkie-talkie, glaring at them from where she'd left it on the table. Her eyes crossed each other, the bright green display doubling itself, filling her head.

"How could he—" Reyna began.

"Oliver, don't move!" Maddy shouted as he shifted out there on the window frame, staring down at the road just below him.

Silence, prickly and heavy.

"I should have told you," the voice cut back in, sputtering at the edges. "There are two of us."

# TWENTY-TWO

One gasp. One scream. One hitch in Red's chest.

There were two of them out there, in the wide-open nothing. Two of them. Two guns. Two red dots. No, this couldn't be happening. This wasn't supposed to happen.

"Get back inside, Oliver!" Reyna was screaming now. "Get in!" A race between her voice and a finger on a trigger.

Oliver tucked his head and rolled back inside, falling against Maddy on the driver's seat, and Reyna just behind. Reyna stumbled, pushing into Red. She tripped over Arthur's feet but he caught her, arms under hers, solid and strong.

"Close the curtains," Reyna was still screaming, the sound cutting through Red. "Close them!"

Oliver righted himself, reaching up and snatching at the curtains, pulling them together. No gap. Shutting the outside away, splitting them into two separate worlds again: the RV and out there. Only a border of thin black material between them.

"It's not fair," Maddy cried, mouth bared, eyes clouded. "We were almost out. We were almost free." Fat tears broke away, rolling to her chin.

"FUCK!" Oliver roared, tendons sticking out across the length of his neck, red and raw, like the puppet strings that worked his head. "Fuck, fuck, fuck!" He beat his fists against the steering wheel, against the dashboard, over and over.

"Oliver, stop!" Reyna lurched forward to take his hands away from him, holding them to her chest. "That doesn't help anyone."

"Two of them." Simon walked backward over a large shard of mirror, doubling the sole of his shoe before it cracked. "Two fucking snipers. You know what this night didn't need?" he called. "Another fucking sniper!"

Oliver was standing again, pushing Reyna out of his way as he stormed through. One of his feet caught on a can of beer, sending it spinning. He roared again, an ugly, scratching sound, as he bent down and wrapped his hands around the closet door. He lifted it up and smashed it back down, the wood splintering, a clean break, clattering back down in two unequal halves.

"Oliver, stop!" Maddy cried. "You're scaring me!"

"I'm scaring you?!" He rounded on her, eyes wild, a fleck of spit foaming in the corner of his mouth. "It's not me you should be scared of right now, Madeline. It's the men with the fucking guns!"

"Oliver, please." Reyna pushed him toward the booth, the side not blocked by the broken mirror. "Please just sit down and calm down."

"We were out," he said to himself, sliding his legs under the dining table, staring at the walkie-talkie. "We were out. I was so close."

Red's eyes shifted to Arthur as he dropped back against the sofa, his eyes on her but not here at all, glazed, far away.

His head fell to his hands and he buried his face in them, whitening halos of skin where his fingers pressed in.

Red reached, stretching out her fingers, each one too aware of itself and of what she was making them do. She rested her hand on Arthur's head just for a moment, near the back of his neck. Mom used to do that to her when she was upset, and Red didn't even realize until right now that she missed it. She shouldn't think of her, why did she keep thinking of her tonight?

Arthur glanced up, her hand sliding off. He caught it in one of his waiting hands, squeezed, his fingers warm against the cool of her knuckles.

Too much.

Red's arm dropped to her side.

She looked around at all of them, at their faces, and there was something new in the air of the RV. Not fear or confusion, they'd had plenty of those. It was despair, plain as she'd ever seen it. And she was an expert in despair.

Reyna was the first to come through it, bending to her knees to pick up the shattered halves of the closet door.

"What are you doing?" Oliver asked her sharply, his finger balanced on the antenna of the walkie-talkie.

"I'm cleaning up," Reyna said, carrying the pieces of wood toward the back bedroom. "Looks like we're going to be here awhile."

Red watched her as she crossed the threshold into the bedroom, chucking the broken door into the gap on the far side of the bed. She returned, making a start on the mirror.

"Maddy?" she asked, gently. "Can you please help me with this? Pick up those larger shards and put them in the trash?"

"Sure." Maddy sniffed, wiping her nose on her sleeve.

"We're never getting out of here." Simon slid down on the sofa, next to Arthur. "This is the worst day of my life."

It wasn't Red's, though, was it? No, she didn't think so, she'd never replace hers. February 6, 2017. It wasn't enough just to lose her mom that way, was it? No, there had to be that last phone call too, still hurting from their argument in the kitchen the day before, about Red not concentrating in school, about her grades slipping. Mom called the home phone at 7:06 p.m., to say she'd be late for dinner. Red was the one who picked up. Red didn't want to talk to her. *Fine,* she'd replied, thinking *Good* instead. Maybe she could go to bed without even seeing her mom tonight, without restarting the fight. But Red restarted it then, she couldn't help it, bristling when her mom called her *sweetie.*

"Don't call me that. I thought I was a disappointment."

Mom never said that, she wouldn't. Red was putting words in her mouth. They'd talk about it when Mom got home, that was what she said. But her voice wasn't normal, and Red thought she must still be angry at her. Disappointed. Did part of her wish Red had never been born? Something interrupted them, a two-tone sound, trilling somewhere in the background behind her mom. A doorbell. Twice.

"Hello," her mom said to someone else, not Red, because she could never just concentrate on Red for one fucking second, could she? Couldn't turn the police captain off and just be Mom. That wasn't fair but Red hadn't felt like being fair.

"Sweetie. Before I go, I need to ask you something. Can you tell Dad to—"

And then it came, the worst part.

"No," Red cut her off. "Stop telling me what to do all the time."

And worse still.

"I hate you."

Red hung up the phone, cutting off her mom's voice as she repeated her name.

And guess what? Mom was dead within ten minutes of that phone call.

"Red?" Oliver said, saving her from the memory, but not from the guilt. That always stayed.

She looked up, just as Oliver reached her, dropping the walkie-talkie into her hand. "Keep cycling through the channels, looking for interference. It's the only plan we have left now," he said, darkly, turning away.

Back to hoping for outside help, because the escape plan had gone out the window, which was a funny way to think of it because that was exactly what the plan had been. Red pushed the + button, skipping to the empty static of channel four, then five.

Channel six. She stopped, waiting there. Mom's channel, from their Cops and Cops game. Stop it, stop thinking about her, Red had no right to be thinking about her. It was her fault Mom was dead, and nothing would fix that, not even the plan. What was it, what was it Mom needed Red to tell her dad? They'd never know, but maybe it would have saved her. It would have saved her and Red said no. Red hung up. Mom was killed, executed, and it was Red's fault. Only her fault, because the police never found out who shot her. Twice. In the back of the head. On her knees. Thinking about how her daughter hated her and how she hated her back just as hard.

Up and up through the channels, the walkie-talkie fizzing in her hands, holding it too tight.

Reyna and Maddy had finished clearing up the broken mirror, and now Reyna was in the kitchen, taking down six glasses from the cupboard. She filled them with water, one after the other, the running faucet filling the RV with a new kind of music, blocking the static for a few moments.

"Here." She passed one glass to Maddy, and another to Oliver at the table, sliding it over. "We need to stay hydrated, it's been a long night already." The next two to Arthur and Simon, who needed it most. The last one to Red, a defeated smile on Reyna's face as Red's fingers cupped the glass.

"Thank you," Red said, taking a sip, and then a long draw, raising the glass, eyes on the overhead lights. She hadn't realized how thirsty she was, and something else too, that yawning feeling back in her gut. Hungry, again. But she couldn't eat. She drained the rest of the water and came up for air.

They couldn't escape. So, what were they going to do now? Red couldn't remember exactly—what was it the sniper had said about that secret he wanted? Would they just wait here, trapped, until Catherine Lavoy gave up the name? She looked to Oliver; he should know what to do, he was the leader.

"We're fucked," Oliver was saying, speaking into his half-empty glass, lending his voice a hollow echo. "We're completely fucked."

Or maybe not.

Arthur took Red's empty glass from her, carrying it back to the counter with his. Two dull thuds as he placed them down. And there must have been something wrong with Red's ears, because now she was hearing an echo of those too, which couldn't be right.

Arthur sighed. "Maybe we should think about the se—" he began.

"Shh," Oliver spat, holding his arms up to silence them all. "I can hear something. I hear . . ."

He drew off, tilting his head to raise one ear.

Red heard it too, a low, clicking, rumbling sound. It was growing, growing, overtaking the static.

"What is . . ." Maddy's voice faded with one sharp look from her brother.

Red looked up, ears straining beyond the ceiling. It was coming from up there, from the sky.

"It's a helicopter," Oliver said, jumping up from his seat. "It's a helicopter!"

Moving closer and closer, like a mechanical roar of thunder. They couldn't see it, but they could hear it.

"It's getting nearer!" Oliver shouted, his eyes glittering, replacing the despair. "We have to signal it somehow. Let them know we need help!"

"The horn!" Maddy said.

"They won't hear that," Reyna told her.

"The lights!" Simon crashed up to his feet. "We can signal SOS, I know how to do it." He jumped across to the light panel, flicking the main switch off and then on again in three short bursts.

"They won't see, the windows are covered!" Reyna shook her head, looking around frantically.

The helicopter must be right above them now, the mechanical drone slicing through the sky.

"Headlights," Red said.

"Headlights!" Maddy screamed. "Simon, go, go, go!"

Simon sprinted to the front of the RV, crashing into the driver's seat as he launched himself into it. Red stood behind him, one hand gripping the passenger seat, the other wrapped hard around the walkie-talkie, the edges biting into her skin.

Simon reached for the lever behind the steering wheel and flicked the headlights on.

A glow filled the covered windshield, around the edges of the pulled-down shade.

"Dot-dot-dot," Simon muttered to himself and he flicked the lever three times quickly. "Dash-dash-dash." He moved the control, leaving the high beams on for a longer stretch between the darkness. "Dot-dot-dot."

"Keep going," Oliver ordered him, leaning past the driver's seat, pulling the shade up so they could see the high beams through the windshield, carving up the night.

The motorized whine of the helicopter was fading, moving away from them into other skies.

"It's leaving," Reyna said, the urgency all but gone from her voice.

"Keep going, Simon!" But not from Oliver's.

The headlights flicked off and on, following the pattern as Simon whispered it to himself. "Dot-dot-dot-dash-dash-dash-dot-dot-dot."

Save our souls. Save us. Please save us.

Headlights on, headlights off.

An idea stolen from another memory. Red's mom used to flash the headlights when she got home from work late, into the windows of the living room. She didn't, though, on the night it mattered most. Red was waiting, angry and hurt, but she was waiting all the same.

"It's leaving, Oliver," Reyna said, placing one hand on his shoulder. He shrugged it off.

"Keep going!"

Simon flicked the lever, back and forward, the world in front of them flickering in and out of existence as the headlights flashed. And Red too, flickering between here and then.

In seconds, the sound faded to a low drone, then a faint hum, until the night swallowed it whole, leaving not a trace behind.

"Gone," Red said.

Simon let the headlights click off, sitting back in his seat. He exhaled, long and hard.

"Maybe it will come back," Maddy said, looking at the back of Oliver's head.

"Maybe," he said. "If it was a rescue helicopter for us."

That was when Red knew for certain that she and Oliver Lavoy did not live in the same world. She could never hear a helicopter and think it was sent for her. No one loved her enough for that.

"Nobody knows to rescue us," Arthur said, looking up at the ceiling as though he could summon it back with the pull of his eyes.

"My mom, maybe." Oliver's voice almost failed him.

"I think it was just passing over," Reyna added, her hand moving to Oliver's shoulder, staying there this time.

"Maybe they saw. Maybe they saw the headlights," he continued.

"Maybe," she said, gently.

"How do you know Morse code?" Arthur was looking at Simon now.

"I mean I don't, obviously," he replied. "Just SOS. I got it from a film. *Panic Room,* I think it was."

"Red, keep going." Oliver turned back to her, mouth tensed in a grim line.

If she was their only hope, then the rest of them really were fucked. Red wasn't getting them out of here. She raised the walkie-talkie and started skipping through the empty channels again.

Oliver sighed, rallying himself, shaking out his shoulders. Red was watching, saw the exact moment an idea hit him, lighting up his eyes.

"Maybe it wasn't all for nothing," he said. "Maybe there's an idea in there, to make some kind of light signal. Here." He darted forward, snatching his Zippo lighter up from the resource pile on the table. "He shot out the tank and the gas has leaked all over the road, right?"

"Right," Maddy answered.

"If I light this"—he flicked up the flame to demonstrate, fire dancing in his too-wide eyes—"and I drop it out the window, it would set fire to that pool of gas. A fire. A signal fire. And maybe someone will see the smoke. Light travels farther than sound, right?"

"Not in the middle of the night," Reyna told him. "No one will see the smoke."

"And you'd set fire to the RV," Arthur said, burying his fingers in his pocket, like he was hiding them from Oliver as he confronted him. "Burn us inside with it."

Oliver was getting desperate now, careless. Maybe Maddy was right, they should be afraid of him after all. Reyna could control him, though, couldn't she? Calm him down, make him see sense.

"The RV is our only cover," she said. "We can't set fire to it."

Oliver ignored her, staring into the flame for one more second before flicking it away, dropping the lighter on the table.

Simon followed him to the table, reaching over the flashlights and duct tape and masking tape and kitchen knife and scissors and lighter, past the pad of paper and pens Maddy had been using earlier, to the bag of still-open chips resting against the side.

He scooped out a handful and placed them in his mouth.

"How can you eat?" Maddy asked him, not really a question.

"Like this," he showed her, opening his mouth in an exaggerated chew so she could see the mulched-up orange coating his tongue.

She didn't react.

"What's our next plan?" She looked at her brother. "What do we do now?"

Silence, other than the sound of static as Red skipped back to channel three and left it there. And a muted crunch from inside Simon's mouth.

"Gu-ys," Reyna said, strangely, the word coming out in two uneven halves, like she'd had to force it through.

Red glanced up. Reyna was staring past her shoulder, out the front of the RV. Something new and unknown in her eyes.

"Guys!" she said in one this time. And then: "Someone's here."

She pointed and Red whipped around, her eyes following the line of Reyna's shaking finger. Out through the windshield into the world beyond. And there, scattered by the dark bodies of the trees up ahead, were two small lights passing through the night. Winking in and out as branches blocked the way.

The lights curved around with the road, breaking free from the trees, two clean white beams, pointing right at them. Coming this way.

Headlights.

"Someone's here."

2:00 A.M.

# TWENTY-THREE

Oliver clambered forward, the white beams reflected in the dark of his eyes as they drew closer, the sound of wheels peeling against the road.

"Who is it?" he hissed.

"No, it's not more of them, is it?" Simon said, one hand up to shield his eyes.

"It could be the police!" Maddy said, her hands clutched to her chest.

Red looked out the windshield, unblinking, filling herself with the white light, like the night had grown its own eyes, staring back into her.

"Turn on our headlights, Reyna." Oliver pushed her toward the cockpit. "So we can see who it is."

Reyna's hand scrabbled forward, reaching for the lever without taking her eyes off those lights. She pushed it and the RV's headlights clicked on, clashing with the others, head to head.

And now they could see what it was. Not a police squad car, but a white truck flecked with dirt, the low rumble of its engine as it rolled forward. Two figures obscured behind the windshield.

It swerved, slowly, to the spare stretch of road on their right, the headlights ripping free from theirs, four distinct beams.

"Who the fuck is . . ." Arthur trailed off, moving forward to stand beside Reyna at the front.

The truck sighed, pulling to a stop right in front of them, almost corner to corner with the RV. The engine switched off, taking the lights with it.

Silence and static, and the after-tick of their engine.

Now that their beams were no longer blinding her, Red could see it was a man and a woman, late sixties or early seventies she'd guess from this distance with two windshields between them.

"Who are—" she began to say.

The static cut away.

"Get rid of them," the voice crackled from Red's hands. She flinched, staring down at the walkie-talkie. "You get rid of them now, or I will kill them."

Not with the sniper, then. Not part of the plan.

"Do not tell them anything," he continued, voice darker and deeper now. "Say you are fine, just broken down. If you tell them anything or signal to them in any way, I will shoot them both."

Not part of the plan at all.

Red glanced up, caught Oliver's eye, staring at her as the keeper of the voice.

"They're not with him," Oliver said. "We can use them to get help."

"He just said not to do that," Arthur spoke up. "He just said—"

"I will kill them," the sniper cut in, as though he had somehow heard. "If you tell them you're in trouble, tell them anything, you will be killing them. I'll do it."

Static.

182

"Get rid of them or they die."

Arthur's eyes widened, his mouth falling open in a silent word.

"But—" Maddy started to say, but the rest didn't matter, because they heard the clack of a door handle slicing through the too-quiet night. Red turned, watched the driver's-side door of the truck fling open, waiting there as the man climbed out behind it. Fur-lined jacket zipped up to his chin, graying hair and red-dotted cheeks.

"Hello!" he called, cupping his hands around the word to protect it from the night. "You folks all right in there?"

He leaned into the truck door and it slammed shut just as the other side opened. The woman stepped out, hair pulled back in a messy ponytail, eyes searching, looking through the windshield. They alighted on Red and the woman smiled, raising a pale hand in a still wave.

Red smiled back, with teeth, just as the voice in her hands said, "Get rid of them or they die. Open the door and tell them you're fine."

"We have to send them away," Arthur said, turning his eyes to the door of the RV.

Oliver pulled him back. "But this could be our only chance to—"

"You heard what he said." Arthur pushed against him. "Do you want to kill these people?"

"We have to do what he says." Reyna walked over, resting one hand against Oliver's chest. "You understand that? He's pointing a rifle at them right now."

"Hello?" the man outside called again, boots crunching against the road as he walked over, toward the door.

"Fine, go," Oliver said, letting go of Arthur's shirt. "Simon, you're the actor. Act like we're fine."

"I'm not going out and standing in that doorway." Simon shook his head. "He already shot at me once."

"He told us we can," Arthur said. "He won't shoot if we're sending them away. I'll do it."

In one quick movement, Arthur slammed down on the handle and pushed the front door. It swung wide open. The man stood just a few feet from the door, a wrinkled smile stretching into his face, skin folding like paper.

"Hello there, folks," he said, eyes flicking up to Arthur as he dropped down the first step, then to Simon and Reyna behind, then Red. She stood back, gripping the walkie-talkie too tight between her hands, like she could make him not shoot by hiding him away.

"Hello, sir," Arthur replied, bowing his head slightly, moving down another step.

"Y'all okay?" the man asked. "We thought we saw some lights flashing from the road back there, drove around to see if anyone was in trouble." He gestured over his shoulder with his thumb. "Looks like you got a couple of flats there at the front."

"Yeah," Arthur said, scratching the back of his head. "We think we drove over something, got a couple of punctures."

"Well, I'll be," the man said, standing back, glancing at the rear tire. "Looks like you got a third out, too."

"And I think I smell gas." The woman stepped forward now so that she too was framed in Red's view of the open door, blocked by Arthur's moving shoulders as he scratched at one of his own arms.

"This is my wife, Joyce," the man said, nodding to her. "I'm Don."

"Nice to meet you both," Arthur said.

"Where are y'all from?" Joyce said, a sweet smile on her face as she stood side by side with her husband. Red tried not to picture it, the red dot floating across their backs, darting unseen between their heads. Eeny, meeny, miny, moe.

"Philadelphia," Arthur answered.

"Thought I recognized the accent," said Don. "Long way from home."

"Yeah, we're on our way to Gulf Shores, for spring break," Arthur said.

"Bless your hearts," said Joyce.

Oliver moved toward the door then, his jaw set, clearly deciding it was safe if Arthur hadn't been killed yet. He pushed past him, dropping down to the final step.

"Hello," he said, voice crisp and clear, back arrow-straight, the full Oliver Lavoy display. "Nice to meet you both. I'm Oliver."

"Don. Joyce," Don repeated. Seemed he recognized that Oliver was the natural leader here. How could you not, with that straight back and those fierce golden eyes? "We live on a farm just yonder, back that way. We were passing by and saw flashing lights."

"What must y'all think of us, coming home past two in the morning," Joyce giggled, hiding it behind one hand. Red noticed the blue polish peeling off her nails. "We were with our daughter, she lives in Jacksonville. She just had a baby this afternoon, our first grandbaby." The words burst out of her, tripping over each other, like she couldn't have not said it, like maybe that was the reason they'd stopped after all.

"Oh, congratulations to you both," Oliver said, and Red could hear the smile pasted over his voice. "New grandparents."

"We're so excited," Joyce said, looking up at her husband. "Aren't we, Don? We couldn't not go and meet the baby right away, could we? She's called him Jacob, after my daddy who passed last year, and he is the cutest little bundle you ever saw. Isn't he, Don?"

"Yes, dear."

"But," Joyce went on, eyes flicking between Arthur and Oliver and Reyna as she told her story, "you know how it is, with a new baby, you don't want your parents hanging around, telling you what you're doing wrong that first night. That's why we decided not to stay the night and drive home, leave her and Thomas to it, you know?"

"I see." Oliver nodded. "Well, I'm sure she appreciated you driving all that way and back to visit."

"We're going to go again next weekend, aren't we, Don?"

"Joyce, will you hush up for one moment?" Don said in answer, an affectionate burr in his voice. "These people don't want to hear our life story, I'm sure." He looked down, grinding his boot into the road, raising his heel to study it. "She's right, you know. You got a gas leak all around here. Looks like the whole tank might've emptied."

Please don't let him look too hard and see the bullet hole in the side there, the one that took out the tank.

"Yeah, we think a branch might have got caught under us," Oliver said, not missing a beat. "Must have dragged it for a while and it punctured the tires, knocked something loose underneath."

Don made a face, gritting his teeth.

"Have you called Triple-A?" he asked.

"Yes," Arthur said, at the same time that Oliver said, "No."

An awkward moment, Don's gaze trailing up away from the two of them. He must have noticed the broken window then, his eyes narrowing, skin crinkling between his brows. The static fizzed and Red held the walkie-talkie behind her.

"We couldn't get a signal," Oliver explained.

"Oh." Joyce smiled; she hadn't picked up on the strain in Oliver's voice. "The service is terrible around here. We're lucky to get one bar in our house, and that's with me hanging out the window in the back bedroom."

"Even worse today," Don added, eyes back on Oliver, though he didn't look as sure and easy as he had thirty seconds ago. "Our neighbor told us that this morning, some truck drove into the cell tower south of Ruby. Knocked out all the networks. Apparently he fled before the police got there. I'm guessing it was a stolen truck and he drove around the turn too fast, lost control. I called AT&T from the road this afternoon and they said their engineers were dealing with it, and service should be back by morning. If they can be trusted," he added with a sniff.

Red swallowed. *They* did that. Drove a truck into the cell tower to disable it. All part of the plan to trap them here. But this wasn't part of the plan. Don and Joyce weren't supposed to be passing at this time. Don and Joyce weren't supposed to find them trapped here, in the wide-open nothing, on their way back late from meeting their first grandchild. Don and Joyce weren't supposed to happen.

"That explains it, then," Oliver said. "Excuse me for one moment." Oliver held up a finger and then backed up the steps, through the door of the RV. He walked toward the dining table, pushing Red out of the way, beckoning to Maddy, hiding by the sofa.

"If you were driving a car," Don was saying, "we might could have towed y'all." He looked around, surveying the giant hulking shape of the RV. Red stepped forward, brushing against Simon at the threshold to outside. "This is quite something, isn't it?" Don said, slapping the metallic side of the RV.

"Thirty-one feet," Red said.

"Is that right?" Don said, a crinkle in his eyes as he looked up at her, pursing his lips to blow out a low whistle. "Well, I'll be."

"It's my uncle's." Simon stepped forward, shooting the couple a smile. Red caught the sideways view, muscles straining in his cheek.

"Really?" Don asked. "And how much does something like this set you back?"

The static spluttered behind Red's back, cutting out.

"Send them away," the voice threatened, low and hissing.

Red held her breath.

"What was that, son?" Don looked up at Simon.

"I said I think it's for people with more money than sense," Simon chuckled, loudly, covering the static. "Like my uncle, I guess."

"Right." Don laughed politely.

"Well, we got no sense and no money." Joyce joined in the laughter, her shoulders hitching. That was when Red's eyes finally caught it, slipping over the side of Joyce's shoulder, hiding in the folds of her tied-back hair. The red dot. Waiting. Ready to put a hole in her.

Red swallowed again, her smile stretchy and tight, pulling uncomfortably at her skin. Keep a straight face, just like she was taught. Give nothing away with her eyes. Face straight, story straight, all she had to remember. *Can you remember all that, Red?*

"How many does it sleep?" Don asked. "There are five of you, right?"

"There's six of us," Reyna corrected, a quiver in her voice that made Red think she'd seen the dot too. Reyna was premed; she knew all the soft and delicate things waiting there beneath Don's and Joyce's flesh, all the horrifying ways they could split apart in the path of a bullet. Insides that would stay inside, because they were going to send them away to save them. Red must have stopped smiling; Joyce was looking at her funny.

"You okay, sweetheart?" she asked.

Red blinked, pasted the smile back on. "Yeah," she said, "you?"

"I'm finer than a frog hair split four ways," Joyce answered. "But I'm worried about y'all and how we're gonna get you on your way."

"What happened to the window here?" Don asked, his feet shifting, eyes too, straying up to the shattered glass.

"Tree branch," Reyna said, almost too quick, like Oliver's lie had been waiting on the tip of her tongue. But it didn't quite fit. "We were too big to come down this narrow road here, but we pushed through because we couldn't turn back, next thing we know, tree comes through the window."

"Right." Don nodded, blinking slowly, like he was trying to picture it in the pitch-black behind his closed eyelids.

Red heard whispering behind her. Not from the walkie-talkie, from Maddy and Oliver, bent over the table, their backs to her.

She sidled away from the open door as Simon asked Don and Joyce about their new grandchild, and how the birth went.

Red stepped up behind Maddy, peered over her shoulder. On a piece of paper, ripped from the pad, Maddy was writing something with the felt-tip pen, waiting for Oliver to tell her the next word.

Red squinted to read the note.

*Help, call the police. There's an—*

"Active shooter," Oliver hissed at her, Maddy turning his words into scratchy black letters on the page. "We are trapped."

"You can't do that," Red said, making Maddy jump, smudging the last word. She hadn't known Red was right behind her. "He said he'd kill them."

"How is the sniper going to know if I pass them this tiny note?" Oliver turned to her, a low hint of rage stirring in his voice. How dare she question him. He was the leader, didn't she know? "He is hundreds of yards that way. He's never going to know."

"He might," Red said, breath stalling in her chest. Come on, she had to do better than that.

"How, Red, how?" Oliver's eyes flashed. "Go on, explain to me how the sniper is going to see this tiny piece of paper."

"When you hand it over," she said, straightening her back too, raising her chin. He was only a few inches taller than her like this. And she couldn't let him do this.

"I have a plan for that, obviously," Oliver spat. "Maddy, fold it, and again, and now on the top, write: *Do not read until you've left this road.* Now, quickly."

Maddy folded the note, her elbow crashing into Red as she did, tongue tucked in her teeth. "Say it again," she said, preparing the pen, shaking in her grip.

"Do not read until you've left this road," he spat, keeping his voice low.

"He said he would kill them." Red watched Oliver watching his sister as she scratched out the words, blocky and big on the small square of paper. "He's going to kill them."

"No, he won't," Oliver replied, ripping the finished note away from Maddy. "I will shake Don's hand and pass it over. If I angle it right, the sniper won't even see the handshake, he'll just see me trying to get rid of them. Don will know something's wrong and not to react when he reads that top part. They won't read the rest until they're safely out of here, and then they'll send help. The sniper will never know, he can't know. This is going to work."

He flipped the note in his hand, unfolding it to check the words inside.

*Help, call the police, there's an active shooter. We are trapped.*

He refolded it, pressing harder than Maddy had, eyes spooling across the words on top, scratchy and desperate. *Do not read until you've left this road.*

"What if it doesn't work?" Red said, hand darting out to hold on to Oliver's sleeve, surprising them both. Maddy too, who gasped behind her. "He'll kill them. That's someone's mom and dad out there. New grandparents. Don't do this. Don't drag them into this."

"Red, be quiet. You don't know what you're talking about." He shrugged her off.

But she did know, she knew better than anyone. If something happened to Don and Joyce, their daughter would blame herself for the rest of her life. Why hadn't she insisted they stay the night? Why couldn't she have had the baby tomorrow instead? Or yesterday? All her fault, dead because of her.

Red couldn't put that into words, though, it didn't belong, wouldn't fit. So she tried just one word.

"Please."

"What's going on?" Arthur was back inside the RV, his voice low, walking over to stand between Red and Oliver. "What are you doing?"

"I'm giving them a note to call the police, passing it over in a handshake," Oliver said, like he was expecting praise for his bright idea.

Arthur looked at Red and she tried to tell him with her eyes. Please understand.

"You can't do that." Arthur turned back to Oliver, and Red breathed out, so glad that Arthur had come back, glad that he was standing right here next to her, on her side. "He'll shoot them," Arthur said.

Oliver rolled his eyes, a muscle ticking in his jaw. "No he won't, he will never know. The sniper hasn't actually taken a shot at one of us yet. Not one. Maybe he's actually bluffing, just trying to scare us into doing what he wants, maybe he isn't planning on killing anyone. Not us, not them." He tried to move past but Arthur stepped in his way.

"What if he does shoot?" Arthur hissed. "You'd be killing them."

"Well, I guess it's four against two. The others would agree with me." Oliver gestured his head toward Reyna and Simon in the open doorway. Then his eyes flicked back to Red and Arthur; they were the two, outvoted, outnumbered.

Unless:

"Maddy?" Red said.

Maddy held her gaze. "They'll be fine," she said quietly. "We can't not ask them to help us."

"You'll thank me when the police turn up and save you," Oliver said, like it was a threat.

The static crackled into silence.

"You have sixty seconds to get rid of them," said the voice, vibrating in Red's hand. A metallic double click from the speaker as he cocked the rifle. "Fifty-nine, fifty-eight."

"Move." Oliver pushed Red out of his way, the note folded small, clutched in one hand.

"No," Arthur whispered, but he didn't move to stop Oliver.

Red tried, grabbing his shirt again. "Oliver, please don't—"

Oliver turned, angry puppet strings up his neck again. His free hand darted out to Red's throat. He shoved her and she fell back onto the sofa.

"You shut up," he hissed, bending over her. "You're going to get us all killed."

But he was going to get them killed, those innocent people outside, and he didn't care, he didn't care because they weren't him.

"Forty-seven, forty-six," the walkie-talkie crackled.

Arthur reached out a hand and Red took it, pulling her to her feet, but it was too late, Oliver was in the doorway, pushing past Reyna to walk down the steps.

"We have a landline at our place," Joyce was saying. "We can give some of y'all a ride and you can call for help from our house."

They walked over to the door, Red's hand in Arthur's and she couldn't remember now, how it had got there.

"Oh, don't worry about it," Oliver said, voice loud and cheery. "We're fine here. We were actually just going to get some rest now; we have a long day ahead of us tomorrow. You said the service should be back in the morning, we'll call Triple-A when we wake up, no problem."

"Are you sure?" Don asked. "It's no trouble."

"Very sure," Oliver's voice boomed. "Think we all just want a good night's sleep and then we'll worry about getting this RV fixed in the morning. Right, gang?" Oliver turned back to look at them, all six of them gathered by the door, Maddy's breath on the back of Red's neck.

"Right," Reyna said with a smile, but she didn't know what was about to happen.

"If you're sure?" Don returned the smile, dipping his head. Could he tell something was wrong? "Come on then, Joyce-bug, let's get you home."

"Before you go," Oliver said with a flourish, "I wanted to say thank you so much for stopping, and a huge congratulations on becoming grandparents." Red watched as Oliver stepped to the left, reangling Don, putting his back to the sniper's position.

Where was the red dot?

"Congrats, sir." Oliver offered his hand to Don in the darkness. Note tucked under his thumb.

"Bless your heart, aren't you sweet?" Joyce said, as Don reached out and took Oliver's hand, shaking it up and down just once.

Oliver's hand withdrew, empty.

Don's face darkened, his eyebrows drawing low as he looked down at the piece of paper in his hand.

Reyna noticed it too, head shifting sideways on her neck.

"Well, it's been nice chatting with you all anyway. Don says I can talk until the cows come home." Joyce laughed, her face up to the sky, and it was too much, this was too much.

Should Red scream at them to get in the RV, or tell them to run? Like she should have before, if she'd only listened to her gut and not Oliver.

Don hadn't moved. His eyes shifted across the note and up, a muscle twitching, pulling at the lines around his mouth. He looked at the broken window again.

"Thank you," he said, nodding at Oliver, closing his fingers around the note. Another nod. Now he must know that something wasn't right here. But he wouldn't know what until he unfolded the note scrunched up in his hand. "That's very kind of you," Don laughed nervously.

Oliver laughed with him. "Well," he said, "you must be tired after such a busy day. We'll let you get to it."

"Sure." Don gritted his teeth as his boots pivoted on the road, keys jangling in his grip. He turned to his wife, straightening out his face before she saw it. He didn't want her to know. "Come on then, honey, we better get out of here."

Maybe it would be okay. Maybe they'd get back in their truck and be out of here before the sniper knew anything was wrong.

Red wasn't breathing, staring as Joyce gave her a final smile, a final wave. The only one who didn't know, eyes kind and crinkled, blue polish peeling off her nails. She turned to go, walking alongside her husband. Red didn't blink, she couldn't, she had to protect them with her eyes.

She could hear Arthur's breath stuttering in his chest, beside her. His hand wasn't holding hers anymore, small movements in his shoulders, disturbing the air around her. Was he shaking?

"You have a safe trip home," Oliver said cheerfully, raising one hand in goodbye as they approached their truck.

*Crack.*

Too quick.

Joyce folded sideways onto the road, a space where the middle of her face had been.

"Joy—" Don said, not panicking yet, because he didn't know, maybe she just fell.

*Crack.*

A plume of blood in the headlights.

A gaping hole in Don's face, beside his forever-open mouth. He fell slowly, knees buckling first, crumpling backward over his legs, bent all wrong. Empty stare up at the stars, a halo of red pooling on the road.

# TWENTY-FOUR

Red wouldn't move.

Simon sprinted past her, back into the RV, tripping over her feet.

"No, no, no!" Reyna was screaming.

"Move!" Oliver spun around and hurtled up the steps, pushing Reyna in ahead of him. That unseen red dot chasing them inside.

The door to the RV slammed shut. Red didn't see who'd closed it, because she couldn't move, but everything moved around her. Flashes and elbows and eyes.

"I have to help them!" Reyna shouted, moving back to the door. "They need medical attention."

"They're dead, Reyna!" Oliver's voice. It seemed far away, even though he was right there. A ringing in Red's ears, static in her hand. "He shot them in the head!"

Two shots in the back of the head.

Red could move now, unsticking her shoes from the ground, peeling herself away.

Maddy was on the floor, crying, head in her hands, hands pinned by her knees.

Knees. Was Don alive when he dropped to his knees, or already gone?

Red turned, the effort of picking up her feet almost too much.

Arthur's face was hidden as well, wrapped in his arms against the refrigerator door. His back shaking.

"Excuse me," Red whispered, her voice not her own. No one was listening. Reyna and Oliver were shouting behind her. Reyna hadn't known about the note, neither had Simon, but they knew now, Oliver telling them in breathless snatches.

"You should have told us first," Reyna said. "We should have all decided together whether or not to do that!"

"Oh, easy for you to say now, Reyna. I had to act quickly!"

Red tuned out, their shouts becoming just noise that she left behind her.

She walked, slowly, past Arthur and the kitchen, her heart too fast, shedding a little more of her every time it beat. Red was surprised there was any left as she passed the bunks and through the open door into the back bedroom. Surely there was just a hole in her chest now, an empty echo against the cage of her ribs.

She placed the walkie-talkie on the bed, laying it down carefully like it could feel pain too. With her other hand, she grabbed a pillow from the top of the bed, digging her fingers into it, the fabric pulling like spiderwebs around her fist. She brought the pillow to her face, held it there with both hands.

Red screamed.

She screamed, the heat of the muted sound hitting her in the face, stinging her eyes. She screamed until it started to snag in her throat, and then she stopped. Put the pillow back in its place, fluffed it up so it didn't look disturbed. She picked up the walkie-talkie, checked it was okay, and then walked back to the others.

Oliver watched her as she returned.

"How did you know?" His voice was hoarse. "How did you know he would do that?"

Red didn't know if she could talk, not until the words were there waiting, raw from the silent scream.

"Because he said. He told us he would kill them and I believed him."

She didn't need to say the rest, it was there, haunting the end of the sentence, finishing the thought. *I believed him, but you didn't.*

"But I don't understand how he—"

The static dropped out, cutting Oliver off.

"That was your fault," the voice said, dark and deep, breaking up at the edges. "I told you to send them away."

Oliver was in front of Red before she realized, taking the walkie-talkie from her hands. Hey, that was hers. Her responsibility.

Oliver pushed down the button.

"You didn't need to kill them!" he shouted, the white of his knuckles pushing through his skin like a prehistoric backbone. "We didn't tell them anything. You were watching, we didn't tell them anything. They were leaving!"

Static.

"You passed them a note telling them to call the police," the voice answered, clipped and clear.

Oliver's mouth fell open.

"Did you think I wouldn't know?" the voice continued. "That was your fault, I didn't want to do that. They're dead because of you."

He paused. A fizzing, metallic breath leaked out of the speakers before the static took over.

"I'm not the one who fucking shot them," Oliver said, voice breaking, but he hadn't pushed the button, and Red couldn't tell if he'd meant to or not.

"Now," the voice came back, "before anyone else has to die, listen to me. Stop trying to escape. You can't. Everything has been planned for. Do what I asked you to." He breathed out, almost a sigh. "One of you has a secret. Give it to me and I'll let the others live. We have hours before daylight. I'm not going anywhere until I get it, and neither are you."

Oliver's brows lowered, a shadow over his eyes.

He raised the walkie-talkie, remembering to hold the button this time. "One of *us* has the secret?" he asked, unsure, tripping over the words. "You're not holding us hostage to get information from someone else?"

This was about him and Maddy, wasn't it, to get that name from Catherine Lavoy? The Frank Gotti case that Red knew backward and forward. Oliver had been so sure before, and Red had followed him right there.

Static.

"This is all about one of you, inside that RV. Give me what I want and your friends don't have to die."

Oliver looked at Red. She tried to hide her realization from him, blink it away. Oliver had been wrong about why they were here. Wrong about the note too. Now two people were dead, right outside, and it was all their fault.

"It's not about using you and Maddy to get to your mom," Reyna said, voice steadier now, speaking to the back of Oliver's head.

"Someone here has a secret, knows what this is about. That's what he's saying. Oliver, it could be—"

Oliver cut her off, raising the walkie-talkie to his lips. "Who?" he asked. "Which one of us?"

A crackle of static followed by a cackle of laughter.

"That's not how this works," the voice said. "You know who you are. I'll be waiting."

Static.

The walkie-talkie dropped to Oliver's side, his eyes dropping with it. Red looked beyond him, at Reyna, then Maddy, Arthur over there and Simon at the back. This was about one of them, about something they knew.

Red coughed, looked away. *You know who you are.* She had a secret too, didn't she? Bigger than most. But this wasn't about her. It couldn't be. No one knew, that was the whole point of it. No one could ever know, not even tonight. That was the plan. Red needed the plan and she wasn't the only one. But she had her answer; it wasn't about that, about her. And if they were talking secrets, Red wasn't the only one hiding something. Clearly Reyna had a secret, something bad enough to think this night could be about that, something Oliver must know too and didn't want out. Red had picked up on that. She had *potential,* see? And before, Maddy had denied having a secret just a little too hard and a little too fast, and Red knew her just a little too well. Which meant there was something she didn't know at all. She didn't like that feeling.

Simon was the first to speak, voice cutting over the static. "Their truck is right there, like twenty feet from the door." He sniffed, turning to look out the windshield. He didn't have a secret he was thinking about, then. Or he was just better at hiding it. "All four tires, working engine, no holes in it. Yet. Doors still open. Ready. It will move. It can drive away."

"I don't think we'd make it," Maddy replied. "At least not all of us. He shot them both so fast."

Simon went on, like he hadn't heard her. "The old man had the keys in his hand, I saw before . . . I don't know if I've ever seen blood like that before. Too much. I didn't know, I didn't think it would look like that." His hands were shaking, pressed against the glass. "It doesn't look real."

Was he in shock? Maybe Simon needed to go back there and scream into the same pillow, trap it in there with hers. Red walked around the others to the front of the RV, coming to stand beside Simon, her arm brushing against his.

He flinched, and Red could now see why.

Out through the windshield, glowing in the white headlights, was Joyce. Right in front of the hood of the truck. She'd almost made it to the open passenger door. Almost. Simon was right, she didn't look real, folded there like an unfinished mannequin, one hand open and reaching. Her head undone, leaking out and soaking into the road. It didn't look red from here, the blood, it looked almost black.

That was what Mom must have looked like, right? Inside that wooden box draped in the Star-Spangled Banner. Had the bullets gone all the way through, like with Joyce? Was part of her face missing too?

The sound of static grew behind her as Oliver approached. He rested the walkie-talkie on Red's shoulder, wordlessly passing it back to her. Hers, her responsibility, keeper of the voice. Her fingers closed around it.

Oliver stared out the windshield too. "Maddy's right," he said. "We wouldn't all make it. He'd be able to take at least two or three of us out before we got the truck moving."

And there were three people Oliver cared about in this RV, so that was a risk too far.

"Especially as the sniper somehow seems to know exactly what we're doing every time," Oliver was still talking. "I can't work out how he knew about the note. There was no way he could even see it, let alone see what was written on it. He . . ."

Oliver's head whipped around, eyes overstretched, too much white showing above and below. He opened his mouth like he was going to say something, then stopped himself, gritting his teeth.

"What?" Red asked him.

He shushed her, head pivoting on his wide shoulders as he looked around the RV.

He charged forward, toward the dining table, grabbing his phone from the surface. He unlocked it, tapped at the screen.

Red walked over, Simon on her heels.

"What are you—?" Reyna began, silenced by the deadly look in Oliver's eyes.

They gathered around him, and Red leaned over to see what he was doing.

On the screen, on a fresh page in the Notes app, Oliver was typing.

*There's only one way he could have known about—*

"Fuck this," Oliver said, irritated, swiping out of Notes, the phone's fault for taking too long, not his. Oliver's eyes flicked to the bottom of his screen, and his thumb followed, pressing onto the music app.

"Oliver, what are you doing?" Maddy asked.

"Wait," he told her, scrolling through the screen, finger landing on a random playlist. *Christmas Songs,* it said. Oliver pressed play on the first song and dragged the volume bar right to the top.

The song began, choral voices singing *ah,* and a high-pitched strum on the guitar. "Rockin' Around the Christmas Tree." In April. Deafening as Oliver held the phone in the middle of the group, speaker facing up. He beckoned them all closer.

Red stepped in, shoulders pressing into Reyna and Simon. The drumbeat of the song ticking half as slow as her heart.

Oliver flashed his eyes at them all.

He started to speak, not loudly, only just audible over the sound of the music. Red had to concentrate, but now she was thinking about the lyrics, and dancing around the tree with Mom before there were two holes in her head.

"There's only one way he could have known about the note," Oliver said, looking at each of them in turn. "The window, yeah fine, his guy on the other side could have seen us climbing out and told him about it. But not the note. There's no way either of them could have seen. So, there's only one way he knew." He paused.

*Everyone dancing merrily in the new old-fashioned way.*

The saxophone burst in, too loud, screaming in Red's ears.

"He *heard* us talking about it," Oliver said. "Because the RV is bugged."

# TWENTY-FIVE

The song continued, saxophone screeching up and down.

"Bugged?" Reyna repeated. Oliver signaled for her to lower her voice, to hide it under the music. "Like with a microphone?"

"How else could he know everything he seems to know?" Oliver replied.

"When would he have bugged the RV?" Reyna returned, just as the chorus did, and Red had to strain to hear. "We haven't left it unattended."

"Maybe when we were changing the first tire?" Simon spoke with the music. "We were all out there, on the other side to the door. Red and Arthur were off somewhere. He could have snuck in then?"

Oliver shook his head. "Not when we were jacking up the RV. We would have felt it."

"When, then?" Reyna asked. "When we stopped for lunch, for dinner at the rest stop? But we double-checked it was locked."

"Maybe even before that," Oliver said. "Maybe before today. You heard him; they planned for everything, they've been planning this awhile. Maybe he planted the bug before Simon even borrowed the RV. Maybe it's something to do with your uncle." Oliver looked at Simon as he said that, a shadow of suspicion in his eyes. Simon sniffed. "Or maybe it's in the stuff we brought onto the RV. In our bags. We need to search everywhere, find it, so we can get our advantage back."

His eyes flashed as the song drew to an end, rallying them all. He dragged the cursor back and restarted the song.

"We'll have to turn the music off so he doesn't get suspicious, but no one mention what we're doing. Just speak normally. Okay?"

Yes, sir, right away, sir. Red blinked. It seemed Oliver had already forgotten that two people just died less than fifteen minutes ago, bleeding out on the road out there, blooms of red around their once-heads. He was already on to the next thing. Moves and counter-moves. Sniper takes a turn, then them. Win-win solutions, as Catherine Lavoy would say, but so far they'd won nothing. It seemed Oliver wanted to avoid the other solution, the most obvious one: finding the secret that the voice on the walkie-talkie wanted. It wasn't Red's he was after, couldn't be. But now Red was starting to doubt herself, dark thoughts slipping in through the gaps, through holes in her head. Was she doing the exact same thing as Oliver, as the rest of them too, maybe, clinging to her secret because she didn't want to lose it? She needed the plan. Needed it. Oliver Lavoy didn't need anything, he already had it all.

"Red, you keep cycling up through those radio channels while you look. Okay, let's do this."

Oliver paused the music, holding his finger to his lips, making sure they all saw. He pointed to himself and Reyna, and then to the back bedroom and the bunks. Red he pointed into the kitchen. Simon the bathroom. Arthur right here at the dining table and sofa bed. Maddy up front in the cockpit. They nodded and dispersed.

Red went to the refrigerator first, pulling it open, pressing her body close to the cool air that seeped out of it. The RV was growing warm and sticky, no air passing through, too many bodies, too much movement, too much fear, and dread and guilt. When would Red's heart stop beating so hard? It couldn't keep this up. It didn't want her to forget—did it?—that Don and Joyce were dead outside. She could have done more. She should have done more. She knew that would happen and she let it. The second time she'd listened to Oliver, chose him, and when would she learn? No time soon, apparently, because she was doing what he told her to right now.

Red moved aside a six-pack of beer, unopened, checking behind it. Cheese slices, salami, butter, beer, oat milk, wine coolers, chocolate. Nothing out of the ordinary. Not that Red knew what a bug looked like anyway, some small black microphone thing, right? Well, there was nothing like that in here. She closed the refrigerator door and turned to the counter, placing the walkie-talkie on top.

Red pulled open the bottom drawer and searched through the saucepans and frying pans, opening each lid and checking inside. Running her fingers into each corner of the drawer to be sure.

Next drawer up, pulling out the stacks of plates and bowls, placing them on the counter and separating each one, the porcelain scraping together, the sound grinding in the bones of her jaw. Nothing there either. Only five sets of each, but there were six of them here.

Top drawer, cutlery. Red picked through the knives, forks and spoons, checking beneath the cutlery holder too. Nothing. An empty space for the sharp kitchen knife that was now sitting on the dining table. Red looked; Arthur was underneath the table, only the bottoms of his shoes visible, sticking out the end.

Nothing around the faucet or the plug in the sink. Red wanted to wash the drying sweat off her face, but maybe that would be a waste of water. How much did they have in that tank below? And how long would the generator keep running? She couldn't remember those numbers, but thirty-one feet was burned into her brain, cropping up when she didn't need it, like right this second.

The high-up cupboard with the glasses. Red stood on tiptoes, pushing them carefully aside to see in, but she didn't really need to. She could see through the rows of glass; nothing black or bug-like in here.

She sidestepped to the oven, swinging the door open. They probably would never have used it on the trip. What could you make using cheese, salami, beer, chocolate and oat milk anyway? Nothing good. She needed to stop thinking about food. She was hungry in the slow comedown from the adrenaline. Scratch that, she'd been hungry before, hadn't she? Or maybe that yawning feeling in her gut meant something else entirely.

"Red?" Arthur's voice interrupted the thought; he was standing behind her. She straightened up and turned.

His eyes were drawn and sad behind his glasses, lashes long and downcast.

He didn't say anything, just raised his eyes to meet hers and then raised one hand.

There, on the back of his hand, written in that same black felt-tip pen against his tan skin, were the words: *YOU OK?*

Beside them were two options. *YES* with a square checkbox drawn next to it, riding up one knuckle. And below that, *NO*, with an empty box.

Arthur gave her the pen, pressing it into her hand, fingers warm against hers as they lingered there. Something passed between their eyes. Red held up the pen, uncapped it. She was always fine, when people asked. Of course she was fine, thanks, yes, she and Dad were doing just great, thank you. Fine, okay, fine. An elaborate lie squeezed into those two tiny words, the greatest gifts to a liar like her. No one asked for more detail if you were fine. But Arthur, he was *really* asking, she could tell. And so Red really answered.

She reached out and held his hand steady, gripped the pen and drew a check mark in the box next to *NO*. She wasn't okay. And maybe Arthur wasn't either. He hadn't forgotten that they just watched two people die twenty minutes ago. Joyce and Don were somebody's someone. Each other's. They had a daughter, a grandchild. But it was the daughter who stayed in Red's mind, between thirty-one feet and the unknown pattern in the curtains. A daughter like her.

"You did everything you could," Arthur said, the marked hand dropping to his side, matching the to-do lists on hers. "You tried to stop it."

No she hadn't, not really. She could have done more. Red shrugged, staring down at the checkbox on Arthur's hand. He'd dropped her hand when Don and Joyce were killed. They were holding hands and then they weren't, and Red couldn't remember the changeover. Maybe if he hadn't dropped her hand, they wouldn't have died, which was a stupid thought but Red had it anyway. Sometimes those small, inconsequential things mattered, like hanging up a phone.

"It wasn't your fault," Arthur said.

But didn't he know? Everything was. All of this.

"I need to pee," Red said, only becoming true as she said it.

It was Arthur's turn to shrug now, a wounded look crossing his eyes. She always did that, didn't she? Whenever he got too close, whenever it got too real. But now she really did need to go.

Red scooped up the walkie-talkie and stepped toward the bathroom door, which Simon had left wide open. She paused as, right then, Oliver and Reyna reemerged from the bedroom. Reyna's eyes shifted, rubbed red, and Red wondered whether they'd been fighting in there, in whispers so the others couldn't hear. How bad could their secret be? Worse than hers? And what about Simon? He was being a little too quiet, wasn't he? Or was that only because he thought the sniper was listening? And, now Red was thinking, Maddy hadn't come over to speak to her in a while, only Arthur.

Oliver clapped his hands to get everyone's attention. "Anything?" he mouthed, lips and teeth moving in oversized strokes.

Red shook her head, saw the others doing the same, a thumbs-down from Simon. Maddy returned to her search of the glove compartment. Arthur was finishing up the kitchen for Red, opening the door to the microwave and checking inside.

Red pressed the button on the walkie-talkie, skipping up through channels four and five, swapping one empty static for another, so Oliver could see she was doing her job.

He wasn't paying attention, though, glowering up at the ceiling.

"Light fittings?" he hissed, mouth overperforming the words again. "Arthur, help me. And can you pass that headlamp?" Oliver's voice had returned to normal levels; clearly he thought the request was obscure enough if anyone was listening.

They didn't need her. Red walked through the bathroom door, bringing the static with her, and shut the door, flicking the lock across. Should she have asked Oliver first? No, she didn't need permission to pee, fuck him.

She placed the walkie-talkie down on the side of the sink, hissing from channel nine, and fiddled with the button on her jeans. Her fingers were too warm and rubbery.

"Simon, hit the lights," Oliver called.

A moment later, the bathroom was swallowed by darkness. Did

they really have to turn her lights off too? Red pulled down her jeans and underwear, feeling blindly for the toilet behind her. She found it and sat down.

"Where's that mop bucket?" Oliver's voice sailed through the gaps under the door. "I need something to stand on."

Well, now she couldn't go, with them all right out there. Red scrabbled through the darkness for the faucet, turning it on so the others couldn't hear her pee.

There was grunting outside, a twisting sound of metal grooves.

"Nothing. Next," Oliver said. The sound of the bucket dropping down somewhere else. "Reyna, you have a quick look in Maddy's bag. Check the pockets."

Red's stuff was in there too. But she would have seen if there was a microphone hidden in her things, when she emptied everything out and gutted the bag. If there even was a microphone anywhere to be found. It was starting to look doubtful. Why was Oliver so certain? The sniper had known about the note. It could have been a lucky guess, seeing Oliver shake Don's hand. But had he even seen that from his position, with the back of Don's jacket blocking his view? And he didn't just know there was a note, he also knew that it was asking them to call the police, he said it like a definite, and that was a guess too far, wasn't it? It had all been so fast.

Red scrabbled in the darkness for the toilet paper, ripping some free and folding it up.

"Next," Oliver said, the plunk of the bucket again.

She stood, pulling her underwear up and fastening her jeans. She flushed and dipped her hands under the cold running water, flicking the faucet off and wiping her wet hands down her legs.

Red stepped forward in the pitch-black, stubbing her toe on the corner of the shower as she searched for the door.

She unlocked it and walked out, closing the door behind her.

The darkness was easier to navigate out here, spoiled by a beam of light attached to Oliver's head as he studied the lights under the kitchen cabinets, removing one of their casings and shaking his head. Simon held the flashlight, and Arthur had the one on his phone.

"Nothing," Oliver said, backing away. "Okay, you can turn the lights back on."

Red was closest, free hands. She flicked up the switches and the inside of the RV reappeared. Maddy was still up front, knees on the driver's seat, eyes level with the glove compartment. Reyna was standing on the sofa putting Maddy's case back, checking the cupboard around it with the flat of her hand.

"Anything?" Oliver repeated, saying it out loud this time.

A low rumble of "No," from Red, Arthur and Reyna.

No bug.

"I don't get it," Oliver said, dropping down on the closest booth. "There must be."

"We've literally ransacked the entire RV," Simon said.

Oliver shushed him.

"What?" Simon doubled down. "There's nothing. We've checked."

"Maddy?" Oliver called to the front, where Maddy was clutching something in her hands, a small rectangular piece of paper, eyes narrowed and thinking as they flicked across it. "What have you got there?"

"Well, not what we were looking for," she answered, holding it up. It was a photograph.

She brought it over, holding it out for the others. There was a family of five pictured there, huddled together on green summer grass, arms looping in and out of each other's, a golden retriever mid-tail wag. The man had gray hair and a bright smile, and his wife and three daughters looked near identical with matching burnt-auburn hair, the same person in four different stages of life, only changed by time.

"This isn't your uncle, is it?" she asked Simon. "I thought he didn't have a family, though. You said he was a loner."

Simon took the photograph, a muscle working in his cheek as he chewed his tongue. "No, that's not him. He's not married, no kids."

Maddy's face scrunched, the look in her eyes replaced with something new, something uneasy. An edge to her voice as she asked: "So why does your uncle have a photo of someone else's family in the glove compartment?"

# TWENTY-SIX

Simon passed the photograph of the happy red-haired family back, not taking a second look.

"I don't know," he said, voice spiking higher, betraying him. He was supposed to be a better liar than that.

"Simon?" Maddy asked.

"I don't know," Simon repeated. "Do you know all the stuff your weird uncle gets up to?"

"We don't have a weird uncle," she snapped back. "Is he, like, a stalker, or something?"

"No," Simon said, though he hadn't leaned into the word like he fully believed it. "No, no, no. Look, I'm sure the RV is just second-hand. Maybe he bought it from that family and neither of them ever cleared out the glove compartment."

"That makes sense," Maddy conceded. "So why are you being weird about it?"

"I'm not being weird."

"Yes you are."

"Maddy," Red warned.

"Simon." So did Arthur.

"It's nothing, really." Simon wiped his forehead with the back of his hand, droplets of sweat by his temples. "Just . . . well, my uncle owns a used-car dealership, right? That's why he had an RV we could use. But, and you know, this is not as bad as it's going to sound . . ." Simon trailed off, clearing his throat. "What I mean is, I'm not sure his business is strictly legal, if you catch my—"

"Stolen?" Oliver barked suddenly. "Your uncle sells stolen cars?"

"Maybe." Simon held his hands up in surrender, taking a step back.

"Maybe?" Oliver demanded.

"Well, n-no, definitely, actually," Simon stammered. "I know because I, well, I helped him once. Couple of times. Few times. Run some scams. Apparently I have a trustworthy face. Good liar when I need to be. Acting is just lying, after all, isn't it?"

Maddy gasped. "Simon, you've stolen cars?"

"No." He shook his head, pointing his index fingers at her. "I've helped. There's a difference."

"Why would you do that?" Maddy stared him down, breathing hard.

"Oh come on, why d'you think?" Simon retorted. "I needed the money."

"Why?" Maddy pressed. "Your parents have money."

"Well, they aren't Lavoy-loaded," Simon said. "I know you never have to think about stuff like this, because your mom thinks the sun shines out of your ass and would support you whatever you wanted to do. But my situation is different. I need the money, in case I want to take a year off and apply to drama schools next year and my parents freak out and refuse to pay for it. I haven't told them yet, I haven't decided yet. It's not that big a deal, really. Just think of it as practice for my first big acting gig. My uncle's been in prison a couple of times, but that was ages ago and he's actually a pretty nice guy. Not everything is stolen, some's legit."

"Wait, wait, wait, forget all that." Oliver stood up, swung his legs out. "Are you saying there's a possibility that this RV was stolen?"

Simon swallowed. "There is a small possibility, yes."

"Fuck!" Oliver smashed his fist down on the table.

"But he didn't say it was when I asked to borrow it, I'm sure he would have told me. He made it all sound legit, said we could use it for free, no charge, before he sold it on," Simon said. "Showed me all the features."

Thirty-one feet long, Red thought.

"You're telling me there's a chance I've been driving across state lines in a stolen vehicle?" Oliver rounded on Simon. "Do you know how bad that is for someone like me?" He bared his teeth. "For me and Maddy, considering who our mom is?"

"*We* didn't steal it," Simon said desperately.

"That's not the point!" Oliver replied. "I thought you said you didn't have any secrets before. This is a pretty fucking big one, Simon. Jesus Christ."

Maddy stepped in front of her brother, asking, "Why would your parents let us use this RV if they know what he does?"

"They didn't, obviously," Simon answered. "They don't know I got it from him. My mom doesn't even like her brother, doesn't know I sometimes go see him. They think we're renting it from a company, that *you* organized it."

"Simon!"

"What, it's not my fault, Maddy!" He turned his eyes on her. "It was your idea in the first place. You're the one who told me we had to keep everything as cheap as possible so that Red could come!"

It was strange, hearing her name like that, forgetting that it belonged to her, that it wasn't just a misplaced splash of color. A second later, Simon's words punched her in the gut, winding her, gnawing at her chest. *Keep everything as cheap as possible so that Red could come.* Her fault again. Simon and Maddy, talking about her behind her back, making Red their problem to solve. And why did it hurt so much that they all knew? Little Red Kenny, poor as dirt and a dead mom, but she had *potential,* hadn't you heard? Everyone was looking at her now, everyone but Arthur. Red's eyes glazed but she blinked the tears back, forcing her eyes open and closed. Don't you dare, don't you fucking dare. She didn't need their pity, she had her plan.

"I'm sorry, Red," Simon said, his voice softening. "I didn't mean . . ."

But he did mean, and that was okay. She was fine. She smiled, waved her hand in front of her face. But she didn't look at Maddy. That betrayal was worse, somehow. No, that wasn't fair. Maddy cared, that was all. Maddy looked after her, looked out for her. Maddy cared.

"And I'm sorry about the RV," Simon continued, looking around at the others. "Look, it probably isn't stolen, I dunno. But whether it is or not, it doesn't really matter now. I don't think someone is threatening to shoot us all over a stolen RV. Killing that innocent couple out there." He stepped forward, pressing one finger into the photo in Maddy's hand, over the man's face. "I don't think that's jolly ol' sniper number one and jolly ol' sniper two." He moved to the woman's face, her auburn hair framing his fingernail. "Husband-and-wife murder team, I don't think so. It's not about the RV, is it? Why we're here."

He finished, breath heavy in his chest, shoulders moving in time with it. He was avoiding Red's eyes, though, wasn't he? At least he finally seemed to have sobered up. Enough.

"No," Oliver said, dropping back down to the booth, rubbing the hand that had punched the table. "But it could be something to do with your uncle. A business thing. Some people he pissed off. Or *you* pissed off."

Simon shook his head. "He's a criminal but I don't think he's *that* kind of criminal. Plus"—he coughed—"killing all of us, including me, wouldn't really be a punishment for him. Not sure he cares. This isn't about him."

"Of course you'd say that," said Oliver. "People have died."

"Yeah, and whose idea was it to pass them a note? That's on you, Oliver."

"And it would have worked," Oliver hissed, "if the sniper wasn't somehow fucking listening to us!"

"He's not listening," Reyna said, voice croaky and unused. "We've checked, there's no microphone planted anywhere."

"You were at this table here," Red said, looking at Oliver and Maddy. "Talking low, so Joyce and Don wouldn't hear. If there was a bug, it would have to be right around here. Around this table."

"Maybe we haven't checked everywhere," Oliver said, studying the table, eyes flickering like he was spooling back his memory, replaying the scene. "Red, give me the walkie-talkie."

That was when she realized; the sound of static had gone. Left her.

Red looked down. It wasn't in her hand, where it was supposed to be. Fuck, where was the walkie-talkie? She must have left it somewhere. She must have—

"Red?" Oliver snapped his fingers impatiently.

"It's—it's gone," she stuttered. "I don't have it."

"What do you mean you don't have it?" Oliver's voice hardened. "Where is it?"

"I—I must have put it down somewhere," Red said, patting the sides of her shirt as though it could have somehow slipped down there. She'd lost it. Of course she had, this was what Red did. Couldn't be trusted with anything. Things erasing themselves from her memory as soon as they were out of sight. Lost keys, lost phones, lost wallets.

Why couldn't they hear the static? Red needed that sound back, anything but empty to her.

"For fuck's sake, Red. Where were you searching?" Oliver pushed up to stand. "The kitchen? Reyna, go check in the cupboards."

"Where've you been?" Maddy said, more patiently than her brother. "Retrace your steps."

Red hated when people said that. That was the whole point, she'd already forgotten where she'd been, there was no trace left to follow. It skirted around her mind, evading her as she tried even harder to think back. And, great, now the *Phineas and Ferb* song lyrics were running through her head again, word for word.

"Everyone be quiet a second!" Oliver shouted, holding his finger to his lips, motioning to listen with his hand by his ear.

Red held her breath and strained to hear. Strained harder. Where had she left it? It was somewhere, it couldn't have disappeared, Red knew. Even though things did seem to disappear around her: headphones, homework, moms.

There was a faint hiss, almost unnoticeable, not much louder than the way the air fizzed when you were scared or alert. But it was there, Red recognized it, coming from beyond the kitchen. Her eyes followed it, to the closed door.

"The bathroom!" Of course. Red darted forward, slamming down the handle and wrenching open the door. The welcome sound of static filled her ears and there, waiting for her on the side of the sink, was the walkie-talkie. Green eye winking as she stepped forward to scoop it up, holding it to her chest. "I've got it!" she called back out to the others. Hers. Her responsibility. Oliver wouldn't take it away from her, would he?

"Bring it here."

Red sidled through the bathroom door, pressing the down button to skip from channel nine—where she'd left it—back to three.

". . . what I say." The voice cut in, midsentence.

Fuck, the sniper had been talking to them.

Red's eyes widened. The other five were over there, too far away. Just her and the walkie-talkie, keeper of the voice.

He couldn't know, she couldn't let him know they hadn't been listening, that they were searching for interference on the other channels.

Red raised the walkie-talkie to her lips, pressed the push-to-talk button. "Understood," she said quickly.

Static.

Of course they hadn't understood, they hadn't even heard what he'd been saying. But that was the only word that came to her, vague enough to fit most places.

"Good," the voice replied. "I'm getting impatient."

Static.

"What did you do that for?" Oliver hissed.

"So he didn't know we weren't listening," she said. "I think it worked."

"Shh. But we have no idea what you just agreed to," he said, holding out his hand for her to bring him the walkie-talkie.

Red hesitated, then placed it in his open hand.

Oliver took the walkie-talkie and bundled it up in his shirt, holding it close in the material, between his tightly cupped hands.

His voice dipped back into whispers. "It's the classic Trojan horse," he said. "Maybe the bug is inside the walkie-talkie, so it's listening even when we think it's not. We always have it around us. And Red, you brought it over when me and Maddy were doing the note. Maybe it's listening all the time."

"Oh, they're clever," Simon said, wagging one finger.

"I can check?" Red offered, voice low. She did not want to believe Oliver, follow him again, even though it made a perfect kind of sense. "I know what the inside of a walkie-talkie looks like, all the parts. I can look?"

"How do you know so much about walkie-talkies?" Oliver asked, not giving it up.

"I just do." Red held her hand out now, waiting for Oliver to pass it back. Her memories did not belong to him. He might be the natural leader, but he didn't know what he was doing here. Red did.

Oliver narrowed his eyes. He unbundled the walkie-talkie and passed it over.

"Shh," he said as he did.

Red slid into the other side of the booth, placing the walkie-talkie down. She would have to be quick at this, so the sniper didn't know they weren't listening again, if he tried to talk. Concentrate. Red's fingers moved to the knob on top, beside the antenna. She flicked it into the off position and the static cut out.

Silence. A buzzing kind of silence, broken up by Maddy's breath as she leaned over Red. It was distracting, in and out and in, a faint whistle underneath.

Red pushed down and slid off the back casing, into the battery compartment. It was empty, other than the three batteries slotted into place. Next she grabbed the screwdriver from the table, inserted it into the first screw on one of the back corners and turned it around, fast as she could. She placed the small screw on the table, spinning around itself, and turned to the next.

The others were all staring, she could feel their eyes on the back of her neck, on her fingers as she unscrewed the next one and placed it down. It almost rolled off the table but Maddy caught it.

"Thanks," Red said, unspooling the next screw.

Oliver shushed her. And was it spiteful that Red wanted him to be wrong about this? For him to be wrong and her to be right.

She undid the final screw, dropping it with the others, and pulled the plastic casing up and to the side, carefully as red and black wires connected through to the batteries. She propped it there and looked down, bringing her eyes closer.

The green circuit board she'd been expecting to see, with small metal parts soldered on. The connection to the antenna, the amplifiers and mixers on an integrated circuit. And what were those small parts called again, oh yeah, capacitors. The tuner, transformers. She remembered the diagrams, the YouTube tutorials. Words and shapes she'd learned long ago, the kind that stayed in her head because they weren't important. Except they were now, and there was nothing here that shouldn't be. She recognized it all, same as the parts inside her mom's walkie-talkie.

"Is there anythi—" Oliver began.

"Shh," Red said this time. She was concentrating.

Slowly, Red's fingers pried up the circuit board, just a tiny bit, so she could lower her eye to the gap and see the parts beyond, sitting at the front of the walkie-talkie. She didn't want to pull anything out of place, she didn't trust herself to be able to put it back together. She didn't know if she could rebuild it if it all fell apart in her hands now. The last time she'd taken hers apart and put it back together had been more than a year ago. Last February 6, just for old times' sake.

Red could see red and black wires connecting to the circular plastic part that doubled as microphone and speaker at the front, beneath the grille in the plastic.

That was it. Nothing here that shouldn't be. No bug that didn't belong. Red lowered the circuit board into position, even more carefully than before, and guided the plastic casing back on.

"No bug," she said, starting on the first screw, forgetting to whisper. Oliver shot her an angry look.

"How do you know?"

"Because everything that's there needs to be there," Red said, tightening the screw and moving onto the next. "There's no independent listening device in there because there's no separate power source. And there's nothing connected to those batteries that shouldn't be. He's not listening to us. Not unless we push the button," she added, slotting in the third screw.

"And we just have to take your word on that, do we?" Oliver asked, also forgetting to whisper now.

"Oliver." It was Maddy who said it this time.

"She could be wrong," he replied. "Or she could be lying to us. How do we know we can trust what she's saying?"

Red wasn't wrong and she wasn't lying, not about this at least. She slid the plastic that covered the battery compartment back and turned the knob to switch the walkie-talkie on. The fizz of static greeted her, welcoming her home. She'd missed the sound. Wasn't that stupid? But it meant the walkie-talkie was working, she hadn't broken it somehow by trying to be useful. Except now she wasn't useful, she was a liar.

Like when she gave her statements to the police over five years

222

ago. Red was trying to be helpful, to be useful, even though the world was ending around them. She described her final phone call with her mom, every hateful part of it. Over and over again, every last detail she could remember. "There was a doorbell in the background. Mom rang the doorbell at someone's house. They answered and she said 'Hello.'" But that couldn't be true, you see, they'd explained to her. Her mom wasn't found anywhere near a residential road, near houses. She was found inside Southwark Generating Station, that old, abandoned power station on the pier. And she was dead within ten minutes of that phone call. They didn't say Red was lying, not like Oliver just had, they said she must have been mistaken, confused, she was only thirteen, she was in shock. Sometimes Red wasn't really sure if she'd remembered it at all. And, now that she thought about it, was she sure about the walkie-talkie?

"What are you talking about, Oliver?" Reyna's turn to look at him, crossing the awkward silence that had followed his words.

"The sniper knew about the note, Reyna." Oliver's face was reddening again, heat in patches up his neck. "He knew what was written on it. He also knew exactly where we were to trap us here. So if we're saying there isn't a listening device somewhere in the RV, then we have an even bigger problem. Because the only alternative is that . . ."

He drew off, eyes circling around the group, finally coming to rest on Red.

"One of us is working with them."

# 3:00 A.M.

# TWENTY-SEVEN

Red couldn't hold Oliver's eyes for longer than two seconds. He won. She dropped her gaze.

"What?" Simon said, voice escaping before he'd even formed the end of the word.

"Don't be ridiculous, Oliver," Reyna said. "No one here is working with the shooter."

"Why is it ridiculous?" he snapped, puppet strings back, spinning his head. "The sniper knows things he couldn't possibly know. What we're saying in here, what our plans are, that fucking note. And let's not forget how we ended up here in the first place." He paused, eyes flashing under the overhead lights as he cracked the bones in his neck. "This road wasn't on our route. We got lost. So either the sniper somehow predicted exactly which wrong turns we'd take, or he was listening through a bug he'd planted and following us, or"—he swallowed—"someone in this RV led us right to him."

He looked pointedly at Simon, Arthur and Red, one hand balling into a fist at his side. He stretched it out, fingers ropy and long, as he studied the three of them. Something tightened in Red's gut, twisting uncomfortably as she watched Oliver's hand bend and flex.

"Not this again," Simon sighed. "We were lost. No signal. None of us directed the RV down this road on purpose."

"I'm not sure that's true anymore," Oliver said. "It was you three, you three giving the directions at the end. I lost the map on Reyna's phone, so we know it wasn't me. Maddy didn't say anything."

"But Reyna was driving," Simon said. "So by your logic, she could be a mole too, right? Because she's the one who physically brought us down here. Or is it just us three that are under suspicion?"

"She only took the turns you were telling her to," Oliver retorted, pointing a finger toward Simon's chest. "And if I remember right, Simon, you were the one who was most insistent."

"I was trying to be helpful," Simon shouted back. "I was drunk!"

"Hm," Oliver said, with a wicked smile. "You seem to only be drunk when it suits you, though, huh? Slipping in and out of it. I thought you were supposed to be the actor here."

"Fuck off, Oliver," Simon spat. "I don't have anything to do with this."

"You're a crook like your fucking uncle."

"Stop, please!" Arthur shouted, stepping forward to place his body between Oliver and Simon, turning his head to look at both of them. "This is fucking stupid. We can't turn on each other."

"And what about you?" Oliver directed his voice at Arthur now. "You were the one giving those last directions, they came from your phone."

Red shook her head. That wasn't fair, Arthur was just the one who happened to lose signal last, on a different network from the others. She should say something. She should stand up for him.

"And I got it wrong, I'm sorry." Arthur held up his hands. "I was just trying to follow the map."

"Red." Oliver's eyes landed on her now. "I remember you were the one who told us to keep going. I wanted Reyna to turn around and you told her to keep going."

She had, he wasn't wrong. Her fault.

"Red didn't do anything," Arthur said, and that was how it felt— was it?—to have someone on your side, on your team. To stand up for you whether it was right or wrong. Red breathed out, gripping the walkie-talkie too hard, like it was Arthur's hand and they were back there standing in the doorway, about to watch two people die. Two people were dead, remember. Right outside. And that red dot was still out there, waiting.

"She was just trying to find the way to the campsite," Arthur continued. "Like the rest of us."

"And in doing so, one of you led us into this ambush, to a man waiting with a fucking rifle! That was no accident!"

Maddy wasn't saying anything. Did that mean she agreed with Oliver, was she taking his side? How many sides were there? Us versus them. Simon, Arthur and Red against Oliver, Maddy and Reyna, splitting the RV in half, and half of thirty-one feet was fifteen point five.

"Oliver, stop!" Reyna grabbed his arm, pulled him back. No, not us versus them, Reyna wasn't taking sides. Lavoy-adjacent, but not a Lavoy, and didn't they both know it. Red certainly did now, gaze creeping to Maddy.

"It doesn't mean one of us is involved," Reyna continued. "If there's no listening device, maybe he planted a GPS tracker somewhere outside the RV and that's why we haven't found it. Maybe that's how he followed us to this road."

"Occam's razor, Reyna," Oliver said, shaking his head. "The simplest solution is usually the correct one."

"This isn't helping," Maddy spoke up. And what did that mean? What side did that come down on? "Please, we have to work together."

The knot in Red's gut loosened a little. She hadn't lost Maddy to the other side. Because they were best friends, almost sisters. Knew each other inside and out. It was in the blood, even, because their moms were best friends before them. College roommates to working side by side as prosecutor and police captain. Would Red and Maddy ever have jobs that went side by side? Probably not; Maddy was going to UPenn and Red was going nowhere. Red couldn't stay Lavoy-adjacent forever, she wasn't sure Maddy would even want her to. But, for now, it counted.

"Lift up your shirt, Red," Oliver said, gesturing, an upward motion with his fingers. "You too, Arthur."

"What are you talking about?" Maddy asked, shrinking back as Oliver returned her gaze.

"I need to check neither of them is wearing a wire," he said.

"Oh, come on," Simon interjected. "This is turning into *Lord of the Fucking Flies.* We're going to end up killing each other, forget about the sniper."

"I'm not wearing a wire," Red said, tucking her arms over each other to protect her chest, walkie-talkie purring in her armpit.

"Great, prove it."

"Oliver!" Reyna hissed.

"She and Arthur came over when Maddy and I were talking about the note. You and Simon were by the door. So if there's a listening device we still haven't found, it's on one of those two."

"Or Maddy," Simon said, hysterical to the point of almost smiling. "Or you. Does it not count if you're a Lavoy?" He slapped his arms down to the side of his legs. Simon got it.

"You're taking this too far," Arthur said, shaking his head, taking a step in front of Red, almost like he was blocking her from Oliver. A barricade. "We all need to step back and take a breather. Everyone wants to get out of here, so let's think about what the sniper has actually asked us to do."

"Why won't you do it, then?" Oliver glared. "If you have nothing to hide."

"Okay, fine, see." Arthur grabbed the hem of his baseball shirt and pulled it up over his chest, the muscles in his bare back heaving and bunching as he did. "See, nothing. This is getting out of hand." He dropped his shirt.

"Now Red."

"No." There was a growl to Arthur's voice now. "She does not have to."

"I'll do it too. Look." Oliver stepped forward, fingers moving quickly down the buttons of his shirt. He reached the bottom and pulled it open, covering his arms like wings. There was nothing on his chest, nothing but the sharp lines of his abdomen. "See. I don't have any secrets. I'm clean." He dipped his head at Red, redoing his buttons. "Your turn."

She didn't want to. Of course she didn't want to. But she also didn't want the others to think she was hiding anything. That would be worse.

"Fine." She gritted her teeth. Her shirt was loose enough that she didn't have to undo it. She gripped the ends, walkie-talkie still in hand, and pulled her shirt up over her bra, flashing the pale skin of her chest and stomach to the rest of the group. She didn't have any secrets either, not on her skin at least. Arthur didn't look; Red saw that. He must not like her like that after all.

Red dropped her shirt, tucking the front tails into her jeans. "Are we done now?"

"I'm sorry, Red," Reyna said quietly, like it was somehow her fault.

"No wires," Simon said, a jagged edge to his voice as he smoothed down his own shirt. "No listening devices. Can we move on, now?"

"Not yet." Oliver shook his head. "Just because there's no wire, doesn't mean someone here isn't somehow communicating with him outside."

"Oliver, come on," Maddy pleaded. "No one here is working with the sniper. He would kill any of us. He killed that innocent couple."

Oliver's eyes were busy, working on some thought alone. Red dreaded to know what it was.

"Phones out," Oliver said, striding to the kitchen and pulling out the bottom drawer, too hard, juddering against its hinges. He selected the biggest saucepan, with a matching glass lid, pulling it out as the other pans shifted and clattered around it. "Come on, I said phones out, everyone. We're going to seal them all in here." He raised the pan.

"There's no signal," Simon said. His phone was out, but his hand tightened around it, like he didn't want to let it go. "How could any of us be communicating with the shooter without a signal?"

"I don't know," Oliver said, brandishing the pan. "Maybe there's still a way to communicate, some kind of app. Or maybe one of them has been hacked and is listening to us. Either way, if you want me to trust any of you again"—his eyes flickered and it was obvious which half of the RV he was talking about—"we are shutting our phones away. All of us. It's not a request."

To prove the point, Oliver pulled his phone out of his back pocket and dropped it inside the saucepan with a dull thud.

"Reyna?" He held the pan out to her. She nodded, not returning his gaze, but she pulled out her phone and placed it inside the pan, on top of his.

Maddy stepped up, dropping hers inside next.

"Simon."

Not a request.

"This is fucking stupid," Simon said, taking two angry steps toward Oliver, letting go of his phone, the device sliding against the others to find its own space.

Oliver didn't need to tell Arthur; he was already leaning forward, phone in hand, placing it vertically in a gap inside the pan, standing guard over the others.

"Red." Oliver held the pan out, everyone's eyes turning to her. She could feel them, every single one of them, like heat on her skin, too long and she might burn. Were they looking at her harder than any-one else? That wasn't good. She reached behind her, hand dipping into the loose back pocket of her jeans, fingers alighting around the cool edges of her phone. She pulled it out and held it in front of her eyes, phone in one hand, walkie-talkie in the other. The home screen lit up. No service. 38% battery now. 3:13 a.m. Strange, how she didn't feel tired at all.

"Red." Oliver prompted again. Not a request, remember? He was the leader and he was leading. Where to, Red didn't want to think about. She hesitated and then slid her phone in on top of the pile.

"No one has a secret second phone, do they?"

Everyone shook their heads and Oliver nodded his.

The phones slid and shifted as he carried them away, putting the pan down on the dining table and then slotting the glass lid over the pan. But that wasn't enough, was it? Next he grabbed the half-used roll of duct tape and pulled a long strip free, cutting it into smaller sections with Maddy's hair scissors. He pressed the pieces of duct tape down from lid to pan, sealing their phones inside.

Then the pan was up in his hands again and he was walking

toward the kitchen, opening the oven and sliding the pan inside. He closed the oven door with a slam that ricocheted around the RV.

He turned back and Red stiffened, catching his eyes for a second before she could blink them away. A shiver passed through her, hiding there just beneath the surface of her skin, even though it was warm in here. Too warm. Was she scared of Oliver, or just scared? Scared of this night and the man outside with a gun. It must be the second thing. She'd known Oliver all her life. A leader had to make hard decisions. He was just trying to make sure they survived. That was all, right?

"Now what?" Simon straightened up, clutching his bony hands in front of his chest, like he was protecting the parts inside. "Are you going to make us strip off our clothes, bend over and cough?"

"Simon, I've almost had it with you!" Oliver exploded. "I'm the only one being smart here. I am trying to make sure we survive. That's all."

"Really?" Simon bit back, tightening his hands. "Because it seems to me you keep avoiding the one thing that we know will get us out of here alive. The reason we're here at all. The secret that the sniper wants."

"Not all of us," Maddy said, shifting uncomfortably, a shadow across her eyes. "Not all of us will get out of here alive. He said that if we give him the secret, he will let the rest of us live. Which means . . ."

She didn't need to finish. Red understood. That secret, the one the sniper wanted, was a death sentence. That was what this was. But it wasn't Red's, it couldn't be, that was the whole point. So, whose was it?

"Well, why don't we concentrate on giving him what he wants, and deal with the consequences after," Simon said, looking at Maddy, because Oliver had started to pace behind them. "He might be bluffing about that part."

"No," Oliver said darkly. "We're not doing that, not playing his game. I'm not letting him kill one of us. Any of us."

The two sides of the RV whole again. Or Oliver didn't want to give up his secret, the one that Reyna knew too. How bad could it be?

Red watched Reyna, her eyes playing across the floor, mouth flickering at one edge, cracking her face. Reyna's hand was fiddling with her top, pulling it into a tight knot at her chest. Tighter, tighter. She took a breath and released her hand, the bunched material staying in place like her heart had burst free of her ribs, trapped there inside the shirt. She shook her head and pressed her lips together, looking up.

"Oliver, we have to—" she began.

"No, Reyna, you keep your mouth shut," he barked, stopping dead still. There was a warning in his eyes. Blink and flash.

"Oliver, we have to," Reyna replied, hardening her voice, a warning in there too. "We have to. This could be about us. About what we did."

# TWENTY-EIGHT

The static hissed and Red wondered whether she could see it now, somehow, stippling across the back of her eyes as she tried to watch Oliver. Danger in the movement of his shoulders, in the widening of his eyes.

"Don't say anything else!" he shouted at Reyna, his breath blowing through her black hair as he came too close. She didn't move, didn't react. Red didn't either, but she had been right, they were hiding something, just like she was. That was what the last few hours had been, Red understood now: escape plan after escape plan, searching for a bug and then a mole. It was all Oliver, trying to hold on to this secret. But his time was up.

"Well, it's too late now," Simon said. "We all know you two have a secret. There's no going back."

"Oliver?" Maddy's voice was small, confused. "What's going on? What happened?"

He didn't answer, because he was staring down Reyna, and she was staring back.

Simon laughed, a hollow sound. "You going around with your witch hunt, accusing one of us of being a mole. And here you are, you knew all along you were the one with the secret."

"This is not about that," Oliver said through gritted teeth, eyes still on Reyna.

"It could be," she answered. "It could be his family out there—"

"Stop!"

"No, Oliver, I won't fucking stop!" Reyna snapped, coming alive, dark hairs sticking to the sweat on her forehead. "If this is about what we did, we have to say! We're the oldest here, we're supposed to be looking after them. They're just kids. He said he'd let them go if we give it up. We have to!"

And maybe Reyna was the most natural leader here after all, standing up to Oliver, unblinking. What could they possibly have done? Something bad enough that a man with a rifle would trap them here to get it out of them. Two men. *There are two of us.* What was bad enough for that? Red could only think of one thing.

"Oliver," Maddy said, shakily. "What is it? What did you do?"

Maddy must be thinking the same thing.

"I didn't *do* anything," Oliver said, and then, suddenly: "Fucking mosquito," slapping his hand against his sweat-slick neck. He stopped, looking back at the rest of them, all eyes on him. He might be Oliver Lavoy but it was five against one here. He paused on Maddy, and Red saw the shift, the moment he gave in, hand sweeping his hair back, stepping forward to drop into the booth. He held his head. "It was an accident," he said, staring back, daring the others to not believe him.

"*What* was an accident?" Maddy pressed, gently, coming to sit down across from her brother.

"It was in January," Reyna said, burying her hands inside her sleeves. "When we went back to college for the semester. We—"

"—I'll tell the story," Oliver cut her off. "You won't tell it right. You won't . . . I'll do it."

He shifted in his seat, the material creaking as he did, or was that the sound of his bones? "Keep going, Red."

"Huh?" she said.

"The channels. Keep going."

Right. Red glanced down at the walkie-talkie, pressing the + button, spooling up, the static flickering out every time she clicked.

Oliver waited, until Red was past channel eleven and still going. Then he cleared his throat and began.

"We went to a bar one afternoon. Near school. Just me and Reyna. We were watching the game, Eagles versus Cowboys. Reyna's not from Philly, you know, but she gets it. Can't miss a game." Oliver sniffed. "We drank a couple of beers, watching the game. I was driving, though, so only two. And as we're watching, I notice this random guy who works there, he keeps looking at Reyna. I don't think Reyna noticed, but I did."

Reyna shifted, fingers fiddling inside her sleeves.

"And that's fine, you know, she's a beautiful girl, people are allowed to notice."

A twitch by Reyna's mouth, pulling at the smooth skin of her cheek.

"Anyway, we watch the game, and stay for a couple of hours after. I've forgotten about the guy by this point. But it's getting later and we're thinking about dinner, so we decide to leave. We walk out into the parking lot, toward my car. There's no one else around. And then I realize I've left my scarf inside. So I leave Reyna in the parking lot and run back inside to find the scarf."

Reyna sucked in a breath, wet through her teeth, loud enough for Red to hear. What was coming? What did they do?

Simon sat down on the sofa behind, watching the story play out, gaze flicking between Reyna and Oliver.

"It takes me a few minutes to find the scarf," Oliver continued. "It's not at the table we were sitting at because someone had already handed it in at the bar as lost property. So it takes a few minutes. And by the time I get outside again, I see Reyna standing by the car. And there's that guy, the one who worked in the bar."

Oliver paused, fingers tapping at the table in an irregular pattern, beating out of time with Red's heart.

"And he's bothering Reyna," he said. "He's up in her face, talking to her. He's even holding her by the arms. And Reyna's trying to break free, push him away."

A silent tear fell down Reyna's face, pooling at the crack in her lips.

"So, of course, I run over and tell this random guy to get lost, to stop bothering my girlfriend. And then this guy, he turns to Reyna and he says, 'Am I bothering you?' So Reyna, of course, says that yes he is."

Red was watching Reyna, and maybe she was wrong, but she thought she saw the slightest movement in Reyna's head, moving side to side. Reyna stopped when she noticed Red's eyes.

"So I pull Reyna away from the guy and I tell him to leave her alone," Oliver said. "And then this guy loses it. He shoves me and I'm asking him what his problem is. And then he hits me, punches me right in the face." He paused, sharpening his focus on Maddy. "He hit me first, that's very important. He hit me first. So I did what any other guy in the situation would do: I hit him back. And maybe it was too hard, I don't know. But I think the guy gets knocked out. He falls back on the pavement and, you know, he's breathing heavy like he's unconscious. He's not bleeding or anything. Just out."

Oliver's fingers flexed and balled again, like he could still feel the guy's face imprinted against his fist. Reyna was crying now, tears racing and crisscrossing each other's tails.

"And we talked about calling an ambulance, or going back inside the bar and telling someone," he said. "But it was only a few seconds, and then his eyes are opening and he's awake again. He seems a bit dazed, but he was fine, started to sit up. So Reyna and I decided to leave before he got up and tried to attack either of us again. We got in the car and drove away and the guy was fine. He was walking away. We saw him. He was fine. He was fine."

Oliver repeated it, like if he said it enough times he could change the past and make it true. Because the guy wasn't fine, that must be why Oliver kept saying it.

Oliver cleared his throat. "So, we go to dinner, we don't think about it again."

Reyna's face tensed. She had, she'd thought about it again, Oliver wasn't speaking for her, Red could tell.

"Everything is fine."

Fine.

"And then two days later, Reyna is working at the local hospital, on this shadowing program Dartmouth runs for premed students to get clinical experience." Oliver paused, wiping the sides of his mouth. "And while she's there, she learns of a patient that just died that morning. It was him. The guy from the bar. He was called Jack something. He died of bleeding on the brain."

"Epidural hematoma," Reyna said, voice thick and her eyes far away, not in the RV anymore, back in that memory that only she could see.

There was silence, only the hissing of static in Red's hands.

"So," Simon said slowly, carefully. "You killed him?"

Oliver's hands slammed down on the table, making them all jump. "I did not kill him!" he shouted, voice spiking at the edges. "He attacked Reyna and then he attacked me. He hit me first. I was only defending myself, defending Reyna."

"Did you tell anyone?" Arthur asked now, his voice low and steady. "After you found out he died, did you tell anyone?"

"Turn myself in, you mean?" Oliver looked at him, blinking too fast. "No, we didn't tell anyone. We said we never would, unless someone asked. I guess there weren't any cameras in the parking lot, because no one ever came to speak to us about it. Maybe the guy hadn't told anyone about the fight after, maybe no one knew. But let me be clear." Oliver rolled his shoulders. "It wasn't my fault. He hit me first. It was self-defense. But we couldn't go to the police, because the right prosecutor might have been able to argue that it was a manslaughter case and press charges against me."

"So you kept it secret?" Maddy asked, voice even smaller than before. "Just the two of you."

"Of course we kept it secret," Oliver replied. "He hit me first. Why should I be punished for him attacking me, attacking my girlfriend? And I couldn't do that to Mom," he added, directing the words to Maddy. "She's about to become fucking district attorney, she's worked so hard. A son with a criminal charge would destroy her career. Not to mention my own legal career. He hit me first."

But Oliver must have hit him harder.

"So," Arthur said, speaking tentatively, careful not to set Oliver off again. "You think it's possible someone knows what happened, or suspects at least. The guy out there with the rifle, he could be a friend, or family? Wants you to admit what you did, how Jack died?"

"I don't know," Oliver said, a small shrug in his too-wide shoulders. "This whole thing is so fucked. It was an accident. I didn't mean to . . ." He drew off, gaze circling in front of him. "I didn't mean to."

Oliver's face rearranged, softening between the eyebrows, a twitch in his lower lip, pulling at his chin. His eyes glazed, almost with the threat of tears, and he looked down before anyone could see. But Red saw, she was watching. And she knew that feeling better than anyone. The guilt a physical pain in your gut, twisting and twisting, like a hunger that never ended. The hot-faced feel of shame. And, despite everything, Red didn't want Oliver to feel that way, to feel like she did. She wouldn't wish it on anyone.

Red stepped forward, to Oliver's side, and he glanced up as the static hissed closer to his ear.

"I'm sorry, Oliver," Red said, looking down at him. "I know exactly what that feels like, that it's your fault someone died. And I—"

"It wasn't my fault." Oliver cut her off, the words rasping into empty sounds in her throat. "He hit me first. I was just defending Reyna. He hit me first. It wasn't my fault." He repeated it, like it was important she understood that. They weren't the same, she and him, and she shouldn't make that mistake again. That was what he meant. But Red hadn't even got to explain what she meant, who'd died because of her.

There was a snuffle to her right. Reyna was still crying, wiping her nose across her sleeve. She didn't look relieved that the story was over, that it was finally all out.

"How old was he?" Maddy was the next to speak, a cautious glance at her brother.

"Don't know, around our age, I guess," Oliver said.

"Twenty-two," Reyna added, a moment later.

Oliver shot a look over at her. Red stepped back so he could see, clearing the way between them.

"How do you know that?" he asked. "From the hospital? You never said before."

Reyna sucked in a deep breath, eyes side to side like there was a war going on in her head, and there she was, stuck between both sides. She blew the breath out through gritted teeth, decision made, one side chosen. Reyna blinked and looked back at Oliver, Red caught in the middle again. She backed away into the kitchen. The story wasn't finished, was it? It wasn't complete. Reyna clearly knew something Oliver did not.

"I'm sorry, Oliver," Reyna said, voice croaky and raw, a new tear dancing down the lines of her face, in and out of the other tracks. "He wasn't a random guy. I knew him."

# TWENTY-NINE

Oliver's mouth hung open, tiny movements in his lower jaw, up and down, and Red imagined she could hear it, creaking at the hinges, creating the sound out of the emptiness of the static.

Oliver still didn't say anything, so Reyna did.

"His name was Jack Harvey, not Jack Something, and I knew him," she said.

Oliver blinked, slowly, the only muscle that moved anywhere on his body.

"Why did you never tell me?" he said with a low growl, voice catching in his throat. But that wasn't the right question. "And how did you know Jack Harvey?"

There it was, the right question. Red's head flicked toward Reyna, waiting for the answer. So was everyone else: Arthur, Simon, Maddy, all looking Reyna's way, backing her into the corner by the front door with their eyes.

Reyna hugged her arms around herself, picking at the wrinkles in her sleeves.

"I knew Jack," she said, slowly, carefully, like her words might cause an explosion if she said them too hard. And, looking at Oliver's face, they just might. "Because we were together."

Simon blew out an awkward puff of air, hanging back, running his hands through his disheveled hair.

Reyna chewed her bottom lip, waiting for the explosion. But it didn't come.

"Together how?" Oliver said, overenunciating the words, sharpening the consonants.

"Together like . . ." Reyna's voice cowered, shrinking beneath an outward breath. "Please don't make me say it."

"How long?" Oliver was too calm, too still, and Red shivered, the hairs standing up across the back of her neck.

"I'd known him a couple of years." Reyna sniffed. "Met him at the bar when I went with friends."

"That's not what I asked."

Reyna shook her head. "Since September. When we went back for fall semester."

Oliver's eyes spooled in his head, working something out.

"Four months," he said, not a question. "You were with him for four months behind my back."

"I'm sorry," Reyna cried. "I shouldn't have done that to you. I know it's awful, and I'm so so sorry."

"And you're telling me now," Oliver continued, still too calm, a clouded look in his eyes, the pupils too large and beetle-dark. "In front of everyone here, in front of my little sister."

Maddy shrank in the booth.

"I'm sorry." Reyna hugged herself tighter. "I wish I could have told you at a better time, just you and me." She shook her head, strands of black clinging to her cheeks, wet with tears and sweat. "No, I wish it never happened in the first place. If I hadn't been such a coward, if I had just . . ." Her words failed, lips pressing together while she tried to get them back.

"If you had just what?" Oliver pressed, and Reyna winced, like he was pressing down on her neck.

"Broken up with you." She said it quietly, almost a whisper, staring at Oliver like there was no one else in the RV. And there wasn't, not really. Red's mind was quiet for once, watching the scene, a strange feeling in her gut. Not guilt, or shame, or hunger, it was something older. Ancient. A primal instinct telling her to keep out of Oliver's way. There was danger outside the RV, and now there was danger inside it.

A low bark of laughter from Oliver as he slapped his hand on the table, making the kitchen knife jump and the flashlight roll toward Maddy. "What?" he said, a deep smile splitting his face, crinkling the skin by his eyes. "You would have chosen *him* over me?" Another quick burst of sound from his throat, halfway between a laugh and a shout, the smile across his face twisting in at the ends, turning cruel.

"I'm sorry. I loved him," Reyna whispered, a pair of silent tears. Red backed up another step. Maybe Reyna shouldn't have said that, not right here right now, but clearly she'd been holding this in for a very long time. It only took a man with a rifle to bring it to the surface.

Oliver was still smiling. Why was he still smiling? "We've been together two and a half years," he said.

"I know," Reyna cried. "And I do care about you, Oliver. A lot. But it was different with him. It was easy."

"Easy, huh?" Still smiling. Hand resting on the table where he'd smacked it, fingers splayed, just a little too close to that sharp knife there. Red tensed.

"Different," Reyna said, with a wet sniff. "Jack didn't feel right about it, what we were doing. I told him I was going to break up with you, I said I'd do it any day now." Her breath hitched in her chest. "I didn't know we were going to his bar that day. If I had I would have tried to get us to watch the game somewhere else. I know that's not the problem here, it's me, what I did . . ." She trailed off, taking a new breath to come back stronger. "That's what he was saying to me in the parking lot. He said he'd waited long enough and I had to choose. I had to break up with you because it wasn't fair to keep doing this."

Oliver didn't speak yet, just that same smile, blinking for her to keep talking.

"And then you came out and saw us, and I panicked. It wasn't how I wanted everything to come out, with both of you there. But I knew it was the moment, whether I wanted it or not, and I had to make a decision, there and then. I had to decide. And, I don't know . . ." She wiped her nose on the other sleeve this time. "I loved Jack, I knew that, but in that moment my head was telling me he wasn't the smart choice, the practical choice, because he worked in a bar and that's all he ever wanted to do. Whereas you . . ." She paused, daring a glance at Oliver.

"I'm going to be somebody," Oliver said, showing too many teeth on that last syllable. "So what, Reyna, it was a battle between your head and your heart, was it?" he mocked her, but Reyna nodded, slowly, up and down.

"I was a coward." She bit her lip. "I made my choice and I pretended not to know him, that he was a random guy bothering me in the parking lot, like you thought. And then everything happened." Reyna winced, like she was seeing it all again, playing just below the surface of her red-raw eyes. "I couldn't find the courage to do it, to choose him. And he was so hurt after, he texted me that night, saying he couldn't believe I'd pretended not to know who he was. And then I didn't hear from him, until . . . until . . ." She didn't need to finish, they knew the rest. "He's dead, and it's my fault, because I was a coward and let it all happen."

Red shuffled, flinching as she made a rustle that drew Oliver's eyes, thinking over it all, sifting through. Reyna hadn't killed Jack, though, had she? It was Oliver who hit him, who caused the slow bleed in his brain. Neither of them meant for him to die. But no one could say Reyna was the one who'd killed him, right? She loved him, and she blamed herself, and that must be a terrible weight to carry. Almost like—

"Yes, Reyna, it is all your fault," Oliver replied after a long pause, voice clipped and flat. "It's all your fault. You made me do it."

"I didn't, I didn't . . ." Reyna puffed out her cheeks to control her staccato breath. "I'm sorry for everything. I didn't mean to hurt anyone." She looked away from Oliver, eyes skipping from Maddy to Red, as though seeing them for the first time, stepping away from that horrible dark memory into the horrible dark here and now, in this RV. "He had four brothers," she explained. "I never met them, but it could be them. He said one of them liked to hunt deer. Maybe they found our messages on his phone, wondered why I never reached out, or went to the funeral. Or maybe they suspected there was more to the story, about how he'd hurt his head, about that last message he sent me. That's the secret they want: how Jack died."

The static seemed to grow louder then, in Red's grip, even though it couldn't have. She was keeper of the voice, and did they now know whose voice it was? Waiting for them on channel three.

Oliver brought his hands together, like a crack of thunder or the clap of a rifle. Twice. Two shots. The sound burying itself inside Red's bones.

He pushed up from his booth. "Well, Reyna, you don't have to worry about *finding the courage* now." He coughed, a smile still stretched across his lips, splitting the near-red flesh into seams. "You and I are over. I could always do better than you."

She nodded. "I'm sorry, Oliver. I really am."

He brushed off her apology, looking away before she was finished. Reyna was no longer welcome on his side of the RV, in the us of *us* versus *them*. A cold shiver passed up Red's spine, even though it was hot in here now, sweat prickling by the seams of her shirt where they pressed into her armpits. The six of them cooking inside this tin can. But the shiver meant something, a realization that Red could put into words. Now there was no one left who could control Oliver. Unless Maddy . . . Red tried to catch Maddy's eyes, but she wasn't looking, picking at the loose skin by her fingernails.

"If that's why we're here"—Reyna was speaking, looking between Arthur and Simon now—"I will face the consequences. I'll tell him what happened, what I did. I'll end this."

"Oh no you won't," Oliver snapped. The smile was gone now, but his mouth wouldn't close, hanging open between words. Pupils still too large in his once-golden-brown eyes. "You're not the one who hit him, I am. If they're looking for a killer, then it's me they're looking for, not you. And I'm not dying because you decided to fuck a bartender, Reyna." A globule of spit flew out with her name. He pointed at the walkie-talkie in Red's hands. "We're not telling him anything. This is your fault, Reyna, no one else's. If anyone should have to walk out of this RV it should be you. But I am not, are you listening?! We don't tell them a thing."

"We have to," Reyna said, a quake in her lower lip. She bit down on it. "It's the right thing to do, tell him what he wants to know. He said he'd let the others go. He might let us go too, if he knows it was all an accident, that Jack wasn't supposed to die."

"I don't know," Simon said, uncertainly. "He killed Don and Joyce out there for nothing. I don't think he's the forgiving type."

"No," Oliver growled. He moved past Red, toward the kitchen, glancing at the timer on the oven. "It's three-forty-five now. We are going to sit here until sunrise, until six a.m., and then his game is over. That's what we're going to do."

"I can't, Oliver," Reyna said, keeping her tone steady, treading around the explosion again. "Someone might get shot. I can't live with that. Red, can you pass me the walkie-talkie, please?"

"No, Red," Oliver barked. "Give me the walkie-talkie." He stretched out his hand, open and waiting.

Red looked, from Reyna to Oliver, the walkie-talkie hissing in her cupped hands, like a coiled snake, like a warning.

Here she was again, standing in the middle of them, trapped in both lines of sight. She clutched the walkie-talkie to her chest.

"Red, don't be an idiot," Oliver hissed, trying to lower his voice. "Give me the walkie-talkie. I'm in charge here. You know me. You don't know Reyna. None of us do, apparently."

"Red, please." Reyna's voice in her other ear. "I'm trying to do the right thing. To save us."

Red's eyes jumped to Maddy's, but there were no answers for her there, only fear, widening, widening.

"Red?"

"Red?"

Left or right.

Move or don't move.

Reyna or Oliver.

# THIRTY

"Red?"

Oliver's eyes burned into hers, past them, into the unknowable things behind, like he could see her thoughts racing back and forth, trying to pull them his way.

The static from the speakers fizzed against her too-tight fingers, tongue pressed against the back of her teeth.

Which one?

She had to choose one of them. Had to make a decision, now, down to her. Two outstretched hands, waiting. Reyna or Oliver?

Red's heart thudded against her ribs, trying to break free, to take no part in this. Red had known Oliver forever, he was right about that. And she'd chosen him once already, four hours ago, coming back to the RV when her gut and her mom told her to run. Should she have run? Where would she be by now? Would Don and Joyce still be alive?

"Red!" Oliver shouted, impatient now, flexing his fingers and taking one step toward her.

The hairs stood up on the back of her neck and her gut told her to move, to peel away from him because there was danger behind his eyes. And this time, Red listened to it. She backed up, eyes still on Oliver, moving two steps toward Reyna by the front door. Quickly, before she could regret it, or double- or triple-think it, she turned on her heels and pushed the walkie-talkie into Reyna's warm hand.

Reyna's fingers closed over it, catching Red's for a moment. A shared blink.

"No!" Oliver barked, charging forward, the RV juddering with his heavy steps.

Arthur darted into Oliver's path, his body blocking them from him, a line of sweat rolling down his temple.

"Stop," he said, voice spiking, his mouth grim and tense as he held one hand up to Oliver's shoulder, pushed against it. "It's Reyna's decision if she wants to tell."

Simon hurried over too, joining the barricade beside Arthur, arm to arm. The Lavoys on one side of the RV, Reyna and Red by the door, Simon and Arthur in the middle. Maddy had gotten to her feet now, watching, chewing anxiously at her thumb.

"It's not!" Oliver stopped in his tracks, spraying the words into Arthur's face. "It's my decision. I'm in charge here. I don't care what Reyna tells him, I am not leaving this RV! No one is leaving this RV!"

A flutter in his voice, hidden just beneath the rage. He was frightened, wasn't he? That was what this was. Underneath those too-wide shoulders and golden-brown eyes, and red-flushed skin, Oliver was scared. By the time it reached the surface, though, it had twisted itself into anger, for cover.

"We have to do what he wants," Reyna called across the barricade. "There's no other way."

"Don't you dare tell him, Reyna!" Oliver shouted back, peering through the gap between Simon's and Arthur's heads. "Don't you dare tell him what I did."

The barricade jostled back as Oliver pushed against them.

Reyna sucked in a deep breath and let it out, the air playing through Red's tied-back hair. She raised the walkie-talkie to her lips and held down the button.

The static cut out.

"Hello?" Reyna said, the word shaking only at the edges.

Static.

"Hello," the voice crackled from the speaker. "I'm here."

Static.

"Reyna, don't you fucking dare!"

"It's Reyna Flores-Serrano," she said, holding down the button, pressing her eyes shut. "I think I have the secret that you're look-ing for."

Static.

"You do, do you?" the voice hissed, dark and deep, giving nothing away. "Let's hear it, then."

"Reyna!"

Arthur dug his heels into the floor as Oliver pushed against him.

"Oliver, stop!" Simon said from the struggle.

"It's about what happened to Jack Harvey, in Hanover, in Janu-ary," Reyna said, her chin bunched and trembling, eyes still closed. "How he died."

Static as she let go of the button, eyes flickering open, backing away against the door as she looked up and saw Oliver's face, the silent threat in his eyes.

The static stretched on and on. Universes bloomed and died in the seconds they waited, listening to the empty hiss. Red willed the voice to come, like she had countless times before, different voice, different reason, but it never worked before either.

"Come on," Simon said, daring a glance back, eyes focusing on the walkie-talkie in Reyna's grip.

A crackle.

The static died.

Silence. It felt strange in Red's ears, after all this time.

"Sounds like a touching story," the voice said. He cleared his throat. "But it's not the one I'm looking for."

A gasp. From Maddy; Red knew without looking.

Reyna's eyes darkened, shadows cast by her eyebrows drawing together, lines of confusion across her forehead. "What?" she whispered to herself, staring down at the walkie-talkie, hissing again.

The struggle in the middle of the RV stopped, Oliver pulling back, straightening up, a new look rearranging his face, red patches slowly receding under his collar. His eyes did the opposite: they lightened.

"It's not about that," he said, voice almost returned to normal, croaking only on the lowest notes. "It's not about what we did, what happened. It's not about me." And as he said that last part, the smile was back playing across his face. Not cruel this time, just unapologetic and there, he didn't try to hide it. He didn't have to be afraid anymore.

The barricade broke apart. Arthur bent forward, breathing hard, wiping the sweat from his hands against the front of his jeans. Simon stretched up, burying both hands in the mess of his dark hair as he said, "Fuck me," followed by a low whistle.

"Not about what happened to Jack?" Reyna said, her voice climbing up at the end, but it wasn't really a question, not one that needed an answer. She couldn't believe it, that was why. She had been so sure; Red could tell by her eyes, by the fall of her mouth.

"It's not about me or Reyna," Oliver said through the smile, turning to look at Arthur, Simon and Red in turn. "We aren't the ones with the secret. It's one of you."

The breath caught in Red's narrowing throat as she studied Oliver's smile. Was the RV getting smaller around them, tighter? It was supposed to be thirty-one feet but they'd never measured. What if it was twenty-nine and shrinking? Oh no, Oliver was watching her as she looked around. It couldn't be her. She had one secret, but no one knew about it, that was the entire point. She didn't even want to think it, in case Oliver could somehow read it in her eyes. Not him. Especially not him.

Simon shuffled, and Arthur hid his hands in his front pockets, glancing up at the ceiling. Was the RV shrinking around him too? Squeezing them all together. Too hot. Too stuffy.

Reyna handed the walkie-talkie back to Red, the weight of it against her skin a small comfort, until the static cut out again.

"I'm starting to lose my patience." The voice crackled back into life. "I have twenty-four more rounds with me." He paused, let that number sink in. It did, sinking right into Red's gut, where it churned with that other, yawning feeling. Twenty-four. Four deadly holes in each and every one of them. "If I don't get my answers soon, I will start shooting at the RV randomly."

Static.

*Crack.*

The microwave exploded.

Maddy screamed.

Simon dropped.

Glass rained down, sparks flashing around the new hole in the back of the machine, a glimpse through into the night beyond.

There was a matching hole in the bathroom wall. Walls, metal, plastic, glass, it went through them all, in less time than it took for Red to blink, to flinch and hold her hands up to her ears, the walkie-talkie hitting the side of her head.

"There's one," the voice said, whispering right into Red's ear. The next second, it refilled with static.

"Fuck!" Simon said, pushing himself up from the floor, brushing off his legs. Patting his chest like he was checking for holes. But he wasn't in its path, none of them were. Oliver had been the closest, and the shot had taken something from him: his smile.

*Crack.*

Red's hands were ready by her ears.

A splintered hole lower than the last shot, in the wall just above the stove, a few inches closer to where the six of them stood. Oliver darted away, knocking into Arthur as he did, the RV shuddering with his feet. He came to stand by Maddy at the dining table, one hand on her shoulder.

"We should take cover!" he yelled.

"Where?" Simon shouted back. "There is no cover. The bullets go through everything!"

Simon was right; there was nowhere to hide. The RV wasn't a shield, it wasn't safety, it was only an illusion, a false barrier between here and the red dot outside. A hot tin can, shrinking, filling with holes. The night punching new eyes through the walls to watch them squirm.

"There's two," the voice hissed, so close to Red's face, it was as though she could feel his breath, blowing through the speaker.

He had twenty-two more bullets to go, how long until one of them found flesh and bone and worse?

"Give me what I want," the voice continued, Red holding it up for the others to hear. "You're getting closer. Yes, this is about someone who died. Someone who was killed, in Philadelphia. You know who you are."

Static.

Red lowered the walkie-talkie, glancing across at the other side of the RV, catching Maddy's eye. They held on for two long seconds. There was something new there, a strange shift in Maddy's eyelids, a glaze like panic across them. A look Red didn't recognize, and she knew all of Maddy's faces. What was wrong? Red tried to decipher it, but Oliver interrupted her.

"Someone who was killed, in Philadelphia," he said, repeating the sniper word-for-word.

Definitely not Red then. She had never killed anyone, not unless you counted her mom, and Red wasn't sure people would. It was her fault, yes, all her fault, and she was the one who carried the guilt, but she hadn't been the one carrying the gun, the one who made her get down on her knees. Two shots to the back of the head.

Simon was shaking his head, running his hands over his torso like he was still checking for holes. Arthur's hands were in his pockets again, or maybe they'd never left. Red wasn't the only one looking; Oliver was studying them too.

"Anything to do with your uncle, Simon?" Oliver asked, pointedly. "He lives in Philly too, right, he ever killed anyone?"

"No." Simon shook his head even harder. "He's not like that. And if he has, I don't know anything about it, it's not my secret. I swear," he said, doubling down on those final two words.

Reyna shifted behind Red and the RV creaked with her weight. A creak, not so different from that muted crack, and Red's hands were ready, halfway to her ears. But it wasn't, not this time. She looked around, at the cockpit, the dining table, the sofa bed, and it didn't matter that Maddy also slept on the left because neither of them would ever sleep on it, the kitchen with the destroyed microwave, the punctures in the bathroom wall. How could she stand here, stand it, knowing that that crack could come any time, and there would be another gaping hole, through the walls, the furniture, her stomach? Blood was red and so was she. The color of her mom's favorite coat, though Red had never worn that one to bed in winter; she couldn't get close to it, in case she took the smell out of it and replaced it with her own. And, anyway, why was Maddy still looking at her like that?

"Arthur." Oliver turned to him instead, narrowing his eyes, the pupils grown too large again, dark and unnatural. "You're the newest here, aren't you?" He didn't wait for him to answer. "Maddy, how long have you known Arthur?"

Maddy jumped at the sound of her own name, finally blinking away that look. "Oh, um," she said, glancing awkwardly across at Arthur. "Maybe six or seven months. Since the start of senior year."

Why was she answering, why was she helping Oliver? Couldn't she recognize the danger back in his eyes? Didn't she feel it up the back of her neck?

"But you go to a different school, right?" Oliver directed the question back at Arthur.

"Right," Arthur said, removing his hands from his pockets, crossing them in front of his chest, the drawn YES/NO boxes visible on the back of one hand, Red's shaky check mark.

Oliver stepped toward him. "You don't like your friends at your own school, then? Or they don't like you? Why is that?"

"I—I," Arthur stuttered. "It's not like that. I have friends. Simon happens to be one of them. And Maddy. And Red."

He said her name last, but there was her mark, right there on his skin, bones rippling beneath it as he tensed.

"What are you doing, Oliver?" Reyna asked.

He ignored her.

"But you live in Philly too." Oliver took another step toward Arthur. "And you're the person here that everyone knows the least. Maddy's been friends with Red since they were born, and Simon since middle school."

"So?" Arthur said, taking a step back as Oliver kept coming, prowling toward him.

"So, are you the one with the secret?" Oliver pulled up, right in front of him, their noses too close.

"No," Arthur said, raising one finger to push his glasses back up.

"Come on, stop wasting time!" Oliver slapped a hand down on the kitchen counter beside him and then he charged, wrapping his hands in Arthur's shirt, driving him backward. "He could start shooting again any second! What's the secret? Who died?!"

"I don't know!" Arthur shouted back, trying to wrestle his arms inside Oliver's grip as they slammed back against the refrigerator door.

"Oliver!" Simon darted forward, trying to pull Oliver away, but he was too weak and Oliver's shoulders too wide. "Can we please remember who the real enemy is?" he pleaded, voice breaking. "The guy outside with the fucking rifle. Not any of us."

"Have you ever hit someone with your car and driven away?" Oliver shouted into Arthur's face, those puppet strings under his skin again, at the back of his exposed neck.

"No!" Arthur said, struggling against Oliver's iron grip.

"Sold drugs to someone? Did someone overdose?"

"No, I've never hurt anyone!"

Arthur bucked, kicking against the refrigerator, pushing away.

Oliver was stronger, shoved him back, forearm pressed against Arthur's neck.

"I'm not like that!" Arthur rasped, the wind knocked out of his chest, trapped in his pinned-down throat.

"Oliver, stop it!" Reyna screamed. But didn't she know? She couldn't control him anymore, no one could. He was loose and he was wild.

"Someone was killed, in Philadelphia!" Oliver roared in his face. "You must know."

"OLIVER!"

That was Maddy. He didn't listen to her either.

"It's not me, we just learned that!" Oliver continued, pressing harder. Arthur's face was turning red. "It's not what me and Reyna did. And it's not about the Frank Gotti case, so it's nothing to do with me or Maddy!"

Arthur's eyes darted across to Red, strained and in pain as he struggled against Oliver's grip. She had to help him.

"Oliver, leave him alone!" Red shouted, daring to move forward. It was useless, Oliver wasn't listening, too focused on Arthur's face, inches from his.

"Just tell me what it is!" Oliver spat. "I am not dying in this fucking RV!"

"M-my br-brother," Arthur managed to hiss, raspy and weak.

"Your brother? Your brother fucking what?"

Arthur looked at Red again, wide and desperate.

Red needed to help him. And they had that deal, remember, the one Arthur didn't know about; that he didn't have to talk about his brother if she didn't have to talk about her mom. Except, for some reason, her mom wouldn't leave her alone tonight.

Oliver's free hand was at his side, fingers balling into a fist, then flexing out. No. *Nonono.* They'd just heard what happened after Oliver punched that Jack. Jack might have hit him first, but Oliver hit him harder and that was all it took. A fatal bleed on the brain. Oliver wasn't going to hit Arthur, was he? Then why was his thumb tucking itself under his fingers, forming a fist that stayed?

No, Red couldn't let him. But what could she do? Oliver was the strongest, the natural leader, the highest-value. Red didn't have the secret. This wasn't about what happened to Jack Harvey, or the Frank Gotti case, which she knew forward and back, Oliver had just said that. It wasn't. The voice had confirmed it: Maddy and Oliver weren't being held hostage for the name of the witness. So what could she do?

But that clue: someone who was killed, in Philadelphia. That fit two people Red knew of. Her mom, killed on her knees five years ago in an abandoned power station. Two shots to the back of the head. And the other, more recent, was . . . unless . . . unless this whole setup wasn't about getting the name, like Oliver had initially thought, holding him and Maddy as hostages. What if they already had the name? No, it couldn't be, that was the whole point, but it wasn't impossible, was it? Oliver said it happened all the time. Which meant that—

"Oliver, stop!" Simon pulled at his shirt. "You're choking him!"

Red had to help Arthur, she had to, his breath now wheezing through his throat in a terrifying low whistle, Oliver's fist raising by his side. Red had to help, and now she knew how. They already had the name, didn't they? That was it. Why hadn't she realized sooner? Why had she blindly followed what Oliver said? Maybe she had realized, part of her, and she'd only wanted to keep it, like Oliver had with his secret. Of course. She knew it now, cold and inevitable. This was all about her. About the plan. If she gave it up now, she'd lose it all, wouldn't she? But she had to help Arthur.

"Stop!" Red screamed, the sound tearing at her throat. "Oliver, leave him! It's me!"

Oliver pulled back slightly, releasing Arthur's throat. His head whipped over his shoulder and he stared at Red. "What did you say?" he demanded.

Arthur coughed, bending over as Oliver finally let go, stepping away from him.

Red looked up and breathed out. "I'm the one with the secret."

4:00 A.M.

# THIRTY-ONE

Red blinked.

Her heart was in her throat, grotesque and swelling, cutting off her airway as she watched Oliver turn to face her, his chest rising and falling. Arthur was still bent double behind, coughing into his hands.

"What did you say?" Oliver asked her again, and she could feel his eyes boring into hers, an almost physical sensation. She didn't like it, him looking at her like that, it might leave a mark.

"I have the secret. It's me," she said, voice almost failing her.

Everyone else was watching her too, Red checked around the RV. There was a look of shock in Maddy's eyes. Wait, was it shock, or that same strange look from before?

The static fizzed in her hands, and Red hugged the walkie-talkie to her chest, purring against her empty rib cage because her heart was still climbing, in her ears now.

She had to give it up.

"Well, what is it?" Oliver spat, puppet strings pulling his head to one side, hanging askew on his neck.

"You okay?" Simon spoke across him, patting Arthur on the back as he finally straightened up.

"Fine," Arthur said, brushing Simon off to look at Red. A question in his eyes, the same as in everyone else's.

"Well?" Oliver took a step forward. "What is it?"

"R-Red?" Maddy said tentatively, tripping over the word.

Red exhaled. Her heart had moved out the top of her head now, somewhere loose in the RV, fleeing from that look on Oliver's face.

"It's me," she said, framing each word carefully, choosing the right ones. "I'm the witness." She paused. "The protected witness, in the Frank Gotti case."

Oliver's eyes snapped open, first shock, then disbelief. "No." He shook his head. "It can't be you."

And how much easier it would be to agree with him. But Red couldn't.

"It is me," she said, treading carefully, like Reyna had before, tiptoeing around the landmines in Oliver's eyes. "I'm the witness in the case." She took one more breath and began. "I was walking in this little park on the waterfront, Washington Avenue Green. This was last August, August twenty-eighth. It was nine o'clock in the evening, not quite dark yet, but getting there. I was walking to the bus stop on Columbus Boulevard, I'd been at the Staples nearby for school supplies earlier. I decided to go through the park rather than walk on the road. It's nicer there."

Red paused, but she didn't need to. Words rehearsed so many times, over and over, she didn't even need to think about them. They followed each other out of her mouth, in their prearranged order, just like in her statements. The way she would have said it all at the pretrial conference in two weeks, and at the trial. She was ready. Keep her face straight and her story straight. All the details.

"I was on the path, going past the back of the industrial complex there. The map says it's for sheet-metal workers," she said. "I didn't know that then, though. There was no one else around at that time, just me. And then . . ." Red did need to pause here, checking that the others were listening, that Oliver hadn't crept any closer while she'd been talking. "I heard two gunshots. One right after the other. *One-two.* It was close by, though. Real close. Somewhere out the back of the parking lot there, near the dumpsters. I didn't want to run in case they started shooting at me too, so I hid in one of the bushes by the path. And I waited."

Red swallowed.

"Keep going," Oliver said, like she needed his permission to continue and he was giving it.

"I heard footsteps on the pavement, and I looked up and I saw him. He didn't see me, but he walked right by me. A white man in his fifties. Dark curly hair. Long, tan coat, even though it was warm out. I later identified him from photographs. It was Frank Gotti," Red said. "Definitely him. There was no one else around after the gun went off. I left about ten minutes later, once I was sure he was gone. Tried to forget about it. But I called in to the police station a couple days later, after I heard about the body they found there that evening. Joseph Mannino. Shot twice in the back of the head. I should have called it in earlier, but I didn't know anyone got shot until it was on the news. I heard Frank Gotti kill him, saw him leaving the scene. I'm that witness."

She finished, daring a glance up at the others. Arthur was looking down, chewing his lower lip with a small shake of the head, like he couldn't believe it. Oliver was staring right at her, Red could feel it; she tried to avoid his gaze, to not fall into that trap. Reyna was watching, tears gone now, a small sympathetic stretch in her mouth, not a smile, but on the way there. Simon puffed his cheeks, blowing out a mouthful of air, not meeting Red's eye. Why wouldn't he look at her, avoiding her gaze like she was avoiding Oliver's? Maddy was behind; Red couldn't see her, so Maddy couldn't see her either and that was lucky. It was half the story, half the plan. But the only half they needed to know. Red couldn't say the rest, not here, right in front of them.

"Why did you never tell me?" Maddy croaked, and now Red spun to look at her, over by the table. Just five feet between them, but it felt longer somehow, different sides of the RV.

"I wasn't allowed to, Maddy," Red said, shrugging one shoulder, just one. "Full anonymity for my agreement to testify in court. I had to sign a lot of paperwork. It was for my own safety, they said. No one knows, that's the whole point. Not even my dad." Red had turned eighteen in the first week of September, when this was all starting. She was an adult in the eyes of the law now, she didn't need to tell him. Not that she was sure it would have registered, anyway. Nothing did anymore, hardly noticing whether she was coming or going, home or not. Maybe he didn't even notice the cold inside their house in winter.

Oliver cleared his throat, eyes back and forth like he was working through her story, sifting through the details. He was prelaw, didn't you know? "Why were you at that Staples?" he asked. "There's one closer to where we live."

Red had been prepared for any question about her testimony, including that, running through them like drills, memorizing her responses so she could make them look natural on the stand.

"Sometimes I go to the waterfront, by the piers," she said, clearing her throat, pausing in the appropriate place. "Because it's close to where my m . . ." She breathed, and that wasn't part of the act; it still hurt to say, guilt churning in her gut beside the fear and dread. "Where my mom died."

No one reacted, faces blank as a favor to Red. No one except Maddy, a rustle as she fidgeted somewhere behind, an outward breath that almost sounded like a sigh. Maybe Red was banned from saying the word too. Sorry.

Oliver raised his head, another question forming on his lips. "What are the chances that it was you, you're the lead witness for the prosecution, and our mom is the lead prosecutor?" Except it wasn't a question, not one Red knew how to answer at least.

"Oliver," Maddy said, stepping forward, voice stronger now. "Don't you see? That's probably why Mom fought so hard to have this case, to make sure it wasn't tried in federal court. It was so she could protect Red. Make sure her name was kept out of all court documents, that she was completely anonymous. She would have wanted to be in charge of all that, for Red."

Maddy was right, her mom had done all that. Red had met with Catherine Lavoy many times over the past six months, not as Red and her best friend's mom, or her dead mom's best friend, but as assistant district attorney and her lead eyewitness in an upcoming case, going over the facts and Red's testimony, practicing for trial. She was safe, Catherine would tell her. Her name would never get out, she promised. Except now it was, promise or not.

Oliver nodded, seeing the sense in what Maddy had just said. "Yes," he said, just to confirm it. "Yes, she would have wanted that. To keep Red safe, anonymous. Make sure no one ever found out who you were. Except"—he paused, a wayward muscle ticking in his cheek—"someone *has* found out who you are. They know you're the witness. That's what all this is about." He gestured his arms around the RV, rolling those too-wide shoulders. Red followed his fingers as he traced them in the air, pointing to the bullet holes in the walls and furniture. "I said—right at the start, didn't I?—that this had organized crime written all over it. This is what they do." He stood still for a moment, staring right at her, through her. "They're here to kill you, to make sure you can't testify at the trial."

Simon gasped, maybe not at what Oliver was saying but that he'd said it at all. But Red knew Oliver was right, the rest of them must as well. The man out there with the rifle knew who she was. And that little red dot, it was meant for her, always meant for her.

"Oliver," Reyna hissed, trying to tell him something with her eyes, but Oliver blinked and looked away from her, back at Red.

"Why didn't you say all this three hours ago, when the sniper told us he knew who we were, that he was looking for a secret?" His eyes darkened, and Red's heart reacted like there was a direct link between them, cause and effect, kicking up in her chest. "You must have known he was talking about you."

But she hadn't, and that was the truth. She hadn't because she'd listened to Oliver once again, over her own gut.

"No," Red said, taking one step back, away from Oliver, toward Maddy. "I didn't. I didn't think there was any way they knew I was the witness. Your mom told me no one could find out my name or any identifying factors, that was the whole point. And then you confused me." Red shook her head. "You said they were holding you and Maddy hostage to get the name from your mom. And I thought you must be right, and obviously I didn't want them to get the name because then they'd know it was me, so I went along with your escape plans. I was wrong, but so were you."

It happened in half a breath, in one flicker of static hissing in her hands. Oliver switched, flipped, face changing around those overbearing eyes. Hard edges and all teeth.

"You should have told us at the start!" he roared, pointing two fingers toward her, like a gun made from the flesh and bone of his hand.

"You knew this was about you. You kept it to yourself, kept us here hours longer than we needed to be! Selfish, Red! Stupid. Those two people out there."

Red bet he'd already forgotten their names.

"They're dead and it's your fault!" Spit flew from his mouth. "You could have ended this hours ago!"

No, not more guilt, Red couldn't carry any more. She'd begged Oliver not to pass that note to Joyce and Don. It was him, not her. Please say it wasn't her.

"You didn't tell your secret back then either," Arthur said, rough and jagged. Was he angry, or was that from Oliver pressing against his throat? "It could have been about you and you held on to it, you and Reyna. You only spoke up when Reyna forced you to."

"Shut the fuck up!" Oliver said, not taking his eyes off Red, trapping her there in his gaze. She shouldn't have looked back, now she was stuck, legs melding into the ground.

"If you die, Frank Gotti walks," Oliver said, voice lower, but the threat was still there, recharging. "That's what they want. They're here to kill you."

"She knows that, Oliver," Simon said, staring at the back of his head. "You don't have to keep saying it."

Oliver blinked and Red moved another step back, closing the gap between her and Maddy. The RV wasn't safety, but Maddy Lavoy was. Maddy looked after her, just like Catherine. Paid for Red's lunch sometimes when she couldn't, though Red had never asked her to. Helped her look for things when she lost them, kept reminders like a walking, talking to-do list. Organized this whole trip so Red could afford to come on spring break. Maddy cared.

"Red," Oliver said, turning her name ugly in his mouth, full of hard edges. "You have to leave the RV."

No one said anything for two seconds, only the empty fizzing static that had made its home in Red's head.

"What?!" Maddy shrieked, voice right behind her, cutting through. "Oliver, what are you talking about?"

"She has to leave the RV!" Oliver looked over at his sister, like Red was already gone and it wasn't up for discussion. "They want her. She's putting the rest of us in danger by staying here. Look. He's going to keep shooting up the RV until he gets what he wants. Some of us will get hit. Some of us will die if we continue. We need to give him what he wants, and he wants Red!"

"No!" Arthur roared now, voice dark and dangerous to match Oliver's. He stretched up to his full height, raised his chin to look Oliver in the eye. "Red is not leaving the RV."

"You can't be serious," Simon was saying. "He'll kill her!"

Oliver didn't answer Simon, instead looking at Red like she was the one who'd spoken. Her heart was fast in her chest, too fast, it knew what was coming and so did she, both unraveling at their seams. She didn't want to die. She wasn't ready. And, oh god, she'd know it was coming, just like her mom did, lifetimes of regret and guilt and anger and hate in those last few seconds of life. No one's world would fall apart without her, though, at least that was one good thing. Would it hurt, or would it feel like relief, when the bullet finally split her open? What should her final thought be? Please, not about the fucking pattern in those fucking curtains, why couldn't she let that go? She was supposed to be thinking about dying, for fuck's sake. She didn't want to die. No, this couldn't be happening. Maddy, help.

"You must have known," Oliver was saying, voice strange and unsteady like he was trying to control it, trying to be reasonable when reason had gone out the window hours ago. His eyes betrayed him, though, wild and overfocused. "On some level. You must have known this was a possibility when you agreed to testify, Red. I mean, this is the Philly mob we're talking about, what did you think was going to happen?"

Not this, never this. No one was ever supposed to find out her name, Catherine told her that.

"But she didn't do anything wrong," Simon said, backing up to stand closer to Red. "She just saw a man leaving a crime scene, she shouldn't have to die for that." His arms tensed at his sides, the Eagles logo on the back of his shirt rippling, mouth opening and closing like it was whispering silent nothings to Red. "I mean, Oliver, you actually *killed* someone and you weren't prepared to leave the RV."

"This doesn't concern you, Simon," Oliver said, darkly, trying even harder to mask it.

"Yes it does!" Simon raised his voice. "It concerns every single one of us. 'No one is leaving this RV,' that's what you said, back when you thought it was your secret they wanted. I see the rules are different for you, then! We're not kicking Red out!"

"Do you want to die?" Oliver let his eyes fall on Simon, and Simon shrank under their weight.

"No one wants to die, that's my point," Simon answered, trying to push back.

"She's not going anywhere," Arthur said, flanking Oliver from the other side, glasses flashing under the lights.

Oliver ignored them both, turning back to Red. "Red, listen to me," he said, softening his voice, but it wasn't soft at all, it was stiff, barbs and thorns at the end of his words. "You need to accept what's happening here. There's nothing the rest of us can do. You know it, don't you, you know you have to leave the RV to save the rest of us.

To protect Maddy. She's your best friend, isn't she? You've known each other all your lives. Save her." His chin moved up and down with those final two words, drilling them home.

"Oliver, no!" Maddy cried. "Stop it, please. Just stop."

"You're all thinking it too." Oliver cast his eyes at all of them, skipping over Red because she didn't matter anymore. There were still two sides to the RV, but this time it was Red against everyone else. A team of one. "Don't pretend. None of us want to die."

"None of us want to throw Red out," Arthur said in answer, and he must have learned it from Oliver, sharpening his words to a point. Oliver even winced, took one step away.

"I know you're all protesting because you have to in front of Red," he said. "Because you care about her." His eyes spun, another circuit of the RV. "That's why we're going to put it to a vote. A blind ballot, so you can vote whichever way you want and no one else will ever know."

The air had grown thorns now too, infected by Oliver's words, pricking at Red's skin, stabbing at the surface of her eyes. It wasn't warm now, it was hot, sweat pooling along the line of her lip, but there was a chill at the back of her neck, hairs rising. She didn't want to die. She didn't want to die.

"A vote?" Reyna asked, shattering the silence, eyebrows pulling together across her forehead.

The static hissed, retreating into Red's cupped hands.

Oliver nodded, just once, that was enough. "A vote on whether Red stays, or she goes."

# THIRTY-TWO

Vote.

Red's mind did that thing again, a word so simple and mundane, yet it lost all its meaning on the trip across her head, unrecognizable out the other side, warped and misshapen. How did you even say it again? What did it mean? Did it rhyme with *note,* and *wrote,* and *quote*? All silly little words, when you thought about them, because thinking about them was easier than thinking about what this vote meant.

"No." Arthur shook his head, teeth bared in horror. "We're not doing that. We're not voting on whether Red gets to live or die. Are you sick?"

"It's the fairest way," Oliver brushed him off. "That's how democracy works, how law and justice work. We each get a vote and the majority wins. That's fair."

Was that fair? Maybe Red's understanding of it was skewed, because it didn't seem fair at all, her life in the hands of five other people. But when had life ever been fair to her, why should death be any different?

"We can't do this," Reyna said quietly, hands disappearing up her sleeves. "This can't be real. We can't do this."

"Does Red stay, or does she go?" Oliver reiterated, setting the rules, the boundaries, the two sides. Stay or go, but really he should have phrased it as *Does Red stay, or does she die?* because that was what they were deciding here, wasn't it? If she left the RV, that red dot was going to find her and she was going to die. That man outside with the rifle was here to kill her, kill her to stop her from testifying. The plan wasn't worth all this after all, was it?

"And you'll listen?" Reyna asked Oliver, her eyes sharpening as they met his. "You'll respect the results of the vote? That's the only way it's fair."

"Obviously," Oliver spat, scrunching his face. "That's the reason we're voting, Reyna." He said her name differently now, cold, doubtful, like it was only half remembered.

"Does Red get a vote?" Maddy asked, her voice thick as she held back tears. Red knew that voice, knew all of Maddy's voices, but still not that strange look in her eyes from before.

"Of course Red doesn't get a vote." He shook his head, like that would be ridiculous.

"I'm not doing this." Arthur folded his arms, gaze hard and disbelieving as he shot it at the back of Oliver's head. "I'm not."

"Then you forfeit your vote," Oliver said without looking back at him. "Maddy." He snapped his fingers in her direction. "Do you have any more pens?"

"Um, yeah, I do," she said, wiping her nose as she forced her feet back toward the dining table and the booth. Her purse was tucked just underneath the table, where she'd been sitting when she and Red played Twenty Questions a hundred lifetimes ago. Maddy bent down and rustled inside. She came back up with four ballpoint pens clenched in her hand. She dropped them down, plastic scattering over plastic, beside the pen already on the table. "Five," she said, the word hollow in her mouth.

"Good, well done, Maddy," he said, stifling a yawn with his fist.

"This is crazy," Simon was saying to himself. "This is crazy."

Red hugged the walkie-talkie to her chest, the vibrations of the static working against her hummingbird heart as Oliver approached.

"Red, you go stand in the kitchen," he said, giving her a push on the shoulder. "You can't see anyone's papers while they're voting."

Of course not, that wouldn't be *fair*, would it? But she did, she moved, her legs following Oliver's instruction before her mind had fully agreed to it.

She passed Simon and Reyna on the way to the kitchen counter, gliding past their downcast eyes. She already felt separate, somehow, her against them, even though it was Oliver splitting the RV up, no one else. She passed Arthur and he didn't avoid her, he returned the frightened look in her eyes.

Her back to the group, Red placed the walkie-talkie down on the counter, its ridges and edges imprinted in her right hand forever, lines and grooves alongside the ones already there. Should she keep going, all the way into the back bedroom to scream into the pillow again? She wasn't sure she could, anyway, this was beyond screaming. This wasn't real.

She spun on her heels slowly, closing her eyes so she could pretend she was anywhere but here. Anywhere was better than this RV. Even at the funeral, Catherine Lavoy's hard grip on her shoulder, bones shattering under the volley of rifle fire, the sad, high notes of the bagpipes. Or under her comforter, all the way under, pajamas, sweater, and a coat, gloves and three pairs of socks, and still somehow cold. Her cheeks weren't, though, because she was crying, cursing her mom for leaving them and letting the world fall apart without her. Cursing herself because, actually, Mom wouldn't be dead without her. It was Red's fault. She broke the world, she took her mom out of it, and didn't know how to put it all back after. What would Mom say to her now? Mom used to fix everything; found Red's keys when she lost them, pulled those silly faces in the mirror to make her snort on a bad morning. Red could almost hear her voice now, the way she leaned into the word *sweetie,* warm and bright, but she pushed it away under the static of all those bad memories. Everything came back to Mom somehow, but Red couldn't drag her into this, she didn't belong. Mom was dead. And now the others were going to decide if Red would die too.

Something touched her floating hand, in the darkness of the backs of her eyelids, the yellow glow of the overhead lights fighting through. Skin, fingers, intertwining through hers. Red opened her eyes, blinking in the new light, and there was Arthur. Not Mom.

Arthur's hand gripped around hers, scribbled checkboxes on his skin to match the ones on hers. Checked and unchecked. Things left undone and unsaid. She was never going to get around to calling AT&T, was she?

"Okay," Oliver said, ripping a fresh sheet of paper free from the pad on the table. He folded it in half, then into quarters, then eighths, pressing his nail along the folds. He opened the page back out and started tearing the paper along the guided lines. An awful sound. "We each get a piece of paper and a pen," he said, concentrating on ripping the pieces. "If you vote for Red to leave the RV, you write *YES* on your paper, okay?" He glanced up to check everyone was listening, eyes stalling as they fell on Red's and Arthur's hands, still holding on. He cleared his throat. "And if you vote for Red to stay in the RV, write *NO* on your paper. Does everyone understand?"

No one answered.

"*YES* to leave, *NO* to stay."

*NO* to live, *YES* to die.

Oliver scooped up five of the small rectangles of lined paper in one hand, the pens in the other. He offered them first to Maddy. She took them, paper fluttering in her grip. Her legs were shaking too, Red noticed, as Maddy slid herself down into the booth.

Oliver handed a pen and paper to Simon next, pointing him toward the front of the RV, in the cockpit.

"We need to stand away from each other, so no one can see how you're voting. By the door, Reyna," Oliver said, dropping the pen and paper above her hand, making sure his skin didn't touch hers. They both fell to the floor, the pen with a small clatter, the paper floating featherlight through the air. Reyna grabbed them both and straightened up.

"Arthur?" Oliver said, holding out Arthur's blank piece of paper and his pen. "Are you voting or not?"

Another glance down at their entwined hands.

There was a twitch in Arthur's cheek, his eyes spinning around the RV, pausing on each person. Was he trying to work out the way everyone would vote, counting them up, the *for*s and the *against*s? Whether his vote was needed?

His hand disentangled from Red's, wet with both their sweat, and he reached out, removing the pen and paper from Oliver's palm.

"Over there." Oliver pointed Arthur toward the sofa bed.

Arthur walked away, dropping down heavily onto the sofa, staring down at the tiny, blank rectangle of paper.

"Excuse me, Red," Oliver said, pushing her out of his way as he bent to open the second drawer down under the counter. He pulled out a cereal bowl, swirling blue-and-white patterns, and pushed the drawer shut with his knee.

"Okay." He took the bowl with him to the dining table, slotting in opposite his sister. His pen and paper were ready in his hand. "Everyone know what they're doing?" he called, too loud, the others flinching. "*YES* to leave, *NO* to stay."

And did Red imagine it, or had he said that first part louder, stumbling over the second? She knew which way Oliver was voting anyway, they all did. He was voting for her to die.

"Once you're done, fold your piece of paper up twice and then come drop it in this bowl here," he said, giving it a shake, the rim thumping on the wood of the table. "Okay. Vote now."

Maddy uncapped her pen, the sound hollow and high, riding up Red's spine as she watched.

Next her eyes darted to Reyna, who was writing something, leaning against her raised leg. Red couldn't tell by the movement of the pen if it was two letters or three.

Arthur was already finished, placing the pen down beside him, carefully folding the paper, pressing down with his thumbs, that muscle twitching in his cheek again.

Simon's pen was in his mouth, eyes up on the ceiling, his piece of paper ready for him against the top of the driver's seat.

Maddy's hand was cupped around her piece of paper as she scribbled something on it, pen flicking back and forth in her grip, tracing the lines of her chosen word.

Red couldn't stand it, the scratching of the pens. She bit down on her bottom lip to stop it from shaking, her eyes darting around too fast that they started to water.

Simon was writing now, and then it was over in less than two seconds, pocketing the pen to fold up his vote.

Red realized she hadn't been the only one watching, studying the others. Oliver had been too, only now turning to his own vote. He leaned over it and pressed the pen down, moving it up and across in jagged lines. Then he laid his pen down neatly on the surface, straightening it so it ran parallel with the side of the table. He folded his vote, once, twice.

"In the bowl, everyone," he said, dropping his own in.

Maddy leaned across the table, placing her vote in next. She didn't retake her seat, standing instead, pacing to the front of the RV, where she brushed past Simon.

Simon sidestepped over, just as Arthur pushed up from the sofa with a fake-leather creak. They dropped their votes in together, at the same time, the small puff of the paper landing.

Reyna was last, walking across from the door, eyes straight ahead. She reached over and let go. It fell, not featherlight this time, into the bowl.

She stepped away, the sofa catching her in the back of her legs, pulling her down.

Simon and Arthur were in that middle space between the kitchen and the front door, Red still behind the counter, separate from everyone else. Maddy up front.

Oliver stood up, a bone cracking somewhere beneath his skin. He sidled out of the booth, coming to stand in front of the table. He reached back to slide the bowl over, dragging it against the wood and against Red's ears. Too loud, every sound was too loud and every breath was too hard, her ribs folding in, one by one.

This was it.

Did she live or did she die?

They couldn't have voted for her to die, could they? These were her friends. Simon, who could always make her laugh, even on this awful, endless night. Maddy, her Maddy. Arthur, not hers, but maybe he could have been. Reyna, and that understanding they had between them, the knowing glances.

Oliver picked up the bowl and gave it a shake, the pieces of paper sliding over each other, whispering and shushing. What did they know that Red didn't? Oliver placed the bowl back down and nodded. At least he was kind enough to not be smiling.

His hand moved into the bowl, shuffling through the papers. He pulled out the first vote, plucked between his finger and thumb.

He unraveled the double fold, eyes skipping across the word written there.

"No," he read aloud.

No. Red's heart leaped to her throat. No. One vote for her to live. Her hands were shaking, but she needed them, sticking out the thumb of her right hand to keep the tally. One vote to live.

Oliver was digging through for the next vote, pulling it out. His lips tensed.

"Yes," he read.

Red's heart sank again, dropping into the acid of her stomach, where it fizzed and fizzed, like a two-way radio. Yes. One vote for her to die. But she'd known that was coming. She knew Oliver was voting yes, she didn't need to be scared. But her heart didn't listen, drowning down there. Red stuck out the thumb on her left hand to match. One vote each.

Oliver picked up the next folded bit of paper, pulling it apart.

"No," he said, dropping the opened vote on the table, beside the others.

No. Thank you, thank you. Red stuck out the index finger on her right hand. Another vote for her to live. Two against one. They'd already had Oliver's vote, wouldn't the rest be *NO*s, filling up her right hand?

Red's eyes dried out, scratchy and raw, staring too hard at Oliver's hands, fingers dipping into the bowl for the fourth vote. He pulled it out and unfolded it.

He breathed in, held on to it just too long.

"Yes," he said.

No, no, no.

Red's throat constricted, cutting her breath in half. That wasn't supposed to happen. Another vote for her to die. This wasn't just fear anymore, was it? This was what terror felt like, her body reshaping around it. But who? Who else voted yes? Her eyes snapped wider, panicked, skipping from Maddy to Arthur to Reyna to Simon. Which one of them was it? Which one wanted to force her out of the RV, out into the wide-open nothing? Which one of them was okay with her dying out there? They all looked shocked, afraid, wretched. Red couldn't tell. But someone wasn't shocked, that vote belonged to someone.

She raised another finger on her left hand. Two votes each. To live or to die.

"Last vote," Oliver said, scraping the final piece of paper out of the bowl.

The deciding vote. Live or die.

He twisted it between his fingers, taking too long. Unpicking the first fold, then the second.

Oliver spun the piece of paper around.

He cleared his throat.

# THIRTY-THREE

"No."

Oliver crumpled the piece of paper in his fist.

That crushing weight lifted from Red's chest, just a little. She could breathe again and she did. No. The final vote was no. Three *no,* two *yes.* Which meant they weren't going to kick her out of the RV, they weren't going to send her out to her death. She was alive.

Arthur sighed, closing his eyes.

Maddy clasped her hands to her cheeks, bottom lip threatening to go.

Simon nodded, his mouth tight, and Reyna looked up at the ceiling, stretching out her neck.

Oliver kept the vote in his hand, fist tightening around it, crushing it.

Something curdled in Red's gut, beside the cool rush of relief, something hot and unwelcome. Two people voted for her to die. Oliver she'd expected, it was his idea after all. But of the four left—Maddy, Arthur, Reyna and Simon—one of them voted for her to go. That hurt more than she could say, twisting through her insides, the feeling making itself a home there beside the guilt and the shame, those hot, red feelings. What was worse, knowing or never knowing who it was?

"Thank god," Maddy exhaled, rushing forward, past the others. She stepped up to Red and wrapped her in a tight hug, trapping Red's arms by her sides. "Thank god," she said again, pressing her cheek against Red's, not letting go. Red could feel her heart too, wingbeat fast in her chest.

"It's okay," Red said as Maddy finally pulled away. "I'm fine."

Maddy stood back and studied her face, eyes brimming with the threat of tears. "You sure?" she asked.

No, Red wasn't fine at all, put another check in the *NO* box on the back of Arthur's hand. She wasn't fine but she was alive and, really, how was that much different from the rest of her life?

Arthur caught her eye across the way. He lifted his chin up, blinking slowly at her, his hands clasped together in front of him, squeezing, like it was her hand he was holding.

Red squeezed back, fist at her side.

"What do we do now?" Simon asked, speaking into the emptiness of the RV, only their breathing and the swirl of the ever-present static.

No one answered, no one knew how to. Especially not Red. Should she thank them for not sending her out, was that what everyone was waiting for? Thank three of them, at least. How was she ever going to stop thinking about that?

Red pressed her elbows into the counter and leaned into them, taking the weight off her feet. Fuck, she was tired. Bone-tired and bone-scared, and when would this terrible night ever end?

Oliver blew out a mouthful of air, cheeks ticking as his mouth flickered. He turned, collecting the unfolded votes from the table, dropping them back one by one into the bowl. Two *yes,* three *no.* It had been close. What if just one more person had turned?

Oliver picked up the bowl and walked toward the kitchen counter, toward Red.

He placed the bowl down, skidding around its lower rim, the ceramic clattering against the surface before it came to a final stop.

Red watched it and then she watched him. He glanced up then, meeting her eyes, dark shadows across his.

"I'm sorry, Red," Oliver said, voice too flat, too normal in this most un-normal time and place.

It happened so fast.

Oliver lunged at her, arms coiling around her waist, iron-tight, pinning down her arms.

"Oliver, no!" Red screamed.

He lifted her off her feet, body braced against his as he stumbled toward the front door.

"NO!" Maddy screeched, inhuman, the sound curling in and out of Red's ears as she writhed in Oliver's grip.

She couldn't move her arms, but she kicked out, trying to catch the wall and push back against him.

Her feet slipped off.

Oliver stretched out one arm, slamming his elbow down against the handle and kicking the door open.

"OLIVER, DON'T!" Arthur's voice roared.

Footsteps crashing.

Screams.

The RV shook.

But it was too late.

The door was open into the wide-open nothing of outside. The black night ready and waiting.

Oliver's arms were crushing her, and then they weren't. He let Red go, shoving her forward, out through the open door.

Red landed on one ankle on the steps. She tripped, falling over herself, the momentum too much.

She rolled down, the final step jumping up to crash against her hip, sending her on.

Red crumpled, facedown, hands-down, against the dirt and gravel of the road. Spitting out a mouthful.

The door of the RV slammed shut behind her.

She was alone.

She was outside.

Not alone, actually, as she raised her head from the road, dirt and grit on her tongue, against her teeth.

There was Don, just a few feet away, folded backward in a way people shouldn't bend. Looking toward his wife, even in death. His head was undone at the back, a mess of blood and bone, hunks of flesh and brain matter on the road.

Only shoes, that was all Red could see of Joyce. The rest of her disappeared beyond the corner of the RV, the full beams carving a path through the black of night, trees waving in the distance.

"OLIVER, MOVE!"

Red heard shouting behind the closed door.

Thumping.

Scuffling.

Red pushed herself up, onto her knees.

She stared out at the scrubland, eyes scanning across the darkness. The grass spoke to her, staggering in the wind, cool on her cheeks.

The sniper was out there, hiding in the night. She couldn't see him, but he could see her.

"GET OUT OF THE WAY, OLIVER!"

Where was the red dot? Was it on her forehead right now, somewhere between her eyes? Last few seconds of having a face.

Her eyes flicked again to Don, those tiny pieces of flesh and skull and brain that would rebuild the puzzle of his head. Which part of the brain was it, the part that told you where you'd put down your keys or your phone? Red must already be missing that part. And where were those red feelings kept, the guilt, the shame? Red hoped those would be the first to blow apart, leave her with some of the good fragments, the better memories.

She waited for the crack, the last sound she'd hear.

There'd be no volley of rifle shots at her funeral. No bagpipes weeping "Amazing Grace."

"Simon, help me!"

Her knees were wet against the road, the sweet, cloying smell of gasoline soaking through.

No, no. She couldn't die like this. On her knees, like Mom. Knowing it was coming.

She tried to push up, but all the strength was gone from her, all the fight, crashing back down.

Red glanced down at her legs. Why weren't they working?

And then she saw it.

The red dot.

Circling there, on her chest. Riding up and down the lines of her checked shirt. Hiding in the frame of her buttons.

This was it.

Soon there'd be a hole there instead, where her heart used to be.

This was it.

Red closed her eyes.

What thoughts should be her last?

The same as her Mom's? Anger. Hate. Replaying that last fight when everything ended, so she lived for eternity in that horrible moment, stuck in the loop. Mom died and she took everything with her. How could she do that to Red? Mom died on her knees and it was all Red's fault, and Red was going to die on her knees and it was all Mom's fault. Blame enough to go around, doubling and doubling until there was too much and Red couldn't bear it anymore. Take those feelings away, blow them out of her head.

She waited.

Waited.

Red opened her eyes, just as dark outside as it was in.

It had already been long. Too long. Lifetimes in seconds. But it had been more than seconds, hadn't it? It had been minutes now.

Why hadn't he taken the shot? The red dot was right there on her chest, ready. Why was she still alive?

Pounding in her ears, but it wasn't her heart. It was coming from the RV behind. Screams and shouts and crashing and—

The sound of the door flying open, whacking against the metal-sheeting side.

Three footsteps.

Arms around her waist again, locking on.

"I've got you, Red," Arthur said in her ear, hoisting her to her feet, dragging her back up the steps, her body pressed against his.

The red dot slipped off her chest, down one leg, and disappeared into the night.

Arthur tripped on the top step, legs skating on the floor to pull them back inside the RV, fingers imprinting between Red's ribs as he dragged her.

"Maddy, the door!" he shouted in Red's ear.

Maddy jumped over them on the floor, darting forward to snatch the T-shirt rope tied to the door. She heaved it, grabbing the handle as it swung back within reach.

The door slammed shut.

Red collapsed back against Arthur, looking down, searching her chest for the red dot, for a hole, for a burble of blood.

Someone was screaming.

It was her.

# THIRTY-FOUR

Arthur drew Red's head back, brushing the wayward hair out of her eyes, and the dirt and the grit.

"You're okay." His words against the back of her head, warm and spreading. One hand against her forehead. "You're okay."

It was hot in here but Red was shivering, winter-night-without-heating shivering. Worse. Muscles vibrating uncontrollably beneath her skin, teeth chattering, crunching the last flecks of dirt in her mouth.

Her breath was too fast, whistling in and out of her chest, agonizing. Why was there pain everywhere? She was alive and it hurt to be alive.

"He didn't shoot," Arthur said, stroking the back of Red's head, because she still had one. "You're okay, you're not hit. You're in shock. Just breathe."

Maddy bent down in front of her, angry red streaks down her face from crying, almost as deep as scratches, like fingernails had put them there, not water.

"You're okay, Red," she said it too, grabbing for Red's hand, squeezing it.

"Here." A glass of water appeared in front of Red. Reyna was holding it out, her hair out of place, bunched up like it had been grabbed. But Red couldn't take the glass, she was shaking too hard, the air quivering around her.

"He didn't shoot you."

Oliver's voice, from farther away.

Red turned against Arthur's chest, looking for where it had come from. Oliver was standing in front of the driver's seat. He was holding one arm across his stomach, bending over it. There was a red mark on his cheekbone, the eye watering on that side.

"He didn't take the shot," Oliver continued talking, confusion in the one eye that wasn't glazed. "I was blocking the door. You were out there for three minutes at least. And yet he didn't take the shot. Why?" he asked her, like Red could possibly know why she was still alive.

Red shuffled, pushing herself away from Arthur, onto her unsteady feet. Her hands were still shaking, betraying her as she pushed against the floor.

Arthur straightened up too, faster than her, holding Red's elbow to guide her up. She glanced down at the point of contact, where he held on to her. There was another mark on the back of his hand now, not just the checkboxes and the *YOU OK?* There was a graze, raw and bleeding, across three of his knuckles. And just to their right, on the floor, the white-and-blue bowl was smashed to pieces, the unfolded paper votes strewn about.

"Why didn't he shoot you, Red?" Oliver said, straightening up with a wince, his voice finding its footing again.

"Oliver, no," Reyna said, a hint of warning, a growl just beneath the surface.

But Oliver couldn't be stopped. He wasn't sorry. That was what he'd said, before he threw Red out of the RV, but he hadn't meant it. He couldn't.

He took a step forward.

"You're the anonymous witness in the Frank Gotti trial, the entire case rests on you, why didn't they kill you?" he said, shaking his lion head. "He had his opportunity. You were right there. For three minutes. Why didn't he shoot you, Red?"

"I don't know!" Red shouted back, rage churning in her gut, taking over all those other red feelings. It was brighter, hotter. "I don't know why he didn't fucking shoot me!"

She didn't. She'd almost wished for it, kneeling in the dirt out there. Now the terror was receding, withdrawing from her fingertips and her limbs back into her gut, and she was just as confused as Oliver. This must be about her, about the trial. It was the only thing that made sense.

"He didn't shoot you," Oliver said again, like saying it would bare the answers, wringing them out of the words. "Why are you immune? He killed that old couple out there. He shot at Simon in the mirror. Would shoot any of us if we tried to leave the RV, but he didn't shoot you, Red. And there's only one reason why."

"What?" Red said, because she wanted to know too.

"You're the one working with them, aren't you?"

"Oliver," Arthur said, low and dangerous.

"Red's the mole," Oliver explained, meeting Arthur's gaze. "Don't you see? It's the only thing that makes sense. They're not going to kill one of their own."

"But she's the witness in the trial?" Maddy said, voice drawing up at the end, making it a question, seeding it with doubt.

Yes, Red was the witness in the Frank Gotti trial, that much was true, but suddenly she couldn't speak to defend herself, because how could she? Her throat was narrowing, narrowing, a blockade, stifling the words before they'd formed.

"She's the one who led us down this road, told Reyna to keep going," Oliver said, raising his thumb, keeping score like Red had before. "The sniper has known things he couldn't possibly know unless someone in here was telling him. Our escape plans, the note about calling the police. Red's been holding the walkie-talkie this whole time, she's the one who told us it wasn't bugged. Why does she know so much about walkie-talkies, anyway? She's outside for three minutes, she's the witness, the one they're here to kill, and yet they don't take the shot. Maybe she's not the witness, maybe she lied. Because she's working with them."

But Red *was* the witness. She might be a liar but that part was true. Then why hadn't the sniper killed her, the small voice in her head asked. She should be dead now. That must have been what they wanted, what all this was about.

"Why would she be working with them?" Reyna spat, and it was clear which side she was taking. Reyna couldn't have been that other *yes* vote, could she? But that left Simon, Arthur or Maddy, and that hurt more.

"I don't know," Oliver spat back. "Money? Everyone knows Red needs money."

Red winced. Everyone did, huh?

"But what does the sniper want if this isn't about Red being the witness?" Simon asked, moving his hands up and down like a weighing scale, shooting Red a sympathetic look so she knew it was only hypothetical. Had he been the *Yes* vote? No, Simon wouldn't do that to her.

"I don't know but—you know what—it doesn't really matter anymore." Oliver's eyes flashed. "Because now we . . . Wait, hold on a second. Red, hold your hands up in the air where I can see them. Do it now!"

Red hesitated, glancing around the RV at the rest of them. No, not again. Were they turning on her again? No, she shouldn't think like that. This was Oliver, all Oliver. They weren't on his side, they'd fought him to open the door so Arthur could come get Red, that must be what happened, reading the signs. And yet there was danger in Oliver's downcast eyes, and Red didn't want to set him off again, the terror stirring in her gut.

She put her hands up by her head, palms open, arms bent at the elbows, glancing back at the kitchen counter, at the walkie-talkie hissing away on top of it. Her job, her responsibility.

"Keep them there," Oliver said, charging forward, but he moved past her, into the kitchen.

Red looked back at Arthur. He was shaking his head.

Oliver went to the oven, pulled it open and reached inside, coming back with the saucepan, lid taped down. He brought it over to the counter and started picking at the pieces of duct tape, peeling them away.

"Oliver?" Maddy asked.

He shushed her, the sound too harsh, like a coiled snake buried there in his throat.

Oliver slid off the lid and reached inside. His hand closed around his own phone, pulling it out from under the rest.

He held a finger up, demanding silence from the rest of them, as he then turned to his backpack on the counter, reaching his spare hand inside. The hand reemerged clasped around a Bluetooth speaker, black and round, dotted in honeycomb holes.

He turned it on with a welcome beep, and then unlocked his phone to connect.

Red watched him scrolling through his music app again, selecting a playlist labeled *Classic Rock*. He pressed play on a song and slid the volume bar all the way up.

The guitar began, deafening, striking up and down. Then the drums, shaking the RV and the very bones inside her.

Red looked at Oliver's screen before he dropped it back into the saucepan, replacing the lid. The song was "Paranoid" by Black Sabbath, and Red must be losing her mind because she almost found that funny, standing here with her hands raised like a fugitive. All because she didn't die.

Oliver grabbed the walkie-talkie, placing it right beside the too-loud speaker. He still thought it was bugged, didn't he? Or he wasn't taking the chance for whatever he had to say next. Oliver moved away, gesturing silently for the others to gather around him by the table. They did. They must have been scared of the danger in his eyes too. Arthur came to stand beside Red, the fabric of his shirt brushing against her raised arms.

"Red," Oliver said, and she could only just hear him over the music blaring behind her. "Keep your hands where I can see them or I will duct-tape them behind your back."

"That's not necessary," Arthur growled back at him.

Red's arms were aching already, elbows drooping, but she kept them up, gritting her teeth.

Oliver's eyes circled the group, skipping over Red. "What I was saying is, it doesn't matter anymore, whatever this secret is that the sniper wants. Because now we have the upper hand."

He paused, waiting for the vocals to come back in on the song.

"We know they won't shoot Red," Oliver shouted, voice still half buried. "She's immune, for whatever reason, whether she's the mole or the witness or . . . it doesn't matter. What matters is that they won't shoot her. And now we know that. And we can use it."

"What are you saying?" Reyna shouted, words almost lost under the noise.

"I'm saying that Red can leave the RV without getting shot!" Oliver replied. "She's immune. We can use that to escape."

"You mean send Red out to go get help?" Simon yelled, hands cupped over his ears.

"No, not Red!" Oliver returned, shooting a glance her way, and she raised her hands a little higher. "I don't trust her. She could be the mole, working with them."

"I'm not!" Red shouted, just as the song was ending, an abrupt and ringing quiet after that last chord.

Oliver silenced them all with his terrible eyes, waiting for the next song to begin. It did, three quick notes strummed on the guitar, followed by another sequence. Red actually knew this song; Mom and Dad used to sing it whenever they were driving on I-95. "Highway to Hell" by AC/DC, and this time Red couldn't not laugh as the drums pitched in. No one else could hear except her, and yes, she must have finally lost her mind, like she lost everything else. Retrace your steps, Red. When did you last see your mind?

"There's enough evidence to suggest Red is the mole, we can't trust her!" Oliver came in with the vocals, showing too many teeth.

"So, what's your plan, then?" Simon shouted. Plan, plan. Red had a plan once. There was a graze on the skin of Simon's hand too, as he swiped the hair out of his eyes, dragging it out of his sweat.

Oliver turned to his sister.

"Maddy," he shouted as the chorus began. "You and Red are the same height. Your hair is basically the same color. If we dressed you up in Red's clothes, the sniper wouldn't be able to tell the difference. You'd look the same through his sights." He stepped forward, looming over Maddy. "He'll think you're Red and he won't shoot. You can leave the RV and you'll be fine."

"I don't —"

Maddy's lips formed around the next words, but she didn't say them loud enough to be heard.

"He'll think you're Red. She's immune for whatever reason; he won't shoot. You walk calmly to the truck out there, get in, turn around and drive away. You'll take a couple of phones with you and as soon as you drive into a signal, you call the police. Or as soon as you find a house and ask to use their landline."

Maddy backed away from her brother, stumbling against the driver's seat. Her face changed, rearranging to make room for the fear: a space between her lips, hanging open, a gap above and below the color of her eyes, stretched too wide. She shook her head.

"I don't think I can," she cried, into the music.

Oliver nodded his head in response, making her go still. "You're the only one who can!" he said. "It can't be Reyna, or me, or Arthur, or Simon. You're the only one who looks like Red. It has to be you. You'll be fine. The sniper didn't shoot Red. She was out there for three minutes and he didn't shoot her. All you have to do is get to that truck right there and drive away and you can send help for the rest of us."

"Oliver, this is too risky," Reyna said. "We don't know why he didn't shoot at—"

"Hands up, Red!" Oliver roared.

Red braced her elbows against her hips, keeping her hands, palm out, by her shoulders. If she'd lost her mind, then Oliver must have lost his hours ago. How could he ask his little sister to do that? To leave the RV in full view of the sniper? It was madness.

"You don't have to do it, Maddy!" Red shouted, staring at Oliver instead. "You don't have to do what he says." But wasn't she a hypocrite, because look at her, standing here with her hands up because he'd ordered her to. The song changed again, to one Red didn't recognize, more guitars screeching in her ears, more drums beating up and down her ribs.

Maddy looked nervously up at her brother. "I don't know," she said over the music.

He stepped forward. "You have to do it, Maddy. You're the only one who can. The only one who can get help for the rest of us. Don't you think I'd go if the circumstances were different?" He stabbed a finger against his chest. "If I could be the one to rescue us all, I would. But that's not how it's played out. You're the only one who can do it. The only one who can make sure we all survive the night."

"This is a terrible idea," Arthur said loudly. "Maddy, you shouldn't—"

"Shut up, Arthur!" Oliver snarled at him, face softening again as he turned back to Maddy. "It will work, Maddy. Do you think I would send you out there, my little sister, if I thought there was any chance of you getting hurt? Of course I wouldn't. They will think you're Red, and she's immune for whatever reason. They will let you go."

Oliver was nodding and then so was Maddy, not quite in time with him.

"Okay," she said, voice wavering, punctured by the screaming guitars. "I think I can do it."

"Good girl." Oliver stepped forward, planting a kiss on the top of her head, pinching her shoulder in his full grip. "Simon." He whipped around. "Where did you say the keys were? For the truck?"

"They're still in Don's hand," Simon replied, gaze darting to Maddy.

"Okay, you just walk to Don, calmly, slowly, like you know they won't shoot you because you're Red." Oliver had both his hands on Maddy's shoulders now, speaking right into her face. "You take the keys, you can do it, just don't look at his head. Then you walk to the truck, get in. Start the engine, pull around and drive out of here. Got it? It's simple."

Maddy was still nodding, she'd never stopped, but Red could tell that she didn't want to do this. She was terrified, almost vibrating with it. And Red wasn't sure now if Maddy was more scared of the man out there with the rifle, or of that look in her brother's eyes.

"I can do it," Maddy repeated, eyes swimming as she looked around at them all. "I can do it," she said. "I'll get help, I promise."

Her eyes latched onto Red. Shifted. What did that mean? Another look Red didn't understand. Did she want Red to step in, to put a stop to this?

"Maddy, you don't have to—"

"Red!" Oliver spun to face her. "Take off your clothes!"

"Maddy's scared, she doesn't want to do this!" she shouted back at him.

Oliver took one step forward, but then so did Red, closing the gap. Fuck it, they'd both lost their minds, they could do this dance together. Oliver didn't listen to her last time, about the note, and two people died. He would listen to her this time. It was Maddy, and she was too damn important.

"Why are you making her do this, Oliver? You don't know it will work. We don't know why they let me live just then, but it's not because I'm working with them, I'm not! I don't care if you believe me, but we both care about Maddy! She is not expendable, just a pawn for you to use in one of your plans. How many of those have gone right for you tonight? Oh, that's right, none of them! You can't send her out there in front of a rifle. If Maddy doesn't want to do this, then she doesn't have to, and you can't manipulate or bully her into it. Or throw her out like you did to me!"

Red's words had sharpened too, razors dragging themselves up her throat as she threw them toward Oliver. He'd made her think her last thoughts, out there on her knees, and he wouldn't do that to

Maddy too. No. Enough was enough. Oliver's eyes flashed, but so did hers, jaw clenched, hands still raised but now they were fists.

"Red, take your clothes off!" Oliver barked.

"Oliver, stop it!" Reyna shouted.

"RED?!"

"No," Red said. "I won't. I'm not listening to you anymore."

If Maddy couldn't refuse her brother, then Red could do it for both of them. She could do that. Maddy took care of her and now it was Red's turn.

Oliver's nostrils flared, eyes flickering as they jumped between Red and Maddy, head hinging on his neck. Dark circles in his eyes like fat beetles, legs skittering up his eyelashes. Red stepped forward again and Oliver moved back, legs knocking into the table. This time he would listen, he would—

Oliver checked behind him, down at the table. In the next second, he lunged for something, wrapping his fingers around it.

Red couldn't see, not until he swung back, the jagged kitchen knife gripped in one hand. Sharp. Reflecting Oliver's distorted face back up at him. Rivulets of sweat dripping down his skin.

Maddy gasped. Simon stepped back.

Oliver raised the knife and pointed it at Red's throat.

"I will only ask you one more time!" he screamed, and the knife glinted at her. "Take off your clothes!"

# THIRTY-FIVE

"Put the knife down, Oliver!" Reyna's voice rang out, louder than the screeching guitars and the thunderous, rifle-crack drums.

Red raised her chin, the tip of the knife only a few inches from her neck, shaking in Oliver's grip. His eyes were wild, too much black, too much red where white should be, bloodshot where the sweat had trickled in.

She didn't move, hands still raised. Red had known Oliver all her life, but she didn't know this version of him, the person the red dot had turned him into, pushing him to the farthest point. But it must have always been there, somewhere inside, this Oliver. Dormant, waiting until he was needed. He didn't even look like himself anymore, hair greasy with sweat, pushed back in chaotic clumps, skin red and blotchy, those puppet strings making his head hang sideways on his neck again as he studied Red back.

Her eyes trailed down the knife in his hands. And the thing was, Red wasn't sure. She wasn't sure this was just an act to get her to do what he wanted. There was a knife in his hands, and part of Red believed he would use it if he had to. He'd thrown her out of the RV once to save himself. She was expendable to him, disposable. And here she stood, in Oliver's mind, between him and his survival. There wasn't a choice.

"Fine," Red said darkly, not loud enough over the music, but Oliver read the word on her lips.

He bared his teeth in a faltering smile that didn't fit his face. He'd won, again.

"Now!" he barked, the knife moving up and down with his voice.

Red inhaled. "Can I at least get some clothes to change into first?"

She gestured with her head, at the overhead cupboards above the sofa, Maddy's case inside with both of their things.

"No, not you!" Oliver said. "You might use it as a distraction to communicate with the sniper somehow. Hands where I can see them."

"I'm not working with the sniper, Oliver," Red snapped back. "I'm the witness, they're here to kill me."

"Except they didn't, did they? When they had the chance." Oliver's eyes left her for a second. "Simon, you go. Get some of Red's clothes out of Maddy's case."

Simon stiffened, looking instead at Red.

"It's okay." She nodded, and her arms were still raised, but she wasn't sure she could feel them anymore. Fizzing, like they were made of static, and Red missed that, the quiet sizzle of the walkie-talkie.

Simon walked the three steps over to the sofa and stood up on it, the plastic creaking under his shifting weight as he opened the cupboard, ducking his head to swing the door fully open. He reached up, the angry wasp sound of the zipper on Maddy's bag.

"Red's stuff should be at the top," Maddy called.

Simon cocked one finger to let her know he'd heard. He reached inside, came back with his hands clasped around a pair of pants, one leg flicking itself up and around his arm.

"Black jeans," Simon called, voice barely audible, trapped inside the cupboard. Well, Red only had two pairs of pants and one pair of shorts with her, and she was wearing one of those. She was glad Simon hadn't gone for the shorts, as hot as it was in this RV, exposed skin would feel like a target, glowing in the night.

Simon reached in with the other arm, shoulder rolling as he rustled inside the bag, picking up one item that Red couldn't see, shaking his head and putting it back to select another. He pulled away, shutting the cupboard door with his elbow and jumping down.

"Here," he said to Red, coming over, handing her the clothes.

"No." Oliver intervened, blocking Simon's way with one arm. "On the floor."

Simon checked with Red. She nodded, what choice did she have? There was a knife to her throat.

Simon dropped the ripped black jeans in a crumple at her feet, and then the top he'd chosen. An old long-sleeved T-shirt in a dark plummy red. It had been her mom's once.

"Red's your color," Simon said to her over the music, an awkward closed-mouth smile on his face. Was he trying to make her feel better with that smile? Or was it masking something else, because he also thought she was a mole? No, Simon couldn't. He knew her. And yet, he could have been the one who voted for her to die. But she wasn't dead, and that was the new problem.

"Red, come on," Oliver shouted, dipping his head to indicate the clothes on the floor.

"At least let her go into the bathroom to change." Arthur stepped forward, tendons sticking up under the tan skin of his neck. Not quite like puppet strings, but close. He was angry, Red could tell. Or scared. Or both. Arthur couldn't think she had anything to do with all this, could he? No, he'd stood by her, all night. Dragged her away from the red dot, held her when the shock set in.

Oliver swung the knife, pointed it at him until Arthur retreated one step. "No," Oliver said. "If we leave her alone, she might get a message to the sniper somehow. She has to stay where I can see her."

"It's fine, Arthur," Red called, fingers too sweaty and swollen as they worked the top button of her shirt and down. "It's fine," as the knife returned to her, followed by Oliver's eyes. What a ridiculous word that was. *Fine.* She was undressing at knifepoint and there was a sniper outside and she was supposed to be dead. But she was *fine,* you know?

Arthur shook his head. He knew it wasn't fine, but he stepped back all the same. De-escalating, the tension easing slightly in Oliver's shoulders as he watched Red undo the rest of her buttons.

"Here, Maddy," Red said, pulling the blue-and-yellow flannel shirt off her arms, standing there in her bra and jeans. She chucked the shirt past Oliver's head and Maddy caught it, clutching it to her chest.

Red picked up the T-shirt from the floor, pulled it over her head. She reached her arms through to the ends of the sleeves and pulled the thin material down over her stomach.

"Jeans," Oliver barked. "Come on, quick. Before he wonders what we're up to."

Red kicked off her sneakers, using each foot to pry the other off. Oliver bent forward, knife still raised, and collected them in one hand, passing them over to Maddy, who started to slip off her own shoes.

Red dropped her eyes and unbuttoned her jeans, pulled down the zipper.

She peeled the jeans down, the dark gasoline stains sticking to her knees, clinging to her pale skin. But she pushed and they gave, falling, bunching around her ankles. She stepped out of them.

Red stood, in this RV, in her underwear and socks, and she looked up at the others. She wasn't ashamed to be standing here in her underwear. Red knew real shame and this wasn't it. Real shame was killing your mom and having to live with it, knowing that she died and the last thing you ever said to her was that you hated her. If Red survived that, she could survive this. She stared around at the others, daring them to look her back in the eye. Could they put a stop to this? If Arthur, Reyna and Simon all stepped up, could they stop Oliver from making Maddy go through with this? There were three of them. But Oliver was the one with the weapon. And he was probably the only one who would use it. Or maybe that wasn't the reason at all. Maybe they didn't trust her either, thought she was working with the sniper. What did Red expect, she *was* still lying to them.

Oliver scooped up her light blue jeans and passed them over to Maddy.

"Go get changed in the bathroom," he urged his sister, over a new song just starting. Notes steadily climbing in threes, entering through Red's ears, biting at her nerves and her exposed legs.

Maddy closed the bathroom door behind her. The last thing Red saw was the look of numb shock in her eyes. Were they really doing this?

Red grabbed her black jeans from the floor and slipped them on. There were rips on one knee and up the thigh of the other leg; she hadn't bought them that way, they were just old. Maddy and Oliver's mom had bought her these ones.

"Maddy's shoes," Red shouted at Oliver. She hadn't packed any others.

He kicked Maddy's white sneakers over and Red wriggled her feet inside, no need to undo the laces. Maddy hated when she put shoes on like that. *You'll break the backs,* she always said, but Red didn't think she'd mind just this once.

The song escalated, high notes on the guitar cascading all around her. And then building again, creeping up the scale.

"You okay?" Reyna mouthed to her, across the RV.

Red nodded, just slightly, so Oliver wouldn't see. The knife wasn't as close anymore but it was still there in his grip, pointing at her throat. People came undone when you stuck a knife in that spot, didn't they? But it wouldn't really matter where a rifle got you, would it? Anywhere and you'd come undone around it, like the scattered puzzle of Don's head.

The bathroom door opened soundlessly, buried under the song, and Maddy stepped out in Red's flannel shirt and her jeans, dark stains at the knees. She had on Red's tattered sneakers too, the laces done up neatly, double-knotted.

"Good." Oliver beckoned her over. "Okay, do you have a hair tie?" he shouted into her ear. "You need to tie yours back in a ponytail, the same height as Red's."

Maddy always had a spare hair tie on her wrist, sometimes more actually. Red often borrowed them, never gave them back because they all got lost somehow.

Maddy pulled up the sleeve of Red's shirt, revealing a black hair tie sinking into the flesh of her wrist. She rolled the band into position over the base of her thumb and fingers, and turning to study Red's hair, she gathered her own up, running her fingers through, pulling the strands to the crown of her head. She secured the hair tie around the ponytail, once, twice, three times, then pulled it tight.

Oliver looked between the two of them, Red and Maddy, and again, frantically, eyes narrowing.

307

"Not quite right," he shouted. "Yours is too long."

Knife still in hand, Oliver backed up to the table, reaching for the scissors with his spare hand. He didn't ask Maddy first. He spun her around, the heels of his hands on her shoulders, and he grabbed the length of her ponytail with his knife hand. He opened the scissors, positioned them about three inches up from the ends of Maddy's hair, and he snipped. It wasn't a clean cut, sliding through, opening the scissors and closing them again and again until the end was hacked off. Uneven, but Oliver seemed pleased with it.

Shards of Maddy's light brown hair scattered to the floor. They glittered, not quite as much as the glass had, but they still held the light.

Oliver moved her back to study her again, dropping the scissors.

The scissors. They were a weapon too, right? Could Red get to them? And then what? She couldn't stab Oliver Lavoy with them. She could threaten to, but he'd know it was an empty threat. And his might not be. Not *rock paper scissors,* but *scissors knife rifle.* Scissors lost every time in that game.

"Yours is too neat!" Oliver shouted. "Red's hair is messy. Can you pull some bits out at the front, and some lumps at the top of your head?"

Maddy nodded, teasing out wispy strands of hair to frame her face like Red's bangs. Pulling at clumps in the ponytail, so they stuck up on her head.

"Better!" Oliver shouted, and that smile was back, the one that didn't belong. "Perfect." He gave Maddy a shake on the shoulders. "You can do this, you know."

He didn't wait for her to disagree. He walked past Red, knife gripped hard in his hand, circling the kitchen counter where the music was loudest. He opened the lid of the saucepan and reached in, removing two phones, one with a marble orange case. He thumbed at the screens, probably checking the battery levels. "Okay," he shouted over the noise. "Take your phone and Reyna's. Actually, take Simon's too, he's on a different network." He pulled out a third phone. "You keep driving until you find a house and some help, or until the first bar of signal appears on one of these phones."

He bundled the iPhones up in one hand and walked over, passing them to Maddy. She nodded, slipping two into her back pockets, one at the front. Oliver was blocking her, Red couldn't see Maddy's face, her eyes, but she could imagine the fear in them. Was this really going to happen?

"Look at me, Maddy," Oliver barked, reaching his spare hand out, knocking a finger under her chin. "You can do this! Walk calmly out the door, turn to the side as soon as you can, that's where you and Red look most alike, in profile. Walk to Don, take the keys out of his hand, then straight into the truck. Shut the door, start the engine. Back up, turn, and then drive the hell out of here. Not fast while you're still in view. But once you're past those trees, you put your foot down, understand? Drive as fast as you can into some signal, or to a house and a landline. And when you call the police, remember to tell them it's an active shooter and they need to send officers right away. Do you know where to send them?"

Oliver shifted and Red could finally see Maddy. She looked frozen, welded to the floor of the RV. A quiver in her lower lip as she searched Oliver's face for the right answer.

"McNair Cemetery Road," Simon was the one to answer. "That's the road we turned off down here. I remember. They'll find us if you tell them that. Tell them to look for headlights."

Maddy nodded, swallowing her bottom lip now, eyes glazed with terror, like she couldn't even listen, like words were just noise battering against her ears.

"Maddy!" It was Arthur now, stepping around the swell of music. "I really don't think you should do this. You shouldn't. It's too risky. There must be another way. Red?" Arthur looked back at her, desperation in the pinch of his mouth.

Red shook her head, tears prickling at the corners of her eyes to see Maddy this scared. Her Maddy.

"Don't go," she said. "Don't do it, you don't have to."

"Shut up, you two!" Oliver roared, puppet head rolling loose on his neck as he whipped back to Maddy. "Don't listen to them, they don't understand. This is going to work, okay? Maddy, Madeline, look at me. It's going to work and you will be fine. You're going to save us all. You. You're going to save us. It will work. It's a Mom plan, a win-win." Oliver's voice was raw from shouting, cracking at the edges, just like his smile. "You get out of here and call for help. And once you're safely gone, we can let the sniper know we still have Red. That will protect us in the meantime. She's obviously worth something to them."

But not to anyone else, clearly. Red once thought Oliver looked at her like a spare sister. She'd been wrong about the second word, though, the one that mattered.

"Don't go, Maddy!" Arthur said, and there were tears in his eyes too. "Don't! Red?!"

She was trying. But Maddy was listening to Oliver, and he had the knife.

"Maddy!" Red cried.

"Oliver, can we think about th—" Reyna began.

"It's okay!" Maddy shouted above their voices and the music, nodding her head too fast, eyes rattling with it. "It's okay, everyone.

I can do it. I'm going to get help for you, I promise. I can do it! I can save you all!"

"You don't have to!" Red yelled back. "Just because Oliv—"

Oliver turned on her, brandishing the knife.

"She's made up her mind, Red, stop trying to manipulate her!"

"It's okay, Red," Maddy said, staring right at her, eyes locking on. "I can do it. I want to do it. I trust Oliver. I'll save us all. I can. I'm not scared."

But she was. She was so scared. Red had never wanted to see that look on her best friend's face and now she'd probably never forget it.

"Right!" Oliver screamed above the song. "I'm going to turn the music off and I want the rest of you to be absolutely silent. Don't say a thing! Red, you keep your mouth shut and you keep your hands where I can see them. Maddy, have you got the phones? Are you ready?"

She nodded.

Arthur was shaking his head.

"Okay!" Oliver shouted. "Go stand by the door."

Maddy did, her feet dragging against the floor, like she was hoping the RV would grow up over them and trap her inside so she didn't have to go. But she'd chosen, and she'd chosen Oliver, just like Red had countless times tonight. He was the natural leader, her big brother, and Red couldn't compete with that.

Maddy waited by the door, fingers raised above the handle, shaking, and she looked just like Red, when you see yourself in one of those dressing room mirrors, see what you look like from behind. Maddy's hair was only a shade or two darker, but the night would hide that. It had to. Because if Maddy was actually going to do this, then it had to work, Oliver had to be right and Red had to be wrong. Had to.

Should Red say goodbye? Tell Maddy she loved her, just in case. She'd had last words before, and she'd regretted them every day since. She could do it right this time. No. No, because they weren't last words, and Maddy couldn't think that either. This had to work. Maddy was going to drive out of here and she would be fine. She was going to save them all.

Maddy looked back over her shoulder, and Red told her as much as she could with her eyes.

Oliver pulled his phone out of the pan and tapped at the screen.

The music cut out, the air hissing in its absence.

No, that was the static, back at last, filling Red's ears. She breathed it in.

Oliver rounded the kitchen counter, standing between Maddy and Red, knife still gripped in his hand.

He looked at his sister and nodded his head. Just once.

"Red? Red?" Oliver said loudly, not looking at her. "Where are you going?"

Then he nodded at Maddy again.

Her lips were gone, sucked back into her face as she pushed down on the handle and the door swung open, inviting in the dark night.

"No," Red whispered, and Oliver shot her a look, knife raised.

Maddy turned, bowed her head and walked down the stairs, the night taking her away. She reached the road, steps crunching beneath her, and then pushed the door of the RV shut behind her.

"Come," Oliver whispered, grabbing Red by her elbow, dragging her with him to the front of the RV.

"Where the fuck has Red just gone?" he shouted, voice grating in his throat and Red's ear.

The others gathered in behind. Just five of them now. Simon leaped over the driver's seat to see. Arthur pressed in on Red's other side. The muscles in his face were flickering, a tortured look in his eyes as he stared out the windshield. He leaned forward, hands fidgeting against his legs, nails digging in. This will work, Red wanted to tell him. It had to, because the alternative was unthinkable. They were wrong, Oliver was right.

He had to be right, holding on to her elbow, knife in the other hand, eyes focused ahead.

Red caught movement in her periphery and whipped around, staring out the windshield into the night.

There was Maddy.

Red's blue-and-yellow shirt glowing in the headlights.

She was walking toward the truck, toward the driver's-side door. Slowly, every step measured and calm, pressing into the road and peeling up.

There was something dangling from Maddy's left hand. The keys. She had the keys. This was going to work. Red was wrong, she was wrong and she didn't need to have said any last words at all, because it was working.

Her heart was in her throat, beating so hard she couldn't hear the static anymore.

She was wrong, it was going to work.

Maddy was just a few feet from the truck now, movement in her neck, ponytail swinging as she glanced up.

"Go on," Oliver whispered, guiding her forward.

Maddy stopped.

She reached out for the door handle.

*Crack.*

5:00 A.M.

# THIRTY-SIX

Maddy folded forward.

She dropped to the road, like her puppet strings had been cut all at once.

"NO!" Red screamed, ramming her elbows down to push Oliver away. "No, Maddy!"

She slammed her fingers and forehead against the cool glass of the windshield, eyes circling the lump of her clothes out there, Maddy's darker ponytail.

Reyna was crying. Arthur too, hands covering his face.

Oliver didn't say a word. Not a fucking word.

Red screamed again, her breath fogging up the window, a cloud to take Maddy away. She screamed, and the glass threw it back at her, echoing around the RV.

No, wait. Red swallowed the scream, forced her mouth shut. The fog receded, but the echo didn't go, muffled, muted, from a different world. Someone else was screaming. Outside.

It was Maddy.

"She's alive!" Red shouted, watching as the lump outside shifted, ponytail falling to the other shoulder. "She's alive!" Red screamed, turning back to the others, to Oliver and his pale face, no longer golden.

The five of them stared at each other, eyes wide, for half a second, the sound of Maddy's scream hammering at the windows. She was hurt. She was shot. Someone had to go get her. Red's eyes locked on Oliver's, but he looked away.

"I'll go!" Red said, shoving Oliver and Simon out of her way. Move, for fuck's sake. She'd been out there for three minutes and the sniper didn't take the shot. Like Oliver said, she was immune for some reason. She was the one who had to go get Maddy. Her Maddy.

Red charged down the RV to the front door. As she reached out for the handle, that small voice of doubt piped up, whispering in her ear. But Maddy was dressed like Red, and he'd taken the shot. Maybe she wasn't immune after all, or maybe the sniper somehow knew it wasn't her. But it didn't matter either way because Maddy was out there, screaming. She needed Red and Red would go. No time for doubts.

She slammed the handle down and pushed open the door. It crashed into the metal side of the RV as Red tore down the steps.

"HELP!" Maddy's scream had found its shape, lingering beyond the edges of the word. "HELP ME!"

"I'm coming, Maddy!" Red screamed back, the soles of Maddy's sneakers beating against the dirt road as Red sprinted toward her and the headlights.

She jumped over the crumpled form of Don.

It was a race. Her against that red dot. Don't think of it, don't think of it now.

"I'm here!" Red shouted, crashing to her knees beside Maddy, dust hovering around them both, held there by the headlight beam.

Maddy was lying there, pitched up by one elbow, face creased in agony. Red looked her over and she saw. The new stain on her jeans. Growing and growing. Around that huge hole there, in Maddy's thigh. A gurgle of blood gushing out, pooling through the material around it. So much blood already, dripping to the road, pouring out in time with Red's heart, battering in her ears.

"Fuck," Red hissed, her hand hovering over the wound, bright red overflowing, darkening as it spread through the jeans. "Fuck."

"Don't leave me, Red," Maddy cried, staring up at her.

"I'm not leaving you." Red lowered her face so they were eye to eye. "I'm not leaving you, okay, Maddy? I promise. Never."

"Okay," Maddy cried through the pain, tears falling into her open mouth. "He shot me. It's bad, huh?"

Red's head wavered, between a nod and a shake. "It's bad," she said, "but Reyna can help you. I need to drag you inside the RV, okay? There's nothing I can do for you out here."

"Okay," Maddy said, the word swallowed by an awful scream as she tried to sit up.

"It's going to hurt like hell, but I need to move you quickly, okay?" Red pushed up to her feet.

"Don't leave me!" Maddy screamed, watching her.

"I'm not leaving you, Maddy!" Red crouched down behind her, where Maddy couldn't see. "I'm right here, and you're coming with me."

Red slotted her arms in under Maddy's armpits, reaching forward until her elbows were locked in.

"I don't want to die!" Maddy cried, her breath rattling through her throat.

"You're not going to die," Red promised her. But she couldn't promise that, she didn't know. That was a lot of blood already. "Okay, three, two, one, go."

Red raised Maddy off the road, her legs bent as she skated backward. Maddy screamed and screamed, her feet dragging through the dirt.

"Stop!" she screamed, the worst sound Red had ever heard. "Stop, Red, it hurts too much!"

"I'm sorry, I can't!" Red said into her ear, checking the path behind her, over her shoulder. It wasn't clear, Don was right there, but Red had to keep going.

She stepped over Don, her sneaker pressing against his empty hand, harder than flesh should ever be. Maddy's feet got tangled in his as Red dragged her over the body.

"Red, stop!" Maddy screamed. "Just for a minute!"

"I can't!" Red screamed back, tightening her grip. She didn't know if Maddy had a minute left. "I have to get you inside!"

Maddy's hands grasped Red's arms, nails biting in.

Heat prickled in Red's cheeks. Was it from the effort of dragging her best friend, steadily bleeding out, or was the red dot poised there, waiting, and she could somehow feel it on her skin?

Red checked behind her shoulder. The steps were right there, a few feet away. She looked back down at Maddy, screaming wordlessly now, a long red streak staining the road, following them wherever they went. Fuck, that was a lot of blood.

"I've got her, Red!" Arthur's voice appeared behind her, crashing down the steps. "You get her feet."

Arthur's hands took over from her, slipping under Maddy's arms while Red darted around to pick up her ankles. The blood had soaked all the way down here, wet against Red's fingers. It just kept coming. How much could Maddy lose before it was too much?

"Go," Arthur said, hoisting Maddy up and climbing the first step.

Maddy's head fell back and she screamed.

Red pushed, carrying Maddy's feet as she tilted, top half going with Arthur, up the last step now, into the RV. Red followed, bringing her legs inside.

"Over here," Reyna called, pointing at the floor in front of the refrigerator. She had a beach towel ready in her hands. "Put her over here."

Simon darted forward and slammed the door to the RV shut as Red crossed the threshold.

"Fuck," he said, catching sight of Maddy's leg, and Red looked again too. So that was what one of those bullets did to flesh and bone. Ripped a hole right through her.

Red looped around with Arthur, laying Maddy down carefully on the floor, sitting up, her back braced against the refrigerator door. She was still screaming, head at an unnatural angle on her neck. Because the strings had been cut.

"I need to put pressure on the wound, Maddy," Reyna said, her voice firm but even, dropping to her knees beside her, pressing the towel down on the gushing bullet hole.

Maddy screamed harder.

"You're okay," Red told her, because Maddy had said it to her before, and maybe it was just the thing you said to people who weren't okay.

She stepped back to give Reyna space, watching. Red's hands floated up to her face to stop it from falling open. One hand was wet. Blood. A handprint of Maddy's blood across her cheek.

Someone grabbed her, spun her around. Oliver's pale face too close to hers, eyes swollen and red, swimming in and out of her vision like a nightmare.

"How did he know it wasn't you, Red?" Oliver spat, shaking her whole body, trying to knock the answers out of her. "How did he know?"

"I don't know!" Red fought him off, leaving another handprint of Maddy's blood on his shirt as she pushed him away.

"Not now, Oliver," Reyna said. She didn't shout, she didn't have to. The look on her face was enough. "I have to stop the bleeding. Does anyone have a belt?" She glanced around at the group, eyes frantic now that Maddy couldn't see them.

"For a tourniquet?" Simon asked, pulling up his shirt.

"Yes." Reyna turned to him. "Do you—"

"I have one," he said, undoing the buckle and sliding the black leather belt out from the loops in his jeans. He passed it over.

"Okay, Maddy, this is going to hurt. I need to tie this above the wound, as tight as it will go, okay? It should slow the bleeding." Reyna held the belt across both hands, moving the towel.

"Okay," Maddy managed to say through gritted teeth. Her skin was starting to look pale and pallid, a tremor in her jaw.

Reyna pushed one side of the belt through under Maddy's knee, then slid the length of it up past the wound. She hooked it around and through the buckle a few inches above the blood-gushing hole, and then she tightened it.

Maddy screamed, weaker this time, breaking into sobs.

"Please, stop," she begged.

Reyna pulled, muscles in her arms and her neck straining. Tighter, digging into the jeans and Maddy's flesh. But that red gurgle of blood, it was slowing, bubbling over rather than pouring out as Reyna secured the tourniquet in place.

"Simon, come here," she said.

He did, falling to his knees.

"Press this towel down directly on the wound." Reyna showed him, and Simon's hands replaced hers. "Harder than that," she directed. "More pressure. More. More. Okay, stay like that."

Reyna pushed up shakily to her feet, wiping the sweat and hair out of her eyes, a pinkish smear from Maddy's blood across her forehead. She stepped over to Oliver and Red and it was written all over her face, in the fall of her eyes and the set of her mouth.

"She's bleeding a lot," she said quietly, under Maddy's groans in the background. "Could have severed the femoral artery, I'm not sure."

"What does that mean?" Oliver croaked.

"It means we need to get her to a hospital as soon as possible, or she could bleed out."

Red's heart fell into her stomach, curdled there in the acid and the shame.

Maddy Lavoy couldn't die. That couldn't happen. Red couldn't let it.

"I'll stop the bleeding as much as I can," Reyna continued. "But she needs a hospital."

Oliver shook his head, and for once, he must be out of plans. His sister was dying and he was the one who sent her out there. Did he feel that guilt, or was he leaving it all to Red? She should have tried harder to stop him, maybe Oliver wouldn't have actually used the knife. Why didn't Red try harder?

Reyna returned to Maddy, taking over from Simon, pressing down with all her weight against the wound.

Plan. Plan. Think of a plan to get away, to get Maddy to a hospital. Red looked around the RV, eyes catching on the pattern in the curtains, she and Maddy sitting beside them just seven hours ago playing Twenty Questions, Red zoning out, forgetting her *person, place or thing.* And now Maddy was dying on the floor over there and Red had to do something. Think. The more she forced it, the harder it was. And, remember, she'd lost her mind awhile back.

Oliver strayed away from her, over to the sofa, dropping down, his face hidden in his hands.

Red breathed in, emptied herself out, tried to listen to the thoughts in her head, but all she found was an empty hiss. Static. The static. She turned around, the walkie-talkie waiting for her there on the counter. Red walked to it, scooped it up, the familiar weight in her hands. Her job, her responsibility. And now she had another one too: saving Maddy.

They'd not found any interference all night, but morning was drawing closer, maybe someone was up and working in a nearby farm or something . . . anything. *Please,* Red begged the device in her hand. There was nothing else Red could do to help Maddy, this was her only job, the only thing she knew how to do. She pressed the + button, cycling up past channel three, through four and five, begging the static to go away, to give her a voice. Any voice. *Please.*

This was all her fault. Maddy was bleeding out in the middle of the RV and it was Red's fault. This was about her, her secret. She was the witness in the Frank Gotti trial, and now Maddy was going to die because of that decision. The men with rifles were here to kill her, no one else. So why didn't they? Red asked herself, spooling up through the channels, static flickering in and out as she pressed. Why didn't they take the shot when it was her outside? Why was she still standing, not bleeding out on the road like she was supposed to be? Why Maddy and not her? Red didn't know, she couldn't understand it. They wanted their secret and they had it, it was her. Why hadn't they killed her?

Unless . . . a thought stirred in her mind, tunneling away as Red's eyes flicked back to Maddy, and the beach towel steadily turning red on her leg. Red looked away and reached for the thought, pulling at it, thread by thread. Unless she wasn't the secret herself. Not the fact that she was the witness. Because she *was* the eyewitness in the Frank Gotti trial, that much was true. But that wasn't the whole story, was it? What if the secret they wanted wasn't just Red, it was what Red knew, the other half of the plan? Maybe they didn't want her, not alone. They wanted the other person involved, didn't they? The name they didn't know, but Red did. Was that why they couldn't kill her, not yet? Because she hadn't told them that name? Was that what they wanted, after all these hours and escape plans and two dead people outside and Maddy bleeding out, did they want that name from Red before they killed her?

Everything slotted into place, sense where there'd been none before.

Red's heart was back, acid-wet, hammering against the back of her teeth. What should she do? She'd already let the plan go a long time ago, said goodbye to it and everything it would give her. But she swore she'd never tell anyone, she swore, and how could she say it here, right in front of them? Cause them more hurt and confusion than they already had. But did Red have a choice? Maddy was bleeding out, surely that undid everything, all the rules of the plan? She would make the same choice, wouldn't she?

And if that was it, the secret the sniper wanted, would he let the rest of them go? Red would have to stay behind, she understood that, but could the others get Maddy in that truck and drive her to a hospital?

She had to try. For Maddy. She would understand, she would forgive her.

Red had cycled up to channel thirteen, but now she switched

directions, flicking back through the channels, toward three, toward the sniper. She was going to give him the name, she had to, if it was the thing that saved Maddy's life. Everyone would want that.

Static fizzed in her ears and behind her eyes, under the skin of her fingertips.

Down through channel ten.

Nine.

Red inhaled.

Eight.

Static.

Seven.

Six.

The static cut away before her thumb pressed the button again.

"—check, over."

A voice broke through the fuzz.

Static.

"What was that?" Simon asked, standing up by the door. "Was that the sniper?"

"No," Red said, staring down at the walkie-talkie. "I'm on channel six."

The static broke off.

"Yeah, the team have removed the truck and the cell tower itself doesn't look too bad. But some of these antennas are damaged, so let's get the engineers up here ASAP now that it's clear. Over."

Static.

Red's breath snagged in her throat.

Interference.

People were talking on two-way radios and she'd found them, she'd found them, and before she lost them she had to—

Red raised the walkie-talkie to her lips, pressed the push-to-talk button.

"Help, call police! There's a shooter down McNair Cemetery Road and one of us has been sh—"

A hand came out of nowhere, colliding with the walkie-talkie, smacking it out of Red's hands.

It fell to the ground, shattering into pieces.

The static died with it.

Red's eyes stayed down there with the broken walkie-talkie, not looking up. Because she knew that hand, the one that came out of nowhere. Knew the black scribbled check mark and boxes by his knuckles, matching the ones on hers.

It was Arthur.

# THIRTY-SEVEN

Red's gaze trailed up from the check mark on Arthur's hand, up the sleeve of his shirt, to his face, inches from hers. Eyes wide and wretched behind his glasses, rubbed raw, mouth open and his breath heavy, shoulders moving with it.

"No," she whispered, shaking her head. "Not you."

Arthur blinked, slow, painful, and that was answer enough somehow.

"What the fuck?!" Oliver was on his feet now, charging over, eyes skipping between the smashed walkie-talkie and Arthur. "It's you!" he roared, taking a handful of Arthur's shirt, shoving him back. "You're the mole. I'm going to fucking kill you!"

In one quick movement, Oliver had Arthur's arms pinned behind his back. Arthur didn't struggle, he let it happen, watching it play out in the dark of Red's eyes.

"Simon, search him!" Oliver barked, holding Arthur in place. "Search him!"

"What the fuck is going on?" Simon said, walking over, pink stains of Maddy's blood up his forearms too. "Why did you do that, Arthur? I don't underst—"

"He's with the sniper," Oliver cut him off. "He's been playing us this whole time. Search him. There's probably a microphone on him. Quickly, Simon!"

Simon's face cracked with the betrayal, shaking his head. But he did what Oliver asked, patting his hands down the sides of Arthur's shirt, moving around to check the back pockets of his jeans. Then at the front, sliding his hand into each pocket.

"Got something," he croaked, pulling out a small, round, plastic device, holding it up for Oliver to see.

"I knew he was listening, I knew we were bugged," Oliver growled, letting Arthur go with a rough shove, grabbing the device from Simon.

"It's not a microphone," Arthur said, but Oliver was already moving, charging across the width of the RV to the window behind the sofa. He pulled a corner of the mattress free.

"No, wait!" Arthur said.

Oliver swung his arm in an arc, throwing the device outside, far into the darkness of this never-ending night. But it had to end sometime; morning was on its way.

Oliver turned back.

"Now we can talk," he said darkly, "without your little friend out there listening."

"He wasn't listening," Arthur replied. "That wasn't a microphone."

"What was it, then?" Simon asked this time, taking a step back from Arthur, so he was shoulder to shoulder with Oliver, bearing down. "What was it?"

Arthur's breath stuttered in his throat, a dry, scratching sound.

He checked in with Red's eyes before answering.

"It's a button," he said. "A remote control. For a light I attached to the top of the RV earlier."

Red remembered him up there, while she was watching the moon cross the sky. She'd seen him climbing up the ladder and, yes, there had been something in his pocket, hadn't there? She'd thought it was his phone. But that wasn't all. She also remembered the way his fingers had fiddled at the front of his jeans all night. He wasn't fidgeting because he was scared, he'd been talking to the sniper. No, this couldn't be happening. Not Arthur. Not him.

"With a light?" Oliver asked, eyes narrowing. "That's how you were communicating with the snipers?"

"Sniper," Arthur said. "There's just two of us."

One sniper. One gun. One red dot. And one liar. This whole time. Red stared at him but he looked like a different person now.

"And, yes," Arthur continued, "with the light. A code we made. Morse code if more detail was needed."

"You told him to kill Don and Joyce?" Simon said, a shadow crossing his eyes as he studied his friend. Who he thought was his friend.

Red couldn't move. She was too close to Arthur and she wanted to be away from him, on that side of the RV, with Oliver and the others, but she couldn't move.

"No, no," Arthur said desperately, voice snagging at the edges. "I told him you'd passed them a note asking to call the police. I thought he'd shoot out their tires and their tank so they were stuck here too. I never thought . . . I didn't think he'd kill them. He wasn't supposed to do that!"

"Did you tell him to shoot Maddy?" Red said, and she couldn't look at him.

"No!" His voice was frantic now. "I told him it wasn't you, Red. I told him to take a warning shot. I thought he'd shoot in front of her, scare her back into the RV. She wasn't supposed to get hurt. I'm sorry, Maddy." He looked at her, voice breaking in half. "I tried to stop you from leaving, because I didn't trust him after what he did to Don and Joyce. I tried, Red, I did. But Oliver forced her out and I didn't have a choice. I didn't want this to happen, any of it. He wasn't supposed to shoot her!" he said, and his eyes glazed again, muscles twitching by his mouth.

Maddy whimpered as Reyna pushed harder against the wound, watching the scene unfold in front of her.

"And who is *he*?" Oliver asked, eyes flicking out the side of the RV, in the direction of the sniper. "Actually, forget that. Who are *you*?"

Arthur sucked a mouthful of air through gritted teeth, eyes darting side to side as he thought through his answer. Red knew that, because she knew his face, the shift in his eyes when he was thinking hard, the curve of his mouth when he laughed. That look he saved just for her. But he wasn't real. And neither were any of those small and not-so-small moments between them. She looked at the check mark on her own hand, and there wasn't a small firework anymore, just a shiver, clawing its way up the back of her neck. Who was he? Was his name even Arthur? Had this been planned from the start, when he first made friends with Simon and then the rest of them? What did he want from them?

"My name is Arthur," he said, pausing, eyes flicking to Red, latching on. "Arthur Gotti."

Simon gasped and Oliver's mouth fell open. Red's heart kicked up, throwing itself around her chest. She doubled back and doubled over, arms wrapping around her ribs to keep her heart from falling out the gaps.

"You're Frank Gotti's son?" Oliver asked, but it wasn't a question, not really. Because of course he was. "So, this is about Red? She's the witness in the trial against your dad and you're here to kill her?"

Arthur shook his head. "No, it's—"

"Why didn't you just shoot her outside her house, if you knew who she was?" Oliver demanded. "Why drag the rest of us into it?"

Arthur ignored him, head twisting on his neck, body following, as he turned to Red. "I tried to keep you safe," his voice croaked. "I've been trying this whole time. I told them I could get it from you, if I became your friend, if I integrated into your life. No need for anyone to get hurt. But you wouldn't, Red. You still haven't after everything that's happened tonight. Anytime I got close to anything real, you would shut down and change the subject. Every time, Red. And then it got too close to the trial and my father said we had to force it. I don't understand why you won't say who it is. That's all we need. It never needed to come to this, I didn't want it to come to this." His eyes widened, pleading with her, one hand buried in the folds of his shirt. "Why won't you say, I don't understand? I told them I didn't think you'd give it up under torture, if we threatened just you, or even your dad. But Maddy's here, the person you care about most in the world. Your friends. She's bleeding out over there and you still won't give it up. I don't understand, Red! Why? Why?"

"What's he talking about, Red?" Maddy's voice was strained, staccato, breathing out through the pain. Her skin waxy and white.

"I—" Red began, but Oliver spoke across her.

"Give what up?" he asked. "She's the witness for the prosecution against your dad, what else do you need?"

"No, she's not," Arthur said, low and steady over the tremor in his throat. "She's not because my father did not kill Joseph Mannino. He wasn't there that day, on the waterfront. And neither was Red."

Red blinked, pressed her eyes closed for a moment. No, she wasn't there. She hadn't seen Frank Gotti, hadn't heard a gun. She'd never even been in that park, but she'd walked it so many times since, memorizing every detail, in case it was needed in her testimony.

"What's he saying?" Simon asked, looking to Red.

"Red wasn't there," Arthur said. "But someone is paying her to say that she was, to set my dad up for a murder he didn't commit. That's right, isn't it?" he asked, and how was his voice still gentle, his eyes still kind? "Someone paid you to do it, to swear under oath that you saw my dad there, to put him away."

Red blinked again, her eyes spilling over, tears hot from the shame, sliding down her cheeks. Yes, that was it. The plan. No one was ever supposed to find out. No one. Red needed that money: pay off their debts, get her dad some real help, have the heating on this winter, maybe even think about college someday. But the money was long gone, the plan over the moment she'd told them she was the witness. Those were the rules.

"It's true?!" Oliver asked, studying Red's face, disgusted by her tears. "That's a crime, Red. That's perjury. What the fuck were you thinking? You can't be that desperate for money!"

"I—" she began.

"Who is it, Red?" Arthur said, and still his voice was soft where Oliver's was jagged and thorny. "Just tell me and it's over. Who is paying you to be the witness? Give me the name."

"I . . ." Red drew off, eyes flicking to Oliver, following the smears of blood to Maddy, then Reyna and Simon. All watching her, backing her into a corner. She'd been about to do it before. She was going to say it on the walkie-talkie before she found that interference. Why did it feel so much harder now with them all looking at her, now that she knew for sure this was what it was all about? Red didn't know if she could. Guilty if she did, guilty if she didn't. A betrayal either way.

"Red?" The calm in Arthur's voice shattered, his jaw tight and tense. "Why won't you tell me? Who is it? Is it one of Mannino's guys? Is it the Russians? Is it one of the New York families because of Atlantic City? Is it Tommy D'Amico? Who is it?"

His voice echoed around the silence of the RV, real silence, now that the static was dead, buried somewhere in the undone puzzle of the broken walkie-talkie at her feet. Her throat was tightening, an invisible hand around it, pressing in from all sides.

Red checked Oliver's eyes, and the danger that lurked there beneath the black, teeth bared and waiting. He didn't have the knife in his hands now, at least. And Maddy, Red looked to her, pale and quivering, biting down on her shaking lip, eyes focusing and unfocusing as she stared back. This couldn't hurt any more than that gaping hole in her leg, could it? Blood everywhere, marking them all.

"Red?" Arthur shouted, voice clawing and desperate.

Red took a breath.

"It's Catherine Lavoy."

# THIRTY-EIGHT

Oliver blinked at her, twin looks of shock in his and Maddy's eyes.

"What?" he barked, stepping toward Red. "What did you say?"

"It was your mom," Red said, looking straight at Oliver. "She's the one who asked me to do it, who set everything up."

Oliver straightened, and Red waited for the explosion, for the landmine to trip in his eyes, taking them all with him. She didn't expect what actually happened next. Oliver snorted, his face creasing as that wicked smile stretched through his skin, curling down at the edges. He laughed, the sound eerie and wrong in the too-quiet RV.

"Don't be ridiculous," he said, slapping himself on the chest. "Our mom is not a criminal."

But she was, if he put it like that, and so was Red. Weren't they all, in some way? Had Oliver forgotten that they all knew his secret now? That he'd killed someone four months ago. How could what she and Catherine did be worse than that?

"She came to me last August, the day after Joseph Mannino was killed, and she asked me to say I'd been there, that I saw Frank Gotti leaving the scene."

"Don't be ridiculous." Oliver laughed again, swinging his head. But Red wasn't smiling. And then came the switch, tripping in his eyes. "Stop fucking lying, Red!" He pointed his finger through her chest, leaving a crater behind. "Stop lying. She wouldn't do that!"

"It's the truth," Red said, picking her eyes up off the floor. "It's the truth, Maddy."

Maddy didn't say anything, wincing as Reyna shifted, the towel growing bloody beneath her fingers.

"Shut up, Red!"

"Let her talk!" Arthur shouted back, rolling his shoulders as he stared Oliver down. "Catherine Lavoy," he said, turning to Red. "And she works in the DA's office? She's the one leading the prosecution against my dad?" His eyes narrowed in confusion.

"Yes," Red said.

"No," Oliver argued over her. "Don't listen to her. She's a liar. I think by now we all know you're a fucking liar!"

"Keep going, Red," Arthur prompted.

"No, you shut up!" Oliver charged forward, pushing Red back against the kitchen counter, the tips of his fingers digging into her arms.

"Oliver, stop!" Maddy screamed, the sound frailer than before. "Let her speak. Please."

Oliver thought about it for a moment, searching Red's eyes, nails digging in deeper, then he let her go, drew back.

Red ran her hands down her arms, placing her fingers in the indentations left by Oliver, too big for her.

"You okay?" Arthur asked her.

"You don't care," she replied.

He looked hurt by that, a flicker by his mouth.

"Go on, then," Oliver said, head hanging off his neck. "Let's hear the rest of your bullshit story, then."

Red coughed, and she didn't know where to look. Reyna was

safe. Simon was safe. "Catherine told me that Frank Gotti was a terrible man. That he killed or ordered the killings of a lot of people. She said she was sure he did shoot Joseph Mannino, but they didn't have enough evidence to prove it in a court of law. That's why they needed an eyewitness."

"And what was in it for you?" Simon asked. He looked drained, wrung out, but there wasn't a war zone in his eyes like everyone else's, so Red focused on him.

"She said she would pay me for the risk," Red said, sniffing. "After the trial, if they got a conviction, she was going to pay me twenty thousand dollars."

Simon whistled.

"Don't be ridiculous," Oliver spat. "Mom doesn't have twenty thousand dollars lying around."

But they did. The Lavoys did have that. And more. Catherine had promised her. Said she could give it to Red, in cash.

"It wasn't just that, though," Red carried on, switching to Reyna, who wasn't looking, she was staring down at the towel, at the color of Maddy's skin. "I needed that money, yes, like you've all been saying, you know I need money."

Simon shuffled awkwardly.

"But it was something else too. Joseph Mannino was shot twice in the back of the head. That's how they executed people, Catherine told me." She glanced over at Arthur. How his family executed people. Now it made sense why he didn't want to join the family business. Not flipping houses, but bodies, drugs. He'd tried to tell her the truth, in small ways. She paused, readying herself for the punch to her gut. "That's how my mom was killed too, five years ago. Two shots to the back of her head while she was on her knees. She was executed. At an abandoned power station on the waterfront in South

Philly, pretty close to where Joseph Mannino was killed. The police never found out who killed my mom, the case is unsolved. But Catherine . . . your mom," she said, eyes finding Maddy, "your mom told me that, though they could never prove it, it was likely someone from that family, someone in the Mafia, who killed her. It was their style. And my mom was investigating the family, looking into their network of crimes, right around the time she died, so that makes sense. Maybe she found out something and they killed her for it."

And if it was Frank Gotti's fault that her mom died, then it couldn't be Red's fault. Except it still was, wasn't it? There was enough doubt left for Red to fill in with her own guilt. They'd never be able to prove who it was, that was what Catherine said, and she knew about these things. But Red needed the money, and she needed somebody else to blame, and there Catherine was, giving her both. Everything she needed, to fix herself, fix everything. But now the plan was gone, dead, it only worked if no one knew.

Maddy winced, gritting her teeth, a high gurgling in her throat.

Arthur shook his head, eyes crinkled with confusion.

"What?" Red asked him.

He sighed. "My dad would never kill a cop. He's smarter than that. It was one of John D'Amico's rules: never kill police. It kept the heat off them. Your mom was captain of a police district." Arthur stared at her. "No one would have touched her."

"B-but," Red stuttered. No, don't take it away from her, she needed it. "Mrs. Lavoy said—"

"She works in the DA's office, right?" Arthur said, face scrunching even farther, chewing on some silent thought.

"She's assistant district attorney," Oliver said, cricking his neck. "Soon to be district attorney, and she'd never do any of the things Red is saying. My mother is not a criminal. Red is lying, do not believe her. That's not the name you're after. It wasn't my mom. And what would even be in it for her, huh? Red? What does she get out of using you to set up Frank Gotti?"

Oliver's eyes were aflame, burning into hers. She wasn't lying, she wasn't.

"Well," Simon stepped in. "You said it yourself earlier, Oliver, didn't you? You said it's a historic case, and that if she gets the guilty conviction she's pretty much guaranteed to be voted in as DA." He shrugged. "She wants to be DA, right? That's what she would get out of it."

"Don't be ridiculous." Oliver rounded on him now, enough fire in his eyes to share around.

But Red was watching Arthur instead, a shadow crossing his face as he looked down, thinking, thinking, chewing the inside of his cheek.

"What?" she asked him, and he jolted back into the room, staring around at the corners of the RV as though it were finally shrinking around them, a countdown to crushing them all.

"It's . . ." He drew off, swallowed, started again. "My family has a contact in the DA's office. Has for years, maybe even ten years now. No one ever knew who it was, though, they always contacted us anonymously, encrypted messaging on a burner phone. Used to talk only to John D'Amico, but then when he started to get sick, they would contact my dad and Uncle Joe—Joseph Mannino, I mean."

Oliver stared at him, horrified. "There's a leak in the DA's office?" he asked. "Working with organized crime?"

Arthur nodded. "For years. That's how we would find out the identity of witnesses in cases against the family, or the locations of members who had flipped and were cooperating with the police. Information about trials and other criminal cases against our competitors. They would get charges dismissed sometimes. Shipments of seized guns or drugs for evidence that we could then intercept. All of that came from this person inside the DA's office. We paid them for their information, into an offshore account, but we never knew who it was. Until . . ." Arthur glanced at Red, an awkward shift in his shoulders, a glint in his eyes. "That's how we got your identity, Red. Just two days after the charges were filed against my dad, when we learned there was an eyewitness, even though there couldn't be, because my dad didn't kill Uncle Joe. My dad told my brother to message this contact, to ask who you were."

"And?" Red and Oliver said at the same time, and she didn't like that. No, they weren't on the same side. The RV was split again, but Red didn't know where she belonged anymore. With Oliver, who had thrown her out of the RV to her death, who had held a knife to her throat, who forced Maddy into his plan and now she was dying over there? Or Arthur, who had been lying to her from the moment they met last September? Because he'd needed to meet her, for his own plan. Of course he'd shown interest in her, laughed at her jokes, offered her rides home, charmed her with kind words and kinder eyes, she'd been his mark. What an idiot she was to think there was anything else there. He was here to get information from her and kill her, that was it. And yet Red found herself standing closer to him, edging away from Oliver, because the danger was in Oliver's eyes, no one else's.

"And," Arthur answered, looking at Red, not Oliver. He had obviously chosen his side. "They told us they needed a day or two to get us the information. And when it came, in early September, it didn't come the normal way, through their burner phone. My father received an email with Red's name and social security and her home address. And the email address that sent it belonged to a Mo Frazer, who works in the DA's office."

"Ugh, of course it's Mo Frazer," Oliver spat. "That makes so much sense. So he's in bed with organized crime, is he?"

Arthur shook his head, unsure. "Well, we assumed he must have been the contact all this time, and maybe he slipped up on this occasion. But it never sat right with me. He sent that from his work email, his name right there in the sender's address. That leaves a trace, somewhere on a server that law enforcement can find. It was so different from all the contact we'd ever had from him before. Careless."

"He got sloppy," Oliver said. "They always do."

"Or . . ." Arthur bit down on his lip. "Or he wasn't the one who sent it, because he isn't the contact. It was someone trying to pin the leak of Red's identity on him. Someone else in the DA's office."

His eyes found Red's, latching on.

"Catherine Lavoy?" she whispered, the word escaping from her at the end, hitching up, turning the name into a question. No, it couldn't be. But something was stirring in her gut, hot, sharp, goring through her as it climbed her spine to whisper in her ear: *Catherine betrayed you, Catherine gave up your name months ago.* No, Catherine couldn't be the one who gave up her name just days after coming to her, asking her to be the witness. Catherine would know what giving up Red's name meant; that they would kill her. It was the inevitable outcome. And Catherine wouldn't do that to her, whether she was the contact working with organized crime or not. She was her best friend's mom, her mom's best friend. There was no way.

Then what was that feeling in her gut? Solid somehow, inevitable, sinking deeper and deeper the harder she grappled to understand it.

Oliver snorted, stretching out his arms, his eyes a battleground, flicking between Red and Arthur.

"Let me get this straight," he said, playing with his chin. "First,

341

Red, you're *claiming* that my mom came to you, offered to pay you twenty thousand dollars to say you witnessed Frank Gotti committing a murder. All so she could get the guilty conviction and become DA," he said, nodding at Simon, mocking his theory. "And now, Arthur, you're claiming that my mom is the same person who has been leaking information to your family for ten years, on the take. And that she must be the one who gave up Red's name, but tried to make it look like Mo Frazer leaked it. How does that make sense?" he barked, striding forward, eyes widening as he passed each of them. "Those two things entirely contradict each other. Why would she ask Red to be the witness for the trial, but then immediately give up her name, knowing Red would likely be killed and the trial would never go ahead? That makes no sense. Come on, think. You have to think before you throw around baseless accusations about my family." He screwed one finger into the side of his head, too hard, his eyes wild again, the uncanny calm before the explosion. "This is such bullshit, all of it. My mom is not your contact, she prosecutes criminals like you." He jabbed that same finger in Arthur's direction, pointed it like a knife. "Your stories don't even make sense. My mom couldn't have done both: ask Red to be involved to win the trial, and then give up her name so the case would never make it to trial. How does that work?"

But Red's mind was circling something, around and around, digging back through the hours of this terrible, terrible night. Maybe there was a way it did make sense, maybe there was a way this all came back to Catherine Lavoy, pulling the strings behind the scenes. Red couldn't believe it, she'd known Catherine for as long as she could remember and even before that, but she also couldn't believe the real Oliver she'd met tonight, that danger flickering just below the surface of his eyes. If he'd done everything that he had tonight, then it was possible Catherine had used Red, betrayed her. Oliver was his mother's son, after all. And what was it, what was the phrase she was looking for? Red looked between Maddy and Oliver, trying to extract it from their eyes, that well-known Lavoy expression that always made Red know she'd never truly be one of them. She dug through the flashes of this never-ending night, Maddy's blood in a handprint on her face, the puzzle of Don's blasted-open head, the fuzz of static, headlights flashing, the red dot on her chest, the check mark on Arthur's hand matching the one on hers, the screaming, the smell of gasoline, shedding each awful part until she found what she was looking for. There waiting for her at the back of her mind, in Oliver's clipped voice.

Red cleared her throat. "A plan must have two parts," she said, repeating Oliver's words, who was in turn repeating his mom. "You have to make sure either way plays out in your favor."

Arthur looked at her, a shift of understanding in his eyes. "That's win-win," he said, parroting Maddy from before. And that feeling in Red's gut twisted, sucking in everything around it. She didn't want to believe it, but it was there, it was all right there and Red had to face it. It was never a plan that belonged to Red, they weren't in it together, the two of them; it was one of Catherine's win-win plans, and Red had just been a pawn, thrown away like she was expendable, disposable. Why? Why her? Did Catherine really not care about her at all? Didn't she see her best friend when she looked at Red; didn't she see the ghost of Grace Kenny there too? How could she do this?

"What are you two talking about?" Oliver spat.

"It does make sense," Red told him, her voice finding its strength from that awful, twisted feeling, deep in her gut. "Perfect sense. Her plan had two parts. In the first scenario, I testify at trial and Frank Gotti is found guilty. Because of the successful trial, your mom is elected DA. And the second part: she gives up my name when asked and Frank Gotti's family kills me, so the trial never goes ahead. But when they investigate where the leak came from, they'll find that email Mo Frazer sent. It will look like he leaked my name. He'd be removed from office, charged with whatever crime that is. You said it yourself earlier, Oliver. Mo Frazer is your mom's biggest competition to becoming DA, her *only* competition. If they killed me, it would take Mo out of the running. In either scenario, your mom wins, she becomes DA." She caught her breath. "Win-win," she said darkly, because in one of those wins she was dead, and somehow Catherine was okay with that. Oliver Lavoy had thrown her out of the RV to die, and Catherine Lavoy had thrown out her name, half expecting her to die, playing that to her favor.

Liar. Catherine Lavoy was a liar. Arthur was a liar too, and so was whoever that second *Yes* vote belonged to, but Catherine was a worse liar somehow. And Arthur had said he was trying to keep Red alive, that this was a last resort. Was that a lie too?

Red felt bile rising up her throat, swallowing it down as she avoided everyone's eyes, wiping a line of sweat from her top lip. Six of them in this RV, and at least five of them were liars, including Red. But she wasn't lying anymore, everything was out, everything was gone.

"This is ridiculous," Oliver said, because clearly he had no other word for it. "None of this is true. My mom didn't do any of that. You know her, Red, how could you accuse her of these things?"

"I'm not accusing," Red replied, and that twisted feeling flipped over, unfolded into rage, and rage was red, just like shame. She felt the heat of it in her cheeks. "It happened. She's the one that offered to pay me to be the witness, told me that Frank Gotti was probably the man who murdered my mom. She manipulated me and then she gave up my name to them."

"Shut up, you stupid little girl!" Oliver spat, switching his gaze to Arthur. "Do not listen to her, she's clearly misunderstood something here. My mom is not the person you are looking for. It's not her! Don't listen!"

"Oliver, stop!" Maddy croaked, her head resting back against the refrigerator door like she was too weak to hold it up now.

"No!" Oliver looked at her, but Maddy didn't shrink back from him; there was nowhere for her to go. "Red's lying!" he shouted. "She's going to get Mom killed and she's lying!"

"What if she isn't lying?" Maddy said, wincing as the words whistled through her throat. "Maybe it's true."

And as weak as Maddy was, bleeding out on the floor over there, skin as soft as ever but far too pale, she was still taking care of Red. Her job, her responsibility, though Red had never asked her to. Maddy wasn't like Oliver, or their mom. Maddy was real and kind and good. If she could stand, she'd be standing on Red's side of the RV, wouldn't she? The two of them, against Oliver. And Red couldn't think right now about where Arthur stood in all of that.

"Maybe it's true?!" Oliver shouted at her, spit foaming out the sides of his mouth. "You think it's true that Mom has been working with an organized crime group for the past decade? Being paid to dismiss cases and give them information? Do you think that sounds like our mom, Madeline? You think she'd fabricate a case against Frank Gotti, pay Red to be a witness, all to become DA? Does that sound like Mom to you?" he demanded. "Any of it?"

"I don't know," Maddy said, pressing her eyes shut.

"You don't know?!" Oliver bent over her. "You think that sounds like Mom, do you? The mom who still cuts your sandwiches into triangles for you? The one who says *whoopsie daisy* whenever she drops anything? Does she sound like a criminal to you, Maddy?" Red could see the red patches climbing the back of Oliver's neck as he bore down on his sister, his head falling to that strange angle, and she knew now that it was a warning sign. An explosion was coming. "The mom who has personalized ringtones for the entire family, sweet family memories, you think she's a criminal? You think the woman who has a doorbell ringtone for you because as a kid you thought you had to ring a doorbell before going in and out of the house, you think the woman who would do something that sweet is a criminal?"

Something caught Red's attention, pulled at it.

"What?" she said, staring at the back of Oliver's head. "Your mom's ringtone for Maddy is the harp."

Red had been with Catherine Lavoy many times over the past six months, meeting in secret, going over her testimony, working out where she could have been before and after the murder without being caught by cameras in case Frank Gotti's defense team checked. Maddy had called her mom a couple of times and Red had heard it, the harp ringtone, plucking up and down. Probably a joke from that time when Maddy was fifteen and insisted she wanted to learn the harp to impress a boy in orchestra, giving up after the second lesson because *no boy is worth that*. Red was sure about it.

"Your mom's ringtone for Maddy is a harp," she insisted.

Oliver glanced back at her, the explosion delayed for now. "Right," he said, breathing hard. "It is now, I think. But when Maddy first got a cell phone, it was the doorbell for a long time, because that's Mom's favorite story to tell about Maddy. I think she changed it a few years ago."

"Doorbell?" Red said, sounding the word out on her lips, like it wasn't a word at all, just a scattering of sounds, nonsense.

Doorbell.

One of the sounds of her shame, that lived there with it, deep in her gut. The sound she'd heard in the background of that final phone call with her mom. Twice. Her mom's strange "Hello," after she'd heard it. Except it was impossible, the police told her, she must have imagined it, or maybe she was confused. Her mom was found in that abandoned power station, no residential roads nearby at all, no houses, no doorbells. It wasn't possible. But Red had heard it, she'd heard that sound and she'd never forget it, never forget that last phone call, not a second of it. "Doorbell ringtone," she said, sounding out the possibility, memories shifting, slotting into new places.

"What are you talking about?" Oliver spat, eyes flashing.

Red didn't know, she didn't know yet, but there was an awful sinking feeling, trying to drag her down. She pushed up against it, feet lifting from the floor as she darted for the kitchen counter, for the saucepan of phones waiting there. Red lifted off the lid and peered inside, looking for her own phone. She pulled it out, the home screen telling her she was down to 12% battery, no service still. That was because the engineers were only just starting work on the broken cell tower. Had they heard her on the walkie-talkie before Arthur smashed it? She had no way of knowing if they had. If one of them had been pressing the button at the same time, then Red's voice would have been lost in the dying night, never found, never heard.

Focus, focus on the doorbell. Something inside was telling her this was important. Maddy might be dying, the police might or might not be on their way, but the doorbell was important.

Red unlocked her phone and tapped into the settings app. Her thumb moved down to the *Sounds & Haptics* menu option and she opened it. She scrolled down to the section labeled *Sounds and Vibration Patterns* and clicked to bring up all the options for ringtones.

Her eyes skipped down the list, past *Cosmic* and *Night Owl* and *Sencha,* thumb spooling the words up the page in a blur. No, it wasn't here. Right at the bottom was another click-through menu, called *Classic.* Red pressed it and a new list appeared on screen. *Alarm, Ascending, Bark, Bell Tower.* Red's eyes kept going, through the rest of the *B*s, past *Crickets,* and there it was. *Doorbell,* sitting just above *Duck* in the list. Red turned the volume on the device all the way up to the top and then pressed her thumb against the doorbell ringtone, heart in her mouth like it already knew the answer.

Her phone dinged, a high double-chime pattern, up then down. Red pressed it again. And again.

That was it.

The doorbell. *The* doorbell.

The exact sound she'd heard during that last phone call with Mom, the phone call that changed everything, ripped the world apart. This was it.

It wasn't a doorbell, because the police were right; it couldn't be. It was a ringtone. Catherine Lavoy's ringtone.

"What are you doing?" Oliver asked her, his shoulders shifting, staring down at the phone in Red's hands.

"Your mom," Red said, her voice breaking, splitting in half. "I think your mom was there."

"Where?" Oliver's eyes narrowed.

Red tried to speak, tripping over her own breath, too fast, throat closing in around it.

"With my mom. When she was killed."

# THIRTY-NINE

Red wished for the sound of static, to cover the awful silence in the RV, and that high-pitched ringing in her ears, two-tone, like the doorbell. Could anyone else hear it? Was anyone else struggling to breathe?

"What are you talking about?" Oliver asked her, brows drawing together, a shadow across his eyes, hiding the fire in them.

"She was th-there," Red stammered. "I heard her. Maybe you don't know this, but my mom called me, only ten minutes before she was killed, that's what the police told me." Her breath was too loud, like a windstorm trapped in her head, pushing at the backs of her eyes. She hadn't said any of this out loud for years, she'd lived alone in the guilt and the shame ever since. "My mom tried to tell me something on that phone call, she asked me to tell my dad something. But we were in a fight, I was mad at her, I was so mad at her, and I can't even really remember why now. But I hung up on her. I told her I hated her and I hung up on her. That's the last thing I ever said to her, to Mom, and then she died. It was my fault, because maybe the thing she needed to tell me, maybe that would have been the thing that saved her. She'd still be alive if I hadn't . . ."

And it wasn't the part of the story Red was supposed to be telling, but she couldn't not, it had sat inside her for so long, festering, a new organ that she needed to keep on living, to remind her every day what she did. Hers and hers alone, her responsibility. But now the rest of them knew too, all eyes on her, and the world couldn't break any more than it already had. No more secrets, not even this, the worst thing she'd ever done.

Red blinked and one tear escaped before she could catch it. "And on that last phone call, I heard a doorbell sound in the background. Twice, before it stopped." She sniffed. "The police told me it was impossible, because my mom was found in that abandoned power station on the waterfront, nowhere near any houses. But I always knew I heard it. It was this." She gestured with her phone, raising it up. "It was a ringtone, your mom's ringtone for Maddy. She was there, behind my mom. My mom said 'Hello' to her, and then I hung up before she could tell me what she needed to." Red's eyes fell to Maddy, her face rearranging. "Your mom was there. You must have called her when she was there. Why did she never say she was there? Mom was dead within ten minutes, so your mom, I don't . . ."

Simon's head dropped into his hands, sucking at the air between his fingers.

Arthur looked across at Red, eyes wide behind his glasses, arm shifting at his side like he might reach out to wrap it around her, hide her away.

"What?" Oliver snorted, shattering the teeming silence, the wicked smile back on his face. Did Catherine ever smile like that, Red tried to think. "Now you're trying to tell me that my mom is the one who killed your mom? They were best friends, Red. Don't be so stupid. And on what evidence? A sound you think you heard when you were

350

thirteen, a child? You're wrong. The police told you you were wrong. My mom wasn't there."

"Mom was investigating the organized crime group when she died," Red said, the words coming out as she thought them. "Your family, Arthur. Maybe she realized there was a leak from the DA's office, maybe she figured out that it was Cather—"

"Do you hear yourself?" Oliver roared, and yes she did, and she wasn't going to tiptoe around that look in his eyes anymore. Because if she was right, if she was right . . . "My mom wasn't there!" he shouted.

Red was about to speak, to push back, the words right there in her throat, wrestling past her out-of-place heart. But a new sound stopped her before she could. A howl, wretched and raw, from Maddy, her face cracking in two as tears slipped from her eyes, fast and free.

"What is it?" Reyna asked, keeping the pressure on the wound. "Does it hurt?"

But Maddy wasn't looking at her, she was looking at Red. She shrieked again, shoulders buckling with it, teeth bared, tears trickling into her open mouth.

Oliver stared blankly at his sister.

"Maddy?" Red said, stepping toward her.

"It was her," Maddy cried, her head nodding in minute movements against the refrigerator. "I—I, she . . . she wasn't home that evening. That's why I called her. I called her but she didn't pick up, went to voicemail after two rings." Her hand shuddered as she raised it to wipe one side of her face, leaving a new smear of blood there, mixing with the tears. "Dad and Oliver were out of town, away for one of Oliver's chess tournaments. I got home after my violin lesson and Mom wasn't there. She wasn't. She didn't get home until past eight-thirty, said she'd been working late. I'd already eaten, leftovers from the weekend." Maddy cried even harder, the words thick and misshapen in her mouth.

Red couldn't move. What did Maddy mean, *it was her*? She watched her best friend and she couldn't move, couldn't breathe, in case that made it true or not true, and Red didn't know which was worse.

"And I remember, Mom said she hadn't eaten, but I remember, I remember, I said to her, 'But you've got sauce there, on your shirt.'" Maddy choked on the words. "It was tiny, but she went and got changed as soon as I said it. I never saw that shirt again, she must have thrown it away." She stopped, spluttering over the tears that just kept coming as she told her story, five years' worth of un-cried tears. "And then the next day, I found out what happened to your mom, Red. That she'd been killed. Shot. I'm so, so sorry. And then . . ." Her voice cracked. "It was all so confusing. Because Mom was saying that she was home at seven that night, that she made dinner for both of us. She didn't, it's not what happened, but she kept saying it, to me, to Dad. But that's not what happened. I called her. The unanswered call was right there in my call log. Why would I have called her around seven if she was at home with me?" Maddy shuddered, wiping the other side of her face. "But I checked again a few days later and the call had been deleted from my log. It wasn't there. And Mom just kept saying the same thing over and over. She got home at seven, right around the time I got in from violin. She made dinner for us both and we watched TV. It was a normal evening. And I couldn't understand why she was lying. But then I started to think that maybe I was wrong, maybe I was confused about which day it was, because she seemed so sure, and why would she lie? And the call wasn't there on my phone anymore. She confused me, Red." Maddy blinked, trying to look at her through swollen, red eyes. "I wasn't sure. I wasn't sure, but I've had this bad, bad feeling all along that something happened that evening. But maybe I was wrong, confused. Half of me wanted to believe her. I'm so sorry, Red. I'm so, so sorry."

The last word broke apart as Maddy bawled, an awful end-of-the-world sound, her face folding in half, eyes pressed shut against the tears.

Red watched her. She didn't move, held in place by the too-hot air, thickening around her in this metal can.

It was Catherine Lavoy. Catherine Lavoy murdered her mom. Made her get on her knees. Shot her twice in the back of the head with her own service weapon. It was Catherine. Mom's best friend.

Red felt fingers on her shoulder, squeezing hard, but there was no one there, because it was Catherine, dressed in black, gripping onto her as the rifles boomed around them at the funeral, splitting the sky in half.

Catherine.

And Maddy . . . Maddy knew. This whole time. Since the day it had happened, the day the world ended around her, February 6, 2017. Maddy knew and she never said anything, in five long years.

It all made sense now, all of it. The way Maddy flinched whenever the word *mom* was said in front of Red. Because she knew what had happened to her. She might have had doubts, but she knew, deep down, she knew who had taken Red's mom away. Maddy always took care of Red, paid for her lunch when Red couldn't, found her lost things, so many lost things over the years, mothered her, all because she knew. Her job, her responsibility.

That was the strange look in Maddy's eyes from before, the one Red couldn't recognize. And this was her secret, the one she thought someone might kill for.

Maddy knew.

"I'm so sorry," Maddy sobbed, repeating the words over and over, until Reyna had to hold her down. "I'm so sorry."

The rifle must have gone off, because there was a hole there in Red's chest, blood pooling through her dark red shirt. But there wasn't. She looked down. There wasn't. But her body didn't believe her, caving in around the wound, rib by rib. Red bent double, agony as her bones cracked in half, cutting through her skin, every piece of the puzzle coming undone. Maddy was howling again, but no, it was closer than that. It was her. A red, guttural sound in her throat, pushing out her eyes.

"No!" Red cried, and it was happening all over again, Mom dying a thousand times in every half second, the world blowing apart and stitching up wrong. "No!"

Red screamed, her hands balling into fists, the hard ridge of her knuckles pressing into her face, marking her skin. Five years of not knowing, not knowing who killed her mom so it could only have been Red, murdering her with those last words. But now she knew. She had the answer. And she was coming undone with it.

Red staggered sideways, one leg buckling beneath her. Someone caught her.

Arthur.

His hands under her elbows, keeping her on her feet. He looked her in the eyes, blinking slowly, twin tears chasing down his face.

"Red," he said, low, soft, almost too soft to cut through the air in this RV. "Look at me."

She was looking at him.

"It's not your fault," he said.

"What?" Red sniffed.

"It's not your fault your mom died."

Red paused, held her breath.

"I know," she said flatly. It wasn't her, it was Catherine Lavoy. They'd all just learned that together.

"Red," Arthur said, fingers gentle against all her broken bones and skin. "It's not your fault."

Red blinked. "I know," she said slowly, the words shaking because she tried too hard. What could Arthur see? What could he read in her eyes?

"Red," he said gently, not looking away.

So Red did, she looked away, anywhere but at him. At the pattern in the curtains over there, please, could she finally work out what it was. *Think.* Or at someone else, but not Maddy, or Oliver, or Simon or Reyna. A distraction, anything, so she didn't think about all that guilt and all that shame, so she didn't bring them out, right here in front of everyone.

"Red," he said again, bringing her eyes back to his.

"Stop, Arthur," she whispered.

"It's not your fault."

That last one did it. Red felt a shift in her gut, something untwisting, something finally letting go. Her face cracked and the tears came. She cried, the sound shuddering in her throat. She stumbled forward, into Arthur's waiting arms, her head against his chest, and Red cried and she let it all go.

It wasn't her fault.

She didn't know what would happen after that phone call. She didn't hate her mom and Mom must have known that, there on her knees at the end of all things, as Catherine aimed the gun at the back of her head. Mom was Red's world, her whole world, and she must have known that, she must have felt it somehow, because that was how love worked.

It wasn't Red's fault.

She'd replaced her mom with the guilt and the shame and the blame. They'd become part of her, a limb, an organ, a chain around her neck. Red thought she needed them to live, but she didn't, because it wasn't her fault and she didn't need them anymore. She cried and it wasn't all because of Maddy or because of Catherine and the truth. She cried because she could finally forgive her mom for dying, and forgive herself too. Enough to go around.

Arthur stroked his hand down the back of her hair, to the ends of her ponytail.

"It's not true." Oliver's voice broke through. "None of that is true. Maddy, what the fuck are you saying?!"

Red pulled away from Arthur, wiping her face. Oliver emerged out of the blur, stepping toward her.

"My mom didn't do any of that!" he shouted. "It's all lies! All of them. I don't know what game you two think you're playing." He glared at Red, and then his sister, dying over there on the floor. "Mom didn't do anything."

"Yes she did," Red said, straightening up to look Oliver in the eye. "She did all of it. And I hope she dies on her knees, scared and alone, like she did to my mom."

"You shut the fuck up!" Oliver screamed. He lunged forward, but he wasn't coming for her, he was going for the table, grabbing for something. He thrashed back around, the knife gripped in one hand, Zippo lighter in the other. A gleam across the metal of both, matching the one on his bared teeth.

"Stop, Oliver, it's over," Arthur said, raising his hands, backing up. "It's over. I have the answer we came for. Red won't testify in court for the woman who killed her own mother. I can use that to convince my brother, he'll listen to me. We were supposed to get the answer and then kill Red, that's what we were told to do, but no one has to get hurt here. No one else." He glanced at Maddy, shivering now, vibrating against Reyna's hands. "I don't have any way of communicating with my brother now, because you threw the remote outside, and the walkie-talkie is broken. But I can go outside." He sniffed. "I'll walk over to him and explain that it's over, tell him to stand down. I'll make sure he does, I promise. Then the rest of you can get in that truck and drive Maddy to a hospital. She needs to get to a hospital. It's over, Oliver. Please, let it be over."

"You're not going anywhere," Oliver growled. "Not with all those lies about my mom. I know what you people do, you're animals. I won't let you kill my mom! None of it's true. You're not going out there and telling your brother her name. It's not happening." He raised the knife, pointed it at Arthur. "You're staying right here."

"Oliver," Reyna pleaded, the towel stained red in her hands. "We need to get Maddy to a hospital. She won't make it. Please, let's do what Arthur says."

"No," he barked, knife swinging in her direction now. "I can't let him leave. I can't let him tell his brother."

"Maddy won't survive, Oliver." Red pushed forward. "She's bleeding out. Arthur is giving us a way out of here. Now."

"I'm not fucking listening to you," Oliver said, voice dark and rasping. "You're a liar! You're going to get my mom killed."

"And you're going to get Maddy killed! We have to go!"

His eyes darted side to side. Because it was a choice, in a way, between his mom and his little sister. That was what this came down to. A life for another. But Oliver Lavoy didn't like making hard decisions. He had everything and more.

"Maybe the people on the walkie-talkies heard you, Red," Simon said, his eyes wide and panicked, sliding up the knife in Oliver's hands. It was over, but it wasn't, because the danger was standing right here, trapped inside with them, and they all knew it, Simon too. "Maybe they called the police, maybe they're on the way."

Red exhaled. "There's no way of knowing for sure," she said. "If one of them was talking at the same time, my interference wouldn't have come through."

"What about if some of us go out the other side?" Reyna suggested, gesturing with her head out the left side of the RV, through the driver's-side window. "We know there's not a second sniper out that side now. Some of us can leave that way and go get help. I'll stay here with Maddy."

"No one leaves!" Oliver roared. "No one leaves until I work out what to do."

What to do. A plan. Oliver was trying to think up a plan, one where he could save both his mom and his sister. A win-win. So like his mom. But Red couldn't see a win-win for him here, and she didn't want him to win, because Oliver winning meant Catherine would win, and Red couldn't let that happen.

"The sniper," Simon said, turning to Arthur. "He's your brother?"

Arthur gave him a small nod.

"Do you have any other way of communicating with him?"

Arthur reversed his head, shaking it instead. "Just the remote for the light and the walkie-talkie."

"Shit," Simon hissed. "I was just thinking, if you had a way of communicating with him, you could tell him to stand down, that we're all getting in the truck. Oliver, would you let us leave that way? If Arthur had to come with us, before he could tell his brother everything. Then you could think about your plan while we're on the way, getting Maddy to a hospital to save her."

Oliver narrowed his eyes, thinking it through. He raised his chin, nodding his head just once. He would allow that.

"But I don't have a way of communicating with him," Arthur said. "I could go outside and look for the remote but I'd never find it in the dark."

"No." Oliver's chin dropped again, eyes flashing. "Arthur does not leave this RV."

"Oliver!" Reyna was crying now, her arms shaking at the elbows. "We have to save Maddy!"

Maddy's eyes were closed now, they hadn't reopened since the last time Red checked.

"Maddy?" Red shrieked, stepping toward her, shoes cracking against something.

"I'm awake," Maddy croaked, and her lips were so pale, blending in with the rest of her face. "I'm awake," she said. "Just resting them, I promise."

The knot loosened in Red's chest, but not all the way. Maddy was dying, Red was going to watch her die if she couldn't get her out of here. Maddy knew, she'd known all along what happened to Red's mom, but she was her best friend, her Maddy, and Red had had enough of guilt and blame. She had to save her.

Her eyes trailed over to Oliver. Could they overpower him? Could she, Simon and Arthur get that knife out of his hands, restrain him? The knife flashed in the overhead lights, pulling in her eyes. It was so sharp. So jagged and sharp. That knife could make someone bleed out too, another person dying on the floor beside Maddy. And Red had no doubt that Oliver would use it; he was backed up against a wall, fight or flight, and she knew which choice he would make there.

Oliver Lavoy was the danger, he had been all along. And now he wouldn't let them save Maddy, not unless they found a way to communicate with the sniper, here, from the RV.

Red shifted and something crunched beneath her shoe, Maddy's shoe. She looked down. It was the walkie-talkie. Smashed to pieces. Plastic and metal and wires. Red's eyes narrowed, skipping over the pieces, slotting them together in her mind, fixing them. Her job, her responsibility.

"I can do it," she said, and she knew she could now, no room for doubt, no time for it. She'd done it so many times before, it was etched there, in the pathways of her mind. Useless, like a lot of things in her head, but not now, right now it might save a life.

"What?" Simon asked her.

"I can rebuild the walkie-talkie."

# FORTY

It was a puzzle, that was all it was. Not like Don's head out there, one Red could fix, one she'd done and undone before. For Mom. Now she could do it for Maddy. She bent to collect them, the pieces of the broken walkie-talkie, dropping them into her open hand.

She took the bundle over to the dining table, passing Oliver as she did. He let her by, but his grip tightened on the handle of the knife as she did. There was heat around him, following him, the smell of stale sweat. The hairs stood up on the back of her neck as she got too close, telling her to stay away.

Red let the pieces slide out of her hands, onto the table, scattering there. She studied them.

"Can you do it?" Simon asked her.

Red breathed out. "If anything's broken, I could take out the RV's stereo system, the radio. They have a lot of the same parts."

She leaned closer to the disassembled walkie-talkie. The green circuit board was cracked down the middle, still holding itself together at the soldered connections. There was a chunk missing from the black casing at the front, by the speaker grille, but that didn't matter. The plastic disk of the speaker was shattered, unfixable, the part that turned radio waves into voices. But that was okay, Red could make a new one out of the paper Maddy had brought. Nothing else looked broken, not the capacitors, or the amplifiers, the tuner, the transformers, not the magnet or the coil inside the broken speaker. She just had to put it all back together again, remake the speaker, reconnect the wires.

She nodded. "I can do it."

"Do you need the stereo?" Arthur asked her, moving toward the cockpit.

"No." She swallowed. "I can do it without."

Red sidled onto the booth and along it, coming to sit beside the window. The same place she'd been sitting almost eight hours ago, staring down at the tiny cars outside on the highway, Maddy chattering opposite her.

"Stay awake, Maddy." Reyna's voice floated over. "You have to stay awake."

"I am." The words rasped out of Maddy's throat. Dry and frail. That sound scared Red more than the screams had. They were losing her.

"Simon, get her some water."

"Sure." He ran to the kitchen.

Red reached across the table, for the scissors, strands of Maddy's light brown hair still clinging to the blades. She pulled a fresh sheet of paper from the pad and sliced into it, moving the paper around as she cut a complete circle, about the same size as the broken plastic part of the speaker.

"Maddy, can you drink for me?" Reyna said. "Can you open your mouth?"

"I'm cold," Maddy said.

It was hot in here, stifling. Red wiped a line of sweat from her temple against the back of her hand as she concentrated, smudging the *Call AT&T*.

She reconnected the circuit board to the antenna, resting it back inside the black casing.

Simon and Arthur were standing over her, watching. What was Oliver doing? Red couldn't see him and that scared her.

"Will you leave Red alone after this?" Simon turned to Arthur, his eyes darkening as he looked at his friend. But they weren't friends, were they? Simon had just been Arthur's way in, to get closer to Red. "You and your brother won't still come for her?"

"You have my word," Arthur said, holding his gaze, refusing to let go. "I never wanted any harm to come to her, to anyone. I tried, I swear, I tried to avoid all this. I don't believe in that, in killing people. I won't do it. Not for anything. That's why my dad says I'll be in charge of the numbers, of the legitimate businesses, because he can't trust me out on the streets, to be a soldier for him. Not like my brother." He paused. "But they will listen to me, both of them, I will make them. No harm will come to Red, ever. I promise."

"Okay."

"I'm sorry, Simon. I'm sorry I had to lie to you."

Simon shrugged. "Always thought you kind of sucked at basketball," he said, with the tiniest hint of a smile in his voice. "And hey, at least I'll never be scared of anything else again after tonight. Makes telling my parents about drama school seem not so scary anymore. But there's something I don't get," and the smile was gone now. "Why didn't you say it was Red with the secret hours ago? Why didn't your brother just come out and ask her who was paying her to be the witness right at the start, when we first found the walkie-talkie?"

Red couldn't see either of their faces, she was concentrating, looping a wire through, reconnecting it to the batteries.

"My dad's idea," Arthur said. "If we didn't say whose secret it was, then maybe we'd learn more than just the information we needed from Red. Find out things they don't want you to know, there's power in that. That's how my dad operates. And we could use those secrets to blackmail you into silence, if my cover ever got blown. Which . . ." He trailed off. "Well, too late now, you know who I am. That's over."

Red glanced up, at Arthur's downcast face, eyes on the floor. His life would never be the same after tonight either, would it? All of them changed, by this RV, by each other. He'd lied to her, he was a liar, but so was Red. And the terrible thing was, she didn't want to hate him. She maybe even wanted to take his hand, the one that matched hers. Her head told her she was a fucking idiot, but sometimes you didn't go with your head, sometimes you trusted your gut. Red had learned that from Reyna.

"How's it going, Red?" Simon asked her.

"Working on it," she said, turning to the speaker, fiddling with the magnet and the coil.

"Stay awake, Maddy." Reyna's voice was higher now, scared.

Maddy mumbled, a croak that didn't make it past her throat.

"Oliver, come on, please," Simon said, running his hands through his hair, pulling at his scalp. "She's not going to make it. Let Arthur go outside and speak to his brother. He says he will let us go. I trust him."

"I don't," Oliver growled. "For all we know, he'll go join his brother, try to kill us all, now that we know who they are."

"What about Red?" Simon pointed at her. "She can go outside, can't she, Arthur? Your brother doesn't know you have the name from her yet, which means he can't shoot Red."

Arthur nodded. "Until I tell him we have the name, Red is untouchable. He wouldn't shoot her."

"Will you let Red go, Oliver?" Simon pleaded. "Will you let Red leave the RV and go speak to him? To ask him to let us go?"

"No." Oliver bared his teeth, brandishing the knife. "Red doesn't leave either! She's a liar. She's trying to get my mom killed!"

"Lights," Maddy rasped, and Red ripped her eyes away from the walkie-talkie, over to her friend. Her eyes were cracked open, barely. One arm was raised, bent at the elbow, index finger shaking as she pointed it. "Lights." The word scratched out of her again.

"What, Maddy?" Reyna said, leaning in closer.

"Lights," Simon said, turning toward the windshield. Red's eyes followed him.

Lights.

Blue and red lights, flickering in the darkness of the dying night. Flashing through the glass, inside the RV.

"Cops are here," Simon said incredulously, like he didn't dare believe it yet. "The cops are here! Red, they must have heard you on the walkie-talkie. They called the cops. They're here!"

Red scrabbled up from the booth, the unfinished walkie-talkie gripped in her hand.

Simon was running up to the windshield, Arthur behind him, Oliver next.

Red followed them, peering through the gaps between their shoulders.

There was a black squad car pulling toward them on the road, red and blue lights spinning from its roof, lighting up the wide-open nothing. But it wasn't pitch-black out there anymore, the sky was stained with the faint pink of twilight.

The police cruiser rolled forward, drawn by their headlights, wheels crackling against the road.

"It's police, Maddy!" Simon called behind him, his voice cracking, breaking open. "We're going to get you to a hospital real soon."

The car peeled to a stop, directly in their headlights, before it reached the back end of the white truck.

"Arthur?" Red said, her breath on the back of his neck.

He turned to look at her.

"Would your brother kill a cop?" she asked.

Arthur's eyes darkened, his mouth tensed as he searched inside for the answer. "I don't know," he said. "He shouldn't, we're not supposed to. But Mike wasn't supposed to kill anyone tonight, except you. I didn't think he'd shoot Don or Joyce, or Maddy. So . . . I don't know. He's unpredictable. He's a soldier, my brother. He knows what the mission is: get the name from you and kill you. He wouldn't let anything stand in the way of that."

"So, he might?" Red said, watching beyond Arthur as the driver's-side door of the squad car pushed open.

"I don't know," Arthur said quickly, turning back as a female officer began to step out of the car in her uniform, dark hair scraped off her pale face, blue shirt, badge glowing on her chest, throwing back the light. She was on her own, looking up at the RV, one hand gripped on the car door, the other by the radio on her shoulder.

Her eyes met Red's for an instant and Red knew what she had to do.

There was no time to think it through. It was instinct, almost, something in her gut where the shame used to live.

She couldn't let it happen. That woman out there might have a daughter waiting for her at home. Maybe they had a fight last night, about homework, about the state of the daughter's bedroom. What had their last words been to each other? Red couldn't let it happen to another little girl, to lose her mom and her whole world the same way she had. Killed in the line of duty. A mom who never came home, never flashed the headlights at the living room windows, never pulled those faces again in the mirror behind the breakfast table. The flag on the casket, the three-volley rifle salute, "Amazing Grace" on the bagpipes.

Red wouldn't let that happen.

The undone walkie-talkie gripped in one hand, Red lashed out with the other, at Oliver. She brought her fist down against his wrist. He wasn't looking at her, he didn't see it coming. The knife flew out of his grip, falling to the floor with a clatter, skidding away under the table.

"What the—" he began to say, but Red was already moving away, charging for the door.

Heavy footsteps behind her, on her heels.

"Don't, Red!" Oliver's voice roared as he sprinted after her.

She didn't look back; she knew what she had to do.

With a last look at Maddy—Reyna watching over Red's shoulder, terror growing in her eyes—Red collided with the front door.

She grabbed the handle and shoved open the door. It crashed into the metal side of the RV with a crack.

"Not one more step, Red, or I'll do it!" Oliver's voice ripped against his throat, battered against her ears.

Red checked over her shoulder.

Oliver was standing by the sofa bed window, the mattress shoved aside. In his hand was the Zippo lighter, open, the flame dancing, fleeing from his breath. He was holding it out the window, pulling the shade up with the other hand.

"I'll drop it, I will!" he screeched, head hanging off his neck again, tendons raw and red, a wild flash in his eyes. "You're not leaving. I'll drop it into the gas, set the RV on fire. I'll do it!" He screamed those last words, foam and sweat around his open mouth, strings of spit hanging from his teeth.

"No, you won't," Red said, one final look at him before turning back to the open door. Oliver wouldn't burn the RV for one reason: he was inside with them. His survival came first, above everything; he was the highest-value here, in his head. Oliver wouldn't drop that lighter, and she knew it.

Red left the RV.

She charged down the steps full speed, shoes crunching against the gravel road as she sprinted to the left. Toward the white truck.

The red dot might be here, following her. But Red was untouchable, he couldn't shoot her. And she had to use that to save this woman.

She leaped over Don's crumpled body, feet skittering as she landed. Could the officer see Don and Joyce from where she was standing? Could she see the blood, the red road?

Red ran, alongside the white truck, around the back of it, toward the police car. SHERIFF CHESTERFIELD COUNTY was emblazoned on its side in bright blues and yellows.

The woman's eyes widened when she spotted Red.

"Stay where you are!" she shouted, drawing her handgun from the holster in half a second. She gripped it in both hands, pointed it at Red.

Red drew to a stop, dirt scattering, bunching around her feet.

But it was okay. She was standing right where she needed to be. Blocking the officer from the sniper's line of sight. Her body a barricade against that red dot. The woman would be safe, because Red was here, and she wouldn't move, she wouldn't move whatever happened. This woman was going home today, and she'd hug her daughter, if she had one, tell her how much she loved her. That was how this ended.

"Hands up!" the officer shouted. "Hands where I can see them!"

Red swallowed, raising her hands, the broken walkie-talkie still in her grip.

"Red!"

Arthur's voice screamed out into the breaking dawn.

Her head whipped back over to the RV.

Arthur was charging down the steps onto the road, his eyes on her as she stood here, frozen.

But there was a dark shape behind him, backlit from the yellow glow of the RV. Faceless, wide shoulders.

Oliver was right on Arthur's heels, leaping to the road after him.

Now that they were both outside, Red could see something new in Oliver's eyes, something final. The explosion must have hit at last, his face disfigured with the rage, eyes black and hollow, not golden brown. And she could see something else too, the knife in his hand as he bore down on Arthur.

"No, Oliver!"

Reyna was outside now too, scrabbling for Oliver's other arm, dragging him back in the same moment he swung the knife.

It caught Arthur in the neck, slicing through flesh.

Not as hard as Oliver had meant it, because of Reyna.

Arthur's hands darted to the gash in his throat, dark blood trickling over his fingers. But he was on his feet, he was still standing.

Oliver noticed that too, righting himself.

He shoved Reyna away.

She slammed into the side of the RV, falling to the road.

Oliver readied the knife, charging toward Arthur to finish it.

*Crack.*

Oliver jolted back. A blast of blood behind him, spattering against the off-white sides of the RV.

He crumpled to the road, knees first.

It was instinct.

Red's hands jumped to her ears at the sound of the rifle, her eyes flicking from Oliver, lying dead still on the road, to Arthur clutching at his neck, to the police officer in front of her.

But the woman wasn't looking at Red. She was looking at the dark shape of the walkie-talkie in Red's hand.

It must have been instinct for her too.

Her gun flashed. A tiny firework.

Something stung Red in the chest, breaking through.

She stumbled back.

Another clap, another firework in the officer's hands. A second punch, lower down, through her ribs.

Red blinked.

Her hand cradled her chest, pressed against her dark red shirt. Her fingers came away and the red came away with them.

Then the pain, a wet kind of pain, gathering around the two holes in her chest. But it didn't stay long, a cool numbness taking over as Red's legs buckled beneath her.

She fell back, onto the road. Legs out straight, arms beside her. A gurgling sound as she tried to breathe.

A beep. A hiss of static.

"Shots fired," a woman's voice said through the fuzz, panicked and high. "Ten-thirty-three. Ten-thirty-three. Requesting immediate backup!"

"RED, NO!"

Arthur was screaming, his voice strange and far away, but he must be close, Red could feel that.

"Stay back!" the officer shouted. "Don't come any closer."

Another gunshot.

The sound of footsteps pounding the road, running away.

"One of them is running. Ten-thirty-three. Requesting immediate backup. We have fatalities. My god. What happened here?"

Red blinked up at the sky.

Dawn was breaking, pale yellows and pinks dissolving the darkness, scaring the night away. But the stars remained, they stayed, blinking back at her.

Red couldn't feel it, the blood burbling out of her chest, nor the road, dirt and gravel hard against her back. She didn't feel anything, except the cool plastic of the walkie-talkie, still gripped in her hand.

She shifted her head, told her eyes to look at it. It was undone, unfinished, broken. But she blinked once, twice, and the walkie-talkie came alive, the green screen lighting up, a glow against her face.

A hiss of static that wasn't there, because it was broken, but it was, she could hear it against her ears. That white noise. Home.

The walkie-talkie wasn't on, except it was, and it was tuned to channel six.

Their channel.

Red couldn't move, she couldn't move to press her thumb against the push-to-talk button, but she didn't need to. Because her own voice was coming through the speaker, Tiny Red, from a decade ago, hiding behind the door as she played Cops and Cops.

"Attention, attention," Red said, voice low and serious. "Officer down. Officer down, requesting backup. Over."

The static hissed, filling up her head.

And then she heard it, clearly, for the first time in years.

Mom's voice.

"Oh no, Officer Kenny," her mom said, that kind lilt at the end of her words that Red missed so much. "Have you been hit?"

"Mom, you have to say: Over."

"Sorry. Over."

Red smiled, watching the walkie-talkie sputter in and out of life, between then and now.

"Yes, I've been hit," Red said. "They got me."

"Oh dear, sweetie," Mom said. "Backup is on the way to administer get-better kisses. Over."

Red coughed, a rattling in her chest that shouldn't be there. But there was something else too, something that did belong.

And here it was, the proof that she'd been wrong all these years. Red knew it was coming, just like Mom must have done, on her knees against the concrete, Red on her back against the road. But it wasn't hate she felt, or regret, or guilt, or blame. They didn't exist anymore, not here in this place, flickering in and out. She wasn't thinking about last words, she was thinking about all the words, all the memories. It was love; thorny and complicated and sad and happy. But it was a red feeling too.

"Aha, there you are, Officer Kenny," her mom said, breaking through the not-there static. "Looks like I got here just in time. You're going to make it."

Red giggled, the radio waves carrying her voice through time as Mom wrestled her to the ground, covering her in kisses.

"Mom, stop," she laughed and laughed and laughed. They both did.

"Love you, Red."

"Love you, Mom."

Red blinked away a tear, smiling up at the wide-open nothing of the sky.

Time must move backward here in this in-between place, reversing, because the night was coming back, darkness reclaiming the sky, taking Red with it. But Mom stayed with her, right here in her hand, at the end of all things.

Mom stayed, and so did the stars.

6:00 A.M.

**Police Radio Transcript from the Chesterfield County Sheriff's Department, SC**

Date: 04/10/2022
Time: 06:06

**OFFICER 1:** What's your 10-20?

**OFFICER 2:** Just coming down Bo Melton Loop, we'll be with you in a few minutes, hold on █████. Are you in immediate danger? Tell me what's going on over there.

**OFFICER 1:** Not sure. It's an RV, there's kids. We have fatalities here. Three deceased. Gunshots, looks like a rifle. We have two in critical condition, they aren't doing well. Need urgent medical assistance.

**OFFICER 2:** Medical is being dispatched as we speak. Can you preserve life? Start CPR?

**OFFICER 1:** . . . Another two here as well. Superficial injuries. They're in shock, they can't tell me what happened. God, there's blood everywhere.

**OFFICER 2:** Officer █████ keep talking to me. We're coming up on your location now, you should be able to hear us soon. The others are on their way.

**OFFICER 1:** There was another one here too. He was bleeding from the neck. He ran, took off east into the trees.

**OFFICER 2:** Dispatch, did you catch that?

**DISPATCH:** Copy.

**OFFICER 1:** It was me, I shot her. She ran at me. I heard a gunshot. I thought she had a gun in her hand. It's not, though. It's not a gun, oh god, what have I done?

**OFFICER 2:** Hold on, I'll be there any minute.

**OFFICER 1:** . . . What have I done?

**OFFICER 3:** Officer ▆▆▆▆ be advised that we just picked someone up close to your location. White male, mid-twenties. He was running down the road. He had a hunting rifle and a tripod on him. We surrounded him and he surrendered. ▆▆▆▆ made the arrest. Uninjured. Just trying to ID now. You think this is your suspect? We got him.

**OFFICER 1:** What have I done?

**MENU**

US > PA > Philadelphia > News > Crime

## Assistant District Attorney Catherine Lavoy Shot Dead Outside Hospital in South Carolina

JOHN HOLLAND April 11, 2022

This morning, Catherine Lavoy, 49, who worked in the Philadelphia DA's office, was shot dead outside the main entrance of Chesterfield General Hospital. She is believed to have been shot in the head by a long-range rifle, killed instantly at the scene. Police and private security guards were attending her at the time.

The local sheriff's department confirmed in a statement that this was likely a planned assassination. The sniper was positioned in the high-rise apartment buildings opposite the hospital. The unknown shooter was not apprehended at the scene and is believed to still be at large. Authorities are appealing for witnesses to come forward with anything suspicious they may have seen, leading up to today's events. The hospital is now on lockdown.

Lavoy had been visiting her daughter, Madeline, 17, who remains in critical condition after an incident that took place on Saturday night into the early hours of Sunday morning, on a small rural road near Ruby, SC. The full details of the night of April 9 are still unclear, but police have confirmed there were multiple casualties. Local residents Donald Wright, 71, and Joyce Wright, 68, were confirmed to have died in the incident. Catherine Lavoy's son, Oliver, 21, was also killed. An arrest has been made, but charges are yet to be filed against the suspect and police refused to give out any more details.

The road where Saturday's incident took place has been cordoned off, but a truck with a flatbed trailer was seen carrying an RV away from the scene into police custody. One eyewitness told *Newsday* that the vehicle had four flat tires and was riddled with bullet holes and broken windows. Another said she could see dried blood inside and outside the RV. More details as this story develops.

It is not yet known whether either of these incidents has any relation to Lavoy's work as a state prosecutor, or any of her ongoing criminal cases. Lavoy's career had been going from strength to strength with a high-profile homicide case against Frank Gotti, 55, which is due to go to trial in a few weeks. Lavoy had very publicly stated her intention to run for district attorney in the elections this year, starting with the Democratic primary election in May.

Her colleague, ADA Mo Frazer, had this to say when asked for a statement about the murder of his coworker: "I just heard about it myself. I am absolutely devastated. With what happened to her kids, and now this. I can't understand it. Catherine was a wonderful woman, a brilliant prosecutor and a terrific mom. I don't know who would want to do this to her, but our office will work around the clock to assist in bringing them to justice where we can. Catherine leaves behind a huge hole and my thoughts and prayers go out to her remaining family."

Dear Red,

It's me. I've never written a letter before, I don't think. Not since they made us practice in school. Now it seems it's the only thing I can do. I need to write this all down, get it out of my head. Even if no one ever reads it.

Because there's a lot I have to say to you, Red. Starting with sorry.

I'm sorry for all of this. I'm sorry for all the lies I told you. I'm sorry for intruding into your life, trying to get close to you. I'm sorry about our plan and I'm sorry about yours. I'm sorry that all of us were thrown together in this mess, because of our parents and everything that happened between them. I'm sorry about your mom, and I'm sorry you had to find out who killed her like that. I'm sorry for everything Catherine Lavoy did to you. I'm sorry for everything Oliver Lavoy did to you. I'm sorry that Don and Joyce died, I should have tried harder to stop it. I'm sorry that Maddy got shot. I'm sorry for everything Mike did. I'm sorry for every hurt I caused you. I'm sorry I didn't try harder to protect you. I'm sorry I never got to tell you. I'm sorry I never kissed you. I'm sorry that I'm writing this letter and it's all too late. I'm sorry I left you there, bleeding on the road. I'm sorry.

I thought you were dead. She shot you twice and I thought you were dead. I'm sorry I ran, I should have stayed and held your hand. It should have ended with you and me.

They took you to the hospital, with Maddy, and I found out you were in surgery and then you were in a coma. I heard a doctor talking about you, they didn't expect you to pull through. Your dad was on the way, on a flight. I thought he would miss his chance to say goodbye, like I missed mine.

That's why I did it, Red. I always promised I'd never kill anyone. That's hard, when you grow up in a family like mine. It's the thing my father hates most about me. But you said you wanted it. I don't know if you were just saying it in anger, because Oliver was there, but you said you wanted her to die on her knees, scared and alone, like she did to your mom. I thought you were going to die, Red. I went back for one of Mike's rifles, where we'd stashed them. I didn't need to practice really, it was easy, with that red dot. One shot and I was gone before they came looking for me. That was my goodbye, I guess, my way of fixing it, taking her out of the world, so at least if you were gone then she was gone too. I wanted you to know but you wouldn't wake up. I didn't do it for my dad, Red. She didn't deserve to live after everything she did to you. I'm sorry if I made the wrong choice, I'm sorry if that's not what you wanted. I'm sorry that any of us had to make these hard choices in the first place.

But you didn't die. You didn't wake up either. I stayed around, waiting to hear. I stitched up the wound on my neck myself, it got infected for a few days. Maddy pulled through, I heard about it on the news. You weren't on the news, though. I wanted to come see you, I knew you were asleep and you'd never know, but I wanted to come see you. Police were everywhere inside that hospital, after Catherine Lavoy died outside. I got through, though, they didn't know they were looking for me. I don't know what Reyna and Simon have told them about that night, about me, but no one caught me. No one even looked. Reyna saved my life that night, I hope I get to thank her someday. I hope it's helped her too, somehow, saving me from Oliver, the way she wished she could have saved Jack Harvey from him. She and Simon must not have told the police anything about me, at least not then, when I entered the hospital. I hope that means Simon forgives me, in his way. I was right outside your room. I could see you there, tubes and wires running all over you. Sleeping. You were only sleeping. I heard they had to remove part of your lung. But you had another visitor already. The door opened and Maddy was there, inside the room with you. She was in a wheelchair still, in her hospital gown. We looked at each other. She must have known it was me, that I was the one who shot her mom. There were police everywhere, she could have shouted, told them I was the one, it was me. But she didn't, Red. We looked at each other and she nodded. She let me go. I never got to see you, though, to hold your hand. It's not for me to say, but I hope you forgive her, Red.

Then it did happen. You woke up. They transferred you to a hospital in Philly, your dad rode with you all the way and I followed you back home. I don't know how long you'll be in there, days, weeks? You'll find this letter when you get back from the hospital. I hope you read it, but it's okay if you don't. I'm sorry I've been in your bedroom, it's just as messy as I thought it would be.

There's something else too. And this is my dad. He insisted, after I told him everything that happened. I know your dad doesn't have health insurance. You'll find the money to cover all your hospital bills and more, hidden in that shoebox in the back of your closet, where you keep the old birthday cards from your mom. It's all in cash, from the legitimate businesses. I insisted about that last part. Please use it to cover the bills and anything else you need to recover. It's yours and yours alone. You don't owe us anything for it, you've already done enough.

Looks like the charges are being dropped against my dad. He'll be out soon. Maybe you already told them what Catherine made you do, that you didn't see him there, I don't know. They caught Mike. I don't know if you know that. They caught him that night—or morning I should say. He's been charged with first-degree murder for Oliver and Don and Joyce, attempted murder for Maddy. Dad's hiring him a good lawyer, but I don't see what good that would do, Mike did those things. He shouldn't have. Oliver, I understand, because he was about to kill me, but the others? Maybe Mike will be better off in prison than out here. His whole life has been a war, that does something to your head, I think. It's done something to my head.

I guess when we were listing outside jobs I could do, Red, we didn't think of Fugitive. Because that's what I am now. They must be looking for me, they must know I played some part in everything. I got away, but I don't know how long it can last. I do spend a lot of time outside, though, if I'm looking for silver linings. And you're alive, that's the biggest one of all. That's all I ever wanted, for you to live through this. But I'm sorry, I hope you know that. I guess none of us—the five that survived—will ever be the same after that long night. I mean, you slept for two weeks after. That wasn't a funny joke, I'm sorry for that too.

I don't know where I'll go next, what I'll do. That feels strange, when there's a whole life ahead of me, and now I have no idea what it looks like. But I know what your life looks like from here, Red. You're the strongest person I ever met. Who else gets up after being shot in the chest, twice? Still standing after everything you've been through. You saved that cop, by the way. She was fine. She has a twelve-year-old daughter. I checked, because I knew that would be important to you. You are amazing. I'm not sure enough people have ever told you that, and I'm sorry about that too. You can do anything you want, be anything you want, and whatever road you go down, Red, I know your mom would be so proud of you.

I'm sorry that this letter is so long. You can stop reading if you want, but there's one last thing. I don't know how long it will be until you're up on your feet. But I'll wait. On the 8th of May, at 8:00 p.m., I'm going to be at Pier 68, waiting for you. To say goodbye, or whatever else it is we have to say to each other. I can say all of my sorrys in person, if you'll let me. I

understand if you don't want to come, if you don't want
to see me, after everything. I will also understand if
you turn this letter in to the cops, if a squad of police
officers turns up at that time to arrest me. I will
understand. That's up to you. It's your choice, Red.
But I'll be there, I promise.
Will you?

YES []
NO []


    Yours,
    Arthur

# Acknowledgments

My first and greatest thanks must go to you, reader. The blank page and the blinking cursor were all the more intimidating this time around, without the safety net and familiarity of my A Good Girl's Guide to Murder series. Thank you for the phenomenal support you have shown that trilogy, and thank you even more for coming with me on another adventure, leaving Fairview, Connecticut, for a creepy, remote road in South Carolina. I hope you enjoyed the intense eight hours you spent in that RV.

A huge thank-you, as ever, to my agent, Sam Copeland, who had to admit that he actually liked this book. Thank you for your bravery—it must have been very hard for you. Thanks also to Emily Hayward-Whitlock for everything that you do, and for taking such good care of my fictional worlds.

It is hard to express my immense gratitude to the team at Delacorte Press for everything they do, taking my stories and characters and turning them into real-life books. I wish there were more synonyms for the words "thank you," but alas, here comes a long list of thank-yous to everyone who helped bring *Five Survive* to life. It takes a village, as they say, and we certainly wouldn't all fit in an RV at the same time!

A massive, massive thank-you to my superstar editor, Kelsey Horton, who is the best partner in crime (fictional) and who works tirelessly masterminding everything to make sure my books are the best they can be. Thank you for trusting me to disappear for months to write *vague RV murdery book*—I'm glad we found a better title for it! And an enormous thank-you to Beverly Horowitz—I'm so happy *Five Survive* found its perfect home with this team!

Thank you to Casey Moses, again, for being a genius designer, and for giving *Five Survive* such an incredible and cool cover. I don't know how you do it. Thank you to Christine Blackburne and your photography prowess. I'm so glad that the first thing readers will see of the book is both of your incredible work. Thank you to Kenneth Crossland for making sure the inside of the book looks just as good as the outside! Thank you to Colleen Fellingham and Tamar Schwartz for your super attention to detail, and for having to go through the book so many times! Thank you to Tim Terhune for your hard work *literally* bringing the book to life.

Thank you to Lili Feinberg, Caitlin Whalen and Elizabeth Ward for your incredible work cheerleading and championing this book, expertly creating buzz and making sure readers have heard about it. Thank you to Becky Green, Joe English and Kimberly Langus in sales for everything you do, working so hard to make sure the book can physically find its way into the hands of readers and into new homes—I'm so grateful. And thanks to Keifer Ludwig for looking after this book on the international stage!

Thank you to my families—Collis and Jackson—for being the very first readers, for celebrating every high with me and for taking me out of the made-up worlds in my head when I need it! Anti-thanks to my dog, Dexter, without whom I would have written this book much faster. And last, but never least, thank you to Ben for sharing every real-life plot twist with me.

# About the Author

Holly Jackson is the author of the *New York Times* bestselling series A Good Girl's Guide to Murder, an international sensation with millions of copies sold worldwide. She graduated from the University of Nottingham, where she studied literary linguistics and creative writing, with a master's degree in English. She enjoys playing video games and watching true-crime documentaries so she can pretend to be a detective. She lives in London.

@HoJay92